Sweet Song,
Bitter Loss

Sweet Song, Bitter Loss

PAUL HENCHER

Matador
Unit E2 Airfield Business Park,
Harrison Road, Market Harborough,
Leicestershire. LE16 7UL
Tel: 0116 279 2299
Email: books@troubador.co.uk
Web: www.troubador.co.uk/matador
Twitter: @matadorbooks

ISBN 978 1803130 996

British Library Cataloguing in Publication Data.
A catalogue record for this book is available from the British Library.

Printed and bound by CPI Group (UK) Ltd, Croydon, CR0 4YY
Typeset in 11pt Minion Pro by Troubador Publishing Ltd, Leicester, UK

Matador is an imprint of Troubador Publishing Ltd

How sweet the thrill of summer song,
The joy of youthful love.
What bitter loss with season gone
When hope lies in its grave.

Prologue

The concave stone walls were windowless so that no natural light could enter the small round room, which also meant that little sound would escape, yet the terrified, injured man was gagged as a precaution. He pulled on the chain by which he was tethered to a metal ring in the wall, but the movement only served to tighten a thin piano wire around his neck. He let out a muffled scream of pain as a burning cigarette was once again pressed into his bare foot. His two tormentors stood back to let the other man in the room, their leader, step forward to face the victim.

'You brought this on yourself Hornet,' he said. 'Rule one of my organization is that nobody – nobody – cheats me. You knew that rule, yet you chose to break it. I might have known you were likely to cosy up to your Colombian compatriots. They will get the message as well, loud and clear. You know why your erstwhile colleague here is called 'the Gardener' don't you.'

Hornets eyes were wide and wild with terror. He shook his head as a gesture of surrender, causing the piano wire to cut into his skin. The man standing closest to the leader pulled a pair of garden secateurs from his trouser pocket and smiled mirthlessly, showing crooked, yellow teeth.

'His hands, Scorpion,' snapped the leader.

The other gang member pulled their victim's tightly-bound wrists upwards, right hand uppermost, and held them in a powerful grip. The Gardener grabbed the man's index finger, looking with satisfaction at the terrified, sweating face in front of him. With calm deliberation he cut through flesh, bone and sinew.

'Strange, I thought it would bleed more than that,' said the leader. 'His thumb as well.'

The gardener re-applied the sharp blades of his secateurs and squeezed hard on the plastic-clad handles. As the man's thumb fell to the floor, his eyes rolled backwards and his body started to jerk in violent spasms. With no control over his movements, the piano wire tightened around Hornet's neck. There was a horrible gurgling noise as blood bubbled from his throat, then within seconds he stopped breathing and his body went limp.

'You know where to take him,' said the leader, as he went to ascend an open wooden stair to the floor above.

At that moment, the heavy oak door swung open and a new arrival, exhausted from running, stumbled into the room, but froze when he saw what had happened to Hornet. The leader spun round : 'what the hell…'

Scorpion was the quickest to react. In a few rapid steps he crossed the room, kicked the door shut, then grappled with the intruder, twisting an arm behind his back with one hand while putting a vice-like hold on the new entrant's neck with his powerful left arm.

'Up here,' ordered the leader, indicating a hatch above the stairway. 'Bring him up here.'

One

With a look of grim determination, the slight, wiry boy scrambled doggedly up the steep bank, hauling himself towards the summit by clinging to branches of shrubs and sturdy tufts of grass. Having reached the top, he swept a hand through his mop of dark, untidy hair as he contemplated the next part of his journey, through the dense maze of brambles and Russian ivy. He was resolute not to give up on his quest, so began to pick his way as carefully as possible through the tangled and thorny vegetation, but, small and careful as he was, his hands and legs were soon scratched and bloody. He jolted with surprise when he disturbed a big green lizard which quickly scuttled off into the undergrowth, then spoke to try and calm a blackbird shrieking a warning of his presence. 'It's alright Signore Blackbird, I won't harm you or your family.'

Giovanni Mirelti was eleven years old, and quite different from his school peers. It wasn't his poor academic results which set him apart, in fact very few of his classmates showed any particular ability in maths, or Italian, or history. One main difference was that he didn't like football, neither playing nor watching. He never joined in with the after-school games on the village sports ground, and was constantly baited for not having a favourite Serie 'A' team. But the main source of ridicule and contempt was his highly unusual passion for the world of nature. In this rural Italian Region of Abruzzo, few people, least of all schoolboys, knew or cared about the names of birds or species of snakes, but for Giovanni it was an all-consuming hobby. He had recently been involved in a fight with several boys at school when he saw them kicking a hedgehog around the yard.

He couldn't wait to leave school, because he knew exactly what he wanted to do afterwards. He would be a park ranger up in the mountains, showing visitors where the wolves, and chamois, and bears lived, and this ambition for the future actually encouraged him to concentrate and perform well at one school lesson – English. His friend, Filippo, had told him that many of the visitors who came to see the wildlife were from England or America, and even those from Germany, or Holland, or Sweden could speak English. As Giovanni stopped to detach yet another length of bramble that had caught on his tee shirt and arm, he imagined a conversation with an English tourist, remembering his classroom lessons:

"Good morning, my name is Giovanni. I am your guide today. What is your name Signore?"

"My name is Mister Smith."

"Will you like that I show you" – no. Another word. Like tree. Wood. "Would you like that I show you where live the wolves, Mister Smith?"

Giovanni smiled with satisfaction at the future scene unfolding in his mind, then pressed on towards his goal.

Eventually he arrived beneath a stand of oak and acacia trees, peering up into the branches before deciding which one to climb. Not the acacia. Hard to climb, and bearing vicious thorns. He picked the oak tree he wanted, and began his ascent, helped by ivy, as thick as his arms, entwined around the massive trunk. Breathing heavily with the effort, and halting occasionally to check his next hand or foot hold, it didn't take long for him to reach a wide bowl about nine metres from the ground where a major branch spread outwards. Secure in his hiding place, he studied the neighbouring tree until he spotted the prize. Ignoring the discomfort of rough bark digging into his knees, and the fly crawling across his face, he waited and watched quietly, patiently, until he heard that beautiful call, those rich, liquid notes of summer song. "Trocadero, Trocadero" it seemed to be singing, then moments later it appeared on a branch, causing Giovanni to hold his breath at the beauty of it. About the size of a blackbird, but showing a dazzling pattern of sharply-defined yellow and black, a golden oriole, that's what Filippo had told him this bird was called. Filippo had explained how they flew back from Africa at the beginning of May to nest once again here in Abruzzo. Heart thumping, Giovanni now saw for himself that the other thing Filippo had said was true. These shy, stunning golden oriole build their nests so that they hang like pockets from a fork in the oak tree's branch. He watched in wonder as the bird carefully wove a strand of grass through the pendulous structure that would soon hold a clutch of three to five speckled pale eggs. Deciding he would return at the end of the summer to retrieve the empty nest for his collection, Giovanni waited until another strand had been woven in before scrambling precariously back down the tree. He jumped the final metre, but realised too late that his shorts were snagged, and heard the sound of ripping cloth before painfully landing belly-first on the ground. Mamma is going to be furious, he thought, examining the torn shorts. He just hoped he would be home in time for pasta, otherwise Papa will be angry as well.

Giovanni made his way as quickly as possible back home, sliding most of the way down the bank in the process, collecting more scratches, before running the final stretch between two rows of olive trees, then scampering through the plastic-beaded fly screen into the main downstairs room of the family home.

Seated at a rustic pine table were his eldest sister, nineteen-year-old Felicita, alongside her fiancé, Mario. Opposite them was his other sister, petite seventeen-year-old Laura. His mother, Anna, was preparing food in the small adjoining galley kitchen area, while his father, Bruno, was ensconced in a well-worn armchair at the other end of the room, watching a television game-show featuring scantily-clad hostesses. Giovanni hustled quickly into the seat next to Laura, anxious to ensure no-one saw his scratched legs and torn trousers.

'Did I tell you I killed a snake this morning,' Mario said to Felicita, but doubtless intended for Giovanni's ears.

'If you mean that poor creature left dangling in the fig tree, it was a slow worm – a type of legless lizard – not a snake. Not very brave after all, Mario,' challenged Giovanni.

'Just in time, my lad,' shouted Anna above the loud volume of the game show, cutting off any riposte from Mario.

Giovanni looked up at the clock on the wall above where Felicita and Mario were sitting. A couple of minutes before seven o'clock. He grinned, knowing his Mamma would have kept the spaghetti and home-made passata warm for him anyway.

'So who's going to win tonight, eh, Giovanni?' smirked Mario.

Giovanni shrugged his shoulders.

'Remind me, who's playing?' continued Mario.

Mario was a heavily-built twenty-three year old, a stubble beard disguising flabby jowls and a weak chin.

'Don't know, don't care,' muttered Giovanni, looking unblinkingly into Mario's full face, and wondering how long the slob would last on a football pitch.

The game show having ended, Bruno turned the television off using his remote, and opened a new can of beer. Beads of sweat glistened on his bald head and high, flat forehead.

'Where have you been?' he asked Giovanni, just as Anna emerged from the kitchen area and placed a large dish of pasta on the table. She would cook a fresh batch for eight o'clock when she, her mother, and Bruno would have *their* evening meal.

'Eh, been looking at little birdies again?' sneered Mario, while Felicita served her fiancé a generous portion of pasta. 'He should be learning to shoot them, not watch them, eh Bruno?'

Giovanni scowled while Laura took over the dishing-up duties.

'Birds, animals, butterflies,' shouted Bruno from his armchair, wiping beer froth from his mouth with the cuff of his grubby checked shirt. 'That's all the boy is interested in. I have one son, and he turns out crazy. What did I do to deserve this?'

'You have two sons, remember?' shouted Anna from her kitchen refuge, angrily pushing a strand of red-dyed hair from her face and tucking it behind her ear.

'Two sons?' responded Bruno. 'I only see one. I don't see two. Where is this other son, eh?'

Felicita, Mario, Laura and Giovanni busied themselves with their bowls of pasta. They were familiar with this argument. Felicita sprinkled more cheese on Mario's dish.

'You know fine well where our first son is. He's in America, working hard, doing well for himself.'

'And what's this son of ours doing in America that's so clever. What's he doing, eh?'

'Building houses in New Jersey. Earning good money. Making something of himself.'

'So why's he building houses in New Jersey? Why can't he build houses in Abruzzo? Come to that, I need a new shed for the rabbits. Why can't he build me a new shed?'

Anna sighed deeply.

'Because you don't pay him. What future does he have in Abruzzo?'

'Don't pay him? What you mean, I don't pay him? I give him food, he's got a room. All free.'

Bruno took a long swig of beer.

'Anyway,' added Anna, Francesco will be married soon.'

'So that's supposed to make me happy, eh? He marries an American slut and I'm meant to jump for joy.'

'Emmy-Lou is not a slut, Papa,' said Laura, unable to stop herself from fiercely joining the argument.

'Oh yes, remind me, why don't you. You and Mamma take all our money and fly to New Jersey to visit our son and this – this American fiancée of his.'

'And you and Mamma will fly to New Jersey for the wedding.'

'We'll see about that,' muttered Bruno, before tipping the near-empty beer can to his mouth.

Having demonstrated support for her elder brother in America, Laura defiantly gave encouragement to the younger brother sitting next to her.

'Did you see anything interesting?' she asked Giovanni.

His face lit up. He adored his sister, thinking her the most beautiful girl in the whole world, and although he suspected she was asking more out of sisterly love than from genuine interest, he proudly explained his sighting of the golden oriole.

'Trocadero, Trocadero,' that's what they're singing,' he enthused.

'Are you sure it's not "you're a hero, you're a hero?"' said Laura.

Giovanni beamed with delight at his lovely sister. She gave him a playful pinch on the cheek, smiling back at him.

Felicita tipped the last of the pasta into Mario's bowl without asking whether Laura or Giovanni wanted any more, while Giovanni twirled the final strand of spaghetti round his fork and scooped it quickly into his mouth.

'How do you know that what you saw was a – whatever you said?' asked Felicita sceptically.

'Filippo told me about them. It was just like he described.'

'Filippo. Him and his biker friends, coming and going at his house,' chipped in Mario.

'Biker friends?' called Anna.

'I don't know them, Mamma,' shouted Giovanni. 'I never see them. I only visit Filippo at his wood-working place, I don't go to his home.'

'Anyway, how come Filippo knows all that stuff about birds and things?' continued Mario.

'Because he's clever. He reads books. He can speak English, and he's been to America, and England, and Spain.'

'If he's so clever, how come a man his age has a pony tail, huh?' taunted Mario. 'And another thing, how come he doesn't have a woman?'

'His wife died.'

'So, his wife died. That's bad luck. Why doesn't he find another wife? There's plenty of women his age around here. Maybe there's something wrong with the guy.'

'Mamma, it's not fair,' shouted Giovanni.

'What's not fair?' she called back.

'If my sister marries a baboon, my nephews and nieces will be baboons as well.'

'Why you little shit,' growled Mario, getting to his feet and scraping his chair on the tiled floor.

'Leave it Mario…'

'Have respect for your elders Giovanni…'

'Be quiet…'

'ENOUGH!' shouted Anna over the tumult. 'Felicita, fetch a glass of wine for Mario. And put the bowl of cherries you picked this morning on the table. Giovanni, finish your water. I won't have this arguing at dinner.'

Bruno switched the television back on. It was half an hour before the football match was due to start, but he would find something to drown out the family arguments. As he was flicking through channels trying to find a half-watchable programme, his youngest son, Giovanni, plonked his glass back on the table, jumped up, and ran to the doorway.

'Hear that, Laura? It's the buzzards. They nest every year in the big trees up on the hill.'

'That pathetic mewing noise?' spat Mario. 'You sure it's not a pigeon farting?'

Mario laughed at his own joke, as Giovanni darted back outside, his bright, dark eyes gazing up into the early evening sky.

Two

The following morning, Tuesday, shortly after eight o'clock, Major Antonio D'Angelo of the Abruzzo carabinieri, Chieti Provincial Division, parked in his usual space in front of the local headquarters, and strode to the station's front door. Standing one metre eighty-eight, Major D'Angelo was unusually tall for an Abruzzese, but, despite an unwelcome widening of his middle-aged girth, didn't lack the typical muscular physique inherited from peasant farming stock, the Abruzzo 'contadini'. His thick, black hair had turned silver at the temples, but his face had not lost the good looks of earlier years, and his twinkling dark eyes remained as mirrors to his emotions. From looking kind and thoughtful, they could change in an instant to show sorrow, or inquisitiveness, or anger. Few people were foolhardy enough to cross Major D'Angelo when anger was reflected in those expressive eyes.

He greeted the civilian secretary, Katia Martorella, in the reception area, then requested the overnight incident report.

'Already with Sergeant Lazzaro,' she smiled. 'He's beaten you in this morning.'

Major D'Angelo returned the smile, and walked the few paces down the wood-panel lined corridor to the office shared by Sergeant Emilio Lazzaro and Trooper Roberto Di Silverio, but finding the sergeant alone in the room. After exchanging pleasantries, D'Angelo asked if there was anything on the overnight report that required attention.

'Another break-in, this time the pharmacy in Ripana,' said Lazzaro, glancing through the printed page he was holding. 'A disturbance outside Bar Sporting in via Frasca – probably to do with last night's football result – a missing boy out at Montenero, and – blah blah blah – oh, a theft from a till in the café in via Roma.'

'Age?'

'Sorry?'

'What age, the missing boy?'

Sergeant Lazzaro looked again through the report in his hand until he found the relevant entry.

'Eleven years old. Last seen at about seven-fifteen yesterday evening when he walked out of the family house alone. Not been seen since.'

'Eleven. Gone to a friend's most likely. He'll turn up sooner or later. What's happening about the pharmacy break-in?'

'I told Di Silverio to go straight there and liaise with the local police vigile, Constable er…,' the sergeant checked a note by his phone, 'Bellini. Constable Bellini.'

'God help us,' groaned Major D'Angelo. 'Our intrepid Trooper Di Silverio will probably line suspects up against a wall and start shooting them, unless Bellini can stop him.'

Sergeant Lazzaro chuckled. Shorter and stockier than his commanding officer, his broad face, flattish nose and large chin reminded the major of a bulldog. The second-in-command was also reliable, loyal, and resourceful. The pair had a successful and informal working relationship, such that at least in private they were on first-name terms.

'Come on, Tonio, he's improving. He might make a decent carabiniere one day.'

'And I'll be the general in Rome,' scoffed D'Angelo. 'He's obsessed with weapons,' – the major glanced at pictures of military hardware which the trooper had put up on the wall, including one with Di Silverio himself smiling broadly with an assault rifle in his hands – 'and he thinks the best thing about his uniform is that it helps him pick up more girls.'

'At least that gives him a reason to look smart. Look Tonio, I know you two don't see eye to eye,' said the sergeant in a more serious tone, 'but he's young, he's got a lot to learn, – and he's well-connected. He comes from a good family, Di Silverio.'

'Which proves that any pool can become contaminated, even a gene pool. And before you start bowing and scraping to the rich and powerful Di Silverio family, bear in mind that they're only where they are because some long-deceased ancestor was adept at bludgeoning his neighbours into submission and stealing their olive groves and vineyards before paying them a pittance to work for him.'

'That may be so, but keep in mind that Trooper Di Silverio's father has – erm – influence.'

'You're not suggesting I overlook the boy's shortcomings just because his papa plays golf with Colonel Battista?'

'I think you should go a bit easy on him, that's all.'

'What is his nickname for me – Virgun?'

'You know about that?'

'You'd be surprised the things I know, Emil. Virgun. The officer with the virgin gun. He thinks I'm wet because I hardly ever carry my personal weapon. I can hear him now, holding forth to his mates : "My commanding officer is issued with a Beretta 92FS pistol, a beautiful hand gun, but he wants to keep it pure, so it never gets taken out. He wants his gun to stay a virgin."

'And when is he going to learn the truth?'

'The truth, Emil?'

'I get to know things as well, Tonio. I heard the story about your time in New York.'

Major D'Angelo felt a cold weight in the pit of his stomach. There were fewer times these days when the memories of his secondment to the NYPD, and the repercussions, came back to haunt him.

'That's history, Emil,' he said coldly.

The awkward moment was rescued by a call on the internal phone, as Major D'Angelo picked it up.

'Yes Katia, what is it?'

'A traffic incident on the ring road. By the parade of shops just before the hospital roundabout. Woman and child injured, don't know how seriously; the ambulance has been called and is on its way.'

'At least it should get there quickly, not far to go. Where are the Civil Police when you want them? Aren't they supposed to take care of the roads? OK Katia, I'll take it myself. Sergeant Lazzaro in command here in the meantime.'

'RTA on the ring road,' explained D'Angelo to the sergeant, grabbing his cap from the top of the desk where he had dropped it earlier. 'Call me if anything crops up that I should know about. See you later.'

When Major D'Angelo arrived at the scene of the accident a few minutes later, the ambulance was already in attendance. The paramedics were carefully assessing the victims and lifting them into the vehicle, flashing blue lights indicating the urgency of the situation, but in the road behind them, chaos reigned. People were shouting and gesticulating wildly as Major D'Angelo parked the Alfa Romeo Giulietta patrol car outside Luigi's hairdressing salon, firmly fixing his peaked cap in place as he marched forward to take charge of the situation. He often wished his compatriots would act rather more calmly in such circumstances. He went first to speak to the senior paramedic to make sure there were no life-threatening injuries, and that her team were in control of their task, noting that a member of the public seemed to be helping with the children. He then studied the scene of the incident. A black VW Golf had slewed to a halt facing towards the curb, several metres beyond a pedestrian crossing, while behind the crossing was parked a blue Fiat Panda, the driver standing by the open door looking anxiously around him. Traffic was building up to both north and south on the single-carriageway road.

'Anyone not directly involved in this incident, or witness to it, please move on,' bellowed Major D'Angelo to the gathering crowd. The shouting and arm-waving gradually diminished, as the ambulance, siren wailing, turned in the road and headed towards the roundabout two hundred metres away, before taking the first right up a long hill to the hospital.

'Who is the owner of this car?' demanded D'Angelo, pointing to the black Golf. A young man, one of the more vocal within the crowd, stepped forward.

'You were driving this vehicle when the incident took place?'

'Yes.'

'Park it there in front of the pizzeria so that this traffic can get moving again, then wait beside my patrol car with your identity card, driving licence, vehicle registration form, and the car insurance document.'

'But this is crazy, it was not my fault,' he insisted, his hands held together as if in prayer, and waving them up and down. 'That idiot there just stopped, I thought he was going to the hairdressers. The fool, he's to blame,' yelled the young man, pointing to the driver of the blue Panda.

'Be quiet,' shouted Major D'Angelo, 'and do as I tell you.'

He then approached the somewhat bewildered-looking man standing beside the Panda.

'Will you explain to me what happened,' demanded D'Angelo.

'What – er – happened? Yes. I – erm – I stop here because, er because…'

'You speak English?'

'Yes,' said the man, I *am* English.'

'OK, I can speak English,' said D'Angelo. 'Tell me what happened.'

'There was a lady, just there by the zebra crossing, with a small child at her side and a youngster in a buggy…'

'Zebra?'

'That marking. Pedestrian right of way. We call it a zebra crossing in UK.'

'I understand. Please continue.'

'Well, they were about to cross the road, the buggy was partly off the curb, so I stopped to let them across, but the car behind me – that VW over there – came straight past me and ploughed into the lady and her children.'

'I see. What is your name please?'

'Fenwick. Jim – James – Fenwick.'

'Are you resident here Mister Fenique?'

'No. No, I have a holiday place here, over at Canosa. I come out three or four times a year.'

'So this is not your car?'

'No, it's a hire car. I picked it up from Pescara airport when I arrived last Friday.'

'Then you don't have an identity card?'

'No.'

'Could I see your passport please.'

'It's in my jacket – in the back there.'

D'Angelo glanced in at the back seat of Jim Fenwick's car.

'Please get it for me.'

Jim Fenwick retrieved his passport from the inside pocket of his jacket and handed it to Major D'Angelo, just as a buzzing from his inside pocket indicated that D'Angelo had an incoming call. Like many of his colleagues, D'Angelo carried a personal mobile phone as well as his carabinieri issue compact radio, which was kept in a small leather pouch on his belt. From a quick look at the screen of his mobile, he could see it was Sergeant Lazzaro calling.

'Yes, Emil, what is it?'

'Just had another call about that boy.'

'Boy?'

'The missing boy. From Montenero. The local vigile rang to say the mother is getting very worried about him.'

Major D'Angelo looked at his watch. Eight twenty-three. If the boy and his pal have gone off somewhere, they could be a while yet.

'Alright Emilio, I'm nearly done here. I'll be back shortly, then I'll look into it. Nothing else?'

'Nothing else Tonio. See you soon.'

D'Angelo ended the call and looked at Jim Fenwick's passport.

'You live in – Sheffield.'

'That's right.'

'But you were born in Germany?'

'Yes.'

'I take it you were on your own when you were driving?'

'No – no, my wife was with me. Nadia. She's Italian. From Rome originally.'

Major D'Angelo looked around ostentatiously.

'Oh, er, she went with the ambulance,' explained Jim.

'She was hurt?'

'No, she's fine. She's a paediatric nurse, you see, and she, erm, she went to help take care of the two small children.'

'Ah. The lady in the blue top?'

'That's right.'

'If you wait here for a few minutes, Mister Fenique, you can follow me up to the A&E, Pronto Soccorso we call it, at the hospital, then we can find your wife.'

'Oh, right, thank you.'

D'Angelo walked to the group of bystanders who were still watching proceedings.

'So, you were all witnesses to the events here?'

The spectators started to shuffle away, leaving just one person, a portly man in his mid-fifties, standing alone.

'Your name please, Signore.'

'De Marco. Gabriele De Marco.'

'Could you tell me where you were and what you saw, Signore De Marco.'

D'Angelo had taken a small black notebook and pen from his top pocket and was writing : Witness, Gabriele De Marco.

'Sure,' said Gabriele, 'I had just come out of the hairdressers there – Luigi's – and I was trying to decide whether to pop across for a coffee and croissant. I was right behind the Signora and her two little kids who were waiting to go over on the crossing. That car there, the Fiat, stopped to let them go, so I thought to myself, yes, I'll follow them across the road while the traffic's stopped, but as I was about to step off the pavement, that other car, the black one, came up behind and overtook the Fiat and hit the lady and her kids. Sent them flying. Terrible, it was.'

'Thank you Signore. Could I have a look at your identity card please.'

De Marco pulled out his wallet and handed over his ID card.

'Address, via Cicconetti, number seven, is that correct?'

'That's right.'

'Thank you Signore De Marco. I shall contact you if it should prove necessary. You may go now.'

Major D'Angelo turned and walked with a determined step back to his patrol car, where the Golf driver stood waiting, looking a good deal less confident than previously.

D'Angelo took the proffered documents and silently checked them.

'So, Signore Valini, Aldo Valini, you admit you hit the lady and her children on the pedestrian crossing?'

'Yes, but…'

'It appears you recklessly overtook a stationary vehicle, ignoring the pedestrian right of way, and caused injuries to three people. Do you have any explanation for your actions?'

'I didn't see the crossing, the paint is all faded, look at it. And nobody stops like that, not unless people are already out in the road. It's the fault of the foreigner, the straniero. They shouldn't be driving on our roads.'

'I see you live in Ortona,' said D'Angelo.

'So what?'

'So, Signore Valini, this is what you're going to do. You will take these documents to the comune in Ortona tomorrow between the hours of eight and eighteen hundred. They will by then have received my report, which will recommend a substantial fine and confiscation of your driving licence. I will further be recommending that you re-take a driving test before being issued once again with your licence. Do you understand?'

Aldo Valini just stared at the major.

'I said, do you understand me, Signore Valini?'

The young man tilted his head back and muttered 'yes.'

'Good, you may go, and kindly drive with greater care.'

Major D'Angelo indicated to Jim Fenwick that he was about to set off for the hospital, and led the way up to the car park outside A&E. They parked alongside one another and entered the building, where D'Angelo asked the paramedic on reception duty the name of the doctor in charge of the recently-arrived RTA victims.

'Dottoressa Cristina Rosello,' he replied.

'And they'll be in trauma suite – room number…?'

'Number fourteen, Signore.'

'Thank you. Follow me, Mister Fenique.'

They ascended a single flight of stairs to the fourth floor. Jim realised that much of the hospital was built at a lower level, so the entrance to A&E was actually on the third floor. They found Nadia Fenwick sitting alone in the corridor outside room fourteen, relieved that her husband had managed to find her.

'This is Major D'Angelo,' explained Jim. 'He wants to check the status of the victims before writing his report.'

'The doctor promised me she would give an update as soon as she could,' said Nadia, greeting Major D'Angelo with a smile and a handshake.

Jim and Nadia both started to recount events since the accident to one another, but within less than a minute, the door of the trauma suite opened, and a lady doctor hurried out.

'Oh, Antonio, hi,' she said, seeing Major D'Angelo.

'Hello Cristina. I need to know if there are any serious injuries to the victims, just in general terms of course, no personal details.'

'They were lucky. Nothing life-changing. We haven't got all the X-rays yet, but almost certainly a couple of fractures, dislocated hip, probable cracked rib, and quite bad lacerations and bruising. We'll need to keep them all in for a day or two, but nothing too serious.'

'Do we need to contact anyone? Partner, family?'

'It's alright, Antonio. Social Department have been contacted, they'll take care of all that side of things. We're grateful to Nadia here for looking after the children until they got here.'

A buzzing from his inside pocket alerted Major D'Angelo to a new call. Lazzaro again.

'Hello Sergeant,' he said quietly, turning away from the other three, but giving notice to Lazzaro with a formal mode of address that the conversation could be overheard.

'More development on the case we discussed earlier Signore,' said Lazzaro circumspectly.

D'Angelo walked a little way down the corridor, his heart beginning to race slightly.

'OK Emil, tell me.'

'The Montenero mayor, Franco Mancinelli, has been on this time, shouting the odds that nobody cares about outlying villages, and that poor people living in the countryside are second-class citizens who don't get any help. He got pretty heated, I can tell you. I said you were on an urgent call, but that you'd get back to him very soon.'

There were a few moments' silence. D'Angelo felt his mouth going dry and his heart thumping more rapidly. Perhaps he had made a mistake, an error of judgement. He could have insisted that the Civil Police come and sort out this traffic accident, and was it really necessary that he came to the hospital to check on the victims? Did he actually want to come and see Cristina Rosello, or was he showing off to the Englishman and his attractive wife? He could imagine how it might appear to someone like Colonel Battista. Dammit, he thought, that he, of all officers in the force, might be accused of neglecting the 'contadini', when at heart he was still one of them.

'Emilio, call the mayor back and tell him I'm on my way to Montenero right now. I'm about to leave the hospital, so give him an ETA. And Emil, find out what you can about the boy, full name, anything about his parents, get the address and co-ordinates, and call me back. Text the co-ordinates. Ciao.'

D'Angelo slid the phone back into his inside pocket and strode back down the corridor towards Cristina Rosello and Jim and Nadia Fenwick. From a few metres distant, he interrupted their conversation to say that he had an urgent call-out, wished them good day, turned sharply around and headed back towards the exit.

Three

Notwithstanding the shocking state of disrepair of Abruzzo's roads, not well constructed in the first place, and never intended for the big trucks that now used them, the generally small volumes of traffic in the countryside meant that there were rarely occasions when drivers on minor roads were held up, except to manoeuvre past tractors and small slow-moving three-wheeled pickup trucks, 'Bees' as they are called. Consequently, journey times could be fairly safely predicted, and Major D'Angelo was due to arrive in Montenero on schedule, although it was unusual for people in Abruzzo to take much notice of agreed times.

Several kilometres from his destination, D'Angelo pulled off the road to make a note of the boy's name, Giovanni Mirelti, and to enter the house's GPS co-ordinates into his satnav. Sergeant Lazzaro had included Montenero's comune phone number in his text message, so D'Angelo decided to call the mayor, Franco Mancinelli, to tell him that he would be going straight to the Mirelti residence, and would he please let the family know. 'But I will come to see you at the comune before I leave Montenero,' promised D'Angelo.

It wasn't long before Major D'Angelo turned off the small road on which he had been travelling onto a track leading to the Mirelti farm. The main house, a three-storey concrete construction, sat alongside a large brick-built barn, behind which D'Angelo could see at least three smaller out-buildings. Beyond the house was a substantial olive grove, leading to a fairly steep hill planted with several rows of vines. The higher part of the hill was covered with dense woodland. Few farmers with that many vines and land to spare were poor, thought D'Angelo as he retrieved his cap from the front passenger seat, especially if, as he had done on his own vineyard, they had planted Montepulciano grapes to take advantage of the increasing popularity and price of Abruzzo's red wine. He looked to the other side of the house, where the nearest neighbouring property stood about a hundred metres away, and in the background rose the snow-capped Apennines and Majella National Park. D'Angelo, feeling the warmth of the morning sun on his back, decided to leave his jacket hanging in the back of his car.

As he crossed the untidy yard towards the house, it occurred to Major D'Angelo how quiet it was, not even the ubiquitous yapping tethered dog. He knocked at the open front door and called out 'Permesso? May I enter.'

Felicita came forward to meet him. 'Please, come in,' she said quietly.

It took his eyes a few seconds to adjust to the relative gloom within the house, compared to the bright May sunshine, but then he quickly took in the cavernous room in which he found himself. It was somewhat sparsely furnished, making the room seem even bigger, and there were two internal doors leading off it. Facing him, seated at the pine table, was Anna. She was twirling a handkerchief around her fingers, and as Major D'Angelo stepped towards her, he could see that her eyes were red and blotchy, with dark rings beneath them. She's had a bad night, he thought.

'Good morning, I am Carabinieri Major D'Angelo. Are you Giovanni Mirelti's mother?'

'Yes, Major. Do you have any news of our little boy?'

'I'm sorry to say I haven't, Signora, but I promise I shall do all I can to try and find him. First, if you'll excuse the intrusion, I would like to ask a few questions. May I sit down?'

'Please, Major. Felicita, would you fetch us some coffee.'

'Thank you Signora. As I understand it, Giovanni left here alone yesterday evening at approximately seven-fifteen, and hasn't returned home. Was he going to meet someone? Did he have anything planned?'

'No, Major, he went out just after eating his supper, on the spur of the moment. I think he heard the buzzards, and went out to look at them.'

'Buzzards?'

'You know, the birds. He loves anything to do with birds, animals, all that sort of stuff.'

'And he didn't say anything as he was leaving, how long he might be, or where he was going?'

'Nothing, Major. He heard the buzzards and was gone. I was up all night, walking round the land, calling him, but he's just disappeared.'

Anna sniffed, and dabbed with her handkerchief at her sore eyes.

'Was anyone else here at the time?' asked D'Angelo gently.

'Oh yes, Bruno, my husband, was here. I think he was watching television when Giovanni left.'

'And where is your husband now, Signora?'

'We have another plot of land just down the road, it belonged to one of my uncles. It's where we grow our vegetables and salad, and he's gone to put in some tomato and courgette seedlings that need planting.'

'I see.'

'Oh please, don't misunderstand, Major. My husband is worried about Giovanni as well, but he thinks the lad is hiding in a barn somewhere and that he'll be back when he's hungry.'

'He might well be right, Signora.'

Anna tugged at her handkerchief and looked sorrowfully towards the door.

'Were just the three of you here,' persisted D'Angelo.

'Sorry? No, oh no, Felicita, my daughter over there, and Mario, her fiancé. And Laura, of course, she's my second daughter. They were all here.'

Major D'Angelo was jotting notes in his book, as Felicita placed a small cup of espresso and sugar in front of him.

'Thank you, Signorina. Where is Mario this morning?'

'He's attaching a spraying machine to the tractor, getting ready to spray the grapes. Shall I go and fetch him?'

'No, Signorina, there's no need. I'll go and have a quick chat with him before I go. And – let me see – Laura, is she here today?'

'She's gone to a friend's house,' said Anna. 'Her friend Maria. Maria has a computer and printer, and Laura's taken her smartphone which has a photo of Giovanni on it so that they can make some posters to say that he's missing, in case anyone has seen him.'

'That could be very helpful, Signora. Do you have any other photos of Giovanni that I might borrow?'

'I'm afraid not, Major.'

'Giovanni won't have an identity card because he's under fifteen,' pondered D'Angelo. 'Could you ask Laura's friend to e-mail the picture to my office? Here is my card with the e-mail address on it. So, yourself and your husband, Bruno, plus Felicita, Mario and Laura, all saw Giovanni leaving.'

'That's right. Mamma was here in the house, but she was upstairs in her room. She spends a lot of time in her room. She's there now.'

'She didn't see Giovanni go? Not from a window, perhaps?'

'No. Her room is on the other side of the house. Her window was open, because when I took her pasta up for her just before eight o'clock, she was moaning about next door neighbours shooting when the hunting season is over, said I should make a complaint to the authorities.'

'She heard shooting?'

'She said she heard a shotgun fired twice, but it was probably just fireworks, a wedding or festa or something.'

'Did she say what time she heard the bangs'

'I think she said it was about twenty to seven.'

'Which would have been at least half an hour before Giovanni went missing,' mused D'Angelo. 'Has he ever gone off like this before, for more than a few hours, I mean?'

'No, Major, never.'

'Does he ever stay overnight with friends, or lose track of time when he's out playing?'

There followed a brief silence. D'Angelo could see sadness as well as grief in Anna's eyes.

'He doesn't really have any friends, at least not his own age. He's a bit of a loner I suppose. He seems – sort of different to other boys.'

'You said "his own age", Signora.'

'There's a man in the village, Filippo, he has a wood-working place, sells carvings, bits of furniture and stuff. Giovanni likes to go and help him, sweep the floor, tidy the stacks of wood, that sort of thing. Filippo pays him a few euros for the work he does.'

'Is he keen on woodworking?'

'Giovanni? No, not really. Giovanni is very interested in nature, birds and animals. I think Filippo is quite knowledgeable, and he teaches Giovanni, especially about birds. Quite a lot of Filippo's carvings are of owls and eagles and such like.'

'Does Giovanni go to Filippo's house?'

'No, I don't think he's ever been to his house. Just the workshop.'

'When did Giovanni last go to help in his workshop?'

'As far as I know, Friday after school was the last time.'

'I think he went on Saturday morning, Mamma,' added Felicita.

Major D'Angelo rested his chin in his large bear-like hand and frowned, drawing his dark, bushy eyebrows down over his eyes.

'Did Giovanni seem in any way different to usual yesterday evening?' he asked.

Anna and Felicita took a moment to reflect.

'I wouldn't say so, no,' said Anna. 'He had spotted some bird or other that Filippo had told him about, and was quite excited about that.'

'So, when he was here, having his tea, nothing happened or was said that could have led to him going out distressed?'

In another moment of silence, D'Angelo noticed a flash of a glance between mother and daughter, then they both looked down at the table.

'There was a bit of a spat between Giovanni and Mario,' said Felicita at last. 'They tend to wind each other up. Mario teases him about liking wildlife and not knowing anything about football, and Giovanni called Mario a baboon.'

'A baboon? How did he react?'

'He was pretty angry, but Giovanni left the house soon afterwards, so nothing came of it.'

D'Angelo rubbed his nose, thinking, wondering, then pushed the empty espresso cup away and stood up.

'I would like, if I may, Signora, to have a look at Giovanni's bedroom. Is that alright?'

'What? Oh, er, yes, yes of course, Major. I'll show you.'

Anna led Major D'Angelo through one of the internal doors to a short passageway and to the stairs, up past one floor to the second. D'Angelo's boots clattered with a ringing sound on the re-constituted stone steps, then on the grey floor tiles as he was shown into Giovanni's bedroom.

The first thing that D'Angelo noticed was that it was a large space, although some of the height on one side of the room was lost because it was beneath the eaves of the roof. The single bed almost looked tiny, as did the bedside table and ancient-looking wardrobe. The white-painted walls were devoid of any pictures or posters, although a dark patch near the window showed where damp had obviously penetrated. There were two posters on show, both attached to the wardrobe doors, but not the type one would expect in a young boy's room, such as footballers or music celebrities. One was a picture of wolves, the other of bears. Inside the wardrobe were shelves of clothes, some flip-flops and a pair of sandals. D'Angelo could see no electronic devices, such as a games console, but the most unusual and striking feature of the room was a table in one corner, or more accurately the objects on top of and underneath the table. There was a huge collection of artefacts that Giovanni had evidently picked up in the surrounding countryside. D'Angelo walked over to the table and looked more closely at the strange collection. There were birds' nests, sloughed snake skins, insects of various kinds, the skull of an animal that D'Angelo guessed was either of a fox or badger, and in the centre of the table, seemingly in pride of place, a carved wooden owl. D'Angelo picked it up and discovered that burnt into the base of the carving was the name 'F. Geniola'. He replaced the owl on the table and walked out of the room, closing the door behind him, to re-join Anna who had been waiting outside for him.

'Is anything missing?' he asked her, 'clothes, pyjamas?'

'No Major, nothing is missing.'

'What shoes would he have been wearing when he left?'

'His green trainers. He wore those trainers nearly all the time, when he bothered wearing shoes at all.'

'And what else was he wearing?'

'Let me think… beige shorts and a faded red tee-shirt.'

'Giovanni's wood-working friend, Filippo. What is his surname?'

'Geniola. Not one of the usual Montenero names. I think it originates from up north somewhere, Milan, Venice perhaps.'

'Mmm. Signora, I wonder if perhaps I might now have a word with your mother, if she's willing.'

They went back down one flight of stairs to the first floor landing, where Anna tapped on a closed door, and called "Mamma".

'Come in Anna.'

Anna opened the door a little way and poked her head through the gap.

'Mamma, Major D'Angelo is here, trying to find out what has happened to little Giovanni. Is it alright if he comes in to speak to you?'

'Here, in my room. A man?'

'He's an officer in the carabinieri, Mamma. He wants to find out as much as he can about our boy's disappearance. Anything at all that you might be able to tell him.'

'One moment then, Anna.'

Anna's mother, Elisabetta, looked older than her seventy-three years, despite having had her grey hair dyed an unconvincing black. Few Italian ladies wished to be seen with grey hair. Her small frame seemed further diminished by a stoop, yet she was still remarkably agile, and could walk with a spritely step unaided by a stick. She rose from the small armchair near her bed and crossed the room to collect a black widow's shawl which had been draped around the back of an upright chair. She placed the shawl around her narrow shoulders, then pulled the door fully open to greet Major D'Angelo. Like many women before her, she was immediately impressed by his tall stature and dark good looks. The major hovered in the doorway before saying "may I enter?" in the customary polite manner.

'Please, come in Major D'Angelo. I would be quite happy to talk to you downstairs, you know.'

'That's quite alright, Signora, I prefer to chat up here. I believe you were here in your room when Giovanni left the house?'

Anna, who had been waiting in the doorway, sniffed, and dabbed her nose with her damp handkerchief.

'I'll wait downstairs, Signore,' she said quietly, and gently closed the door behind her.

'What on earth can have happened to my grandson, Major D'Angelo?' asked Elisabetta in a firm voice.

'In all honesty, Signora, at the present time I have no idea, but I am determined to find out.'

D'Angelo walked across to the open window and looked out, taking in the neighbouring property and the mountains in the background.

'A lovely view you have from here, Signora.'

'I love it, Major. And in answer to your earlier question, yes, I was up here when Giovanni disappeared. I spend quite a lot of time on my own. Perhaps more than I should, I don't know. It's just that since I lost my husband... the place doesn't seem the same any more.'

'This was your family home?'

'Yes. Anna grew up here. Bruno, that's her husband, his family come from a small village about eight kilometres away. He did well for himself when he married Anna.'

D'Angelo looked around what was yet another large, square room. There was a dressing table with a mirror in front of it against one wall, and a wash basin in the corner. There were several prints of rural scenes hanging on the other walls, a well-stocked book-case, and above the bed a religious icon with a Palm Sunday cross tucked behind it. Next to the bed was a small table on which sat a large analogue alarm clock. The air was scented with an old-fashioned perfume. It struck Major D'Angelo as a room that was comfortable and lived-in without being cosy.

'You seem fairly self-contained, Signora.'

'Oh, I'm content with my own company most of the time, Major. When you get to the stage where there's not a lot to look forward to, you find satisfaction in the simple pleasures, a new book to read, a visit to church, even taking flowers to the cemetery. Unless Rodolfus comes to visit, of course,' she added with a twinkle in her eye.'

'Ah, Rodolfus and the Princess,' smiled D'Angelo.

'You know the story?'

'I read it in my sister's book when I was very young. There was a beautiful Princess who lived at the top of a tower in her father's castle, but the jealous and vengeful witch of the mountain' – D'Angelo stole a quick look through the window at the snow-capped mountains – 'put a curse on the Princess, turning her old and…'

'Old and ugly, Major.'

'So she hid herself away, never leaving her lonely garret. Then one day Rodolfus came along, and was lifted up to her window by a giant eagle. Rodolfus kissed the old woman, broke the curse, and she was once again young and beautiful.'

'Bravo, Major, well remembered. Isn't it amazing how we can remember stories like that from when we were six or seven, but struggle to remember things that happened last week. You're not Rodolfus by any chance, are you? I always imagined he was wearing uniform.'

'I'm afraid not, Signora. The nearest I get is that my middle name is Rodrigo.'

'Then if I may be so bold, Major D'Angelo, I shall call you Rodrigo. You will call me by my first name, Elisabetta. In this house I'm always either Mamma or Nonna, or in the case of Bruno and Mario, nothing at all. It would be nice to be called by my name for a change.'

'And a beautiful name it is too, Elisabetta.'

'I do so want you to find Giovanni, Rodrigo,' she pleaded in a voice suddenly sad and serious. 'Anna's first son went to live in America, you know. She must have a son. It would be dreadful for her to lose both of them. I don't know if I can be of any help, but I will try.'

'I just wanted to confirm you didn't see Giovanni after he left the house, after seven-fifteen in the evening.'

'No. I think the last time I saw him was yesterday lunch-time.'

'Anna told me you heard what you thought were gunshots.'

'Two. About five seconds apart. They were definitely from a shotgun.'

'They couldn't have been fireworks perhaps?'

'No, Rodrigo. I was married for nearly fifty years to a hunter, and I know what a twelve-bore sounds like. But my husband, unlike our neighbours, only shot what was legal, and within the hunting season.'

'Who are your neighbours?'

'Pietro Fiorito and his wife Federica Mancinelli with their son, Leonardo.'

'Mancinelli? Same name as the mayor. Same family?'

'Same family. I think they might be cousins. There are quite a few Mancinelli around here. The son, by the way, is – how shall I say – backward.'

'I think we say 'having learning difficulties' these days.'

D'Angelo walked once again to the window and discreetly looked at his watch. It was just before ten minutes to eleven.

'Where were you when you heard the shots being fired, Elisabetta.?'

She put her thumb and forefinger to her mouth and thought for a few moments.

'I was over there,' she said, 'sitting at my dressing table. I might eat my supper alone, but I wanted to be sure I looked tidy. Old habits die hard.'

'Would you sit there for me now?'

'Oh!' Puzzled, Elisabetta hesitated a moment. 'Yes, alright.' She sat on the straight-backed chair facing her table and mirror.

'Can you remind me what time you heard the gunshots?'

'It was – it was twenty to seven. I wanted Anna to report them, and I thought it was important that I remembered the time they were shooting.'

'I notice, Elisabetta, that you don't wear a watch.'

'No, it broke ages ago. It was a present from my husband. I have my trusty alarm clock to tell me the time. I can see it now.'

'In the mirror?'

'Yes.'

'Without turning round, can you tell me what the time is now?'

'Yes. It's ten past – er – eleven.'

'Might you have checked the time just like that, looking at your clock in the mirror, when you heard the shots?'

'Very likely. I was doing my hair, you see, and I wouldn't have wanted to muck things up by turning round.'

'Would you turn round now and check the time.'

'Oh – good gracious, it's – it's ten before eleven. I said ten past, didn't I.'

'Is it possible you could have made the same mistake yesterday evening? That it may have been twenty *past* seven when you heard the shotgun being fired, not twenty *to* seven?'

'Oh – oh my goodness. You mean – you mean maybe the shots were fired *after* Giovanni left the house?'

D'Angelo looked across at the neighbouring property, biting his lip in thought.

'Well, Elisabetta, we have to consider it a possibility.'

Four

Major D'Angelo tactfully explained to Anna about the possible discrepancy in the time of the two gunshots, and told her that he would be opening a case file on Giovanni's disappearance, even though it was usually standard procedure to wait forty-eight hours before taking such action. He needed to return to his office at the carabinieri station as soon as possible, but would first speak briefly to Mario and, as he had promised, would also call on the mayor, Signore Mancinelli, to explain what was happening. One more thing he wanted to know : Anna said she had gone outside several times during the night to look for Giovanni, but had Bruno, her husband, also gone out, either with her or on his own?

'No,' responded Anna, 'he didn't leave the house. Except to shut the door of the rabbit shed, of course, which he does every evening, to prevent foxes getting in.'

'What time would that have been, Signora?'

'Normally he would do it about eight o'clock, but he was watching the football, so he went out at half-time, around eight-thirty.'

'And at that time, you weren't worried about Giovanni not being in the house?'

'No, we didn't start worrying until quite a lot later.'

'How does Giovanni feel about you keeping rabbits?'

'Hates it, thinks it's cruel. He's refused to eat any rabbit meat for about three years.'

'Who kills the rabbits, Signora?'

'Sometimes I do, sometimes my husband or Mario. We have more than enough for ourselves, so we sell quite a lot of them.'

'How do you kill them?'

'There's an iron bar just inside the shed. We use that.'

Major D'Angelo found Mario in the big barn near the house, wearing a safety mask while pouring chemicals into a tank on the back of a small tractor. From a few metres distant, avoiding any noxious fumes, D'Angelo introduced himself, and asked Mario if he would briefly stop what he was doing in order to answer a few questions. Mario tipped the last of the container he was holding into the tank, screwed a cap on to the tank opening, pulled the mask up off his face so that it sat on his forehead, and walked casually to where D'Angelo was standing.

The carabiniere explained that he was investigating Giovanni's disappearance, and noticed that Mario showed no discernible sign of emotion or concern.

'Do you live here, Signore?' asked D'Angelo.

'No,' replied Mario. I will live here when Felicita and I are married, but at present I still live with my parents.'

'Did you go home to your parents' house last night?'

'Yes.'

'What time did you leave here?'

'Soon after having some supper. About seven-thirty,

I suppose. I wanted to be home in time to watch the football.'

'And you went straight home?'

'Yes. Well, that is, after I'd finished a small job I had to do in here.'

'What job was that, Signore?'

'I needed to fix the fuel pipe on the tractor. The old one had split.'

'Which involved what? You have a spare hose?'

'Yes. There's a section of rubber hose on the bench over there. I cut off the length I needed and attached it to the inlet on the tractor.'

'What did you use to cut the hose?'

'A clasp knife. From the shelf at the back.'

'Please, show me.'

Mario glared disdainfully at the major for a few seconds before plodding languidly to the back of the barn where he picked up a folding knife from a shelf on the wall.

'Would you open the knife for me, Signore,' said D'Angelo.

With another impertinent look into the major's eyes, Mario pulled open the knife with more force than was necessary. D'Angelo looked at the clean blade, and nodded to indicate that he was satisfied. While Mario snapped shut the blade and replaced it on the shelf, D'Angelo looked at the rest of the tools, and realised how many potential weapons were at hand. There was a sharp-looking billhook, a half-metre jemmy, several screwdrivers, a lump hammer… anyone with the intent in mind could cause mayhem in this place.

'Thank you, Signore. I'm sorry to have interrupted

your work. By the way, are you worried that Giovanni has been missing for so long?'

Mario shrugged his shoulders.

'I don't know where he is, but to tell you the truth, officer, he's such a weird little kid, he could be anywhere.'

'What do you mean by that?'

Mario tilted his head to one side, and looked towards the barn entrance, through the open doorway to the yard outside.

'OK, I give you an example. A few days ago, and I swear this is the truth, I saw that kid out in the yard, he picked up a worm, a worm for God's sake, and put it in the grass over in the field where it was safe. That boy ain't right in the head.'

D'Angelo was silent for a few moments, remembering having done similar things himself when he was young, and even not so young.

'He likes animals, doesn't he?'

'Pah. The kid wasn't normal, not by a long stretch.'

With that remark, Mario snapped his mask back over his face and strode back to the tractor, questioning time over as far as he was concerned.

Once more out in the warm, sunlit yard, D'Angelo paused to think. Mario clearly didn't like Giovanni, or at least had no time whatsoever for the young member of his future family, and although Mario was less sharp than many of the tools in that barn, would he actually be capable of extreme violence, if indeed any harm had come to Giovanni. Yet D'Angelo felt sure that Mario, with his final remark, had referred to the boy in the past tense. There were other worries nagging at the major's consciousness, including the proposition that Giovanni's father, Bruno, seemed to be showing very little concern for his missing son. The last time Bruno had left the house yesterday evening was to deal with the rabbits, an issue which must have caused friction between the two of them.

D'Angelo turned and walked back the other way, skirting the barn until he stopped outside a shed from which emanated the distinctive pungent smell of caged rabbits. Entering the building, he found hutches positioned all around the inside perimeter, some stacked one on top of the other, containing rabbits of varying ages and colours – white, brown, black and grey.

Beside the door, leaning against the wall, just as Anna had described it, was the iron bar, the purpose of which was to despatch the unfortunate animals. D'Angelo picked the bar up, realising immediately by its weight that it was in fact lead rather than iron, being a section of old water pipe, one end of which had bits of fur stuck to dried blood.

On the short drive to Montenero's municipal building where he would speak to the mayor, D'Angelo wished that he was instead heading straight back to his office in order to open a 'missing person' case file on Giovanni Mirelti. From all that he had gleaned about the boy from family members, Major D'Angelo was now sure that this wouldn't be a simple case of Giovanni staying overnight with a friend. It was possible that the lad had fallen and hurt himself, unable to make his way home, or, and this was less likely, that he had strayed too far and got lost. The only other possibilities that D'Angelo could perceive were that Giovanni had run away, or that he had been abducted, or that he had been killed, accidentally or deliberately. D'Angelo found himself gripping the steering wheel tightly while considering the latter option.

He parked immediately outside Montenero's comune building, where parking was not normally permitted, and ran up the stairs to the mayor's office on the first floor, where he found Franco Mancinelli in conference with the local civil policeman, Maurizio Bordoni. D'Angelo gave a brief resume of his conversations at the Mirelti family home, then asked if any information had come to light within Montenero itself.

'Nothing at all,' said Franco, with a shrug of his shoulders.

'I've been asking around, in the café, pharmacy, post office,' said constable Bordoni. Nobody has seen him. I checked at the school, but he hasn't attended this morning. It's as though he's simply vanished.'

'We will have to conduct a search around the area of the Mirelti place,' stated Major D'Angelo. 'I shall be returning here this afternoon to speak to the neighbour, Signore...'

'Fiorito,' prompted Franco. 'Pietro Fiorito.'

'Fiorito, yes. Meanwhile, I will instruct my sergeant to organize a search party. Can I ask him to liaise with you, Bordoni, for local knowledge?'

'Of course, Major.'

'There are doubtless a fair number of abandoned buildings in the vicinity, perhaps also some disused open wells. Now, Signori, if you'll excuse me, I need to go and set wheels in motion from my office.' D'Angelo started to leave. 'Incidentally, Signore Mancinelli,' he added, 'I understand that Pietro Fiorito is married to a cousin of yours, Federica Mancinelli. Do you know anything about Pietro allegedly shooting out of season?'

Maurizio Bordoni kept his eyes fixed on the table top, while Franco Mancinelli waved his hand dismissively, as though swatting an imaginary fly.

'The son, Leo, is a bit wayward at times, Major. Bordoni here has had to have words with him on a few occasions, but nothing serious, you understand, nothing we can't sort out ourselves.'

D'Angelo stopped briefly at the Bar Emme-P near the village's central piazza to buy a salami panino to eat on his way back to the carabinieri station, then hurried on in his journey back to his office.

He entered the reception area of the station to find Katia surrounded by piles of documents which she was sorting and then returning to the large grey metal cabinet that stood against the wall behind her desk.

'Having a clear-out?' asked D'Angelo.

'Oh, hello Major. I was actually searching for something, but I'm doing a bit of tidying at the same time.'

'And what were you looking for?' D'Angelo picked up two certificates that he had spotted lying at the front of the desk. 'Would it have been these?' he enquired, holding the certificates up in the air.

'We… that is, Sergeant Lazzaro, felt they should be on display, not hidden in a cabinet.'

'On display?'

'It was a significant achievement for this Division, you winning the regional shooting competition two years running. We agreed the certificates should be up on the wall where they can be seen.'

D'Angelo dropped the certificates back on the desk.

'Tell Sergeant Lazzaro,' he said, 'that I was shooting at cardboard targets on a range, so it counts for nothing and won't impress anyone. But thank you for the thought. Katia, I want you to send a message to all roadside vehicle-checking units to be on the look-out for an eleven year-old boy, Giovanni Mirelti, either hitch-hiking or possibly abducted. We should hopefully be receiving an e-mail with his photo attached, so use that image. And put a message on our facebook page.'

'What category, Major? Routine?'

'No, Katia, make it Priority.'

'You don't think it's like…'

'Like the Tommaso Sparanza case? I don't know. We never found the perpetrator.'

'That must have been six, maybe seven years ago.'

'One month short of six. It doesn't mean he won't do the same thing again. I was there, Katia. I saw the poor kid lying in the rocks near the beach at San Vito where he was found. He looked like a broken little doll, except the crabs and seagulls had already had a go at him. If Giovanni Mirelti is still alive, I don't want him to end up the same way. Is Lazzaro back from lunch?'

'Not yet.'

'I have to send a damn road accident report to Ortona, but I'll get that out of the way as quickly as possible, then as soon as Sergeant Lazzaro returns, I want him in my office to initiate a 'missing person' file.

Twenty minutes later, D'Angelo had finished his accident report and checked his secure personal inbox, only to find another reminder from HQ that he had not yet conducted his cost-saving audit for the station, and that his proposals should have been sent in by now. The 'helpful' suggestions included : 1) Reducing the hours worked by civilian staff, 2) Cutting or down-grading one of the vehicle fleet, or 3) Sharing staff with other stations. D'Angelo's happy vision of sending Trooper Di Silverio on job-sharing duty to somewhere in Sicily was interrupted by a tap on the door followed by the entrance of Sergeant Lazzaro. D'Angelo closed his secure file and put cost-cutting out of his mind, while he and Lazzaro planned what actions were required on the Giovanni Mirelti case. Lazzaro's initial responsibility would be to organize a search in the vicinity of Giovanni's home.

'Any civilians to be drafted in to assist?' asked Lazzaro.

'Not at this stage. I want you to recall Corporal Gattone from roadside-checking duty, then with him you will have Di Silverio, Carrea, and Di Stefano in your squad. Your office will be the incident room, but I want someone based here full-time to liaise. Where's Rossi?

'Working at Chieti on an IT system. She sounded pretty bored last time I spoke to her.'

'OK, get her back here, as from tomorrow morning. Your contact in Montenero is the local vigile, Maurizio Bordoni. He seems alright for a poliziotto. I'm going to arrange to meet Carlo from Forestry Police out at Montenero this afternoon, if he's available.'

'I'll get cracking straight away, Tonio.'

D'Angelo gave a 'thumbs up' sign as he put in a call to Carlo at Forestry Police.

Five

Within the grand, pillared Headquarters building in Abruzzo's premier city of Pescara, Colonel Edoardo Battista was studying figures relating to the previous month's expense claims by officers under his command. Battista was a man who liked figures and statistics, because they told him what he wanted to know about the efficiency of his force, such as how many kilometres were being driven, how much the fuel was costing, and how many roadside checks were being conducted. Columns of figures were neat and orderly, just like Colonel Battista himself. His uniform was always immaculate and perfectly pressed, his short, dark hair was trimmed regularly, as was his clipped moustache, and he would frequently look through his wire-framed glasses to make sure there was no dirt beneath his well-manicured finger-nails.

Colonel Battista didn't like being disturbed when he was checking figures, and nobody liked being the one to disturb him, but sometimes needs must, and today that task fell to Lieutenant Alberico, who knocked nervously on Battista's office door, then waited the customary five seconds before being commanded to enter. Battista just looked at the young officer without speaking, awaiting an explanation for the disturbance.

'Sorry Signore,' mumbled the lieutenant, 'but there's been another killing. Thought you should know, Signore.'

With no change of expression, Colonel Battista slowly placed the pencil he was holding on to his desk, then carefully turned it so that it was perfectly aligned to the straight sheaf of papers.

'Go on, Lieutenant.'

Anyone unfortunate enough to report a serious offence to the colonel was made to feel that they were personally responsible for adversely affecting the crime figures, and Alberico could already feel his mouth beginning to dry, and sweat dampening his armpits.

'The body's been found behind a unit on a small industrial estate, Signore, half a kilometre from the airport.'

'Shot?'

'No, Signore. Garrotted.'

'Garrotted? Different MO to the last one then.'

'Yes, Signore. One other thing.'

'Go on.'

'The body apparently has multiple cuts and burns, possibly cigarette burns, suggesting the victim was tortured before he was killed.'

'Who's over there?'

'Sergeant D'Alessandro was the first to respond, Signore. Captain Luciani is there now to take command of the scene. The spacemen – sorry, Signore, the scene of crime officers are on site, as is Dottore Sibona.'

'Alright, Lieutenant, take me there.'

'Me Signore? I was just…'

'You were just?'

'Nothing Signore. I'll take you there right away.'

'Bring a car round to the front. I'll wait for you there. And Lieutenant.'

'Signore?'

'Your shirt sleeve button is undone. Kindly dress properly before you leave the building.'

'Signore.'

Lieutenant Alberico was tense with nerves as he drove the patrol car round the side of the building and along the street to the bottom of the marble steps where Colonel Battista was waiting for him. He could feel sweat now trickling down his sides and his back as the colonel climbed into the front passenger seat, and slightly nauseous at the smell of Battista's cologne. Fortunately, the colonel opened his window and lit a cigarette, holding it carefully upright between two fingers at the open window, occasionally taking slow and delicate drags.

Alberico successfully manoeuvred the busy and somewhat congested city-centre roads, despite a short wait at one junction where Battista told him to 'just go, they'll stop for us.' The Alfa Romeo squad car was soon out on the E80 metropolitan autostrade, travelling at speed past the junction for Pescara West, then alongside the airport runway on their left where Alberico saw a plane coming in at low altitude to land. He thought briefly about his forthcoming trip to London with his partner, Fabio, a relationship he kept secret from his colleagues. He found it hurtful that he had to listen to details of other officers' holidays with wives or girlfriends, when he felt unable to tell anyone about Fabio. Except Olivia, of course. He could tell her. The station gossip was that he and Olivia were an item, but he was Livvy's 'safe' gay friend, and Livvy was his confidante.

Alberico saw the big shopping mall to the west of the airport, and slowed down to take the Sambuceto exit. The slip road took them under the autostrade and on to via Adigo, then right on to via Po. Alberico drove slowly, looking for an electrical distributor on the right hand side where he knew there was a small road leading off to the industrial estate. He didn't want to miss the turning, not with Colonel Battista sitting alongside him. Sure enough, he turned into the little road, past several units, following the bend to the right, then pulled up where three vehicles, a huddle of people, some of whom were wearing white protective suits, and a stretch of hastily-erected tape, indicated that they had arrived on site.

While Alberico went to speak to Captain Luciani, Battista sought out Dottore Sibona who had been in conversation with one of the Scene of Crime Officers, and asked for his assessment.

'Come, Colonel,' said the pathologist, 'I will show you.'

They walked round to the back of the empty and scruffy-looking unit where one of the officers was taking close-up photographs of the body. The victim was lying on his back, mouth open and his head arched backwards, his left arm across his torso. Colonel Battista was a firm believer in the validity of first impressions, and he quickly summed up in his mind his first impressions of this victim. Some dead people look as though they died peacefully, others as though they met a violent end. The young man lying in this patch of weeds and long grass looked as though he had died in agony. A number of blood stains showed red on his cream-coloured chinos, and as dark patches on his blue polo shirt. Clearly visible was a red line around his neck. His feet were bare.

'As you see, Colonel,' said Sibona, 'the victim is male, probably in his mid-twenties. He wasn't carrying any means of identification, so we can't be sure of age. He clearly didn't die here, but he's been dead for, I would say, a little over twelve hours. I'll have to carry out an autopsy, of course, but I'm reasonably certain he died of strangulation, by means of a length of fine wire, which looks to have cut through the trachea. You'll have noticed the small wounds on the chest and legs, all inflicted pre-death, but there are also small round burn marks on his feet and on the arms. He suffered before he died, Colonel. Now, something else you might find interesting. Panzera, would you please hold up the victim's right hand.'

The officer responsible for photographing the body duly lifted the corpse's stiff right arm. Sibona looked at Colonel Battista for a reaction, with almost an expression of excitement on his white-bearded, bespectacled face.

'Yet more agony, Dottore,' said Battista silkily. 'So, our young victim was on the take. I had assumed he was being tortured for information, but it looks like punishment, for breaking the crooks' code of conduct.'

Battista looked at the grisly mess of the man's right hand, at the raw stumps where his thumb and forefinger had been cut off, then indicated he had seen enough, allowing the officer to lay the man's arm back in the grass.

'Was he a drug user, do you know, Sibona?'

The short, stocky pathologist turned his mouth down and shrugged his shoulders, hands raised in the air.

'I'll have to check all the usual places for puncture marks, and carry out toxicology tests,' he said, 'but he appears to have muscle wastage, causing him to look gaunt, and skin and hair are in poor condition, so my guess, Colonel, would be that he's been using narcotics of some sort.'

'What's that mark, Dottore, on his left wrist?'

Sibona looked at the arm which lay across the man's stomach.

'A small tattoo, Colonel. Believe it or not, it's a hornet.'

'There was certainly a sting in the tail for him, eh Sibona.'

'Shocking.'

Battista glanced at the corpse and nodded.

'I mean your sense of humour, Battista, or what passes for one.'

With a stern expression on his face, Battista walked back round to the front of the concrete unit, passing one of the Scene of Crime Officers carrying a body bag, in which the corpse would be carried to Sibona's pathology lab. 'No dignity in death,' thought the colonel. No sooner had he made his way round the side of the building, than Captain Luciani strode to meet him, with Alberico and a corporal in his wake.

'We still don't know who he is, or where he was killed, or why,' said the captain in his clipped Roman accent, 'but we've made a breakthrough of sorts. Tumini here discovered that one of the larger units round the corner, the one being used as a distribution hub, has CCTV cameras installed, and one of them is trained on this access road. He's just been looking through last night's images. Between the hours of eleven o'clock last night, and what was it, Corporal, five o'clock this morning, only three vehicles came along here. Two were cars with young couples inside, and both stayed in the close for a considerable period of time, so we think… well, we're sort of discounting them for the time being. The third was a van, Citroen…'

'Renault, Signore. A Renault van,' corrected Tumini.

'Renault van, that's right, was recorded passing the distribution centre coming this way at three twenty-seven, then returning in the other direction at three thirty-one. Four minutes, Signore. Just enough time to dump a body and scarper.'

'Did you get the registration number, Tumini?' asked Battista.

''Fraid not Signore. Won't even get it with enhancement. We would only have got a number if it had turned in towards the distribution unit.'

'Colour?'

'Not white, Signore. Probably blue or green.'

'Well, it's something I suppose. Find out if a similar vehicle has been picked up on camera anywhere else in Pescara in the three to four o'clock time frame. Will we get any positive ID on the driver?'

'Not very clear images, I'm afraid Signore, but we've sent the stick to IT to see what they can do with it. There were two in the front, driver plus passenger, both believed to be male.'

'Captain Luciani.'

'Signore?'

'The body's about to be cut apart in Dottore Sibona's path lab. I want you to attend, find out what you can. Then your priorities are to discover who he is and where he was killed. The why he was murdered, and by whom, we'll find out later. You might try and find out, though, if there could be any significance in him having been dumped here. It may be worth checking who owns and who previously used this unit. I want a progress report by eighteen thirty.'

Six

Major D'Angelo had agreed to meet Captain Carlo Bottini of the Forestry Police at the bar in Montenero at fifteen-thirty, so having arrived just after three o'clock, he decided to have an aperitivo while waiting for his friend. He shunned the prosecco, choosing instead a non-alcoholic sanbitter, but ordered the usual small plate of cured meats, cheese cubes, and pastries when the waitress came to his table in the corner of the piazza. Wearing his service-issue dark glasses in the bright afternoon sun, D'Angelo looked around at the people, vehicles and buildings in this central area of the village, when his attention was drawn to a girl pinning an A4-sized poster to the public notice board outside the pharmacy. He could see that the poster featured a picture of a tousle-haired boy, and D'Angelo knew instantly that the girl was Giovanni's sister, Laura. He removed his dark glasses and walked over to where she had just finished putting up her notice.

'Excuse me, Signorina,' he said, 'are you Laura Mirelti?'

Laura squinted and shielded her eyes with her hand as she looked up at the tall carabiniere.

'Yes. You must be Major D'Angelo, trying to help us find our little Giovanni.'

She glanced with sad eyes at the board, and the poster she had put up, requesting information on the whereabouts of the missing eleven year-old. D'Angelo could see in her face the same haunted, desperate look that her mother had worn that morning, the same welling of emotion that suggested she might burst into tears at any moment.

'Please, Signorina, come and join me in an aperitivo.'

'No, no I can't. I still have all these posters to put up and hand out.'

'It's an important job you're doing, Signorina, and very worthwhile, but a short break won't hurt, and you may be able to give me some fresh information. Please, my table is up there in the corner of the piazza.'

While Laura made her way reluctantly to the table pointed out by D'Angelo, the major stepped briskly into the bar to order a second aperitivo before going to join her. Laura sat bolt upright in the metal chair, yet looked as though she was in a trance, her eyes unfocused, hands clutching the wad of posters in her lap. D'Angelo wondered how much of her attention he would be able to attract. As he looked at her properly for the first time, he couldn't help but notice her petite but well-proportioned figure, and how attractive her face would be if it wasn't masked with grief.

'Signorina, may I call you Laura?'

'What? Oh, yes, Major D'Angelo.'

'Laura, I first of all wish to express my sincere sympathy that your brother has gone missing, and I hope very much that we find him soon. Has anyone yet reported a possible sighting?'

Laura stared down at the image of Giovanni on the top poster of the pile and slowly shook her head, as a few tears gently rolled down her face. D'Angelo clenched his teeth, wishing desperately that he could do or say something to ease the girl's pain, but knowing he had to conduct a careful, objective investigation which may not end happily.

'Laura, can I ask you to think for a moment about the last time you saw Giovanni, when he left your house after the meal yesterday evening. I know he and Mario exchanged some harsh words, but how would you describe his mood when he went outside?'

Laura slowly raised her head and looked straight into D'Angelo's enquiring eyes.

'Giovanni is a beautiful boy, Major. He has the sweetest nature, but he lives – he lives somehow in his own little world. All he has ever wanted is to be left in peace, with the birds and animals that he loves so much. This world doesn't suit people like that, does it Major? My sister's Mario, the kids at his school, even Papa, they don't understand him, think he should be like them. And people can be very cruel to outsiders, to those who don't fit in.'

The waitress emerged from the bar and transferred the aperitivi from the tray she was carrying to the small round table where D'Angelo and Laura were sitting. They waited in silence as glasses and plates were set on the table, including two small glasses of water, and remained silent while the waitress disappeared back inside the bar.

'I'll tell you what I found the other day in the back of one of his school exercise books,' Laura suddenly said. 'He had written "I would rather die, not finding, than live, not looking." A strange thing for an eleven year-old boy to write, wouldn't you say, Major?'

D'Angelo cupped his chin in his hand, wondering what to say. Giovanni must be like a fish out of water in this isolated, rural community. It seems the only two people who love him are his mother and Laura, and probably only Laura makes the effort to try and understand him. Then there's Filippo. What about Filippo?

'I take it he's quite a sensitive boy,' said D'Angelo at last, choosing a cube of sheep's milk cheese from the plate in front of him. Laura fiddled with her glass of sanbitter, but without drinking. 'What sort of things can upset him?' he prompted.

Laura sighed, thinking. 'I suppose the thing he hated most of all was cruelty to animals. Strangely enough, he could cope quite well with the jibes and bullying he himself was subjected to, but couldn't stand seeing animals mistreated.'

D'Angelo took a rolled slice of prosciutto and then a sip of his drink.

'Does Giovanni ever show signs of temper?' he asked.

'At times, when goaded enough. That's only natural, isn't it. Major D'Angelo, I really want to get on with distributing these posters, if you don't mind.'

'Of course, Laura. I'm grateful you could spare me some time. How are people reacting to them, by the way?'

'Some are sympathetic, quite a few not really interested. The most positive reaction was from Filippo, of course. He's devastated that his young friend and helper is missing. He's put three posters up on his own premises, and taken some more to put up elsewhere. He's going to tell everyone he meets to search their outhouses and any empty buildings they know of. I've promised to let him know as soon as I hear anything.'

Major D'Angelo stood up and handed Laura one of his cards.

'I would appreciate it if you would keep in touch with myself as well, Laura. Anything, anything at all. Good day.'

'Good day to you, Major.'

As Laura crossed the piazza towards a small row of houses, D'Angelo looked down at the table and saw that, apart from having drunk a little of her water, Laura's aperitivo and plate of buffet food were untouched. But tucked under the edge of the plate, smiling up at him, was the picture of Giovanni on one of the posters.

Ten minutes later, a Forestry Police Land Rover pulled up in front of the pharmacy, close to D'Angelo's patrol car, and the burly, jovial figure of Carlo Bottini limped around the vehicle to wave a greeting to D'Angelo. The two men exchanged smiles and handshakes.

'How are you, old buddy?' said D'Angelo.

'Bearing up. The leg's giving me a bit of grief. It normally eases off a bit when the winter's over, but this year... the doc thinks they might have to put another pin in it. Enough of my woes, what's going on here?'

While Carlo ate the morsels of food left on Laura's plate, D'Angelo briefed him on Giovanni's disappearance.

'So you want me to come with you to check on these neighbours, Fiorito and son, eh?' said Carlo as he popped the final pastry into his mouth.

'That's right. Suspicion of shooting out of season, and while we're there, have they been cutting any trees after the end of March.'

'Someone heard a chainsaw?'

D'Angelo grinned impishly. 'Nothing certain. Just want to check, that's all. Have you brought your toy with you?'

'My 'toy' will save you a fortune from not having to use the helicopter, *and* it'll do a better job.'

'I must remember to point that out to Accountant Battista. "Part of my cost-reduction programme, Colonel, and more efficient to boot." Come on Carlo, I just need to nip into the bar to settle up, then you can follow me to the Fiorito place.'

D'Angelo and Carlo arrived in convoy at the Fiorito holding to find Pietro and his son, Leo, replacing a stretch of broken wire in their vineyard. Pietro stood watching them park and get out of their vehicles before pulling off his protective gloves and walking slowly to meet them. Two dogs in a small enclosure were barking furiously and running up and down along the high enclosure fence.

'Good afternoon, Signore Fiorito is it? I am Major D'Angelo, and this is my colleague Captain Bottini of the Forestry Police. I wonder if we might have a few words.'

Pietro Fiorito gave a response which D'Angelo understood in part only.

'I am from this area,' said Carlo Bottini, 'and I can speak Dialect, but we will please conduct this conversation in Italian. And in answer to your question, which for Major D'Angelo's benefit was : "what the bloody hell do you two goons want, I've already had some of your lot tramping over my land this afternoon," the other officers were searching for a missing boy, we are here to ask whether anyone on these premises has recently discharged a firearm outside the legal hunting season.'

Pietro glared at Carlo for a few seconds.

'Haven't you got better things to do, eh?' he sneered. 'I suppose that old bitch over there's been moaning again.'

'So you acknowledge that shots were fired?' said D'Angelo.

Pietro turned and glanced briefly at Leo, who was still standing in the vineyard, watching the three of them, his nose wrinkled and mouth open.

'My son is, well, he's not all that smart,' explained Pietro, in a more gracious manner. 'I tell him he can't shoot after the end of January, but he can be a bit – wayward, sometimes, you know? I'll try to make sure it doesn't happen again.'

'Two shots. From a twelve-bore. Is that correct Signore?' persisted D'Angelo.

Pietro pulled his mouth down in a thin line, irritated that his disclosure had not terminated the discussion.

'Yes, a couple of shells, to scare away some wild boar that had come down from the wood up there. Like I said, the lad gets muddled, but I'll make sure the guns are locked away where he can't get at them. Will that be all, Signori?'

'Not quite, Signore Fiorito. Captain Bottini would like to inspect the firearms and the shells you use, as well as last season's hunting licence.'

'Is this really necessary? I've got a lot to do this afternoon.'

'If you please, Signore.'

Pietro took a deep breath and exhaled through his bulbous nose.

'Leo, pull that wire tight,' he shouted to his son, trying to make himself heard above the baying dogs. 'Use the tool there, like I showed you, then twist the wire round the post and tie it off.'

Pietro led the two officers along the front of his house, where D'Angelo caught a glimpse of a woman peeping at them from the corner of a window, before she ducked hurriedly out of sight.

'It's just yourself, your wife, and your son living here, is that right Signore?' asked D'Angelo.

'That's right,' snapped Pietro, as he stomped down some breeze-block steps to the basement, where he pushed open the sliding door. A cat darted out and ran off between their legs. Inside the basement, Pietro opened the door of an ancient oak cupboard from which he took out two fairly old double-barrelled twelve-bore shotguns, one of which he handed to Carlo. 'This one's mine,' he explained.

Carlo pushed the catch and broke the gun open, then lifted it towards the light to look into the barrels. He grunted, snapped the gun shut, and handed it back to Pietro, taking the second shotgun in exchange, repeating the inspection procedure. He saw straight away traces of burnt powder on the inside of the barrels, indicating recent use, unlike the smooth, shiny barrels of the first gun.

'This is your son's, eh?' said Carlo.

'That's Leo's, yes.'

'The shells?'

As Pietro opened the cupboard door again, D'Angelo, standing behind him, could see two boxes of shells, and noticed that Pietro reached over and took out the box at the back, which he handed to Carlo. While Carlo was studying the box and the cartridges, which he noted were the small number nine size shot, typically used by bird shooters, D'Angelo reached inside the cupboard and brought out the other box, which he gave to Carlo. There was an instant reaction.

'Number one size shot. Well well. Pretty heavy duty. Similar to what the Americans and English call BB shot,' he added by way of explanation to D'Angelo, who raised his eyebrows.

Carlo opened the box to find that it was half empty.

'What do you use these for, Signore?'

Pietro shrugged, his hands held upwards.

'Hares.'

'Hares?'

'And foxes. We get a lot of foxes around here. They have to be kept under control.'

'You could kill a wild boar with one of these, no, Signore Fiorito? Can I see your licence please.'

D'Angelo was deep in thought. If these shells could kill a wild boar, they could certainly kill a young boy.

Pietro sullenly pulled open the drawer at the bottom of the cupboard and took out his hunting licence.

'Sixty euros. For hunting hares and listed approved game birds, during the period September to the end of January. Not for hunting wild boar, and certainly not out of season.'

'The boy was scaring them off, not killing them.'

D'Angelo found a piece of cloth in the drawer and wrapped it around the upper part of the stock of Leonardo's shotgun in order to pick it up.

'I'll keep hold of this for the time being,' he said. 'I'll give you a receipt for it.'

The three men went back outside and up the rough steps to the front of the house, Pietro sure that this time the visit was truly over.

'I noticed a large stack of logs drying out between your vineyard and orchard,' said Carlo. 'You know it's illegal to cut trees down after the end of March?'

Pietro stood still and put his hands on his hips. 'I cut those trees from my own woods in January,' he spat. 'This is beginning to feel like harassment, just because my son, who has learning difficulties, popped off a couple of shells, and my nosy neighbour complained.'

Carlo went to his Land Rover and fetched a drone and control unit from the back of the vehicle, while D'Angelo put Leonardo's gun in the boot of his car.

'And what the bloody hell is that thing?' yelled Pietro, as Carlo prepared the drone for flight.

'It's going to take some pictures from the sky,' explained D'Angelo calmly, 'so we can be sure there's been no recent tree-felling, either on your land or anyone else's. A good wide area please Carlo.'

Pietro watched as the drone rose into the air like a giant mechanical mosquito, then he and D'Angelo followed Carlo who walked to a rise in the land, all the while concentrating on manoeuvring the drone with the levers on his control box.

'You mentioned your neighbour,' said D'Angelo, 'you know the son didn't return home last night?'

'Ha, no great surprise. He'll be back for his tea. Like a wild thing, he is.'

'You know Giovanni do you?'

'Know him? I wouldn't say I know him. He runs around all over the place, then he yells at me to stop shooting birds. I just ignore him, or sometimes tell him to bugger off.'

'When did you last see him?'

Pietro puffed out his cheeks and blew out through pursed lips. 'When did I last see him. Let me think. Probably four or five days ago.'

'You didn't see him yesterday?'

'No. Definitely not yesterday. I was doing some grass cutting for the comune most of yesterday, and I would have remembered if I'd seen him from the tractor.'

D'Angelo and Pietro had gone a little way down the slope away from where Carlo was standing, where D'Angelo spotted some large feathers on the ground, patterned with bars of dark and light brown. Some smaller feathers lay amongst them.

'Do you keep chickens, Signore Fiorito,' asked D'Angelo, picking up one of the larger feathers.

'Chickens? No. Used to have some a few years ago, but I kept losing them to the foxes. That'll be where a fox has brought a bird that it's killed elsewhere,' he added, looking at the feathers. 'I sometimes find rabbit skins on my land as well. Leo made a duster for his gun with one of them.'

The drone had travelled out of sight, Carlo still concentrating on using the on-board digital camera to take both long-distance and close-up images. D'Angelo looked around, trying to spot the drone, when he noticed the roof of a building in a hollow a short distance to the north of where they stood.

'Who lives there?' he asked Pietro.

'Holiday place. English guy and his South African wife. Pots of money, by all accounts. Don't see them very often.'

'Are they there now?'

'Might be. I've seen a car going in and out over the last few days. Like I said, we don't see them much. Keep themselves to themselves.'

They stood in silence for a while, scanning the horizon, then heard the buzzing sound of rotors before the drone came into view, finally landing a couple of metres from Carlo.

D'Angelo and Pietro walked back up the slope to join Carlo, who was reviewing some of the images on the small screen of the on-board camera, which he had detached from the drone. Satisfied with the quality of the pictures he had captured, Carlo picked up the drone, and the three men walked back towards where the vehicles were parked. Pietro stopped when they reached the vineyard.

'That will be all for now, Signore Fiorito,' said D'Angelo, as Carlo carried on towards his Land Rover, 'but I may wish to speak to yourself and your son again.' He looked across at Leo, who seemed to be floundering with a long length of unruly wire. 'I take it you have no plans to leave your home in the next few days?'

'No plans. I'll be here.'

'Thank you for your co-operation. Good evening, Signore.'

Pietro watched D'Angelo's departing back through narrowed eyes. D'Angelo glanced over his left shoulder towards the house, and could swear he saw a face peeping again through one of the windows. He reached the Land Rover, where Carlo was storing the drone in its carrying case, before strapping it into the back of his vehicle. The two men then wandered towards the front of the Land Rover, where Carlo handed D'Angelo the small RAM card which he had removed from the drone's on-board camera.

'You'll be able to download the file on to your PC and look at the high-res images on the computer screen,' explained Carlo.

'Thank you, my friend,' said the major, putting the card safely into the top pocket of his shirt. 'I owe you for this.'

'We'll go halves if you find what you're looking for, which I presume is a patch of recently-disturbed earth?'

D'Angelo grimaced, and looked out across the green countryside with its beautiful backdrop of the Apennine mountains.

'Yes, Carlo, that's what I'm looking for.'

'You think he's dead?'

'I'm sure he's dead, much as I don't want to believe it. I think his mother knows, as well. I'm going round to see her again now.'

'Incidentally,' said Carlo, as he opened the driver's door of his Land Rover, 'why are you holding a buzzard's feather?'

D'Angelo looked at the big feather he still had in his hand.

'Buzzard's feather? Is that what this is?'

'Put it this way, it's from a large bird of prey, and the most common one round here is the buzzard. Let me know if you find anything of interest among those pictures. See you Tonio.'

D'Angelo watched Carlo drive away, then slowly climbed into his own vehicle. As the carabinieri officer was starting his short drive along the road towards the Mirelti household, Pietro Fiorito walked into the kitchen of his house where his wife, Federica, was waiting for him.

'That was about next door's boy, wasn't it?' she challenged.

'They said they were looking for out-of-season tree felling.'

'Don't be a fool, they were looking for the boy. Do they know he was here yesterday evening?'

'Of course they don't, so we're all going to keep quiet about it, aren't we,' he said threateningly.

Husband and wife glared at each other, as Leo hovered anxiously in the doorway.

Seven

It took only a couple of minutes for Major D'Angelo to drive round to the Mirelti house, but it was sufficient time to call Sergeant Lazzaro for an update on the search.

'Nothing doing I'm afraid Major,' said Lazzaro in formal 'on-duty' mode. 'Mind you, we could do with a tank to get through some of this undergrowth.'

'I'll put in a request to the colonel. Meantime you'll have to make do with the service-issue machetes. Update me if you find anything, but bear in mind that for the next little while I'm going to be with Giovanni's parents. Over and out.'

D'Angelo felt uncomfortable as he approached the open front door with its plastic fly-screen curtain of beads, and a sepulchral silence greeted him when he was invited in to the large living space of the house. Once again it took several seconds for his eyes to adjust to the relative gloom within, but the gloom of the atmosphere was far more oppressive. The family members were all present, including Elisabetta, who was in the kitchen area. Felicita was laconically sweeping the floor, Anna sitting at the table, her hands on either side of the phone as though she expected it to ring at any moment. Bruno was standing a little way apart from the others. Laura had been the one to invite Major D'Angelo inside, and only Mario was missing. They had all noticeably tensed as D'Angelo entered. Anna sat bolt upright in her chair, Bruno stared at the major, his arms at his sides. Felicita clutched the broom in front of her as though it was some sort of defence.

'Forgive my further intrusion,' said D'Angelo apologetically, 'I understand what a difficult time this is for you all.'

'You have news for us, Major?' said Anna in a tone part hopeful, part fearful.

'Nothing so far, but please, regard it as being nothing negative as much as nothing positive. Sometimes no news is good news.'

This brought on a fit of sobbing from Anna.

'Something bad has happened to him, hasn't it Major?' said Laura. 'There's been no response to my posters. Nobody has seen him.'

'We're still conducting a 'missing person' enquiry. There's nothing so far to suggest that situation should change, so let's all stay positive.'

D'Angelo hoped his words of encouragement were hiding his own feelings of foreboding.

'He never had any sense, that boy,' shouted Bruno suddenly, shattering the subdued atmosphere like a sledgehammer. 'Going here, going there, chasing after bloody birds, he was bound to get into trouble.'

With that angry riposte, Bruno stormed out of the house, leaving behind a silence that was even heavier than before. Nobody seemed to know what to say or do, until at last D'Angelo spoke.

'I notice Mario is not here. Is he busy outside?'

The silence continued for a few moments longer, until Felicita quietly gave an explanation.

'We decided it would be best if he stayed away for a few days,' she said. 'Until – until we know what's happened. He and Giov…'

She seemed unable to finish what she was trying to say.

'Yes, I understand, Signorina.'

'Have you spoken to Fiorito and his son?' asked Elisabetta, handing D'Angelo a glass of water.

'Yes, Signora, I have.'

'And? Had they been shooting?'

'Leonardo, or at least Pietro on his behalf, claims he fired a couple of shots to scare away some wild boar.'

'Do you believe him?'

D'Angelo took a sip of water. 'At the moment I don't have cause to doubt him, but I may wish to speak to them both again. They say they haven't seen Giovanni for several days. Apparently Giovanni has tried in the past to stop Pietro and Leo shooting at birds. Do you know if that is correct?'

'Giovanni hates the hunting, Major,' said Laura. 'He can't understand how it can be right for hunters to buy a sixty-euro licence that allows them to walk wherever they like, over anyone's land, providing it's not fenced, to shoot, allegedly, Snipe and Woodcock, when in fact they shoot at any birds they happen to see. And I, for one, tend to agree with him.'

'They're also not supposed to shoot within a hundred and fifty metres of a house,' added Elisabetta, 'but we sometimes hear lead pellets landing on our roof.'

'I'll mention it to the Forestry Police,' offered D'Angelo, which reminded him of the file of aerial photos that he needed to look at. He tapped the pocket of his shirt to reassure himself that the card was still safely inside.

'Just beyond Fiorito's house, there's a place that's apparently used as a holiday home. Do any of you know the owners, or whether they're out here at the moment?'

'An Englishman and his wife own it,' said Anna. 'I know what they look like, I've seen them in the village, but I can't say I know them. His name is Ren something – Renson, that's it. Martin Renson. His wife's name is Zoe. I believe her second name is the same as his – Renson.'

'English women take the same family name as their husband, Mamma,' said Laura.

'Oh, I see. But she's not English, you know.'

'I understand she might be from South Africa,' suggested D'Angelo.

'That's right, South Africa. Sometimes he comes over on his own, without his wife. When they're not here, which is most of the time, a couple in the village look after the place for them. The woman's name is Claudia Sabatelli. She has a key, keeps the place tidy. Her husband, Roberto, looks after the garden and pool.'

'Pool? They have a swimming pool?'

'Yes, Major. They're not short of money, I believe.'

'And if the Rensons are not here, where will I find Claudia Sabatelli?'

'In the village. Via Santa Rosa, number – let me see, she's two doors along from the mayor .'

'Number six, Mamma,' said Felicita. 'The red door, number six.'

'Thank you,' said D'Angelo. 'Something else you might be able to help me with – where would I go if I wanted to buy some unusual meat, not just the usual pork or chicken, but perhaps wild boar meat, for example?'

The four women exchanged furtive glances.

'You mean illegally-shot wild boar meat, Major?' said Elisabetta.

'Possibly. But I shall be very discreet. My source of information will remain a secret.'

'There's a good butcher here in Montenero, Major. Bianca di Lello. Her shop is in via Adriatico, that's the road on the hill going down out of the village. It should be open about now for the afternoon.'

'Thank you. I may call in there, get some nice meat for dinner. Now, if you'll excuse me, I should be going.'

D'Angelo left in the same silence that had greeted his arrival, but Laura spoke as she saw him to the door.

'We don't know what else to do, Major D'Angelo. We feel so helpless.'

'You're doing very well, Laura,' he assured her. With a glance back inside the room, he wanted to add that she should stay strong for her mother, but instead he gave a small nod of his head and walked out into the yard.

As a sudden gust of wind plucked at his shirt, D'Angelo looked beyond the house up to the mountains, to see black clouds billowing from the west, curling around the already obscured peaks and rolling down across the intervening countryside, promising heavy rainfall before too long. He started on towards the car, then heard a strange noise coming from the barn, so stood still, listening, and decided to investigate the source of the sound. Entering the barn, he couldn't at first make out where it was coming from, then noticed the head and arms of Bruno, slumped across the bonnet of the tractor, standing on the far side of the vehicle. Between long bouts of noisily sucking in air, he was sobbing with utter wretchedness, a truly pitiful sight and sound. D'Angelo walked quietly around the front of the tractor and stood just a metre away from Bruno.

'Signore,' said D'Angelo softly. Bruno lifted his head suddenly with the surprise of being found, looking at D'Angelo with startled, tear-filled eyes.

'Signore, believe me, I understand the pain you are feeling. There is no shame in showing it.'

Bruno's head dropped once more onto the tractor bonnet. He remained motionless for several moments, then with a huge force of will, he pushed himself upright so that he stood sideways-on to Major D'Angelo, with the look of a man completely defeated.

'We've lost him,' he muttered. 'I've got one son in America, and now we've lost the second.'

'Bruno, we don't know that, we…'

Bruno flapped his hand in front of him, silencing D'Angelo.

'You know it and I know it,' said Bruno, with a strained, breathy voice. 'He was a strange kid, and I don't think I tried hard enough to understand him, but he was my son, and I loved him. I suppose I just wanted him to be more like other kids his age, so he wouldn't get bullied, get hurt, but it stopped me seeing all the good things in him.' He turned to face D'Angelo. 'It takes guts to be different, you know. My son had guts, and I never gave him credit for it.'

D'Angelo felt instinctively that Bruno was displaying genuine grief, not remorse. He had seen both emotions in the past during similar circumstances, indeed he had sat alongside a father pleading in front of assembled journalists for the safe return of his daughter three days after he had hidden her body in a disused wine press. That man had sobbed, but without genuine tears, it had seemed to D'Angelo, a charade for public consumption. Bruno's tears, on the other hand, had been shed in private, not intended to have been witnessed either by a family member or an outsider. D'Angelo decided there was little point in trying again to convince Bruno that Giovanni might still be found safe and well. He put an arm out, half intending to put his hand on Bruno's shoulder in a gesture of comfort, but decided the move was inappropriate, so let his arm drop back to his side.

'It's strange,' said D'Angelo gently, 'how sometimes we can be hardest on those we care for the most.'

'We should tell Francesco what's happened,' said Bruno distractedly, more to himself than to D'Angelo. 'He might come over from America to be with us for a while.'

'And remember,' added D'Angelo in what was almost a parallel conversation, 'that you have a wife and two fine daughters. Whatever the outcome may be, you will be better able to face it if you stay strongly together.'

Bruno looked at D'Angelo again, with distant, haunted eyes, as the carabinieri major retreated from the barn.

'Major D'Angelo,' he called. D'Angelo stopped and turned round. 'You will find out what happened to our little boy, won't you?'

'I'll do my very best, Bruno, I promise. My very best.'

Eight

D'Angelo parked on the roadside in front of a row of lime trees, a short distance from the butcher's shop on via Adriatico. As he walked down the hill to the shop, he heard a distant rumble of thunder, and noticed that the clouds sweeping down from the mountains had become heavier and blacker than last time he looked. He turned his head as a three-wheeled 'Bee' truck chugged across the road and pulled up alongside a Fiat in front of the butcher's premises. A ruddy-faced man with short, thinning hair, and a frame almost as broad as his height, clambered awkwardly from the front of the vehicle and seemed to roll past D'Angelo towards a large brown bin that stood against a wall next to the shop.

'Evening officer,' he said cheerily on the way past. 'Scraps,' he added, nodding towards the bin. 'Boil it all up for me pigs. Ultimate in re-cycling, eh?' He grinned, showing several gaps where teeth were missing.

D'Angelo flicked his head backwards in acknowledgement, and watched as the barrel of a man lifted the heavy-looking bin with considerable ease.

'Can I have a look inside?' said D'Angelo on a sudden whim.

Raising his eyebrows in puzzlement, the man lowered the bin to the ground and obligingly pushed back the swing lid. A few flies buzzed out, along with the smell of blood and offal, but D'Angelo's attention was immediately drawn to the tips of feathers bearing exactly the same pattern as the feather he had picked up on Fiorito's land. He tugged on them, and quickly realised they were the wing tips of a large bird. He carried on pulling, shaking off bits of fat and gristle, until the bird, about the size of a thin chicken, was dangling in his hand above the bin. Except it clearly wasn't a chicken. With barred light and dark brown colouring, hooked beak and sharp talons, it immediately struck D'Angelo as a bird of prey, although he had never seen one up close before.

'Don't worry, officer,' said the bin collector, 'we get rubbish sometimes, but we sort it before it goes in the pot. Never had anything like that before, though,' he added as he stooped forward, inspecting the bird.

'What is it?' asked D'Angelo.

'Search me. Looks like an eagle or something. Mind you, now I come to think of it, isn't it one of those birds you quite often see sitting on a branch or a post by the roadside? They look quite big when they fly away.'

'A buzzard?'

'Buzzard. Is that what they're called. Vicious looking thing isn't it? You can chuck it back, officer, I'll get rid of it.'

'You carry on, Signore. I'd like to keep this.'

The cuboid pig farmer shrugged his shoulders before flipping back the lid of the bin, which he then lifted once again and waddled over to slide it onto the back of his 'Bee'.

Holding the bird a little away from himself, D'Angelo entered the butcher's shop. Two customers stood inside the premises, both of them women, one of whom was a sturdy middle-aged lady standing immediately in front of the counter, the other a tiny, wizened elderly lady who was waiting a little way behind the first.

'Good evening,' they chorused together.

'Good evening,' replied D'Angelo, aware that the women were staring with rapt interest at the bird he was holding. The silence that followed was broken only by the hum of an overhead fluorescent light strip, and the occasional pop as an insect was incinerated on the filament inside a blue-lit trap on the wall behind the counter. D'Angelo noticed a ticket machine, so strode across to peel off the next number, as the two lady customers continued to stare at the carabinieri officer and his strange trophy.

Moments later, a large metal door on the street side of the counter opened, and a woman wearing a white apron and red-banded white hat emerged, carrying a large pork loin. She glanced quickly at D'Angelo with a forced smile and gabbled 'good evening,' then dropped the pork on a large board that was below the level of the counter.

'You said five chops, Signora Giuniari?'

'Yes,' said the first customer, forcing herself to turn away from D'Angelo. The butcher, Bianca di Lello, selected a suitable cleaver and with considerable ease cut off five chops from the pork loin.

'And half a kilo of mince was it?'

'Half a kilo, that's right, twice minced.'

The butcher picked up a lump of beef from inside the counter, sliced off a portion, cut away the fat with a small knife, and weighed it. She then cut a little more meat from the lump of beef and put both pieces in the bowl of a mincing machine on a shelf behind her to her right, switching the machine on as she did so. She caught the minced beef on a sheet of grease-proof paper, which she then put back in the bowl to be minced a second time. She worked quickly and dexterously, finally weighing the end product which she declared to be just a fraction over the half kilo, then wrapped it in a second sheet of paper.

'Is that all for today, Signora?'

'That's all, thank you Bianca.'

Bianca dropped the chops and mince into a small plastic bag which she handed to Signora Giuniari, then went over to the till to collect the customer's money.

'And don't forget your receipt,' she said, looking conspicuously in D'Angelo's direction.

The small elderly lady stepped forward to request half a chicken breast, sliced, frequently glancing at D'Angelo as though seeking reassurance that she was allowed to be served while he was waiting. 'There we are, Signora Cristini,' said Bianca. She hurriedly paid and took her meat, still snatching glances at D'Angelo, then tottered from the shop with a final 'good evening.' Finally, D'Angelo was left alone with Bianca di Lello.

'A strange choice, officer,' said the butcher, 'would you like me to exchange it for something a little more edible, a chicken, perhaps, or a rabbit?'

It was only now, as he looked at her properly for the first time, that D'Angelo realised what a striking looking woman Bianca di Lello was. Strands of chestnut-coloured hair peeked out beneath her unflattering white hat, her intelligent blue eyes and high cheek bones emphasised a strong but attractive face, and her tall frame moved with an almost athletic grace and ease. D'Angelo guessed her age at somewhere in the mid-thirties.

'I'm keeping this, Signora di Lello, but what I would like to know is how come it ended up in your scraps bin?'

'I was never going to be able to sell it, officer...'

'D'Angelo. Major D'Angelo.'

'As I say, Major D'Angelo, I was never going to be able to sell it, so I threw it out. But if you insist on keeping it, at least let me give you a carrier bag to put it in.'

'What sort of bird is it?' asked D'Angelo as he dropped it into the proffered opaque plastic bag.

'There you have me, Major. All I know is that I've never seen a chicken with a beak like that, so it didn't pass my quality control check. Now if you'd like a nice bit of beef...'

'Could it be a buzzard, do you think?'

'A buzzard. Hmm. Are they the birds you sometimes see going round in circles high up in the sky, looking for prey on the ground?'

'I repeat my earlier question, Signora di Lello, what was it doing in your shop?'

'Not a lot, seeing as it's dead.'

'Don't play games. I want to know.'

'Look, Major...'

'D'Angelo.'

'Of course. Major D'Angelo, I didn't try to pass it off as something else, it was obviously delivered here by mistake, I got rid of it, no harm has been done. If you would like a few chops to take home...'

'Who delivered it?'

'I could look through my paperwork, but somehow I don't think I'm likely to find a delivery note saying : "One buzzard, fresh," with the name of a supplier underneath.'

She noticed a glint of anger pass over the major's face.

'Alright,' she continued, 'I'm being flippant, but I really don't see that there's much of a problem here.'

'It depends what else you've got out there in the cold store. I could organise a search of your premises, get some experts here who could find out whether you're selling any unlicensed meat – wild boar, perhaps, or wild geese. We could revoke your licence to trade.'

A bell chime on the door announced the arrival of another customer, a man with a large white moustache wearing shorts and a vest.

'Sausages, Signore Ricci?'

'Aye, couple of spicy sausages if you please, Bianca.'

She quickly wrapped two sausages and handed them over the counter.

'Pay me tomorrow, Francesco.'

As Francesco Ricci was leaving the shop, Bianca spotted the mayor's wife parking her car outside. She quickly flipped over a sign on the door to show 'closed' rather than 'open', then darted outside to intercept the new arrival. Hastily explaining that the shop would be closed for a short while, Bianca asked the mayor's wife for her order, and promised to deliver it to her house within half an hour, then locked the door and pulled down a blind when she returned inside the premises.

'If you think *my* presence is bad for business,' said D'Angelo calmly, 'wait until the inspection.'

Bianca held her hands in front of her, palms facing forward, in an act of surrender.

'Alright, you win, not that there's much to tell.'

'Tell me anyway.'

D'Angelo felt a slight lurch in his stomach as Bianca stood close to him. He caught a sensation of fine scent as he looked into her deep azure eyes.

'This is a very traditional, very conservative community, Major D'Angelo. Nothing much changes here from generation to generation.'

D'Angelo's heart seemed to skip a beat as he noted that this time she remembered his name.

'People around here still kill geckos if they see them, because they believe geckos turn into tarantulas. And many of the older people, brought up with the lira, offer handfuls of coins for me to take the correct amount as they don't understand euros and cents. I have proper suppliers to my business these days, so I no longer need to rely on local farmers and smallholders bringing in the occasional pig carcase or a few chickens or rabbits. But it's part of their way of life, so yes, I still take them.'

'Animals slaughtered on the farmers' premises, not in registered slaughterhouses?'

'Meat hygiene rules issued by the EU have as much meaning in these parts as a Chinese guide to cooking rice.'

'And what about other meat, the non-domesticated variety? Gun meat, I think they call it.'

Bianca was silent for a few seconds, looking into D'Angelo's eyes.

'Be straight with me, Major D'Angelo. Are you really interested in small-scale supply and demand of wild meat in a remote rural community? It's not exactly on a par with Mafia drug dealing or money laundering.'

'Nevertheless, it's illegal.'

'What is it you're after?'

'I've asked you several times already, who brought this in, and when?' demanded D'Angelo, holding aloft the plastic bag with the buzzard in it.

'There's a local farmer, Pietro Fiorito, who every now and then brings in a wild boar that I butcher and sell to certain customers. Fiorito has a son called Leonardo who also likes to shoot, but he's not that bright. He shot the buzzard yesterday evening and brought it here first thing this morning. That's all there is. I'll come quietly officer.'

Bianca put her arms out in front of her with one wrist on top of the other.

'I won't take you into custody just yet,' said D'Angelo with a mirthless smile, 'because I believe you're telling the truth. But I suggest very strongly that you stop this trade in wild meat, otherwise the forestry police will get involved and people *will* be prosecuted. You've had your warning.'

Bianca unlocked and opened the door for D'Angelo to step outside.

'Do you manage this place on your own – I mean, you don't have a partner to help you?'

'Are you asking if I'm married, Major D'Angelo?'

'It must be a lot of work for one person,' said D'Angelo, slightly flustered.

'My husband drives one of those big tankers that takes wine up to Germany, so he's away a lot of the time. He's on a trip at the moment, actually, but no, he doesn't help in here when he's home. He prefers to put his feet up and recover from the stress of those long journeys. Good evening, Major D'Angelo.'

'Good evening, Signora di Lello.'

Heavy drops of rain fell on D'Angelo, and splashed off the pavement, as he hurried back to his car under a black sky.

* * *

In Pescara, Captain Alberto Luciani was heading back towards carabinieri headquarters from the quiet, tree-lined suburb which was home to the university, and where a part of the medical science block was given over to Dottore Sibona's pathology laboratory. Although he didn't regard himself as particularly squeamish, Captain Luciani had felt the bile rise in his throat a few times while watching the autopsy on the murder victim, thankful at least that he was in a viewing gallery behind glass, so he was saved the smell if not the sight of the ghastly process. Two white-coated students alongside him in the gallery were enthusiastically scribbling notes and drawing diagrams, listening intently to Sibona's commentary as each organ was in turn removed from the cadaver, watching with fascination as the skull was sawn open and the brain removed. Luciani was feigning professional objectivity, glad that the young students were too engrossed to notice him frequently shutting his eyes.

When it was finally over, he didn't feel he had learned anything particularly relevant, but had gone down to speak to Dottore Sibona, while the pathology assistant was removing the corpse and cleaning the lab.

'You should go to an optician and get your eyes checked,' Sibona had said. The look of puzzlement on Luciani's face prompted the pathologist to tease the captain about how many times he had closed his eyes during the post-mortem. But Sibona had helpfully recounted what he considered to be the relevant points arising from the examination, which Luciani had summarised in his notebook, and would now impart to Colonel Battista.

Captain Luciani arrived at Carabinieri headquarters, leaving his vehicle in the underground car park at the back of the building, then went by lift up to the third floor. At the end of the corridor, Luciani took out his notebook and re-read his notes from the meeting with Sibona, making sure he understood what he had written. Satisfied, he pocketed the notebook and strode down the corridor to Colonel Battista's office. He tapped on the door, and counted to five in his head before hearing the command to enter. Battista checked his watch, noting with satisfaction that Luciani had come to present his report with ten minutes to spare.

'Yes, Captain, what have we learned about the victim?'

Luciani cleared his throat and pulled the notebook from his top pocket.

'I have noted what I believe to be the salient points from the post-mortem examination, Colonel.'

Battista smiled. Nobody achieves advancement, he thought to himself, without occasionally taking the credit for someone else's ideas. The 'salient points' would surely have been suggested by Dottore Sibona.

'It was confirmed that the knife wounds and cigarette burns were inflicted pre-death, as had been the removal of the thumb and forefinger from his right hand, while abrasions on the wrists and ankles indicated that the victim had been constrained by rope or thick twine, approximately eight millimetres in diameter. His last meal had been taken some seven hours before death occurred, at which time he had eaten pasta with tomato and meat sauce, something like a ragu, or possibly...'

'Yes, yes, Captain, I get the picture. We're conducting a murder investigation, not a culinary quiz. Continue.'

'Time of death was put at between seven and nine o'clock yesterday, that is Monday, evening. The build-up of tar and other substances in the lungs indicated he was a smoker, and the fatty, degraded liver showed a higher than average intake of alcohol, probably including spirits. Death had been caused by asphyxiation due to penetration of the trachea by a thin wire.'

'He was garrotted, in other words.'

'Quite so, Colonel. It is not inconceivable, however, that the wire had been placed around the victim while he was being tortured, and that an involuntary spasm due to severe pain had caused him to inflict the fatal wound himself.'

'I think we'll leave that one for prosecutors to decide. Anything else?'

Captain Luciani cleared his throat once again, then looked back at his notes.

'It is conjecture, nothing more, on the part of the examining pathologist, that the victim was not from the local area, or even from Italy.'

'How come?'

'Dottore Sibona has taken blood, urine and tissue samples for toxicology tests, which he believes will show that the deceased was using illegal addictive drugs. Dottore Sibona also noted that the victim had been suffering from herpes, with related sores on his lips and gums. These symptoms are typically associated with a ritual sharing of homemade pipes to smoke cocaine base paste, or paco as it's commonly called, within Latin American communities. Paco is very harmful and highly addictive, and is distinct from the free-base and crack cocaine such as is produced in Europe and the USA.'

Colonel Battista remained seated impassively at his desk, resting his chin on steepled fingers, while Captain Luciani, feeling uncomfortable, slipped his notebook back in his top pocket.

'I have known Dottore Sibona for some time, and have heard his evidence on several occasions,' said Battista quietly, 'and I have found his theories to have been remarkably accurate. Now, you were going to check on the ownership of the industrial unit where the body was found.'

'My apologies, Colonel, I asked Lieutenant Alberico to look into that matter, and hoped he would have reported to you directly.'

'As it happens, Captain, he has done so. He sent me an e-mail shortly before you arrived, and I took the trouble to print it. Here it is.'

The colonel handed Luciani the printed e-mail which had been lying face down on his desk.

'Please read it, Captain.'

'Signore Colonel, my enquiries to date have revealed that the commercial premises behind which the murder victim was discovered were last used approximately a year

ago by an import-export company which had trading links with...'

'Carry on.'

'Which had trading links with South America.'

Nine

Major D'Angelo had driven a short way out of Montenero when the heavy rain turned into a full-blown thunder storm. Flashes of lightning were accompanied by a torrential downpour, followed by hail. Hail stones were bouncing off the surface of the road, and beating an incessant rhythm on the bonnet and roof of his vehicle, until even with windscreen wipers working at full speed, visibility was too restricted to continue driving, so D'Angelo found a suitable place to pull over and stop until conditions improved. He looked back at the village, perched on top of a wooded hill, dark under the stormy sky. "Montenero," he said to himself, "Black Hill. Now I understand why the place is so named."

He sat in his stationary car for twenty minutes, astounded that several vehicles passed him in the atrocious conditions, until the storm vanished as suddenly as it had arrived, and the countryside was bathed once more in bright evening sunshine.

D'Angelo called Sergeant Lazzaro on his carabinieri radio.

'That was some storm, eh Sergeant? Did you manage to find shelter?'

'We're fine. Di Silverio is complaining because his uniform got wet.'

'It'll dry, and he's too young to worry about rheumatism.'

'If that kid is still out there…'

'Yes, Emil. If that kid is still out there, he's going to be in a bad way. Keep going while there's still daylight, and I'll see you back at base in the morning for a de-brief.'

'Understood, Tonio. Over and out.'

D'Angelo continued on his way, and at a little after seven-thirty he was sitting alone in his office, with the card holding the images from Carlo's drone inserted in his computer, clicking his way through the photos. He came to shots of the holiday home, distinctive with its new roof and bright blue swimming pool alongside. Examining each picture carefully, he realised there were no vehicles or people visible, but could see a bright red towel over the back of one of the reclining chairs beside the pool. He was staring at the photo, trying to spot any other signs of occupancy, when his personal smart phone buzzed an incoming call.

'Hi Adriana, sorry, I'm a bit behind, I'll be home soon,' he said quickly, having seen his wife's name appear on screen as the caller.

'Have you forgotten we're supposed to be going to Rosalinda and Giovanni's for a pizza this evening?'

'Shit. What time?'

'Eight o'clock. Any minute now.'

'Christ. I'm on my way love. Sorry.'

D'Angelo's wife ended the call. She looked in the mirror of her en-suite bathroom and added a little mascara to her long eyelashes, then patted her newly-shampooed shining black hair. She picked up the stick of orange lipstick, puckered her lips, then changed her mind and put the lipstick down again. It would take Antonio at least fifteen minutes to drive home, even putting his foot down, then he would have to change. So she went downstairs and poured herself a nice cold glass of white Pecorino wine from the fridge, and wandered out onto the portico to sip while she waited, seeing dark storm clouds being blown away in the distance. When the crunch of tyres on the gravel drive heralded D'Angelo's homecoming, Adriana emptied her glass with the final mouthful of wine before calmly walking upstairs to belatedly apply her gloss lipstick.

Moments later, D'Angelo rushed into the bedroom, his shirt already half unbuttoned.

'Are the girls coming?' he called, while snatching a clean shirt and a pair of jeans from the wardrobe. He was greeted by a silence while Adriana put the finishing touches to her lipstick before dabbing her lips with tissue.

'Just Gabriella,' she replied, checking the final result of her make-up in the en-suite mirror. 'Marianna is out with Patrizio.'

D'Angelo grunted in response, as he buckled the belt on his jeans and pulled on a pair of slip-on shoes.

'Presumably Gabri's ready. I didn't see her anywhere when I came in.'

'In her room with her iPhone, I suspect. She was ready half an hour ago. What happened, some old dear lost her handbag?'

D'Angelo winced at the barb, but didn't rise to it, mainly due to feelings of guilt and inadequacy. He knew that Adriana had harboured dreams of being a senior officer's wife, hosting cocktail parties in Rome or Milan, not a major's wife in a rural backwater. She didn't miss too many opportunities to remind him of her disappointment. What was it she liked to say to her friends : "I thought I had married a high flyer, but ended up with a turkey".

'Missing boy,' he said evenly, 'out at Montenero.'

'You mean like…'

'Like Tommaso Sparanza, yes. I'm ready, let's go. Oh, by the way, there's a carrier bag with a buzzard in it in the freezer.'

'A what?'

'A bird. I'll explain later.'

D'Angelo banged on his younger daughter's bedroom door and shouted that they were ready to leave. By the time he was poised to set the alarm system, and Adriana had collected the tray of cakes she had bought to take for their hosts, seventeen year-old Gabriella was gliding down the stairs, still transfixed by the screen of her iPhone.

'That stays here,' ordered D'Angelo.

'But Papa…'

'No buts. We're going for a social evening with our friends, not playing with smartphones.'

'I bet you're taking yours,' she said grumpily.

'I am taking mine, yes, in case I get any urgent calls, not to exchange text messages with my mates.'

Gabriella tossed her long dark hair and stomped out to the car, while D'Angelo rolled his eyes at Adriana.

'I presume Francesco will be there this evening,' said Adriana, once they had turned out of their drive onto the quiet road.

'I wonder if he likes pouting fish impressions,' mused D'Angelo.

Gabriella smiled, despite her determination to show her feelings about the iPhone ban, then tried to check her reflection in the car's rear door window as she contemplated seeing Rosalinda and Giovanni's good looking son, Francesco, all thoughts of missed chats with her friends suddenly forgotten.

Less than five minutes later, the two families were greeting each other with kisses and handshakes, a bottle of Prosecco was opened with a 'pop', and Francesco was adding a few more chips of oak to the outdoor pizza oven, studiously checking the thermometer to make sure the temperature was spot on for baking the pizzas in the exact requisite time. Rosalinda added various different toppings to the rings of pizza dough she had prepared earlier, while Giovanni took charge of sliding them into the oven, using his watch to ensure perfect timing. The operation was run with military-style precision, until the pizzas were cooked and sliced, wine was poured, and a rowdy free-for-all ensued.

The six of them were seated at an outdoor table on a stone patio, surrounded by the wide expanse of Giovanni and Rosalinda's plot of land. The wine was flowing, the conversation increasing in volume, when Gabriella suddenly squealed with delight, bringing to an abrupt halt the talking and laughing.

'Look, look over there,' Gabriella shouted excitedly, pointing towards the grass meadow. Everyone turned to see what had caught Gabriella's attention.

'Ah, the fireflies,' said Rosalinda. 'They are beautiful, aren't they.'

Everyone watched, and the longer they looked, the more of the tiny, dancing lights became visible in the darkness.

'You used to call them little fairies,' recalled Adriana.

'They remind me of the party we had after your confirmation,' added Giovanni. 'You decided that night they were angels, come to look after you.'

'What year was that?' asked D'Angelo.

'Let me see – it was six years ago, that's right isn't it, Adriana?'

'Six years, yes. Gabriella was eleven when she was confirmed. She looked so pretty in that white dress, trimmed with little blue flowers.'

'Eleven? She was only eleven when she was confirmed?' said D'Angelo, 'it seems very young to be making all those vows and promises.'

'They know fine well I wouldn't make them now,' chipped in Gabriella, 'they like to catch you when you're young and malleable.'

'Yes, but eleven, you're just a child. Is that the usual age for being confirmed? How old were you, Francesco?'

'About that age. Eleven, twelve maybe.'

D'Angelo looked back at the fireflies, his thoughts a long way away.

'You were both confirmed by Father Ignazio, weren't you?' asked Giovanni.

'Ignazio. Wasn't he the one they got rid of?'

'Moved elsewhere, more likely. The Church doesn't have a great track record when it comes to getting rid of rogue priests.'

'So he might be interfering with young kids somewhere else?'

'Unbelievable isn't it. Anyone found guilty of that kind of offence in your organization or mine, it'd be instant dismissal.'

D'Angelo turned to his daughter, a look of horror on his face.

'Gabri, he didn't...'

'No, Papa, he didn't touch me. Anyway, I think boys were his particular predilection.'

The adults all turned towards Francesco, who held up his hands in denial.

'It's alright, he didn't touch me either. I think Roberto and Massimo were his favourites.'

'Giovanni,' said D'Angelo quietly.

'What is it?' asked his friend.

'No, sorry, it's nothing. I was just thinking of something – of someone – else.'

* * *

At around the same time, in Pescara carabinieri headquarters, Colonel Battista was standing at the window in his office, hands behind his back, watching the coming and going of carabinieri officers on a shift change. He had made several phone calls, and as he watched people on the pavement below moving between pools of light cast by the street lamps, decided that it was time for him to go. Slowly he walked to the door and turned the key to lock it, then moved with the same deliberate steps to a large grey filing cabinet. He opened the bottom drawer and removed a pile of clothing which he placed on his desk, then took off his uniform which he fastidiously arranged on a hanger that he then carefully placed on the side of the cabinet. First he pulled on a white tee-shirt, hesitated briefly, then unlocked a drawer in his desk and lifted a body holster which held a small, snub-nosed .22 pistol. He checked that the hand gun was loaded, then strapped the holster over his left shoulder and around his chest. Next, he put on a dark blue loose-fitting shirt which was decorated with yellow and red spots, then a pair of charcoal grey chinos over his boxer shorts, a light-weight cotton jacket and a pair of black trainers. He took off his wire-frame glasses, to be replaced by square, blue-framed spectacles from the desk drawer, and finally he donned a red baseball-style cap. Beneath some documents in the drawer, he found a brown leather wallet, the contents of which he carefully checked. He counted ten fifty-euro notes, fingered a VISA credit card, and opened an identity card with his photograph inside, opposite which was printed his alter ego – Dottore Lorenzo Profico, Administrator of the Isolation Department, Chieti Hospital. He put the wallet, a packet of cigarettes, and a box of matches into the side pocket of his jacket.

After another glance from the window, Battista slipped out of the door, re-locking it as he went, dropping the key ring into his trouser pocket, and strode down towards the lift. Seeing a light flash on the lift's call button, he darted along a short corridor to the right and took the stairs down to the basement car park, keeping his eyes firmly fixed on the steps without raising his head. He traversed the dimly lit concrete floor of the car park to a green metal door to the right of the exit ramp, then pulled the key ring from his pocket, checking that alongside his office key was a key which enabled him to later re-enter the one-way locking security door back inside the building that he was about to exit. Pleased to escape the heady smell of petrol and diesel fumes, Battista gave the peak of his cap a tug so that it was low over his face, then, hugging the walls of roadside buildings so that he was outside the arcs of light from street lamps, he hurried down the third turning off the main street, down towards the river. Walking at a brisk pace, keeping to the shadows, he followed the side street along the north side of Pescara river towards the sea.

Crossing the busy thoroughfare of Corso Victor Emanuele II, he soon reached Piazza Italia where he left the riverside behind and cut through a series of small side streets before opening out onto via Nicola Fabrizi. Here he walked round a block in a three hundred and sixty degree manoeuvre, but before turning back in the direction he had been heading, he ducked into the dark doorway of a church where he stood silently watching for several minutes, making sure he hadn't been followed. Satisfied that he would no longer be recognized as Colonel Battista of the carabinieri, he continued on his way, but acting in a more natural manner, taking the persona of someone probably going to meet friends in a café or trattoria. He would be unremarkable and unremembered by anyone who happened to see him. He slowed his walking pace, and even lit a cigarette, becoming invisible in full view.

Close to the wide beach-side road of the Lungomare Matteotti, he sauntered down the short, unassuming via

Parso where he took off his baseball cap and rang the bell of number eight. He looked up into the top right corner of the doorway at the pinprick of a red LED and discreet CCTV camera, then pushed the door open and stepped inside when he heard the click of the lock being released, quickly closing the door behind him. Within seconds, a large, flamboyantly-dressed woman came through an internal door to join him in the subtly-lit hallway.

'Good evening, Signore Profico,' she greeted him, 'how nice to see you again. You wish to see Carla, I believe?'

'That's correct, Signora, Carla will be expecting me.'

'Regrettably, Carla is still with a – er – client, but Diana is available. Diana is a very nice girl…'

'I have arranged to see Carla, Signora.'

'Yes, well, she shouldn't be long, if you don't mind waiting. But don't worry, Signore Profico, Carla will be nice and clean before you see her.'

'I pay full price for your services, Signora, for which I expect discretion and not having to wait. Please don't let this happen again.'

'I'm sorry, Signore…'

'Dottore.'

'Dottore. I'm sorry. If you'd like to wait in here. What can I get you? A cold beer, a glass of wine…'

'Water.'

'Water. Yes, of course. I'll send someone out with a glass. Would that be still or sparkling?'

'I don't care. Just water, Signora.'

The large woman bustled out of the small, cosy room into which she had guided Battista, who ignored a comfortable armchair and glossy magazines, and stood waiting irritably in the middle of the floor. Finally, the muscular young man who had earlier brought Battista's glass of water, re-appeared, and quietly led Battista up a single flight of stairs and tapped on the door of a first-floor room. At an answering call from inside the room, the young man put his open hand out to indicate that Battista could enter, then discreetly drifted off back down the stairs.

Battista entered the perfumed, dimly-lit room which was dominated by a large four-poster bed. Carla was sitting in a small armchair near the foot of the bed, a glass of Prosecco in her hand, the bottle and a spare glass on a delicate table at her side. A small art deco style lamp threw soft, pink light onto Carla's luxuriously long red hair, and seemed to make her red-painted lips glow. Her long, shapely legs, bare but for a minute strip of skirt, were elegantly crossed, her feet enclosed in black patent stiletto heels. Her lacy white blouse did little to conceal full breasts and dark, prominent nipples.

'Renzo, darling,' she said, lifting the tall, narrow glass, 'how wonderful.'

'You seem to be on a tight schedule, Carla. I've had a long wait.'

'Not that long a wait, my dear Renzo. A glass of fizzy?' Carla pointed to the bottle and empty glass.

Battista ignored the offer and remained standing.

'Well,' he said, 'do you have something for me?'

'When you find out why I kept you waiting, darling, you'll be pleased with me. Very pleased indeed. But do sit down, you make me feel nervous.'

Reluctantly, Battista sat in a chair similar to Carla's, settling with distaste into the red velvet upholstery.

'So tell me what it is that will make me pleased with you.'

'I've been trying, very subtly of course, to glean any little snippets of information from the other girls. Diana had a few bits and pieces of gossip, and Bianca told me some stuff I already knew.'

'And what did Anna have to say?'

'Renzo, you know Anna?'

'A stab in the dark,' said Battista, feeling rather smug. 'There's Bianca – B, Diana – D, you're C, I guessed at Anna for code A. What's your real name, Carla?'

'I'll tell you my real name, darling, if you tell me yours.'

Battista jerked his head slightly, wondering whether this informant was becoming too inquisitive, too close.

'But then your last client told you something more useful.'

'Bravo, darling, you're so clever. You're like that Englishman, what's his name – Sherlock Holmes.'

Battista looked at the prostitute with a blank expression.

'Who was your client, and what did he tell you?'

'He said his name was Otto, but I doubt if many clients give their real name, eh Lorenzo?'

She looked at Battista with a little smile playing on her lips.

'He was one of those men who wanted to impress, despite the particulars of our relationship. The more I flattered his ego, the more he was willing to divulge. He told me how much money he was making, all cash in hand.'

'Drugs?'

'Wow, Otto, I said,' continued Carla, ignoring Battista's interjection, 'how do you do that? "Nothing bad," he replied, "not drugs or weapons or anything that's going to hurt anyone."

I help get people into the country, give them a new start in life." I thought it was drugs where you made the real money, I said. "Yes," he replied, "big profits. The boss wanted to get into that market, but here in Pescara it's pretty much tied up. Run by a guy called Rex, and they're vicious, those drug boys. They'll beat up or even kill anyone who steps out of line. Word is, they gave someone the chop yesterday. Not my scene, Carla." So really what you're doing is helping people, I said. Isn't it dangerous?' "For me, not really," he answered, "I don't go in the boats or anything. They land the migrants at night, I take them to a safe place where they spend a day or two, then they get carted off to all different locations where they disappear, and I get a cut of the take. Easy money. As a matter of fact," he added, his mouth by now in overdrive, "they're bringing in a fresh consignment Thursday night. Tell you what, I'll come and see you again at the weekend, and I'll take you out for a meal into the bargain."

'That's the sort of stuff you like to know about, isn't it darling?' she said, her recounting of the earlier conversation at an end.

Battista was mulling over what Carla had told him.

'He told you someone called Rex was running the drug business. That sounds like an Anglo-Saxon name. Where's he from? Where does he live?'

'That's all I know. If I'd started pushing for more information, he would most likely have clammed up.'

'Hm. And no more details about the boat drop, such as where, what time.'

'I listen to what they tell me, and I tell you,' Carla retorted, anger creeping into her voice. 'I get any more involved, I'll end up getting slapped around, maybe hurt, and not able to work for a while. How would I live with no money, huh?'

'OK Carla, you've done well. If you hear anything more, anything at all, ring me at that number I gave you.'

Battista stood up and took out his wallet, counting six fifty-euro notes, which he placed on the little table, next to the Prosecco bottle. Carla ran her tongue lasciviously over her top lip.

'You know, darling Renzo, for a couple more of those you could have a nice little bit of sex.'

Despite himself, Battista's usually neutral expression showed a hint of distaste.

'Don't forget, call me if you hear any more. There's one thing you can do for me before I go.'

'Renzo! Say it.'

'Look out of your window, as if you were expecting a visitor, and tell me if there's anyone down in the street.'

'Oh,' said Carla, crestfallen. 'I thought you wanted another sort of favour.'

She put her glass down, went over to the window, pulled back the heavy velour curtain, and looked up and down the short, narrow street below.

'Nothing. No-one.'

'Thank you. Until the next time, Carla. Good night.'

Battista went back downstairs and pressed a button in the hallway. He knew the routine. A call would be made to

Carla to make sure she was alright and had been paid, but he only had to wait a matter of seconds before a buzzer on the door indicated he could pull it open and step out into the sea-scented night air.

Battista was deep in thought as he began to retrace his steps back to the carabinieri headquarters. From what 'Otto' had told Carla, it seemed as though the murder was some sort of dispute within the dominant drug gang, which was run by someone called Rex. On the other hand, he had a lead on a people-smuggling operation, which he knew existed, but hadn't been able to penetrate or break up. Tonight's information gave him a chance to do just that, assuming 'Otto's boast to Carla was correct. A success on that front would offset the black mark for the drug gang murder.

Battista was so busy planning his move against the people-smugglers, he was unaware that a moped which had disappeared round the corner at via Bologna had only just come out behind him on via Firenze. As Battista walked into the dark, quiet alley that was via Calabria, the moped zoomed up alongside him and came to an abrupt halt. The rider's face was mostly hidden under a helmet and visor, but the speed with which he jumped off the machine and pulled a knife on Battista, along with the stubble on his chin, suggested he was a young man, probably late teens or early twenties.

'Your wallet, quick, or you get this,' he demanded, in a thick Abruzzese accent, waving the knife in front of him.

Battista's anger that he had allowed himself to be cornered in this way was tempered slightly by the realisation that his attacker was an opportunist scumbag mugger, not connected to his meeting with Carla and the information he had gleaned.

'I haven't got any money,' protested Battista, backing into the wall behind him and pretending to fiddle nervously with his jacket, while actually undoing a middle button on his shirt.

'Liar, you got money alright. Where you been, some nice restaurant for a meal. Come on, bastard, give me your wallet, quick, or I slash your face with this.'

He was now holding the knife threateningly close to Battista's eyes.

'OK, OK, it's in my inside pocket, you can have it.'

The mugger, sure of a quick robbery, glanced briefly to his left to make sure the coast was clear for a quick getaway, and in the instant he did so, Battista pulled the Beretta hand gun from its holster, put the barrel to the young man's hand, and pulled the trigger. The crack of the gun as it was fired was amplified within the alley's enclosed space, followed by a scream of pain, and the clatter of the steel-bladed knife falling to the pavement. Battista considered for a moment taking the moped to put distance between himself and the scene of an attempted robbery, but decided instead to leave hurriedly on foot, gauging he would have plenty of time before an alarm was raised and acted upon. He disappeared into the darkness, leaving behind a young man bent double in agony, his right arm tucked into his midriff, squeezing the injured hand which a .22 bullet had just passed clean through.

Ten

D'Angelo woke the next morning as the first tinge of colour from a new dawn was showing through the bedroom window. He pressed a button on his bedside alarm clock to light up the face, and saw it was a little before five o'clock. His thoughts immediately turned to Giovanni; if the boy was still alive, had he survived a second night, wherever he was? Three words kept going round and round in his mind – home, school, church. One of those must hold a clue to his disappearance. D'Angelo's efforts thus far had been concentrated on the boy's home life and associated connections, such as the neighbours, and his tendency to wander off looking for wildlife. Apart from the local policeman's visit, no proper investigation had taken place at the school, and it was only since last night's talk about confirmation that D'Angelo had wondered if the church had played any part in Giovanni's life. But the harsh reality was that if the boy had been abducted, he could be anywhere, a deeply troubling thought. There was still so much work to be done. D'Angelo lay still and quiet in bed for a while, anxious not to disturb Adriana at such an early hour, but eventually restlessness defeated him, and he crept out of bed, taking his clothes with him to the bathroom so that he wouldn't have to return to the bedroom.

Downstairs, he brewed himself some coffee and ate a bowl of cereal, before leaving the house as quietly as possible for the drive to his office, where he spent two hours alone, looking once again through Carlo's aerial photographs, and committing whatever thoughts he had to the computer file dedicated to Giovanni's disappearance. From eight o'clock, he heard increasing levels of noise and disturbance from Lazzaro's team setting up the incident room, thankful to hear Sergeant Rossi's voice among the melee. He had a feeling that Rossi's input would be valuable, possibly crucial, to this case.

D'Angelo shut down his PC and ventured along the corridor to the newly-created incident room. He was pleased with what he found. On the far wall, alongside a large, and for now clean, whiteboard, was displayed an equally large and detailed map of Montenero and the surrounding area, upon which Corporal Gattone was shading certain sections with a marker pen, and pushing coloured pins in it to highlight buildings. In front of the whiteboard, Sergeant Rossi was arranging a large central desk to her required layout, including laptop computer, two phones, one landline, the other mobile, and trays for paper documents. Meanwhile, under Sergeant Lazzaro's supervision, Troopers Di Silverio, Carrea and Di Stefano were moving desks and chairs from other locations to a star pattern across the floor of the room. Major D'Angelo helped himself to a cup of water from a cooler that was positioned half way down the side wall, while he waited for the arrangements to be completed. With a final buzz of chatter and scraping of chairs while D'Angelo had a brief word with Rossi, silence fell as the major stood facing the room with the whiteboard behind him.

'Good morning, team. Thank you for your efforts yesterday, I appreciate the difficulties of the terrain you were working in, and the sometimes adverse weather conditions. I would like to welcome back Sergeant Rossi; it's good to see you here again, Sergeant.'

There was a murmur of concurrence with that remark from around the room.

'I take it, Sergeant Lazzaro, that the shaded portions on the map here are those areas already searched?'

'That's correct, Major. And the green pins indicate occupied properties, red pins show empty or abandoned buildings that have also been checked.'

D'Angelo studied the map and found a red pin he was searching for.

'There's a property here,' he said, 'close to the Fiorito place, a holiday home that I believe is currently empty.'

'Is that the one with the swimming pool, Major?' asked Corporal Gattone.

'That's the one. Did your team check it out, Gattone?'

'Yes, Major. No-one at home, no car in the car port. All windows shut, all doors locked. A separate small block, probably used as guest accommodation, but that was all closed up as well. I checked inside the pool pump housing and round the garden, then gave it the all clear.'

'Has co-ordination with the local constable – what's his name?'

'Maurizio Bordini.'

'That's it, Bordini, has that worked out alright?'

'No problems, Major. He knows the area well, so he's an important asset.'

'Good. Corporal Gattone, can you put in a call to him to find out if there's been any development since yesterday evening.'

Gattone went to the back of the room to make the call, while D'Angelo continued to address the remaining officers.

'Sergeant Lazzaro, I want you to add some civilians to today's search. Liaise with Bordini on who might be suitable, and make sure they work under the supervision of a carabiniere.'

'Will do, Major.'

Di Silverio looked across at Lazzaro and coughed conspiratorially.

'Oh, yes,' continued Lazzaro, 'Trooper Di Silverio came up with a suggestion. Would it be possible for us to get a sniffer dog and handler, maybe out from Pescara?'

D'Angelo bit his lip for a couple of seconds.

'That's a damn good suggestion, Di Silverio. It's certainly worth a try. Anyone have any contacts in dog section, help us short-circuit the official channels?'

Sergeant Rossi raised a hand in front of her face.

'I met a guy while I was at Chieti.'

There were good-natured jeers from around the room.

'He handles a Springer Spaniel, swears by her,' continued Rossi, smiling, 'she's been trained for doing people searches as well as finding drugs.'

'See what you can do. If he agrees to help us, I'll contact Giovanni's family and ask them to let us have an article of clothing, or whatever it is the handler needs for scent purposes. Yes, Gattone?'

'Nothing new, Signore. No sighting, no more information.'

'Thank you, Corporal. As you know, Sergeant Rossi has come in to co-ordinate everything here, but I'm making a change to today's plan. We have to work on the assumption that Giovanni is still within the Montenero area. If he's been taken by someone, then God knows where he might be by now, but I'll ask HQ to distribute the lad's description on a wider scale. I'm going to check today whether there might be a church connection. Apparently, it's not uncommon for kids of Giovanni's age to be confirmed, which would mean confirmation classes, and therefore possible contacts outside the areas of home and school that we need to look at. And on the subject of school, we know very little in that area. Bordoni went there yesterday morning just to confirm that Giovanni hadn't turned up, but although the boy was a bit of a loner, he must have had one or two pals, someone he might have confided in – perhaps even a teacher that he felt able to talk to. So Sergeant Rossi, I would like you to go to the school this morning, see what you can dig up, but clear your visit with the head teacher before you go. Have you brought any civvies with you today? I don't want you going in there in uniform.'

'No, Major, sorry. Oh, wait a minute though, there might still be some civvy clothes in my locker.'

'If not, stretch the budget and go out and buy a cheap top and a pair of jeans. My daughters assure me you can get stuff at a reasonable price at the Chinese emporium on via

Tripio. Now, transport. Sergeant Lazzaro, your team will be taking the Forester and the old 159, correct?'

'Correct, Major.'

'Sergeant Rossi, you take the AR Giuli. I'll use my own vehicle today. Any questions? Good, let's go.'

Several pairs of eyes followed Sergeant Rossi as she picked up her phone and speed-dialled a number at Chieti station to talk to her dog-handler friend, laughing and joking, but at the same time seemingly receiving assurance that he would bring his dog to come and help in the search. She gave Lazzaro a thumbs-up sign. Teresa Rossi was popular with junior and senior officers alike, in fact she was liked by almost everyone she met. With a ready smile, she had an open, cheerful face with engaging grey-green eyes, while her physical presence demanded attention. Tall, and with an athletic build, Teresa Rossi was captain of the town's netball team, and had been inter-divisional ladies Tae Kwando champion for the past three years. Not only that, she was a good communicator, and probably the most competent IT expert within Chieti Region. D'Angelo had her marked for rapid promotion. She ended her call to a chorus of cheers from her colleagues, and left the room to check her locker with a broad grin on her face.

It didn't take long for Lazzaro to get his team organized and on the road, himself driving the Subaru Forester in the lead, followed by the Alfa Romeo 159 driven by trooper Di Silverio.

D'Angelo waited for Rossi to re-appear, changed from uniform into jeans and tee shirt, and called her into his office. While Rossi stood waiting, D'Angelo rang the Mirelti house phone, to be answered at the other end by Laura.

'We're continuing the search today,' he explained, 'and we're going to be helped by a dog, trained to find missing persons. One of my officers, Sergeant Teresa Rossi, would like come to your house with the dog handler, and, if you don't mind, borrow an item of clothing belonging to Giovanni so that the dog has a scent to seek. Would that be alright?'

'Anything that will help, Major D'Angelo. Mamma is unwell and still in bed, so I shall find something suitable for your officers.'

'I'm sorry to hear about your mother, Laura. How are the rest of you coping?'

'Nobody's talking much. My other brother is coming over from America, so that might help a bit. We just don't know what to do any more. We feel so helpless.'

'Teresa Rossi will explain what is happening with regard to our search, Laura. If she thinks of any way you may be able to help us, she will let you know.'

With the call ended, D'Angelo confirmed with Rossi that she knew what was required of her.

'The Mirelti house first, with your dog-handler friend, then the school. Laura will find the article of clothing for you. She's a bright, competent girl, you'll like her. You have the co-ordinates for the house?'

'Yes, Major. I'll report later.'

Shortly afterwards, D'Angelo watched from his office window as Rossi climbed into the Alfa Romeo Giulietta squad car, and he smiled to himself as she revved the engine and spun out of the parking bay with a squeal of tyres. The car would be in for harder driving than it had yesterday, when he was at the wheel.

Having checked his inbox, in the calm of a quiet station, and preparing to set off to Montenero, there was a gentle tap on his door. Slightly puzzled, he called for the visitor to enter, and Katia crept tentatively into his office. He could see immediately that something was wrong. She wore a worried, almost tearful, expression, her face pale and taut, her demeanour cowed. D'Angelo stood up and pulled a chair to the side of his desk, indicating for Katia to sit down, while he resumed his place in his own chair.

'I'm very sorry to trouble you, Major D'Angelo,' she said in a quiet, wavering voice, 'I know you're very busy looking for this missing boy...'

'What is it, Katia? What's wrong?'

She looked down at her lap, where she was twisting her fingers in agitation, and her wavy, brown hair fell across her face.

'I don't like to ask, Major, but I think I need some help.'

'Katia, of course I'll help, if there's anything at all I can do. You're one of us, and we look after our own, as you know. But before you tell me what it is, stay there and I'll go and fetch us each a coffee.'

When D'Angelo returned to his office with two small cups of espresso, Katia was looking slightly less pained, her cheeks showing a hint of colour. After taking longer than was necessary to stir the sugar into her coffee, she began to speak, not looking up, and in a voice barely above a whisper.

'You're going to think this is very silly, a woman of my age, but a few weeks ago I met a man. It all started at the supermarket, where he offered to help carry my groceries out to the car. We got chatting, then started meeting at a café, or bar, and then one evening he took me out for a meal. We went to that new place, you know, the one just off the Piazza della Vittoria. Anyway, one thing led to another, and he started staying nights at my apartment.'

D'Angelo saw a patch of red rising on Katia's neck.

'What must you think of me, Major?'

'Katia, you're still young, you're an attractive woman, why on earth shouldn't you have a male companion?'

'You're very kind, Major.'

Katia half smiled, but at the same time, D'Angelo noticed a small tear roll gently from each brown eye.

'He works away quite a lot, so we can't see each other all that often, but I really look forward to the times we can be together. Anyway,' she continued, 'last week he asked if he could borrow some money, just until he was paid, so I gave him a hundred euros.'

D'Angelo's face tensed slightly. He looked, as though for inspiration, beyond Katia to the far wall where there hung a photograph of Rocco 'Rocky' Marciano, a famous son of Abruzzo.

'Then last night he said he wanted to borrow more. I asked him why, and he became very agitated. "I didn't want to tell you," he said, and he banged his hands above his head against the wall. "But I suppose you should know. I damaged a van at work, and because it was my fault, they told me I had to pay to get it repaired. I borrowed the money from a lender, but I've been struggling to pay it back, and now they've told me that if I don't make the payments on time, they'll send someone after me to beat me up, and the beatings will get worse until I pay them. I'm desperate, Katia," he said to me, "and I'm worried that if they find out about you, they'll come after you as well." I had to give him the money, Major D'Angelo, but I'm frightened. I'm frightened about what could happen to him if he doesn't pay up, and I'm worried that if I lose my job here, I won't be able to lend him any more money.'

'What do you mean, lose your job here?'

'I know that Colonel Battista has been on at you to cut costs, and the civilian secretary at Guardiagrele has been dismissed, and Angela in Lanciano has had her hours reduced. I'm worried the same thing might happen to me.'

'Katia, you do a vital job here, and I'll fight tooth and nail to keep you full time. You look after your mother, don't you?'

'Yes, Mamma had a stroke two years ago after Papa died, so now I take care of her.'

'Tell me a bit more about your man friend. What is his name?'

'Giorgio. Giorgio Pellegrini.'

'And where does Giorgio live?'

'In Orsogna. I don't know his address, I've never been to his home.'

'That's alright. Do you know who his employers are?'

'No. He doesn't like his job, so he never wants to talk about it.'

'Katia, please don't take this the wrong way, but are you sure he gave you his correct name?'

'Oh yes, quite sure. He had dropped his ID card one morning on the kitchen floor, and I saw his name on the front of it when I picked it up.'

'You didn't look inside it?'

'No.'

'Can you give me a brief description of Giorgio.'

'He's forty-four, about one metre seventy tall, short dark hair, thinning a bit.'

'That's fine. Leave this with me for the time being, Katia. If you want to go for a stroll outside, or…'

'No, thank you Major, I would rather stay and get on with my work, keep myself busy.'

'Fair enough.'

Katia stood and went to the door.

'Oh, Katia,' said D'Angelo just as she was about to leave his office, 'how much did you give – er – lend Giorgio yesterday?'

'Three hundred euros. I'm going to be a bit short this month.'

Once Katia had left, D'Angelo looked at his watch and cursed to himself. This was going to take up precious time, but on the other hand he had to do something to help Katia. He hoped it wouldn't take too long. He called Orsogna comune and asked them for the address of Giorgio Pellegrini. He heard the clicking of a computer keyboard, then the rustling of paper. Eventually, the clerk in the mayor's office came back on the phone.

'I'm sorry, Major D'Angelo,' she said, but we don't have a Giorgio Pellegrini in the Orsogna comune.'

D'Angelo then immediately called central records in Chieti, and asked if anyone named Giorgio Pellegrini lived within the Chieti Region. He bit his lip and tapped the desk with his left hand while he waited for a response. If this drew a blank, he would have to try Pescara for a check covering the whole of Abruzzo, but after that…?' At last, the nasal voice of the young man in Chieti records came back to D'Angelo.

'Two residents of that name in the Region, Signore.'

'Their comunes and ages, please.'

'First lives in Francavilla, age seventy-six.'

'And the second?'

'The second lives in Ari, age forty-four.'

'Full address of the second, please.'

'Via Morio, number fifty-seven.'

'Thank you. Good day.'

D'Angelo gritted his teeth. Still, it could be worse. A trip out to Ari shouldn't take too long. With a reminder to Katia to call him with any important messages, D'Angelo went out to his Toyota RAV4 car and set off for the small town of Ari. Via Morio was a long, sprawling road of mainly modest residential properties, interspersed with a few businesses, including a hardware store and a hairdresser, and even an olive press. D'Angelo slowed down when he spotted number sixty-three, and pulled up behind a white van. He found number fifty-seven, a small, terraced house amongst a line of dowdy, street-side properties, and saw on a hand-written strip above the doorbell the name Vitullo. From within, he could hear the raucous, non-stop noise of daytime television. He pressed the bell and waited, but without response. He pressed it again, holding it down for longer, and this time the door was opened by a heavy, doughy-faced woman with lank hair. An equally unprepossessing girl of nine or ten lurked behind her.

'Eh?'

'Good morning, Signora. I have come to see Giorgio Pellegrini.'

She looked at D'Angelo for a few seconds, her slack jaw open, showing an incomplete set of poor teeth, then turned and pushed open an internal door to her right.

'He's in there,' she said in a voice used to competing with loud noise from a television. D'Angelo stepped inside, while the woman trundled off towards her own lair in the kitchen, with its competing television.

'Shouldn't the child be at school, Signora?'

'Off sick,' she said, without looking round. 'This one's always sick.'

D'Angelo was left at the open door to a small, shabby room, where a man with short, thinning hair was watching a ubiquitous game show in which the host was assisted by semi-clad young girls. He turned round with a start as D'Angelo entered the grimy den, and watched, speechless, as the carabiniere calmly picked up the remote from a small table at the side of his chair and switched the television off.

'Signore Pellegrini? Signore Giorgio Pellegrini?'

Still wide-eyed, but emerging from his state of shock, the man nodded.

'If it's about that speeding fine, I'm going to pay it. Today. I'm paying it today.'

'I suggest you do so, or you're going to be in even more trouble.'

'More trouble? What do you mean?'

'Taking money under false pretences, with no intention of repaying it.'

'Kat…'

'Yes, Katia. I presume she's not the first victim of your scam, but she's going to be your last. You're going on a list to be watched, and if there's any hint of your little game being played out again, you'll be arrested and put on trial. Ever been to prison, Giorgio?'

'No. I'm not a criminal.'

'A presiding judge might think differently. Give me the money you took from Katia.'

'But the speeding fine…'

'The money.'

Pellegrini pulled a wallet from his back trouser pocket and took out three hundred euros, which he sheepishly handed over to D'Angelo.

'And the hundred you took from her last week.'

'That's it. I'm cleaned out.'

'Give me the wallet.'

Pellegrini reluctantly handed D'Angelo his wallet, where the officer found a further seventy euros, which he added to the three hundred.

'Regard the thirty as still owing, but I shall give Katia the full amount, so you'll be owing it to me,' said D'Angelo, 'and you will never attempt to contact Katia again. Incidentally, the name on the door is Vitullo.'

'The wife's name. This house is hers.'

'So you've been leeching off women for a long time. It hasn't exactly propelled you into the jet set, has it?' commented D'Angelo, looking around the small, scruffy room. With a further warning to Pellegrini to end his career as a con-man, D'Angelo returned to his car, angry and upset. He was going to have to explain to Katia that she had been taken in and cheated, and that her short-lived romance was over, an explanation which was going to be very painful for her. She didn't deserve to be treated like this. But it was a conversation that would have to wait, because D'Angelo headed towards the town centre, then took a left turn in the direction of Montenero.

Eleven

As agreed in a phone call, Sergeant Rossi met up with Davide, the dog handler, a couple of hundred metres before the turn into the Mirelti property so that they could arrive together. True to her word, Laura had found an unwashed fleece that Giovanni wore during the winter, and Davide stayed just long enough to collect the fleece and return to his van with the dog inside, and by the time he was turning back into the road, he was already talking to Lazzaro on his radio to check where they should meet up before Davide joined the search.

Rossi stayed at the house for a while longer, introducing herself to the family, and explaining to them that she was taking on a co-ordinating role in the search, so they could contact either herself or Major D'Angelo, who was lead officer in the enquiry.

Twenty minutes later, having taken her leave of Giovanni's family, Sergeant Rossi had parked fifty metres down the road from the entrance to Montenero Primary School, not wishing to draw attention to the carabinieri squad car. She sat for a few moments, contemplating the sad atmosphere she had just encountered, before walking back up to the school building, where she was directed to the classroom in which the head teacher was taking a history lesson. The head teacher left her class briefly to greet Rossi, and check she was the officer who rang earlier, then directed her to the staff room where Giovanni's form teacher was waiting, temporarily relieved of teaching duties by courtesy of an experienced assistant. The teacher, Signora Recchia, insisted that Rossi call her by her first name, Carolina. Rossi reciprocated by asking that she be called Teresa, helping retain the image of a civilian, possibly a new recruit to the teaching staff.

'We're very anxious about Giovanni's disappearance,' said Carolina, 'how might I be able to help?'

'I want to try and build a picture of him,' replied Rossi. 'I gather he's rather a loner. Does he have many friends here at school?'

Carolina twisted her mouth and glanced away, towards the window.

'Not really. He's quite often with Enrico, a quiet little boy who has very poor hearing, and who avoids the rough and tumble of playground games. But he's closest of all to Evelina. They're almost inseparable. They sit next to each other whenever they can, and they hold hands while waiting for the school bus. I can easily envisage them going out together at high school, and probably even getting married in years to come.'

'Can I meet Evelina, have a quiet chat with her?'

'Not today, I'm afraid, Teresa. Evelina was devastated when she heard that Giovanni had gone missing, and she hasn't come to school today. Her mother rang to explain her absence.'

'Was Giovanni bullied by any of the other boys?'

'Oh no, we don't allow any bullying here,' said Carolina defensively. 'But you know what children are like. If there's one who's a bit different, they, well – they can be a bit unkind.'

'Do you think Giovanni enjoys school?'

Carolina once again thought about the question before answering.

'I think he's rather neutral about it. He isn't overly enthusiastic, he does just about enough to get by, but his attendance is good. He doesn't take lots of days off sick like some of the children.'

'But as far as the other pupils are concerned, you would say he's on the fringe, not one of the crowd, so to speak.'

'That more or less sums it up, yes.'

'And you said he does just about enough to get by. Does that mean his school work is average"

'I have the record book here, Teresa. You can see the typical grades he gets from the three of us who teach his class – generally between five and seven, six being regarded as the pass mark. There we are look, Maths : 5, History : 6, Italian : 6,…'

'But two notable exceptions,' observed Rossi quickly, 'Natural Sciences and English.'

'That's right. Signore Orsatti takes him for sciences, and he tells me that Giovanni loves Natural History, in fact he thinks the boy knows more about fauna than he does himself. His excellent knowledge in that area pushes up his grades for the whole subject to eight, nine, even ten. Eleven is the highest possible grade.'

'And English?'

'Our English teacher is Signora Treddenti, and she teaches across nearly all the classes. English is her only subject, and yes, she gives Giovanni between seven and nine, and here, look, another ten on that report.'

'How much longer will Giovanni be at this school?'

'This is his final term. In September, after the holiday, he's due to go up to the Lower Secondary.'

'Which will presumably involve a longer bus journey, and being with older pupils. Does that prospect worry him, do you think?'

'He's never said anything to suggest he's bothered about it. Like a lot of our youngsters, I think he's looking forward to freedom and the end of school days, although it's surprising how many look back on life here with fondness. It's an odd thing, that they'll rebel against discipline, but their lives can be happier and more structured when they have rules and regulations to obey.'

'I greatly enjoy my job,' said Rossi, smiling, 'and it's all about strict rules and regulations. Is there anything else about Giovanni you think might be helpful, anything we should know about?'

'Not really. Oh, except I have here his Italian exercise book, which he handed in on Monday.'

'Monday? The last day he was in?'

'Yes, that's right. Anyway, I had asked the class to write an essay of about two hundred words on any subject they chose, and this is his essay. The grammar is moderate, some of the words he uses are good, but the subject matter most unusual. Normally, pupils will write about something they've done with their friends, visiting a festa, perhaps, watching the marching band or the firework display.

Giovanni has written a fantasy story about some birds that get together and decide to do something because a hunter has been shooting their family and friends. They fly up to the mountains, and persuade a bear to come down in the night and kill the hunter while he's asleep.'

'Shows imagination.'

'Oh yes, it shows imagination, and it's quite graphic, but I would never ask him to read his essay aloud to the class.'

'Too graphic?'

'Not that so much. Some of the games they play on their smartphones and tablets are truly gruesome. No, it's just that the fathers of some of the pupils in his class are themselves hunters.'

'I see. Yes, I can understand how sensitive that would be. Could you prepare a list of the hunters' names for me, just in case? And can I keep hold of the exercise book for now?'

'Yes, please do.'

'Thank you. And I would like to go and see Giovanni's friend, Evelina, if you could give me her address.'

'No problem,' said Carolina. 'Her home is not too far from here.'

D'Angelo decided to try and cover two bases with one visit. He wanted to know whether Giovanni had any connection with the church, and in particular whether he had been attending confirmation classes, but he was reluctant to add to the family's distress by calling on them yet again without any positive news. At the same time, he wanted to meet Giovanni's friend and part-time employer, Filippo, so he was hoping that Filippo might be able to answer the question about confirmation, as well as covering any other unknown aspects of Giovanni's life. Laura had described the location of Filippo's workshop, and with his growing knowledge of Montenero's layout, it didn't take long for D'Angelo to find the small but functional premises. The ornate door was partly open, watched over by a carved wooden owl that sat in a recess in the stone doorway. D'Angelo pushed the door further open and stepped inside, where he found most of the floor space taken up with blocks and sheets of seasoned timber, and all four walls covered with shelves, some of which held a wide variety of hand tools, others loaded with carvings. In the middle of the space was a large, floor-standing lathe being worked by a middle-aged man with a full beard and long hair tied back in a pony tail. The scene was lit by a beam of sunlight, falling as though from a theatre spot lamp, from a high window behind the man's back, a myriad motes of dust dancing in the bright glow. D'Angelo walked the few paces to watch as the man carefully turned his block of dark wood, the newest carving gradually taking shape. For a while the man continued concentrating on his work, not lifting his eyes for a second, until he stopped and examined his creation. Apparently satisfied with progress made, he switched off the lathe and put down his carving, looking at D'Angelo for the first time. In the sudden silence, D'Angelo became more aware of the surroundings and smells inside the workshop. The scent of newly-cut wood mingled with the sweetness of linseed oil, the slightly acrid smell of tobacco, and beneath it all something else, a bitter-sweet odour that could never be disguised, weak but unmistakable, the smell of cannabis.

D'Angelo remembered his time as a high-flying young captain leading drug busts in Rome, before becoming one of the youngest majors in the Italian carabinieri, destined surely for the very top. But that was all before…

Returning from the past, he introduced himself to Filippo.

'Ah yes, of course,' responded Filippo, 'Laura told me about you. You're leading the hunt to try and find Giovanni. Do you have any news?'

'Unfortunately not, but the search goes on. I gather he sometimes came to help you in here?'

'I'm sure he will again when he's found. I look forward to his visits. He reminds me a bit of how I was when I was his age.'

'But you have no idea what could have happened to him? Where he might have gone?'

Filippo looked down at his lathe and shook his head.

'None at all. It's a complete mystery.'

'Did he ever visit you at home?'

'No, he never came to my house, only here at the workshop. But I'm sure he knows that if he's in any sort of trouble, he can come to me for help.'

'Where is your house, incidentally?'

'It's a place on its own, half a kilometre below Contrada Castagne.'

D'Angelo looked around at the wooden carvings on the surrounding shelves, many of them depicting animals and birds.

'I saw one of your owls in his room at home. He must love all these.'

'Anything to do with nature, Major D'Angelo.'

D'Angelo's eyes rested on a particularly prominent carving of a snake, set on its own small shelf in the middle of the wall. Its coiled tail formed the base, its hooded head with red glass eyes raised as if to strike. D'Angelo walked over to examine it.

'That's very impressive,' he said. 'How much would you charge for a carving like that?'

'I'm afraid that particular one is not for sale, Major, but if any of the others take your fancy...'

'Another time, perhaps. Tell me, Signore, do you happen to know whether Giovanni was visiting the priest for confirmation classes?'

Filippo picked up a piece of cloth and wiped his hands, an almost symbolic gesture of absolving himself of responsibility, it occurred to D'Angelo. Filippo threw the cloth back on the shelf where he had found it.

'We didn't talk about it much. I suppose I tried to dissuade him from it – I've never been a great lover of the church myself. All those strict rules and humble obedience, not my thing, Major. Too much of a free spirit.' Filippo grinned briefly for the first time, but the smile soon disappeared. 'My mother told me she had a bad time at a convent school when she was young, so she hated anything to do with the church.'

'But Giovanni...'

'Giovanni was attending confirmation classes. He's due to be confirmed in a few weeks' time. He asked me if I would go to the ceremony, but I declined. I tell him that a lot of cruelty to animals results from the church's belief that all life other than human is inferior, because only humans supposedly have souls, but he just quotes Saint Francis of

Assisi at me. It's been the closest we've ever got to arguing. When all's said and done, it's his life, his decision.'

Filippo picked up a packet of cigarettes, but seemed to change his mind and put them back down.

'So he's determined to continue with his confirmation?'

'As far as I know, yes.'

'Does he tell you about his home life, or school?'

'Yes, he's quite a chatterbox when he gets going. I don't think he finds life particularly easy either at home or school. Odd one out, if you know what I mean. I get the impression he's fond of his mother, but has a difficult relationship with his father, and he doesn't get on at all with his future brother-in-law.'

'Mario?'

'Mario, that's right. The real loves of his life are his sister, Laura, and his girlfriend at school, Evelina. Always talking about one or other of them, and neither can do any wrong in his eyes. And of course, he's always wanting to know about animals and birds.'

'How did you get to know Giovanni?'

'He was staring at the owl in the doorway when I arrived one day. He asked me if I had carved it, so I told him I had, and there are more of them inside if he would like to see them. He started to come here sometimes after school, so I got him to help tidy up, sweep the floor and so on, for a bit of pocket money.'

Filippo pulled back the cuff of his long-sleeved shirt, revealing what appeared to D'Angelo to be an expensive watch. He also saw a small part of what looked like a tattoo.

'I don't want to rush you, Major, but I need to go and see a customer soon.'

'Of course,' said D'Angelo, 'I won't hold you up any longer.' He looked again at the display of carvings. 'Do you sell many of these?'

'I sell enough to get by. Mustn't complain.'

'Mm.' D'Angelo moved towards the door. 'By the way, some civilian helpers have joined the search for Giovanni today. Your services not required?'

'I would gladly have gone to help if I'd been asked. I presume the candidates were selected by Maurizio Bordini, in which case I'm not surprised my name wasn't on the list. I suspect that in Bordini's opinion, I'm not the right type to be given much responsibility.'

Filippo shook his head, so that his pony tail swung from side to side. D'Angelo smiled with understanding, and left the workshop.

Filippo stood still for a short while, then went slowly to the door and pushed it shut. He walked back to where the lathe stood, and once again picked up the cigarette packet. Inside the pack, along with a number of cigarettes, was a spliff he had rolled for himself earlier. He started to draw it from the packet, then pushed it back down, chose instead one of the cigarettes, and lit up. Deep in thought, he blew smoke into the beam of sunlight, like a billowing cloud across a summer sky.

D'Angelo walked past where he had parked his car, looking up to the impressive bulk of the church of San Bartolomeo, which stood at the highest point in Montenero, the summit of the Black Hill, surrounded by a ring of pine trees. He pulled the small but efficient radio phone from its leather pouch and called firstly Lazzaro, for an update on the ground search, then put in a call to Rossi. He could hear that she was using hands-free, so was obviously in the car.

'I'm on my way back to base,' she explained. 'After visiting the school, I went to see Giovanni's little girlfriend, who was at home today.'

'Learn anything of interest?'

'Not really. Some unusual schoolwork that I'll show you later, and the girl is very upset, I think she's made herself ill with worrying. It's a shame, she's a sweet kid. One thing I did get from her. It was a struggle, Giovanni had told her it was a secret, and she wasn't to tell anyone. You know what kids are like, when they've promised to keep a secret. Well, girls anyway. I'm not sure boys are quite so principled. Sorry boss. Eventually I persuaded her to tell me this secret. Giovanni had seen his sister's fiancé, Mario, stealing money from his nonna's purse. Giovanni had apparently challenged him, but Mario told him to "keep his trap shut" or he'd suffer the consequences.'

'Do you know when this happened?'

'I got the impression it was quite recently. In the last week or two.'

'Thank you, Sergeant. I've had a word with the guy Filippo, and now I'm off to see the priest.'

'Your day for confession, Major?'

'Ha bloody ha. You go and man the fort, I'll catch up with you later. Over and out.'

Having climbed the numerous steps leading up to the church, D'Angelo realised he was a bit out of shape, not as fit as he used to be, and promised himself he would do a bit more exercise now he was approaching fifty. Fifty. Good god, he thought, nearer the end than the beginning, what a depressing prospect. Perhaps he should re-think this religion idea, maybe there's something in it after all.

The large main door of the church, covered by a newly-constructed portico, was open, so D'Angelo let himself into the cool, incense-scented interior of the building. His footsteps echoed on the large stone flags of the central aisle as he made his way towards the altar, where he could see a side door leading to the vestry. He had thought he was alone in the huge space, but a movement beyond the gap between the rows of pews suddenly caught his attention. He walked between two of the pews to discover an elderly, diminutive woman fussily arranging some flowers beneath one of the stations of the cross. D'Angelo felt sure he had seen her somewhere before, and when she turned to look up at him, he remembered her face. One of the customers in Bianca Di Lello's shop. D'Angelo was blessed with a good memory for names, but he was struggling to recall this woman's name. In the space of just a few seconds, he visualised the scene at the butcher's, and played back in his mind the moment she had taken the bag of meat from Bianca. Cristini. That was it, he was sure. An appropriate name for someone in a church.

'Good morning, Signora Cristini, I trust you are well. Busy with the flowers, I see.'

The woman blinked a few times, and glanced at her floral display.

'Yes officer.' She paused, remembering the strange sight of this carabinieri carrying a dead bird. 'Always work to do in the Lord's house.'

'Indeed, Signora. I was wondering if the priest was here this morning, Padre – er…'

'Padre Falcone.'

'Padre Falcone, that's right.'

Signora Cristini's eyes opened wide and she stumbled backwards against the white-plastered wall.

'Are you alright, Signora?'

'Yes – thank you,' she squeaked, putting her hand up to her mouth. It had just occurred to her that the dead bird this officer had been carrying was some sort of hawk, like the priest's name. She didn't understand the significance, but she had heard stories of strange and frightening rituals.

'Can I get you anything, Signora? Some water, perhaps?'

'No – no, really, nothing, thank you.'

'Can you tell me where Padre Falcone is now?'

Signora Cristini, ghostly white, pointed towards the back of the church with a shaking hand.

'The community room, next door,' was all she managed to say.

Puzzled by the woman's reaction, and looking at her carefully to make sure she hadn't some sort of stroke or seizure, D'Angelo thanked her, and went back up the aisle and out of the church. Behind the church he found a modern, flat-roofed building with a notice on the wall alongside the door, stating that it was the community room, keys in the care of Padre Orlando Falcone.

Finding the door unlocked, D'Angelo went inside. The first thing he saw was a square beam of bright light projected between several rows of plastic chairs on to a screen at the front of the room.

'Nearer, it'll have to come a bit nearer,' somebody said.

The light beam wobbled, then overlapped the edges of the screen.

'Too far, Andrea, back a bit.'

The voice came from a man in a black cassock, not immediately visible in the darkened room, standing in front of the screen just outside the path of the light source. A young man towards the back of the room eased backwards a small table holding the projector until the screen was perfectly lit.

'There. That's it, right there, Andrea. That should be spot on. Try a slide.'

Andrea picked up a small white remote and pressed a button, and with a short whirr and click a picture appeared on the screen showing a cluster of bright red toadstools with yellowish spots. The priest who was directing operations took a few steps backwards and examined the projected toadstool photo for a few seconds.

'One more, Andrea.'

Another whirr and click changed the picture from red toadstools to a ring of dainty white ones, looking like little parasols. After another careful examination, the priest seemed satisfied.

'Good. Yes, that's going to be fine, just like that. Now, let's have some light.'

The priest and the young man each went to a window either side of where D'Angelo was standing and tugged on a short cord to release the blinds that had been shutting out the daylight. While Andrea went to the other side of the room to release two more window blinds, Padre Orlando Falcone greeted Major D'Angelo, who in turn introduced himself.

'Sorry to have kept you like that,' apologised the priest, 'we have an expert coming in this evening to give a talk on fungi, which ones are edible, which ones to avoid. I want to make sure we're ready for him. I'm not sure how many people will be coming to listen to him, but I think we'll be alright.' He distractedly looked around at the chairs, trying to decide whether a sufficient number had been set out. Padre Falcone was round-faced with red cheeks and short, dark hair, turning to steel grey. D'Angelo was trying to avoid looking at the man's stomach, an enormous protuberance which made him appear nine months pregnant, slightly, but not sufficiently, disguised by the head to toe covering of cassock.

'I believe some fungi are quite seriously poisonous,' said D'Angelo.

'Absolutely right. A family of three tragically died up in Le Marche just last year from eating the wrong ones. We don't want that to happen to any of our citizens.'

D'Angelo remembered the strange-looking mushrooms he had on his pizza yesterday evening, and felt his stomach lurch slightly.

Padre Falcone started counting the chairs, still not sure there were enough.

'I've come to ask about a boy who I believe is due to be confirmed soon,' said D'Angelo, trying to gain Padre Falcone's undivided attention.

'Ah, yes, young Giovanni,' said the priest, turning back to look at D'Angelo. 'Bad business, where can he have got to?'

'That's what I'm trying to find out, Padre. Has he been attending confirmation classes with you?'

'Yes, yes. That'll be all for now, Andrea, I'll see you this evening. Come about seven thirty, if you will. Our guest is due at eight. Come, Major D'Angelo, it's a beautiful morning, let's take a stroll outside, breathe in some lovely fresh air. The pine trees give off such a wonderful scent, don't you think? Come along, this way.'

Padre Falcone, surprisingly nimble on his feet considering the handicap of his distended stomach, led D'Angelo out onto the wide, stone-paved piazza overlooking a large part of Montenero.

'Splendid views from here, Major D'Angelo, don't you think?'

'Excellent. And your lovely church occupies the nearest point to heaven.'

Falcone laughed. 'Quite so, Major, quite so.'

'Do you know Giovanni well, Padre?'

'As a matter of fact, I have got to know him quite well, yes. An unusual boy. Of course they're all on best behaviour for my benefit, I realise that, but I've prepared a good number of youngsters for confirmation in my time as a priest, and Giovanni Mirelti stands out as being different, not just among the six candidates I'm currently preparing.'

'Not six boys?'

'No, no. Two boys, four girls. They're due to be confirmed by the bishop of Lanciano, Monsignor Iacovella, at a ceremony next month.'

'You say Giovanni is different. In what way is he different?'

Padre Falcone puffed out his cheeks and tried to think how best to answer the question.

'Apart from Elisabetta, his nonna, I don't see his family at church on a Sunday, so there won't be any pressure from home on his decision to be confirmed. One of the other candidates, a girl called Evelina, is a very special friend of his, and perhaps that is a contributing factor, although I honestly think he has decided that being confirmed is important to him, and that he would have come along anyway. But there seems to be a constant battle going on in his mind.'

'How do you mean, Padre? What sort of battle?'

The two men continued walking in silence until they reached the edge of the piazza. D'Angelo worried that the priest, with so much weight in front of him, might topple over the edge and roll down the hill.

'How about that for a view, Major. This is the best time of year for this view, before the heat of summer makes it too hazy. There, look, you can see the sea from here.'

D'Angelo looked out across woodland and vineyards, olive groves and dotted farms and hamlets, thinking, hoping, that somewhere out there he would find Giovanni. But would he be alive or dead.

'Yes, the battle in the boy's mind,' said Falcone, prompted by the silence. 'He keeps questioning things, are the words in the Holy Scripture right or wrong. "Do Christians love animals," he would say. "Of course we do," I tell him. "But a snake was blamed for being evil and tempting Eve to steal an apple that she shouldn't have had. Why should a snake get the blame?" What can I say, Major? I try and explain that the Book of Genesis in the Old Testament is now regarded as largely allegorical, and we don't take it too literally, so he asks how much of the rest of the bible is not true. "So is it true or not that animals have been put on earth just for the benefit of humans," he says. "That's open to interpretation," I tell him. "Do animals have souls?" he asks me. "No, only humans have souls." "So when I die and go to heaven, there won't be any animals there?" "Well, the state of rest in God's heaven is different to the toil we suffer on earth," I explain.

D'Angelo glanced sideways at the priest and wondered how much toil he was suffering on earth. The theological discussions between Giovanni and Padre Falcone sounded to him like game, set and match to the boy. "I wouldn't want to be in heaven if there aren't any birds and animals there." As you must have gathered, Major, Giovanni is very fond of the natural world. I tell him that it's very important to live a good and Christian life here on earth, whatever our role in society happens to be. Last week he wanted to know if God would punish people who steal. I told him that we all need to know what's right and what's wrong, and explained that after confirmation, if we know we've done wrong, we should confess our sins to receive absolution. He pursued the point, and said that if the thief wasn't caught, and he didn't go to confession, would God then punish him. I got the feeling he had someone specific in mind. It's both a joy and a trial having Giovanni in my confirmation class, Major D'Angelo. I welcome him into the family of the holy church, but I sometimes dread what topics of conversation might arise on the journey.'

'It sounds to me as though he has quite a lot of doubts about his faith, Padre.'

'I like to think he just needs reassurance, and his faith will be all the stronger once he has been reassured.'

D'Angelo couldn't help but feel sceptical on that point, but kept his thoughts to himself.

'So as far as you are aware, Padre, Giovanni and your other five students will all be confirmed by the bishop next month.'

'Absolutely. And for now, I shall be praying for the swift and safe return to our fold of our dear Giovanni.'

'Amen to that, Padre.'

Twelve

The Citroen C4 People Carrier rounded Pescara's via Di Vestea into via Bardet and stopped after thirty metres outside Party Pieces For All, a brightly modern, glitzy shop selling a wide variety of low-cost fun items, especially popular with children and young adults. Two Vietnamese girls, one aged sixteen, the other seventeen, climbed out of the back seat of the C4 and entered the shop, as the driver of the vehicle, a heavily-built Chinese national sporting a buzz haircut and Aviator sunglasses, continued on his journey without so much as a sideways glance.

Inside the shop, the elder of the two girls went straight to take over duty behind the till, while her younger companion began tidying shelves and checking whether any items needed re-stocking. This was one of the three shops the girls worked in, and after several months of harsh discipline and instruction, they were familiar with the routine of their duties. They worked hard and for long hours, but it was supposedly worth it. Admittedly, they didn't receive any pay, but they were given food and somewhere to sleep, and they had been promised that if they worked well, and became completely fluent in Italian, they could go on to better things, and eventually they would get citizenship and identity cards, so that they could live and work anywhere they wanted within the European Union. It was a dream that kept them going. Signore Lau himself, who had made his fortune with a casino in the gambling mecca of Macau, had come to speak to all the girls in the house, and told them that the lucky ones among them would be selected to work at his casino here in Pescara. The casino girls lived in another house, with only two in each room, so it was rumoured, and they had special privileges. But it was also rumoured that some of the girls had to work as escorts, a prospect that frightened the younger of the two girls in the shop, who called herself by her new name, Maria. She didn't like the look of European men. They had hard faces, and most of them were overweight. She had come to Europe on a long and difficult journey because she had promised her grandma in Ho Chi Minh city that she would come and earn plenty of money, enough to send some back home to help look after her little brother, because Grandma's pension wasn't enough. But so far, Maria hadn't been able to send a single euro, and week by week she was becoming increasingly anxious. When would she be able to earn some money that she could send home?

Now something else was worrying her. There was a tiny room in the house that no-one talked about, as though they pretended it didn't exist, but Maria knew it existed and she had seen some of the ones who had been locked up in it. They were mostly very young, she guessed about eleven or twelve years old, and usually girls. She didn't know where they came from – she had seen two that were definitely Asian, and one who was black, perhaps from Africa. Each of them was only ever kept in the little room for one or two days, then they were taken away and Maria didn't see them again. This morning she saw a boy being put in the room. He seemed a bit older, perhaps thirteen or fourteen, and he looked as though he might have been European. But it had been Maria's turn to sweep the corridor, and she had overheard a little of the conversation between the woman who was in charge of the girls, and the woman who did the cooking. The cook had asked where the boy was from and what would he eat. The supervisor replied that he was Muslim, and she thought he was from Libya, but definitely North Africa. "That's good enough for me," the cook had said. "North African Muslim diet."

Maria couldn't understand what was happening to these younger ones, or where they went after they left the house. They were surely too young to be working, unless they were somewhere unseen, perhaps washing dishes in a restaurant kitchen. As she picked up some small pads of coloured notelets, carelessly knocked from the shelf by an indulgent child, Maria thought again about her secret plan. An elderly customer had left their mobile phone on the shop counter one day, and although Maria was racked with guilt for having stolen it, nobody had seen her slip the phone into the pocket of her jeans. It was an old-fashioned phone, and when Maria had tried ringing the shop number a few days later, it had worked, so she guessed it was pay-as-you-go rather than on contract. She had hidden the phone among her few possessions at the house, intending to use whatever credit was left on it to contact her grandma so that she could explain why she hadn't yet sent any money, but another idea had formed in her head. She didn't like the fact that children were being kept in that tiny room at the house, and she was trying to think of a way to let the authorities know, but without jeopardizing all the other residents. She knew a number to ring, because a police car had stopped outside the shop one evening to deal with a drunken tourist, and the number 112 was on the car door. If only she knew what to say to them.

* * *

At carabinieri headquarters, Colonel Battista had received a very unwelcome message. The deputy minister of sport and culture would be arriving at Pescara airport on a scheduled flight from Barcelona at eleven a.m. The deputy minister's office had booked a suite at the Hotel Sabbia D'Or, and "he requires to be collected by car from the airport and from there taken to the hotel. At two thirty, he wishes to be collected from the hotel and taken to the closing events of the international beach volleyball competition, at which he will be presenting the cup and medals to the winners."

Battista slammed his hand down on his desk. It was bad enough having to send an officer to pick him up from the airport, but surely to God the deputy minister of sport is capable of walking about two hundred metres from his beachside hotel to the sports lido? He called Captain Luciani on the internal phone, and told him to report to his office. Less than a minute later, the captain was standing in front of Battista's desk, feet slightly apart and hands clasped behind his back.

'A plane from Barcelona carrying our esteemed deputy minister of sport and culture will be landing at Pescara airport at eleven o'clock, which is,' said Colonel Battista, looking at his watch, 'in twenty-six minutes' time. You are to fetch the deputy minister and transport him from there to the Hotel Sabbia D'Or.'

'Yes, Colonel.'

'Then at half past two, you will collect the said deputy minister and take him to the sports lido where he will have the important duty of presenting medals.'

'You mean that patch of sand where they play beach volleyball, Colonel?'

'That's the one.'

'But from the hotel it's only...'

'I don't care how near or far the journey is from his hotel. You will ensure he arrives safely at his destination.'

'Yes, Colonel. Do you happen to know the deputy minister's name, Signore?'

'That I can tell you, Captain. It is Signore Sartolini. I suggest you make a start, Luciani.'

The captain moved towards the door. 'One thing before you go. Has there been anything significant on the morning report?'

'Nothing particularly important, Colonel. There was, however, a slightly strange incident reported overnight. A twenty year-old male presented himself at the hospital A&E with a hand wound. He said he had fallen on a metal spike that had gone right through his hand, but the doctor who treated him notified us of the incident because he was suspicious. Apparently, the doctor has worked with the charity Medecins sans Frontieres in Yemen, and he noted that the young man's wound was very clean, which reminded him of bullet wounds he had dressed while working for MSF.'

'Any calls to report hearing a gunshot?'

'No, Colonel.'

'Very well. Take good care of our deputy minister friend, Luciani.'

Captain Luciani hurried back to his desk and entered the words 'Sartolini, deputy minister of sport and culture' into the search engine on his PC. Several headings came up on the screen, including some newspaper articles, but Luciani soon found what he was looking for, which was 'Images of Carlo Sartolini.' He clicked on the most suitable photo in order to enlarge it, and felt sure he would have no trouble in recognizing the deputy minister. He was looking at the picture of a haughty man, with full, fleshy lips, a prominent nose, and black wavy hair. Even if the photo had been taken a few years ago, vanity being one of a politician's vices, and the hair was now not quite so jet black or abundant, and there were a few more creases around eyes and mouth, Luciani was sure there would be no mistaking him. He grabbed his cap and ran down the stairs to the ground floor, where he marched briskly to the transport desk and booked himself a squad car, and by the time he was driving the Alfa Romeo up the ramp into the street, he noted with satisfaction that only three minutes had elapsed since he left Battista's office. Twenty-three minutes, plus however long it might take for Sartolini to collect his luggage and reach the arrivals hall, should give Luciani plenty of time to be waiting, like a faithful servant of the state, for the appearance of the deputy minister of sport and culture.

* * *

In the tiny room at the house where Maria and the other girls were boarded, the fourteen year-old Libyan boy had dressed himself in the smart Italian clothes that one of Signore Lau's employees had brought in for him, and he was now undergoing inspection by the house manager.

'The shirt's probably a size too big for him,' she was saying, 'but the style is fine. It'll do. Now, you're going to be a good boy, aren't you?'

'Yes, Signora. When will I see my parents? I want to be with them.'

'Soon, very soon. They'll be so pleased to see you. Be nice to the important gentleman who's coming to meet you. Remember what we told you – be polite, and do everything he asks you. You'll do that, won't you?'

'Yes, Signora.'

'Good. Come with me, and Hue Li will take you in the nice big car to the hotel. Perhaps tomorrow your parents will be here to collect you. Come along now.'

Once ensconced in the back of the C4, the Libyan boy gazed in awe through the window at well-dressed people and expensive-looking shops, full of luxury goods, as the Chinese man with Aviator sunglasses drove slowly through the busy streets towards the sea-front and the Hotel Sabbia D'Or.

* * *

On his way back down the hill's steep steps into the village of Montenero, Major D'Angelo flipped through the last few pages of notes in his little book, until he found details of the previous afternoon's conversation with Giovanni's family, just before he had visited the butcher, Bianca Di Lello. He had asked about the holiday home with the swimming pool, and he had noted the name and address of the house's caretaker – he had written the name Claudia Sabatelli, living at via Santa Rosa, number six. Finally descending the last flight of steps back down into the cobbled via Roma, D'Angelo spotted a woman leaning on the railing of her first-floor balcony overlooking the street, keeping her eye on the comings and goings of anyone walking in the street below her.

'Can you tell me where via Santa Rosa is please, Signora,' D'Angelo called up to her.

'Santa Rosa? Are you looking for the mayor?'

'I'm looking for via Santa Rosa, Signora.'

The woman clucked like a hen. 'Down that way,' she said, pointing towards the centre of the village, 'take the turning just before you reach the pharmacy. That's Santa Rosa.'

'Thank you, Signora. Good day.'

Set back a little way from the next door property, its two balconies festooned with hanging baskets of geraniums and petunias, D'Angelo rang the bell of red-doored number six.

'Signora Claudia Sabatelli?' D'Angelo enquired of the stout, middle-aged lady who opened the door.

'What's happened? Is it Roberto? What's happened to him?'

'No, Signora, please, it's alright. It's nothing to do with your husband.'

'It's not? You sure? Oh, thank God. Thank God for that.'

'May I come in? Perhaps you should sit down, have some water.'

'Yes, come in. You gave me a bit of a fright. I think I will sit down for a minute. Oh dear.'

D'Angelo gave Claudia Sabatelli a few moments to drink some water and recover from the shock of his arrival on the doorstep.

'I'm sorry I gave you a scare, Signora. My name is Major D'Angelo. I presume you're aware that the Mirelti boy has been missing since Monday evening?'

'He still hasn't been found? His poor Mamma, she must be worried sick. What can have happened to him?'

'We've been checking nearby properties in case he climbed in and can't get out. I understand you look after a holiday home owned by an Englishman.'

'Signore Renson, yes. I tidy it up when he has gone, and have it all ready for him when he next arrives.'

'Is he there at the moment?'

'No. He was here last week, but he's gone now.'

'Was he alone, or with his wife?'

'He was on his own. Quite often it's just him.'

'When did he leave?'

'Monday night. He flew back from Pescara airport.'

'Monday night? So presumably he hires a car from the airport to drive out here?'

'Yes. He told me he has a long drive back to his home in England from wherever the plane lands, but he prefers to do that rather than drive all the way from Rome to here.'

'I understand. Have you been to the house to tidy it since he left?'

'Not yet. My son and his wife called to see me yesterday, so I didn't get a chance. Roberto went over just before the storm to make sure nothing had been left outside. I shall go this afternoon when Roberto is back with the car.'

'I wish to go there myself to have a look, Signora. I would be grateful if you could let me borrow the key.'

Claudia sat bolt upright in her chair.

'Oh, I'm sorry, no, I don't think I can do that. Signore Renson is very particular about his privacy, he told me he didn't want anyone apart from Roberto and myself to go into his house when he's not there. He was very clear about that.'

'I'm sure you wouldn't want to impede a carabinieri search for a missing boy, Signora. But I would be perfectly content for you to accompany me to the property. I don't think Signore Renson would object to that, would he?'

'Oh, oh dear, I'm not sure. Well I suppose, under the circumstances...'

'If you could collect the key, Signora, my car isn't far away.'

Thirteen

In Pescara, Colonel Battista was about to chair a meeting of his Divisional Commanders in Room 2A. Three of his DCs had already arrived at headquarters, and they were waiting for the fourth, the 'old fox', Major Camponelli. He had been delayed because he had spent the previous two hours contacting his most reliable informants, letting them know he wanted to hear any word from the street about a drug gang leader called Rex, and any talk about a possible imminent landing of illegals. Battista had offered him only the barest information, hoping for corroboration on the Thursday night landing, and possibly an idea of arrival point.

Moments after coffee and biscuits had arrived, Camponelli swept into the room, rocking in his usual side to side motion, his white-bearded chin jutting forward as though in a chase.

'Morning Signori,' he growled in his gruff voice, as he helped himself to an espresso and settled himself into the empty seat.

'A snippet on my way here on the drug boss,' he continued, as he stirred two spoons-full of sugar into his strong coffee, before swallowing it in virtually a single gulp.

'Please share it with us,' prompted Battista, ensuring he took back control of the meeting, slightly irked that Camponelli had grabbed the initiative and everyone's attention without deference to his Commanding Officer.

'All I can tell you is that some guy called Rex has pulled together a few loners and small-time operators, and he's starting to run a pretty efficient organisation. Bit of an enforcer, by the sound of it.'

'Nothing else?'

'Nothing so far. Except he's reckoned to be based out of town.'

'Out of town? You mean from a distance, Rome, Naples?'

'No, it sounded to me like he's local, but not shacked up in Pescara itself.'

The officers started discussing whether Rex could be living on the outskirts of Pescara, or perhaps he has a villa on the coast, down in Francavilla, maybe, or even as far as Ortona. Their discussion was interrupted by an incoming call on Camponelli's personal phone, which was sitting on the table in front of him. He held up a hand for silence before accepting the call. Camponelli's colleagues could only sit and listen to a series of grunts and 'uh-huhs' until he ended the call and replaced the phone on the table.

'Looks like it's on for tomorrow night, Signori, but we still have no idea where they will be landed.'

'In that case,' said Battista, 'we will now make practical and logistical plans on the basis that at some time on Thursday, between midnight and five a.m., within let us say twenty kilometres to north or south of Pescara, we shall attempt to intercept a people smugglers' boat landing some illegal immigrants. As for Rex, the drug baron, I'm minded to hand over investigation to one of the peripheral commands. I have one or two possible candidates in mind, and I shall announce who will be taking the lead once I have made a final decision.'

'Will that include the murder investigation, Edoardo?' asked one of the younger, ambitious Divisional Commanders.

'Most probably. I shall give the matter some thought,' replied the colonel.

At the airport, Captain Luciani had been right about being able to pick out the visiting deputy minister, Signore Sartolini. He looked as arrogant as his photograph suggested, coming through the swing doors into the arrivals hall in splendid isolation from the common herd. He handed his bag to the greeting carabiniere with all the grace of a bull elephant, and climbed into the back seat of the waiting squad car while Luciani held the door open for him. After receiving a few one-word responses to his attempts at polite conversation, Luciani gave up on further pretence at interest in how the deputy minister's journey had gone, and drove the remainder of the way to the Hotel Sabbia D'Or in silence.

Parked in a nearby side-street, a pair of eyes shielded by Aviator sunglasses watched as Captain Luciani dropped Sartolini off at the hotel, and once the squad car had disappeared into the distance, the Chinese chauffeur flicked his fingers to indicate that the man in the back of the C4 could now escort the Libyan boy into the hotel.

* * *

As Major D'Angelo walked alongside Claudia on the gravel path towards the front door of Renson's holiday home, he could see immediately that, although not large, the single-storey house had been renovated to an exceptionally high standard. The stone walls, probably having been coated in plaster for many years, were exposed and expertly pointed with an appropriately-coloured mortar, the roof had clearly been renewed, yet the original Roman-type terracotta tiles had been cleaned and replaced on top, and the solid wooden door matched the window frames. Tasteful but expensive, was D'Angelo's initial assessment.

Claudia Sabatelli turned the key three times to release the three-lever mortice deadlock, and stepped smartly into the entrance hall to neutralise the alarm system. The internal finishing and décor confirmed D'Angelo's first impressions, as he crossed the threshold onto beautiful patterned black porcelain floor tiles.

'You want to look around the whole house, Major?' asked Claudia, with a hint of pride in her voice.

'Yes please, Signora.'

'Alright, we'll start here,' she said, leading D'Angelo into the first room to the right of the entrance hall. It was a bedroom with a small en-suite bathroom. The room contained a good-sized double bed with bedside tables on which stood reading lights that matched the main central ceiling light. The bed was neatly made up ready for use. On one wall there was a wardrobe, which D'Angelo opened, finding it empty except for a number of coat-hangers on the rail. Against another wall was a substantial chest of drawers, on top of which was a china pot-pourri holder and an English-language paperback book. On the walls were a mirror and three paintings depicting African scenes.

'The guest bedroom,' explained Claudia, confirming the assumption D'Angelo had already reached.

The next room they entered was the kitchen-cum-dining room, with French windows leading out onto a semi-circular patio with outdoor table and chairs. Unlike the first room they had looked in, the kitchen bore evidence of having recently been used. There were dirty plates on the worktop near the sink, and used glasses and mugs on the central island. Claudia, conscious of her duty to restore order, went to collect the plates, but D'Angelo held up a restraining hand.

'Please don't touch anything for the time being, Signora.'

He moved slowly around the terracotta tiled floor, trying to picture the scene in this room on Monday evening. He looked inside the dishwasher, where there was other crockery and cutlery waiting to be washed, then he opened the fridge where he found a large part of a cooked leg of lamb sitting in a cooking tray. In the door was a carton of fresh orange juice, some milk, and about a quarter of a bottle of white wine, a good Passerina from one of the area's top cantinas, D'Angelo noted.

'You said Signore Renson's wife was not here this time.'

'That's right, Major. She's a very busy lawyer in South Africa, she can't always come over.'

'But it looks to me as though Signore Renson was not here alone.'

Claudia shrugged her shoulders.

'I don't know, Major. Maybe he left stuff for a couple of days, or he might have entertained friends for the evening, who can tell.'

'Friend, singular, perhaps Signora. Only two dirty plates, both used for the same meal, by the look of it. And I can't imagine many people cooking a leg of lamb when they are eating alone.' Claudia shrugged again. D'Angelo flipped open the lid of a waste bin and spotted an empty red wine bottle. On the worktop were two wine glasses larger than the others, and D'Angelo could see that they had both contained red wine. Using his private smartphone, he took several photos of how everything had been left.

'Shall we continue the tour, Signora?'

The next room on the itinerary was the bathroom, with attractively tiled walls and marble finishing around the shower cubicle and hand basin. The room had been left clean and tidy, not too much work here for Claudia to attend to. D'Angelo didn't waste much time before moving on to the living room. A comfortable suite of furniture comprising a sofa and two armchairs was arranged around a highly-polished coffee table. There was no television in the room, but in one corner stood a drinks cabinet, on top of which sat a framed photograph of two people, a man and a woman. D'Angelo went over to look more closely at the photo.

'Signore Renson and his wife, I presume?'

'Yes, Major.'

D'Angelo was looking at the image of an attractive, tanned woman with short blonde hair, smiling into the camera, alongside a powerful-looking man with a square jaw and swept back light brown hair. They both seemed to have a confident, reassured look, a couple for whom life had been good.

'A recent picture?'

'I would say it was taken a couple of years ago.'

'But their appearance hasn't changed?'

'No, they look just the same now.'

Similar to the kitchen, this room also had French windows, but they led out on to a covered portico, beyond which was the swimming pool. D'Angelo noticed that the pool-side chairs he had spotted on the aerial photo had gone, doubtless stored away by Roberto during yesterday's visit. He continued his walk around the room, stopping in front of a small table and high-backed chair set against the wall. In the centre of the table was a laptop computer, on one side of which were three paperback books, and on the other side some papers. D'Angelo had a quick look through the papers, which included electricity and water bills, a bank statement, and an invoice from a swimming pool maintenance company. He bent down to pick up a small shop receipt that had fluttered to the floor, a receipt which seemed to be for various food items. He nonchalantly turned it over before replacing it on the pile of other papers, but froze when he saw what was written on the back. There were few words, but he had to read them twice more to be certain of what they said. The words were : Mirelti – pay next week. He placed the piece of paper back with the rest, and asked to be led to the next room.

'Only one more, Major. This way.'

As soon as Claudia's back was turned, D'Angelo quickly picked up the shop receipt with its apparently incriminating message and slipped it into his pocket, then followed her into the main bedroom. The layout and décor were not dissimilar to the guest bedroom, with large double bed and a slightly more luxurious en-suite, but there were obvious signs of more frequent use. The bed had been hurriedly re-made, and a shirt was draped over one of the two chairs. A pair of ladies' slippers had been left on the floor beside the chest of drawers, and the double wardrobe contained a selection of men's and ladies' clothes, suitable for both warm and cold weather. In the en-suite, a range of toiletries graced both the hand basin and shower cubicle. D'Angelo could smell a lingering hint of cologne. He looked into the shower cubicle and saw, curled around the water outflow hole, a single long hair. He picked it up to examine it. Holding it against the mottled green and white wall tiles, he could see that it was fairly dark, and certainly not blonde. On re-joining Claudia in the bedroom, he announced that he would also like to see inside the separate guest accommodation, which was at the far end of the pool. She sighed audibly, and muttered that she would have to fetch the key from the drawer in the kitchen. Once she had left the room, D'Angelo pulled back the bed's top cover and sniffed the pillows, and as he suspected, he could smell ladies' perfume. It was a scent he vaguely recognized; perhaps it was one that his wife used occasionally. He replaced the cover, and went to join Claudia for an inspection of the guest accommodation. The compact self-contained unit appeared not to have been used for some time, probably since the previous summer, evidenced by a scorpion sitting undisturbed on the wall. It wasn't long before the visit was completed, and Claudia was re-locking the door behind them.

'That'll be that, Major. I'll return this key and lock up the house, then perhaps you can take me back home.'

'Just a few minutes, Signora, I would like to have another look in the living room. You can start clearing up in the kitchen, if you wish, but please leave the two large wine glasses exactly where they are.'

Back in the living room, D'Angelo lifted the lid of the laptop computer and pressed the power button. He could hear clattering noises from the kitchen as he willed the computer to hurry through its start-up procedure. A picture of an idyllic lake or fjord surrounded by trees suddenly filled the screen, then the date and time appeared in the lower left corner. The latter subsequently disappeared, then came back again, along with the name Martin Renson in bold letters in the upper centre of the screen, along with the picture of a man on horseback in a small circle. Then D'Angelo's heart sank. Below Martin Renson's name, a small box appeared, along with the instruction to enter PIN. It flashed expectantly, as D'Angelo's shoulders slumped in defeat. He turned the power off and closed the lid, but his mind was racing. He took the shop receipt out of his pocket and read it yet again. Mirelti – pay next week. As bizarre as it seemed, this case was now looking like a kidnap situation, with Giovanni being held for ransom. But held where? Had Martin Renson really returned to England, and who was the woman who had shared his bed? Was *she* holding the boy captive? He heard another clatter from next door, and suddenly realised how important those two glasses might now become, with possible requirement for DNA evidence. He almost ran to the kitchen to make sure his earlier instruction had been obeyed, and was relieved to find that not only were the wine glasses still in situ, but the mugs were also still there.

'Signora Sabatelli, please leave everything alone now. I would like one of my colleagues to come and look at the house, but in the meantime I shall take you home. I'm afraid it means I will have to keep hold of the key for the time being.'

'Oh but Signore Renson…'

'Leave Signore Renson to me, Signora. I shall explain to him that you were merely doing as instructed by the carabinieri. If you would like to wait by my car, I shall be with you shortly.'

As Claudia Sabatelli walked disconsolately to the car, D'Angelo locked the house door and used his secure radio to call Sergeant Rossi.

'Rossi, I know you've only just got back to the station, but I need you here again in Montenero.'

'So long as you sign off the petrol receipts, Major.'

'Let's hope the colonel's in a good mood. Would you be able to get into a PC bypassing the security PIN?'

Rossi was quiet for a few moments.

'Possibly, but it wouldn't be strictly legal.'

'It's a bad connection, Rossi, I didn't catch that last bit. Make sure there's an evidence kit in the car before you leave.'

'Will do, Major. I'm still in civvies, does that matter?'

'Not at all. Might actually be a good thing, I'll explain when you get here. I shall be at the Englishman's holiday home. The co-ordinates are already saved in your satnav. See you soon. Over and out.'

After dropping Claudia off at her house, D'Angelo went to the café for an espresso and croissant, sad to see on his way that two of Laura's posters had been defaced with beards and glasses. "Bloody kids," he thought to himself.

Not long after arriving back at the holiday home to wait for Sergeant Rossi, Lazzaro reported in with a call.

'Still no sign, Major. The dog is dashing around all over the place, but hasn't come up with anything. Davide is worried that any scent trails might have been washed away with yesterday's storm. I told him the rain had been very heavy. There are still a few outlying hamlets to cover, and progress is fairly slow.'

'There's a change of plan, Lazzaro. Davide's probably right. That rain and hail will have made any chance of picking up a scent virtually zero. Confidentially, I have reason to suspect a possible kidnapping, so I want you to switch your search to Montenero itself. Do a door to door. The guys can go solo to cover the ground quicker, but stand the civilian helpers down. You're looking for a female, aged between twenty-five and forty, long darkish hair, but not black. Anyone fitting that description, see if you can get their OK to have a dog do a quick search for a missing person, indoors and out, then call Davide in with mutt.'

'What if they object, which some probably will.'

'Make a note of the address, and we might have to go back heavy-handed. Best to do it with their agreement if possible.'

'Sounds a bit of a long shot, Tonio.'

'It's a hell of a long shot, Emil. I'll call you later for a briefing, so leave Gattone in command when you leave.'

'Understood, Tonio. Over and out.'

D'Angelo made a slow tour of the grounds before letting himself back into the house and re-familiarising himself with each of the rooms, then opened the French doors in the living room and waited on the portico, watching sand lizards dart around the low stone wall, or bask in the warm May sunshine, until Sergeant Rossi arrived, carrying the evidence kit.

'I'll know this journey well by the end of today, Major. Wow – nice pad isn't it.'

'Very smart, Rossi. Now this, as you see, is the kitchen. Gloves on, and bag up those glasses and mugs please.'

'I take it you suspect a crime scene here, Major,' she said, as she carefully placed each item into a sterile bag.

'Possibly. There's a bit more evidence I want collected from the bedroom. This way.'

D'Angelo led Rossi to the en-suite in the master bedroom and pointed out the hair on the floor of the shower cubicle.

'There's another one here on the shampoo bottle.'

'Well done, Sergeant. What colour would you say they are?'

'I would think they're probably chestnut. Not red enough to be auburn.'

'I'll bow to your knowledge of such matters. Let's go and have a try at this computer.'

In the living room, D'Angelo and Rossi went straight to the table with the laptop.

'This was on that pile of papers,' said D'Angelo, handing Rossi the shop receipt.

'Some food items purchased on – what's today? – er – two days ago – on Monday.'

Rossi turned the receipt over.

'Ah. Now I understand, Major. But why would he write this on a little bit of paper and leave it lying around? And it's in Italian. Surely he would have jotted it in English?'

'Perhaps. Most probably it was written by whoever is in this with him. The anomaly is that Giovanni's family claimed not to know Martin Renson. They've seen him around, but that's all. Yet here we have the Mirelti name cropping up in the man's house.'

'Another Mirelti?'

'Maybe, but Mirelti isn't a common name in Montenero.'

'The family reported him missing in the first place, didn't they?'

'They did, but presumably that was before hearing from Renson. Laura put posters up yesterday morning, but since then, as far as I know, they've just been staying in their house.'

'So you think there might be something on the computer?'

'I believe it's worth a look, if we can get into it.'

'I'll see what I can do, Major. As I said, it's breaking a few rules, and I'll probably need to contact one of my dodgy 'friends' for some help, but I'll give it a shot.'

While Rossi concentrated on the laptop, D'Angelo wandered back out to the portico and called Lazzaro.

'Any joy, Sergeant?'

'Only one possible contender so far. She was naturally very puzzled by the intrusion, but we drew a blank anyway.'

'Rossi is with me. She thinks the hair colour could possibly be described as chestnut.'

D'Angelo looked back into the living room, and saw the drinks cabinet with the photograph of Renson with his wife.

'One other thing, Sergeant. I imagine the mystery lady is good looking, judging by the one she's usurping.'

'I'll bear that in mind, Major.'

It took Rossi a remarkably short time to hack into the laptop.

'My contact says it would have taken quite a lot longer to get into the Pentagon. Good job he's on our side, eh Major?'

D'Angelo shook his head in disbelief.

'Can you have a look around in it, see what's on there.'

With what seemed to D'Angelo to be mind-boggling speed, Sergeant Rossi delved into the various files on the computer.

'Basically, he uses the Office applications – Word, Excel and e-mail, to manage his company while he's here on holiday,' she said after a few minutes of searching and reading. 'The e-mails are between himself and clients, and to someone called Dan, I think he's the factory manager, or something like that. The spreadsheets hold a lot of data on cabling, so I guess that's his company's product. There's some private stuff in there too, but nothing untoward. A list of restaurants, for example, with a brief description of each, and a contact phone number. Then there's information about the pool, cleaning instructions and so on. From what I can see, all very innocuous.'

'You've looked at the latest e-mails?'

Yes, I've seen everything sent and received up until around mid-day on Monday. Nothing after that.'

D'Angelo walked back over to the French window and stared out for a few moments.

'There's nothing else we can do here. Close the computer down, and don't forget the evidence bag. I have to take the key for this place back to Signora Sabatelli, so wait for me just outside here on the road. We're going to call in to see Giovanni's family again, you and me together. I want it to be as relaxed as possible, hence it's better you're not in uniform. I want you to ask them again whether they've ever had any dealings with our English friend. Maybe they're holding something back.'

Fourteen

Having informed Claudia Sabatelli that he had removed two glasses and two mugs from Renson's holiday home, D'Angelo returned to where Rossi was waiting, and the two of them drove back to the Mirelti house. Both had to steel themselves to enter once again the gloomy main room with its heavy and depressing atmosphere, and D'Angelo found himself apologising for yet another intrusion at such a troubled time. Anna had come downstairs, but she looked unbelievably frail. Her hair was straggly and unkempt, her face pale, and the shadows beneath her eyes were darker than ever. She sat at the table nursing a cup of orzo drink of powdered roasted barley. It looked as though it was all she was able to ingest in her current state. Elisabetta was obviously now spending a lot more of her time downstairs rather than up in her room, and seemed to have taken back her more influential role within the family in this time of crisis. When D'Angelo and Rossi entered, Elisabetta was busy preparing food in the kitchen area, giving instructions to Laura, who was helping her.

Judging by the hammering noises that could be heard from outside, Bruno was fixing some machinery in the barn, and Felicita, explained Laura, had gone to visit Mario.

Presenting the excuse that he wanted to go and see Bruno, D'Angelo left Sergeant Rossi with the three generations of women from the household.

'Was the fleece helpful?' asked Laura.

'We think the rain might have made it difficult for the dog,' said Rossi, trying to hide the strain in her voice. 'We're checking some of the houses in the village now.'

'We had a visitor a short while ago,' said Anna in a weak voice. 'The priest from San Bartolomeo came round. We think your Major D'Angelo has been to see him, which probably prompted him to visit.'

'He wouldn't have thought of it otherwise, the fat lazy bugger,' spat Laura.

'Laura, that's enough.'

'Sorry Nonna, but what does he actually do for any of us?'

'If you came to church occasionally, young lady, you might find out. And it was rude of you to go upstairs when he was here trying to give us some comfort.'

Laura snorted with derision.

'The thing is, Teresa,' interrupted Anna, trying to calm the waters, 'apart from Mamma, none of us go to church much, except for weddings and – er – christenings,' she muttered, looking down at her cup of orzo. Rossi felt a stab of pain, knowing that 'funerals' was the missing word, the dreaded word that hung in the air like a plague. The silence that followed was oppressive.

'It was good of him to come, though,' said Rossi eventually, embarrassed by the weakness of her comment, clearly only uttered in order to break the silence.

'There's a nice holiday home not far from here,' she continued, 'owned by foreigners.'

'Yes, Martin Renson and his wife.'

'Do any of you know Signore Renson?'

'No,' said Anna, 'as we were saying to Major D'Angelo yesterday, we know what he looks like, but none of us have ever spoken to him.'

'I said "good day" to him once in the pharmacy,' corrected Laura.

'So you've had no other contact from him?'

'No,' said Anna, clearly puzzled by the question. 'Why do you ask?'

'He's one of your nearest neighbours, and we're interested in anyone who might have seen Giovanni on Monday evening,' said Rossi, thinking on her feet. 'Signore Renson was at his home until Monday night, and if he had seen Giovanni wandering around on his own, he might have let you know.'

Anna looked at her mother and daughter, and all three shook their heads.

'As I said, Teresa, we've never had any contact with the English signore.'

'It's the Fioritos you should be questioning,' said Elisabetta forcefully. Pietro and that son of his. They'll have the answer.'

'We need to look at all possible scenarios, Elisabetta. Is there anything you feel you need, a support counsellor, for example?'

'A support counsellor won't bring my son back. I'm sorry. That wasn't polite. My elder son will be arriving from America tomorrow, so he'll be able to help us see this through. Thank you for the thought, Teresa.'

'Well, don't forget you can contact myself or Major D'Angelo at any time.'

D'Angelo and Rossi met up by their respective vehicles at almost the same time.

'Bruno says he's never had any contact with Renson – how about the rest of the family?'

'Laura said "hello" to him in the pharmacy, but that's all. Elisabetta is insistent that we should be questioning the Fioritos.'

'I'm going to call Lazzaro and tell him to meet us back at the station. The way you drive, you'll be first there, so can you get some panini for the three of us?'

* * *

In Pescara, Captain Luciani was kicking his heels and looking at his watch every few minutes. He knew that whatever he got involved in, he would have to break off to go and fetch the arrogant deputy minister and drive him a couple of hundred metres to the sports lido. He knew it was too early, but he decided to go to the hotel and wait there rather than at his desk. At least there might be some nice-looking female tourists to watch while he waited. He parked once again on the yellow line right outside the hotel entrance and stood on the pavement, ready for his charge to appear. A few of the hotel customers were coming and going, some of them in beach gear, but Luciani's attention suddenly focused on a man and boy coming through the large glass double door. What he noticed was that the man momentarily froze with a look of panic on his face when he saw the captain standing beside a carabinieri car. The boy, who Luciani took to be the man's son, wore a very strange expression, somewhere between trauma and fear. Luciani watched intently as the man grabbed the boy's upper arm with a rough hold and twisted him to the right, before guiding him at a brisk pace along the street. At the first intersection, Luciani could see the nose of a car, which appeared to be black. The man with the boy flicked his head backwards before the two of them disappeared around the corner, then moments later the car reversed back up the side-street. Alarm bells started to sound for the carabinieri officer, so he ran to the junction, just in time to see that the black car, a large Citroen, had reversed into an alley to turn, and was now speeding away from him along the small side-street. All he could make out from the registration plate was that it began with what looked like DF, but he wasn't even sure of that. Frustrated, Luciani strode back to the hotel and entered the lobby. The receptionist was trying to explain to an elderly American couple that the shops were closed between one o'clock and four o'clock, that this happened every day, not because it was a holiday. Luciani interrupted the conversation.

'Just now, a man and boy left the hotel. Could you tell me which room they are staying in please?'

The receptionist looked towards the entrance as though an image of the two might still be visible.

'A man with a boy? I'm sorry, I didn't see them go.'

'The man, slight build, aged about forty, the boy, possibly his son, somewhere around thirteen to fifteen. They're most likely Italian rather than foreign.'

'We have quite a few families staying with us, but I can't think who those two might be. Would you like to see the hotel manager?'

'Yes please.'

Luciani had an equally fruitless discussion with the hotel manager, and short of demanding access to the CCTV files, he decided he wasn't going to get any further with trying to find out who the man and boy were. Ten minutes later, deputy minister Sartolini stepped out of the lift, checking his cufflinks were straight, and, as taciturn as he had been previously, he was taken on the very brief journey in the back of Luciani's Alfa Romeo patrol car to the beach volleyball arena.

* * *

On arriving back at the station, Major D'Angelo quietly asked Katia to come into his office for a moment. He handed her four hundred euros, explaining that Giorgio had repaid the money he owed her.

'He's sorted things with his creditors, and he isn't in any danger, but I'm very sorry to tell you that you won't be able to see him again.'

Katia gave a little gasp, and put her hands up to her mouth.

'He didn't know how to tell you, because he's genuinely fond of you, and he wishes things could be different, but, you see, he's married, so...'

D'Angelo waved his hands in the air as though in submission to an impossible situation.

'I'm really sorry, Katia.'

'Thank you, Major,' she whispered, and with a sniff and quick wipe of her eyes, she left his office.

In the incident room, D'Angelo and Rossi had finished eating their panini by the time Lazzaro arrived, so they each gave their de-brief on the day's meetings and events before Lazzaro brought them up to speed on the search.

'Officially this is still a missing person enquiry,' said D'Angelo, 'but I want it treated as a criminal investigation.'

He picked up a marker pen and stood in front of the whiteboard.

'Let's review the situation as it stands. Giovanni Mirelti went outside his family home at seven fifteen on Monday evening, approximately forty-three hours ago. This briefing is for us to consider two possibilities regarding the case, homicide and kidnapping.'

On the left side of the whiteboard, D'Angelo wrote the heading Homicide.

'We can only address motive and opportunity from the point of view of potential perpetrators.'

D'Angelo wrote the name Mario on the board.

'Mario, engaged to Giovanni's sister, Felicita. There was considerable enmity between Giovanni and Mario, in fact the two of them had been arguing moments before Giovanni left the house. Plus, you found out something else, Teresa.'

Taken slightly off-guard by D'Angelo's use of her first name, Rossi didn't react for a few moments.

'He told his friend, Evelina, in confidence, that he had seen Mario stealing money from his grandmother's purse. Mario was using threats to prevent Giovanni from reporting the matter.'

'Perhaps Giovanni told Mario he was going to report it anyway. Sufficient motive?'

'You said you thought Mario could be fairly volatile,' added Lazzaro.

D'Angelo rubbed his chin and pondered the thought.

'I got the impression he could be tricky. He made it quite clear he didn't like answering my questions. He's been keeping away from the house recently, so I haven't seen him since yesterday morning. We'll give him a three out of five for motive, now let's consider opportunity. He was out in the barn, alone, apparently repairing the fuel pipe on the tractor not long after Giovanni was last seen.'

'How about four for opportunity?' suggested Rossi.

D'Angelo wrote a four alongside the existing three.

'Next, the trigger-happy neighbours, Pietro Fiorito and his son, Leonardo. Elisabetta heard two shots being fired which may, or may not, have been shortly after Giovanni went outside. Pietro has admitted that Leo used his shotgun on Monday evening, allegedly to scare away a group of wild boar, but we know that at some time on Monday he shot a bird, a buzzard, which I still have in my freezer at home.'

'I bet your wife is pleased with that.'

D'Angelo smiled as he wrote the names Pietro and Leonardo beneath that of Mario.

'Possible motive? Giovanni hates hunting, especially the shooting of birds, and has harangued the Fioritos for it in the past. A row, a sudden loss of control, and Leo turns his shotgun, loaded with heavy duty cartridges, on Giovanni. How does that sound?'

'I'd give that a four to Leonardo, father accessory,' said Lazzaro.

'I agree,' added Rossi.

'Opportunity?'

'Five,' said Lazzaro and Rossi together.

'Anyone else on the radar for homicide?'

'Are we ruling out the father?'

'No real motive, other than the lad didn't conform, perhaps an embarrassment. We'll put him there for now, with just a one for motive and four for opportunity. Agreed?'

There were nods from the two sergeants.

'Now, today we've discovered the other possibility.'

D'Angelo wrote a second heading, Kidnapping, on the right hand side of the board. Beneath it he wrote the name Martin Renson, followed by a plus sign and a question mark.

'I take it the question mark is for the mystery lady we're looking for in Montenero?' asked Lazzaro.

'That's right. Renson was at his holiday home until Monday night, when he flew back from Pescara to Stansted in England. There was a woman staying with him, but it wasn't his wife. It'll be difficult to check with the flight manifests whether she returned with Renson, as we don't have a name, but I put in a call to airport security to find out if there's any record of a young boy travelling with Martin Renson. It'll probably draw a blank, but, Teresa, do you have our shop receipt in that file of yours?'

'Right here, Major.'

'Show it to Emilio, will you.'

Lazzaro read the note on the back of the receipt.

'It was in Renson's place, beside his computer. Thing is, Emil, none of Giovanni's family admit to having had any contact with this English guy, so why would he write that they have to pay him next week?'

'Weird. I don't understand it,' said Lazzaro.

'That makes three of us. As far as I know, the Mirelti family aren't particularly well off, so an odd choice for a ransom demand, but we've all been involved in some bizarre cases.'

There was a murmur of consent from the other two.

'And this note is all we've got? Asked Lazzaro.

D'Angelo shrugged and spread his hands.

'Not much, I grant you, but we have precious little else to go on. We bagged up some glasses in case it comes down to a check for DNA, but there was no obvious evidence that Giovanni had been at the house, and there was nothing on Renson's computer.'

D'Angelo looked at the names he had written on the whiteboard.

'Strongest candidate for homicide is Leo Fiorito, but at this stage we haven't got enough to pull him in for questioning. We have to speak to Martin Renson, but I doubt if the British police will take us very seriously, so I can't think they will be sufficiently motivated to conduct any sort of a meaningful interview.'

'So we have to send someone over there?'

'I don't see any alternative, Emil.'

'Would the British police allow that?'

'You're right, it has to be official, but if we keep it low key, just between myself and an equivalent rank in whichever force we're dealing with, I dare say we'll manage to get away with it. If we take it up the chain, especially if politicians get involved, then I wouldn't be too optimistic.'

'Have you thought about who could go?'

'That's another tough one. Whoever goes will have to be able to speak decent English, which, unless we borrow someone from outside our area, narrows the choice down to Teresa or myself. I want to keep a handle on things here during this vital initial period, yet Sergeant Rossi is acting as liaison with the family and is taking on responsibility for co-ordinating the investigation.'

'I don't mind going,' said Rossi, after a brief silence. 'After all, I've hardly started the co-ordinating job yet. How long will I be away? Two days, three at most.'

'Makes sense,' chipped in Lazzaro.

'Alright, Teresa goes,' agreed D'Angelo. 'Are you able to go at short notice?'

'No problems, Major.'

'Good. The comune at Montenero will be able to tell you Renson's home address in England and hopefully some contact details.'

'I made a note of his e-mail and business address from the laptop.'

'Well done, good thinking. Check which police force is based in that area, and I'll liaise with an appropriate officer – I think their Inspector is roughly equivalent to my rank. I'm going to request a budget for you to go with an oppo, but don't worry, you'll be going on your own. I'll show afterwards that I slashed the operation budget in half as part of my cost-cutting initiative. Get a gold star from the colonel. I'll put Katia on to arranging your travel, so let her know as soon as possible what your eventual destination in England will be. We might as well try and land you as close as possible.

Fifteen

Colonel Battista had ordered that an empty office be turned hurriedly into a temporary makeshift incident room, as control centre for Operation Seahawk. A map of the Abruzzo Adriatic coastline had already been pinned to the wall, a map which Battista was studying carefully, his finger moving from one location to another. His mind was juggling with how many possible landing sites required what level of resources. It was an area of expertise in which Battista took great pride, ever since he achieved top grade in his promotion exam for the module 'Allocation of Resources'. As he looked at the map, he began to have doubts about his earlier assumptions. Perhaps it would make more sense to land the illegals at one of the small bays further south, then take them by road up to the Pescara area.

Battista tried to put himself in the mind of a people-smuggler. All down this coast, the beaches shelve gradually out to sea, so a boat with an inboard motor wouldn't get close enough to shore to be able to disembark a group of migrants, in which case it would have to tie up at a small fishing jetty. It might be possible to come ashore unseen and unnoticed in the early hours of the morning, but the downside would be that all fishing vessels are known and accounted for by the local community, and an irregular landing would attract attention, especially if a truck was on hand to transport the illegals further north. Then the truck itself being driven at night would add risk to the enterprise, depending on how far it was from landing point to safe house. At one of the bigger ports or marinas, on the other hand, there would obviously be more potential witnesses to the landing, but the coming and going of fishing boats and pleasure craft is more normal at these entry points, and therefore less likely to attract notice. Battista tapped the map with his finger, as though expecting it to provide the answer for him. He came to his decision. Rather than having mobile patrols covering stretches of coast, he would place officers on look-out at the five most likely landing spots, with two mobile teams ready to respond to any report of a landing.

On cue, his Divisional Commanders filed into the incident room for the Operation Seahawk planning meeting, at which Battista began by giving orders for the overall plan.

'Two officers at each of the following possible landing zones,' he explained, then, referring to the map, he stabbed his finger on each of the marinas at Silvi, Montesilvano, Pescara, Francavilla, and Ortona. 'Two rapid-response mobile teams, one here, and one here.' He indicated points on the main coast road, just to the north and south of Pescara.

'The operation will commence tomorrow, Thursday, at twenty-three thirty hours until apprehension of suspects. If no landing is sighted, the operation will stand down at zero five thirty Friday morning. Communication between sighting officers and back-up will be strictly by secure radio. No mobile phones operating on a commercial network provider will be carried by any of the officers involved. Is that clear?'

There were nods and murmurs of consent.

'Good. I will now leave Major Camponelli to chair the meeting for details to be arranged and specific personnel allocated to the operation. For now, good day, Signori.'

* * *

Marco could feel damp patches on his shirt beneath his armpits, then a tickling sensation as a bead of sweat ran down the small of his back. He was guided past double doors, which in the evenings were opened to patrons of the Blue Diamond Club, leading them to the hall where these wealthy businessmen and professionals, and the occasional visiting Mafia boss, could gamble their earnings at the blackjack, roulette, baccarat and craps tables, or on the house-advantage gaming machines.

Ahead of Marco was another polished door with a brass handle, but not for him the mirrored, carpeted elevator. The Macauan Chinese at his side, who moved with the ease and grace of a gazelle, yet was rumoured to be able to kill a man with a single karate blow, swerved down a corridor to the right, then stopped to enter a four-digit code into a wall-mounted keypad. Marco, as a European and therefore not entirely trustworthy, was not even allowed to know the code. The steel door clicked open, and without a word or change of expression, the Macauan held the door open to allow Marco through to the utilitarian staircase on the other side, which provided access up to the first floor.

Marco fingered the open neck of his shirt as he climbed the stairs, wishing he had been allowed time to put on a tie, knowing the value Signore Lau placed on his employees being properly dressed. Marco also gave himself a reminder to call his employer 'Sir' and 'Meester Lau' rather than Signore. The idiom of 'when in Rome...' didn't apply to Meester Lau. Marco looked up into the small lens, then tapped nervously on the polished oak door as it clicked open.

'Permission to enter, Sign – Meester Lau?' he said, in a rather squeaky voice. He coughed discretely to try and clear his constricted throat.

The man who sat regally behind his walnut desk merely indicated with an open hand that Marco was permitted to sit in a high-backed oriental-pattern chair in front of the desk.

Lau was fifty-four, and beginning to show the signs of the over-indulgence that came with comfortable living, despite the careful cut of his tailored shirt and raw silk suit. He had the broad face and straight, black hair of an Oriental, but less narrow eyes and sharper nose as evidence of the mixed Portuguese with Chinese heredity. He slowly replaced the cap on his Parker fountain pen, an early gift from his parents, which he still favoured when signing letters or writing notes, and placed the pen in the ivory holder on his desk.

'I understand you were compromised while delivering a service to one of our important clients.'

Marco found some of his duties distasteful, in spite of the handsome renumeration. He found it extraordinary that his boss was able to compartmentalise aspects of his business empire. He made the provision of innocent minors to sexual predators sound like take-away pizza delivery.

'I wasn't expecting a carabinieri officer to be waiting outside the hotel, sir. I'm sorry. I'll be more careful in future.'

Marco's breathing was erratic, causing his words to come out in fits and starts. He knew how pathetic he must sound, as he surreptitiously wiped his damp palms on the tops of his trouser legs.

'I pay you well to do a simple job, but you can't even do that properly.'

Marco tried to swallow, but his mouth was too dry.

'How many times have you been told,' continued Lau, 'that discretion is a key element of our service. Mister Sartolini hopes to become deputy Minister of the Interior before too long. A client in that position would be extremely helpful for our business, but your stupidity and carelessness have resulted in a serious breach of security. I take it the carabinieri man saw both you and the boy quite clearly?'

'It was very brief, sir. He only had a few seconds to see us.'

'But he followed you along the street, and saw our vehicle drive away.'

'We were long gone by the time the officer peered round the corner. He is a good driver.'

'A good driver with a useless courier.'

Marco could feel prickles of sweat on his top lip which he attempted to lick away.

'That vehicle will be out of service until we know

whether or not it is being sought. You will personally dispose of the other asset.'

'You, you mean the boy, sir?'

'Deal with it.'

'Shall I send him back to Libya, sir?'

Lau blew through his nose and leaned back into his leather-upholstered seat.

'If I were to write on a piece of paper something that would incriminate you, would you drop it in the bin or burn it?'

'But sir, I'm not a… I don't do that, I don't know how. And he's just a boy.'

'In that case, it shouldn't be too difficult. Your mess, you clear it up.'

Lau pressed a button beneath his desk, releasing the door with a faint click, then retrieved his pen from its stand and picked up a printed sheet of paper from the sheaf in front of him.

Marco stood up on wobbly legs, his temples throbbing, and made his way to the door, which he closed behind him as he left the room. He staggered down the stairs, frightened he was going to either pass out or vomit, and once he was back on the polished marble floor of the club entrance, he half ran, like a drunk heading for the toilet, until he barged through the front door and out into the street. The Macauan was watching Marco leave, then Lau's voice came through his bluetooth ear-piece.

'Make sure he completes his final duty, then terminate his contract.'

* * *

Sergeant Lazzaro took the call from Gattone.

'We've done most of the centre. A couple of vague possibles, but they didn't come to anything, and now Davide and the dog have to return to Chieti. Shall we carry on, or call it a day?'

Lazzaro quickly conferred with major D'Angelo, then passed the message on to Gattone.

'Wrap it up, mate. Di Stefano asked me this morning if he could knock off a bit early because his wife's not well and the kids will be back from school. We'll see you, Di Silverio and Carrea back here shortly.'

D'Angelo stood staring at the floor, rubbing the back of his neck.

'Christ, Emil, we're not getting anywhere. We're going to lose this one.'

Lazzaro leaned on the stone sill and stared out of the window.

'He's out there somewhere. Alive or dead, he's out there, and someone knows where. You sure we shouldn't be pulling in Fiorito and son?'

'You know the score. We pull someone in without enough evidence, they walk free, we're left looking incompetent, and the whole enquiry grinds to a virtual standstill.'

'We've still got the lead on this English guy.'

'Let's see what Teresa comes up with on her visit to UK. If we draw another blank, then we'll get Fiorito and his boy in for questioning.'

D'Angelo was busy with some overdue admin work when Gattone, Di Silverio and Carrea returned from Montenero, and within minutes of their arrival, the red warning light flashed, giving notice that an emergency call was being routed through to the station. Lazzaro picked up the call.

'… the post office. She put up a struggle, but he pulled a knife and slashed her with it. Someone's helping her, but he's got her money, and now he's getting in his car.'

'Outside the post office? Which direction is he facing? What's the car?'

'He's going. It all happened so quick. He's heading for the Lanciano road. Old grey Peugeot 206 Estate.'

Lazzaro pushed the phone into Gattone's hand, and ran out to the reception area, where Rossi was in discussion with Katia.

'You still got the Giulietta key?' he shouted.

'This is it,' said Rossi, picking up the key that she had put on the desk. Lazzaro snatched it out of her hand and dashed to the entrance, just as Di Silverio was coming in through the door holding an espresso in a paper cup. Lazzaro spun him around, sending the coffee flying.

'Knife attack. With me, now.'

'I left my pistol…'

'No time. Come on.'

Rossi had left the patrol car right outside the building, so it took just seconds for Lazzaro to jump into the driver's seat while Di Silverio scrambled in alongside him, pulling the passenger door shut as Lazzaro fired the engine, thrust it into reverse, then slammed it into first gear and gunned the motor out of the car park before swerving straight out into the main road.

'Siren,' he yelled at Di Silverio, as he himself switched on the flashing warning lights.

Just as he reached the junction with the main street on which, further along, the post office was situated, a grey Peugeot estate was hurtling towards them and the comparative safety of the twisting Lanciano road. Lazzaro pulled into the centre of the road, cutting off the Peugeot's exit route. The Peugeot driver braked, then spun to his right, up the hill of via Cadolini towards the industrial estate.

Lazzaro thrust the screaming engine into second gear and followed mere seconds behind the Peugeot. The road narrowed at the top of Cadolini hill to a virtual single track as it threaded through some houses and a garden centre, then both cars successfully negotiated a sharp left turn followed by an equally sharp right hander as they careered along the back of the ridge. Di Silverio looked to his right down the steep, unprotected slope, and wished he was the one doing the driving. He felt relief as the road straightened on to a broader, flatter tract of land past two side roads, both of them dead ends awaiting possible future commercial development. Very quickly they were into the heart of the industrial park, with factory units, distributors and repair shops flashing past, workers stopping what they were doing to watch the high-speed chase.

Suddenly, the Peugeot driver swung to the left down one of the side roads, but instead of following him, Lazzaro braked and screeched to a halt past the turning. He calculated that the man's best chance of escape was to double back the way they had come, then get onto his original route to the Lanciano road.

'Does this road go left or right at the end?' asked Lazzaro.

Di Silverio remembered coming down this way to investigate a break-in at a paint factory.

'Right, then comes back out just past the tyre place.'

Lazzaro nodded, turned off the siren and executed a racing start, cursing the wheel-spin until the tyres found traction on the smooth tarmac. As he reached Full Service Tyres, a lorry was approaching in the opposite direction, and with metres to spare, Lazzaro cut in front of the lorry and slewed to a halt across the side road. Expecting to see the Peugeot within seconds, Lazzaro and Di Silverio jumped from their vehicle, pumping adrenalin, and stood in a quiet, empty road. Ten long seconds passed in an eerie silence. Lazzaro and Di Silverio looked at each other and shrugged. Both were thinking the same thing : there must be another exit leading back onto the spine road. They would probably find the Peugeot, doubtless having been stolen earlier in the day, abandoned or burnt out on a patch of waste ground somewhere, with no clue about the identity of the knife attacker, unless they happen to get lucky with an eyewitness back at the post office.

They stood and waited for a further ten seconds, adrenalin rush subsiding, then went to get back in their vehicle. Di Silverio slid into the passenger seat while Lazzaro stood by the door on the driver's side, taking one last look down the empty stretch of road. As he turned to climb in, there was a screech of tyres as the Peugeot roared out from behind a low building thirty metres away. It continued to accelerate until it slammed into the back of the carabinieri Giulietta, opening a gap between the patrol car and the iron railing which encircled Full Service Tyres.

Lazzaro was hit by the turning vehicle, knocking him to the ground, while Di Silverio, briefly disorientated, staggered from the car. The impact had caused the Peugeot to stall and roll backwards, the driver frantically turning the ignition key to try and re-start the engine. Di Silverio would later claim he knew exactly what he was doing, but in truth he was in a slight state of shock. He went to the back of the patrol car, not sure what to do next. The boot had flown open on impact, and he peered round it at the still stationary Peugeot, its front nearside wing badly smashed, then something else caught his eye. He couldn't quite believe what he was seeing. There, in the boot of the patrol car, was a double-barrel shotgun. He grabbed the gun, pulled the stock into his shoulder, and advanced on the Peugeot, aiming the weapon at the driver's head. The small-time criminal knew that the situation was now way beyond his control. He had intended to frighten the lady with his knife, but had slashed her in a fit of panic, desperate for the money that would buy him another fix. He was shaking as Di Silverio pulled his door open and ordered him out of the car, wide-eyed with fear as he stared into the twin barrels of the officer's shotgun, unaware that it wasn't loaded.

Lazzaro had scrambled painfully to his feet, blood streaming down his face from a gash in his forehead, moving with difficulty due to a trapped nerve in his back. He took one look at the damaged rear of the Giulietta and called Carrea at the station to bring the Forester to collect them, and a low-loader recovery vehicle to pick up two damaged vehicles. While Carrea drove, Di Silverio travelled back to the station alongside the arrested man in the back of the Forester, the shotgun propped between his knees, grinning joyfully.

Sixteen

While Lazzaro was being patched up in A&E, Sergeant Rossi handled the custody arrangements for the post office knife attacker. Major D'Angelo owned up to having taken the shotgun from Leonardo Fiorito the previous day, and had forgotten to remove it from the boot of the Giulietta. He congratulated Di Silverio on the arrest, and instructed Trooper Carrea to fetch some beers for a post-work celebration.

Meanwhile, Katia had struck gold. While trying to find flights to the UK that would take Rossi as close as possible to North East England, she contacted the PA of Signore Damiano, who owned the big family-run pasta factory out near Casoli. Katia had remembered that Signore Damiano had promised Major D'Angelo a favour after the safe return of one of his delivery trucks that had been stolen two years ago, and she knew that he quite frequently travelled in the company's helicopter, either to Rome to catch a commercial flight, or to Pescara where a private jet took him to meetings within Europe. The PA informed Katia that the timing of her call was perfect. Signore Damiano and his daughter, Patrizia, were due to fly the following morning on a business trip to Manchester, and she would ask her boss if it would be possible to take Sergeant Rossi with them. She had rung back fifteen minutes later to tell Katia that Signore Damiano and his daughter would be delighted to take Sergeant Rossi to England, and they would be leaving the factory at seven o'clock sharp in the morning.

D'Angelo had managed to make contact with Inspector Richard Armstrong of Northumbria Police based in Sunderland North, ironically part of Southern Area Command, on whose patch Renson's company was located. He took some persuading that a carabinieri officer could travel to England to interview a UK resident, but finally agreed to the arrangement, providing the purpose of the trip was solely for gathering information relating to security issues at Renson's Italian residence. Inspector Armstrong said he would inform his colleague at Alnwick in Northern Area Command about Rossi's visit, as Martin Renson lived in the Alnwick area.

Relieved that Rossi's impending visit to England had been approved, D'Angelo was completing a budget request form for two return flights to UK plus internal travel and two nights' accommodation, when he heard cheering and clapping coming from the direction of the incident room. He went to investigate the cause of the uproar, and found Lazzaro had returned from A&E with a large pad taped to his forehead.

'I didn't realise they could perform a frontal lobotomy so quickly,' joked Rossi.

'Did they stitch it?' asked D'Angelo.

'No, they glued it, would you believe. The real problem's my back, I can hardly bloody move. They gave me a prescription for some pretty strong painkillers, but I think I might have to take a few days off. Sorry, Major.'

'No, that's OK. Get yourself fit. You're no use to us in that state anyway.'

D'Angelo looked at his watch. 'A bit early,' he said, 'but let's have a beer to celebrate the return, and imminent departure, of the wounded warrior.'

While bottles were being opened and a festive mood descended on the station, Rossi wandered over to where D'Angelo was standing.

'All set for the morning, Sergeant?'

'All set, Major. I was wondering, my car's been playing up a bit lately, and I don't want to risk missing the ride, so is it OK if I take the 159 over to the pasta factory?'

D'Angelo bit his lip. With Lazzaro out of action for a few days, and Rossi away in England until the weekend, his chain of command was beginning to look a bit thin. Added to that, the Giulietta would have to go to the repair facility after being smashed by the Peugeot, and now another vehicle would be out at Casoli. Yet he could hardly deny Rossi's request.

'Sure,' he said, 'no problem. I'll give you the English Inspector's number in case you need to speak to him while you're over there, and keep me informed of whatever you find out from Renson.'

'Will do. Just a friendly chat at this stage, eh, Major?'

'That's what I've agreed with Inspector Armstrong, and I always keep my word,' said D'Angelo with a wink and a smile.

* * *

Maria was supposed to stay in the communal room after their eight o'clock meal, and she knew it meant punishment if she was caught breaking the rules, but she heard voices from down the corridor outside the little single room, and her inquisitive nature got the better of her. Slowly and quietly she opened the door and peeped round the door frame to see what was happening. The man who ran errands for Mister Lau was talking to the lady in charge of the home.

'I know it wasn't scheduled, but he has another appointment. Ask Mister Lau himself if you want to risk interrupting him at this time of the evening.'

The lady was facing away from Maria, so she didn't catch the response, but then the man spoke again.

'He was due to move on tomorrow anyway, so no, he won't be coming back here. You can lock up at the normal time.'

Typical of Europeans, the man always seemed to speak in a loud voice, but Maria thought he sounded anxious and agitated. She waited and watched as the boy was brought out from his room, then led away by the man. She carefully closed the door and went back to sit on her bed. Maria was overcome with the usual feeling of homesickness, wishing she was back in Vietnam with her gran and her little brother, but suddenly, inexplicably, she also felt frightened and vulnerable. She looked at the small cupboard where she had hidden the stolen phone, wrapped in underwear, as tears started rolling down her cheeks.

'I'm taking you somewhere nicer to stay,' said Marco, 'you'll be much happier at this new place while you wait for your parents to come for you.' He knew he was gabbling, but felt the urge to keep talking. 'I forgot to ask your name, what is it?'

'Yousef,' the boy replied.

Marco immediately regretted having asked. He wanted the boy to remain anonymous, just another illegal immigrant who could easily have died anyway on the journey from Libya. He fingered the length of cord in his pocket with a sweaty hand as he and the boy made their way towards the harbour. Following their progress from an inconspicuous Fiat Panda was the watchful Macauan.

The sea was calm, especially within the shelter of the harbour wall, where reflected lights bounced and sparkled on the tops of lazy waves. There was barely sufficient breeze to rattle the pennants and rigging on the dark shapes of moored boats, as Marco and Yousef crossed the road to overlook the harbour.

'Your new place is over there,' said Marco, tilting his head vaguely in the direction of the line of sea-front buildings. 'It's a bit early for bed, so let's go out on the sea-wall and watch for any boats coming in.'

The Macauan parked within metres of the beach-side road, then left his car to cross on the southern side of the harbour wall, where sand and rocks stretched twenty metres before shelving gradually towards deeper water. Dressed in black, he was virtually invisible as he climbed silently over the last few rocks, where he stopped to listen. Just audible above the sound of small waves lapping gently around his feet was a gurgling sound, frantic choking, then silence. He crouched in the darkness of the rocks as the sound of running feet went past him up on the wall, then a retching noise and the splashing of vomit on water as Marco lay on the far side of the wall, his shining, wet face reflected on the bobbing harbour waves as he coughed up the final, foul-tasting bile. 'So weak, these Western men,' thought the Macauan to himself while he waited. He pulled himself tighter against the stone wall when he heard Marco jump down onto the beach, then a scraping noise as Marco lifted a lump of rock which he carried back along to the seaward end of the breakwater. Half a minute later, a splash was the Macauan's signal to retreat hurriedly back up the beach and cross the road, to hide in the shadows close to his parked car. He remained hidden for several minutes, expecting Marco to return the same way that he had arrived. A middle-aged couple walked past where he waited, and a group of noisy teenagers had gone in the opposite direction, but there was no sign of Marco. He remained calm. The job could wait until tomorrow night if necessary, but he knew that Mister Lau would prefer that things were tidied up tonight.

Keeping his gaze fixed on the ground, he slid effortlessly into the Fiat, drove the short distance to the junction with the seafront road, then turned left and stopped after twenty-five metres, overlooking the harbour. A quick scan in both directions confirmed that Marco was not in the vicinity, so the Macauan drove to the next turning on his left and travelled up the narrow street, then took the next left again and completed a circuit of the block by coming back down the road where he had first parked the car. Although he felt inconspicuous in an off-white Panda, a ubiquitous vehicle throughout Abruzzo, he didn't want unusual patterns of behaviour to draw attention to himself, but he nevertheless decided that a reasonably slow tour of the same route would be safe enough, so long as he didn't stop this time. Out on the pavement were two of the gang of teenagers, chatting and smoking – outside a bar. The Macauan preferred certainty to speculation, and he couldn't go inside the premises to check, but he decided to take a chance on the probability that Marco had gone straight in for a drink to dull his conscience. He continued driving round to the street where he expected Marco to pass on his way home, but this time he turned right instead of left, and parked about a hundred metres along the street on the right hand side. He pulled on a dark baseball cap, slid down in the seat, and began what could be a long vigil.

The Macauan had to keep changing position to ensure his blood was flowing properly and his limbs weren't seizing, then almost an hour later his patience was rewarded. Having angled the rear-view mirror so that he could watch for anyone approaching from behind, he saw Marco walking towards the car with the over-careful tread of the drunk. Between checking in the mirror and looking forwards along the street, the Macauan made sure no-one else was in sight, and meanwhile Marco steadily drew alongside then passed the Panda, concentrating on each step he took. It was imperative not to let Marco walk too far ahead, so quickly and quietly the Macauan opened the car door, and on soft rubber-soled trainers, he stepped up behind the oblivious Italian. With movements of extraordinary speed, the Macauan first dug his straightened fingers into the kidney area of Marco's back, causing him to arch and throw his head backwards, then chopped with the side of his hand into the man's exposed trachea. Marco's body began going into convulsions, and, unable to breathe, it would take about a minute for death to occur. The Macauan had to move quickly. He bundled Marco into the back of his car, then drove a route he knew, dodging up and down side streets, to the multi-storey car park beside Piazza della Marina. He went directly to the top floor, stopping briefly by the few parked cars to make sure they were empty, then pulled up beside the low wall overlooking via Marco Polo. He pulled the unconscious man from the back of the car, thankful for his slim build, then, careful not to let Marco's legs scrape the concrete wall, tipped him over the top onto the tarmac below. It would only be a matter of time, thought the Macauan, that the comune would fix a railing around that low wall. This was the third suicide jump from here just this year.

At the Blue Diamond Club, deputy minister of sport and culture, Carlo Sartolini, was an honoured guest for the evening, delighted to have been given five hundred euros' worth of free playing chips by the beaming, generous Mister Lau. A while later, Lau retired to the smoking lounge where he was enjoying a large Cuban cigar with his third balon of Courvoisier. The Macauan, attired appropriately in dinner suit and black bow tie, briefly entered the room, caught Lau's eye, and gave a slight nod. Lau emptied his brandy glass and clicked his fingers at the barman for a top-up. As he swirled the freshly-poured liqueur around his glass, Signora Leporini entered the lounge and came to speak to Mister Lau.

'Our special guest is enjoying his evening,' she said, 'shall I choose a girl for him?'

Lau chuckled and swallowed a mouthful of brandy.

'I think not, my dear,' he said, still smiling broadly, 'unless she happens to have an arse like a young boy.'

Seventeen

Sergeant Rossi thought that she would be one of the first to arrive at the Damiano pasta factory at six forty-five on Thursday morning, but she joined a queue of cars entering a car park that was already half full. She parked at the far end, facing the crystal clear water of the mountain-fed river from which some of the water was carried by aqueduct into the factory, and was the reason for the plant having been sited here in the first place. Carrying her small hold-all, which held everything she needed for her trip to UK, she followed the signs to reception, where she announced herself to the receptionist. Having been asked to take a seat while she waited, Rossi felt a mounting sense of excitement about the forthcoming day, which promised two significant 'firsts'. She had never previously flown in either a helicopter or private jet, and was greatly looking forward to both experiences, which she felt sure would cap the two unusual modes of transport on her current list, namely an armoured personnel carrier and a marine landing craft, during exercises in conjunction with the regular army.

When Signore Damiano and his daughter Patrizia came down in the lift to the reception area shortly before seven o'clock, Rossi jumped from her seat to meet them, grinning broadly.

'I would like the three of us fellow travellers to be on first name terms,' said Damiano, introducing himself as Giuseppe.

'I'm Teresa. Thank you so much for letting me come with you.'

'It's a pleasure,' said the stocky fifty-six year old millionaire businessman. 'I'm sure Patrizia will be glad of your company, instead of having to talk to her boring old father all day.'

'It'll be good for us both,' added Patrizia, 'we usually just talk shop the whole time.'

Patrizia and Rossi fell into easy conversation during the short walk around the side of the factory to the helipad, where their pilot was waiting for them, standing next to the gleaming silver-coloured helicopter.

'It's a bit noisy in the air, so we need to wear head-sets,' explained Patrizia, as they climbed into the passenger area and strapped themselves into the seats. Giuseppe chose to sit up front with the pilot.

'You've plotted the slightly amended route?' he asked.

'All cleared, no problem,' smiled the pilot.

Giuseppe turned to see that Teresa was settled in the right hand side seat.

'Keep slightly to left of the designated building,' added Giuseppe, as the pilot fired the motor into life and the rotor blades began to turn, slowly at first, but soon picking up speed. He gave a thumbs up signal, and Teresa felt a strange sensation in her stomach as the helicopter lifted into the air, then banked to the right to begin its northward journey towards Pescara airport.

Between chatting excitedly to Patrizia, Teresa was fascinated to watch the patchwork of landscape above which they were flying, when suddenly she gave a little yell of surprise.

'I live just back there. That's the road I go in to work on – this is – look, look, our station. Oh my God!'

Patrizia smiled as Teresa stared silently, open-mouthed, from her window. Her carabinieri colleagues, having climbed through the skylight on to the roof of the station, were grouped around an Italian flag which they had stretched out across the tiles, and were waving frantically up at the helicopter. Teresa craned her neck so that she could watch the scene until it disappeared from view, then turned back to see the smile on Patrizia's face. Giuseppe had turned in his seat to watch her reaction, and both he and the pilot were smiling with pleasure that their little act of co-operation with Major D'Angelo had produced an enjoyable result. Teresa didn't know whether to laugh or cry, but she just kept on grinning.

The journey from pasta factory to airport took less than twenty minutes, and it was only as they were hovering to land that Teresa suddenly asked about security procedures.

'Another advantage of travelling privately,' said Patrizia, 'we don't need to be checked.'

'So you could take something – or someone – out of the country without the authorities knowing?'

'I suppose so, although we're screened by immigration in the country where we land.'

Teresa was wondering how easy it would be to by-pass that particular procedure, and made a mental note to find out whether Martin Renson flew by commercial airline or private jet.

The helicopter bumped lightly to the ground on its skids a short distance from a hangar, in front of which a small jet stood waiting. They remained seated until the rotor blades had stopped turning, then the three of them walked over to the aircraft, which was a level of comfort up from the helicopter. Giuseppe, Patrizia and Teresa settled into three of the four comfortable leather seats that faced one another, each with its own retractable table.

After a short delay while they waited for an incoming Alitalia plane from Milan to land – they were, explained Giuseppe, still subject to normal Air Traffic Control take-off and landing protocols – the small jet taxied to the runway for a subsequent smooth lift into the morning sky above Pescara, sunlight glinting on the swept-up wing tips. After reaching their cruising altitude, Patrizia went forward to retrieve from a small insulated cabinet some croissants, coffee and fresh orange juice that had been stowed for them earlier.

'Should keep us going till our first meeting,' she said.

'What time will that be?' asked Teresa.

'Eleven fifteen UK time. They're an hour behind us. Today and tomorrow we'll be meeting the distributors who handle our products in the north of England and Scotland.'

'Do you sell a lot of your pasta in the UK?'

Patrizia laughed. 'You don't think of the English eating pasta, do you? Fish and chips or pie and mash. But believe it or not, the UK is our number one market in Europe. All thanks to my brilliant work of course,' she said, for her father's benefit. 'But lately we've been squeezed a bit by some of the supermarkets' own-brand products, and the growth of low-cost retailers such as LIDL and Aldi. So we want the wholesalers to push our brand a bit harder, and we've got something of an ace up our sleeves. Our development people have come up with a new pasta shape. It's designed to hold more sauce than the traditional orecchiette pasta – more closed and crimped. We're calling it 'cowrie shell', and hoping it'll give us an edge on the competition.'

'I take it you're in charge of sales?'

'Export, yes. My brother looks after Italy. I suppose you're not allowed to tell us the purpose of your visit?'

Teresa shrugged and smiled apologetically.

'By the way,' continued Patrizia, covering the slightly awkward moment, 'do you want to come back with us on Saturday morning?'

'I'd love to, if that's alright.'

'Of course. We'll be flying from Edinburgh, seven o'clock again. I suggest we exchange mobile phone numbers so we can get in contact nearer the time.'

* * *

The Sundberg family were down on the Pescara beach bright and early, determined to enjoy their final morning of swimming and sunbathing before heading to Rome for three days of sightseeing and culture. They would then be heading back on the long journey to their home in the city of Orebro in central Sweden. Parents Aleksander and Franciska were enjoying simply lying on the sand, while twelve year old Hannah was walking along the beach, splashing through the shallow surf and examining the odd seashell. It was too early in the season for Italians to be swimming, the Adriatic not yet up to optimum summer temperature, but it didn't deter ten year old Claus from participating in his latest favourite hobby of snorkelling. He had discovered the pleasures of observing aquatic life through his newly-acquired mask, while slowly flapping his fins to drift out close to the rocks stacked against the harbour breakwater. He had even mastered the technique of diving beneath the surface, which he had done in order to examine more closely some sea urchins and an octopus. Absorbed in his search of underwater life, he was making his way further and further out to sea. He had been told not to go too far, but the end of the harbour wall was beckoning, and the temptation was too strong. He wouldn't go right round into the harbour, but there might be some really big fish in that deep water just off the end of the wall. Claus felt that he was swimming through patches of water colder than the rest, now that he couldn't see the sea floor, but on the water line the rocks were covered with swathes of blue mussels. He decided to go for one final dive, so he took a deep breath and thrust his head down into the water, beating his fins to push his way into the depths. His ears popped as he went as deep as he could, had a look to his right, then to the left, where he saw a head, not just a head, a whole body, eyes staring up at him, hair waving in the current, arms outstretched with lifeless hands reaching towards him. In his panic, he let out a silent scream which dislodged his breathing tube. He was gulping bitter, salty seawater, but thrashed his feet to get away, to escape to the surface. He reached the top, coughing and choking. Disorientated, he didn't know which way to swim, then looked above the waves until he could see the distant line of buildings and the beach in front of them. His breathing tube was gone, but he kept the mask on his face as he swam as fast as he could away from the horror, towards the safety of the beach.

'Aleks, look, what's happened, why is Claus swimming back so fast?' said Franciska, rising quickly to her feet.

'Perhaps he's been stung – a jellyfish or something.'

They both ran to the water's edge, then Aleksander took a plunge and began swimming towards his son. By the time they reached one another, Aleksander found that he could still stand on the sandy seabed.

'What is it, what's the matter?' he said as he lifted his son onto his shoulder. Claus was crying and coughing up seawater as his father began the painfully slow process of wading back to shore.

'Out there – someone in the water – dead,' Claus managed to say between sobs.

When Aleksander was walking in water about thirty centimetres deep, he put Claus down. Claus immediately pulled off his fins and mask and ran to his waiting mother, flinging his arms around her neck. Hannah had witnessed the unfolding drama and had run back to join the rest of the family.

'He says there's a body out there in the water,' said Aleksander quietly.

'Should Claus go to the hospital?' asked Franciska, cuddling her distraught son.

Claus had finally stopped coughing up water, but was now shivering.

'He's in shock. Wrap a towel round him, and let's get

him back to the hotel. If necessary, we can get the hotel manager to ring for a doctor or an ambulance.'

By the time they reached the hotel, Claus had more or less recovered, and asked for a Fanta to try and get rid of the taste of salt water.

'It was horrible,' he said. 'There was a boy out there under the water. He didn't look dead, but he must have been dead, mustn't he?'

Aleksander asked to see the hotel manager, to whom he explained as best he could that they needed to call the police, because his son had seen a body in the sea. The manager was obviously sceptical, saying he would 'sort it out later,' but Aleksander insisted that his son wouldn't have made up such a story, and the police must be called immediately. With a reluctant sigh and shrug of his shoulders, the manager finally agreed to call the police, who told him that it was not within their remit, and that he should contact the carabinieri instead.

It was Sergeant Mascetta in Major Camponelli's command zone who received details of the call, and he, unlike the hotel manager, was very much interested. He informed the major of the reported incident, and decided to investigate the matter himself, not being directly involved with preparations for Operation Seahawk.

To the manager's utter amazement, Sergeant Mascetta turned up at his hotel barely ten minutes after his phone call. He apologised for wasting the carabiniere's time, explaining how the foreign father of a young boy had insisted he make the call, but of course ten year old boys have vivid imaginations, and what he probably saw was an old coat or something similar drifting in the water.

'Can I offer you a coffee to make up for it, officer?'

'Later perhaps. I would like to speak to these people if I may.'

'Signore and Signora Sundberg, yes officer. Their son Claus reported having seen the body. Please come into my office, you can talk to them in there. I'm afraid their Italian is not that good.'

A short while later, the Sundberg family joined Sergeant Mascetta in the hotel manager's office. With a fair amount of gesticulating, Mascetta asked the Sundbergs if their son could show him where the sighting took place, so while Franciska and Hannah remained at the hotel, Claus led his father and Sergeant Mascetta along to the end of the harbour wall, where he pointed down into the sea. Mascetta donned dark glasses and peered into the water, but could see nothing. Hardly surprising, he thought, as the body must be several metres below the surface. He thanked Aleksander and Claus, explaining that they could now continue with their holiday. Alone on the harbour wall, Sergeant Mascetta made some phone calls, until he managed to track down one of the Command's trained scuba divers. He explained the location, then waited the half hour it took for an inflatable with two men on board to appear from the other side of the harbour. He watched as the man in wet suit and diving gear flipped backwards from the side of the inflatable and disappear beneath the waves in the area he had pointed out, while the diver's colleague kept the small boat turning within a restricted area. It wasn't long before the diver's masked head popped back up to the surface, his raised hand giving a signal with thumb and forefinger together to form a circle.

'Success,' shouted the man in the inflatable, 'he's located the deceased person.'

Mascetta exhaled with a low whistle. Accident, he wondered, or homicide.

'Bring the diver to the beach,' he called in reply, and strode back along the harbour wall.

The inflatable with its outboard motor came within metres of the shoreline, allowing the diver to walk the short distance through shallow surf to meet Sergeant Mascetta, who was waiting on the damp sand.

'Young male,' said the diver, anticipating Mascetta's question. 'There's a cord round his ankle tied to a rock.'

'Almost certainly homicide then.'

'I would say so. Most suicides follow fairly predictable patterns, and while we both know that some are more imaginative than others, a youngster tying a rock to his leg and heaving it out to sea? I don't know.'

'Seems unlikely. How long will it take to recover the body?'

The diver looked out beyond the harbour wall.

'Shouldn't be too difficult. I reckon we could have him on dry land within an hour. Can we hand him over to you once we're ashore?'

'I'll have a vehicle waiting.'

The diver started to splash back through the water to the inflatable.

'Make sure the cord and rock stay intact,' called Mascetta.

The diver raised his hand in acknowledgement and clambered aboard the waiting craft.

Mascetta decided he would take up the hotel manager's

offer of a coffee, and let the Sundbergs know that the unfortunate victim had been found, before he made preparations to take charge of the boy from the sea.

Eighteen

Having taken her leave of Giuseppe and Patrizia Damiano, astonished how easy it had been to enter the UK after a flight by private jet, Sergeant Teresa Rossi hired a car at Manchester airport in order to undertake the drive up to the north east of England, making clear she would be dropping the car at Edinburgh airport on Saturday. She made sure that the Ford Fiesta she hired was equipped with satnav, a precaution for which she was very grateful as she negotiated the fast and busy English roads, very different to the roads of her native Abruzzo. Her lunch break consisted of a filled roll and a fizzy drink; she remembered only too well from a previous visit to England when she was competing in a Tae Kwando competition that the service station coffee was virtually undrinkable, the food bland and stodgy.

After another session of driving on the unfamiliar left hand side of the road in difficult conditions, especially having run through a couple of fairly heavy showers of rain, it was a great relief when she turned off onto smaller town roads and the satnav eventually informed her that the next right turn from Station Road would be into Henry Robson Way and the South Shields Business Works, the address of Martin Renson's factory unit. She stopped in front of a large board at the roadside which listed the units and their occupants, prominent among them being M R Cabling, with premises at the centre of the industrial park. The factory itself was easy to find, and Teresa ran through in her mind the forthcoming discussion with Martin Renson, as she parked in one of the bays reserved for visitors, and walked the short distance to the factory entrance. A cold gust of wind coming off the North Sea reminded Teresa how far she was from home, causing her to feel a rare moment of insecurity and isolation in a foreign land and alien culture. She paused for a brief couple of seconds until she felt a resurgence of her customary confidence, before marching through the doorway and straight up to the receptionist's desk.

'Can I help you?'

'I would like to see Mister Renson please.'

'Do you have an appointment?'

'Oh, er – no.'

The receptionist was trained to deal with cold-calling sales reps.

'Can I ask the nature of your visit?'

'It's – er – private.'

'You're personally known to Mister Renson?'

Teresa Rossi was thrown by all this formality. If Renson was out having a coffee, why doesn't the receptionist just say so, and ask her to wait? What a strange, guarded race these English are.

'Well, you see…'

'Could I suggest you telephone for an appointment, and we'll see if it's appropriate for you to meet the managing director. Mister Renson has a fellow director who usually sees sales representatives.'

'Oh I'm not a sales repres… er, person, no, I'm here to see Martin Renson on a personal matter. I'm from Italy, you see, and I've come to discuss a thing that is – how do you say – disresolved to do with his holiday home.'

The receptionist could see there was an incoming call that she needed to answer, just as Dan Ingham, the works manager, came into reception via the metal door leading from the shop floor.

'Dan,' said the receptionist, 'this lady is a personal friend of Martin's, she's called in to see him, can you have a word?' The receptionist immediately turned her attention to the incoming call. 'M R Cabling, how can I help you?'

'So you're a friend of the boss?' said Dan.

'Well, you see…'

Dan's phone was playing an electronic version of a tune Teresa didn't recognise, but it might have been an old Elvis Presley number.

'Sorry, Pet. Won't be a mo. Yes, Gary? Noo, the Hereford Health Trust job is all done and dusted like, ready to ship. You and Michael can get yer sennes away onto the Fire Service job, the new one. I knoar it's in section three, but yer'll no get the bloody plague, man. H'away. Sorry, Pet, all bloody go today like. Did Martin no tell yer, he's away with the Sweaties.'

Teresa looked at him blankly. 'Sorry?'

'Jocks. Meetins in Scotland, Love, all day.'

'Oh, I see,' said Teresa, crestfallen.

'Tell yer what, the boss has got just the one early meeting tomorrer mornin like, then he'll gan stret hooam, should be there 'boot eleven. Why divvent yer meet him there?'

'At his home?'

'Aye. I'll give him a call if you want, mek shooer it's OK. I might get him between meetings.'

'No, don't worry, Dan, I'll call him myself later.'

'You shooer? It's nee trouble like.'

'No, honestly…'

The door from the factory floor swung open, where a young lad wearing regulation navy blue trousers and polo shirt with MRC embossed in white above the breast pocket was hovering in the doorway.

'Ken says there's not enough ethernet for the four-eight junctions,' he called across to Dan.

'Fer foock's sake… check bloody Goods In, man, there was a delivery this morning.'

The youngster disappeared quickly.

'Sorry, Pet, busy day like. I'd best go.'

'No, that's fine, Dan, really. Thank you for your help.'

Teresa drove a kilometre away from South Shields Business Works before parking in a side street to make two phone calls. She rang Inspector Armstrong of the Northumbria Police to let him know that she had visited Martin Renson's factory, and that she was going to meet him at his home at eleven o'clock the following morning. He told her that he would let his colleague at the Alnwick station know about the arrangement. She then rang major D'Angelo.

'So you'll be seeing him in the morning?'

'That's right. At his home. I hope I find it easier talking to him than to the works manager.'

'What do you mean?'

'I could hardly understand anything he said. I think he

was speaking English, but perhaps it's like Abruzzo where some people still speak dialect. He kept calling me a "pet." Isn't that the word they use for a dog or cat?'

'Pet? Yes, I think it is. How strange.'

'Still, he was a nice enough guy, and he did let me know when Martin Renson would be home.'

'Teresa, don't forget that Renson is a possible suspect in what could be a serious offence. Keep on your guard. What's your plan now?'

'I'm heading north of here to Alnwick, the town near where Renson lives. On google map it looks like Aln-wick, but they seem to call it Annick. I'll find somewhere to spend the night and have a nice relaxed start in the morning. Any developments over there?'

'Afraid not. We've been sent a few names by a teacher at Giovanni's school, someone by the name of Carolina Recchia. Was she the teacher you saw?'

'Yes, the names she sent will be the fathers of some of Giovanni's classmates who are hunters. Giovanni is very anti-hunting, and no doubt lets his feelings be known. There's an exercise book in the file. If you read the last thing he wrote in it, you'll see what I mean.'

'Are you coming back with Giuseppe Damiano?'

'Yes, all arranged. I'll be back on Saturday.'

'Good. Take care, Teresa, and keep in touch.'

* * *

'What time do you have to leave?' called Fabio, from the kitchen of the smart two-bedroom apartment close to Pescara's sea-front.

'I need to be in Ortona by ten.'

'And it's an all-night operation?'

'Yes. I don't know what time I'll be home, it depends how things go.'

Lieutenant Giorgio Alberico was playing with Mitzi, their much-loved cat, on the sofa in the adjoining living room. He was thinking about his forthcoming night's work, having been allocated the responsibility of watching from the harbour wall for incoming boats into the port of Ortona, in command of a two-man back-up team waiting near the quayside, as his role in Operation Seahawk.

'It's ready,' called Fabio. He had insisted that Giorgio should have a good dinner before his night-time vigil, so had prepared a ten-layer fresh pasta lasagne for their evening meal. Giorgio gave the purring Mitzi a kiss on the top of her head and left her on the sofa, then joined Fabio at the kitchen table. Fabio was opening a bottle of Montepulciano d'Abruzzo, bought at the local cantina, to go with the lasagne.

'Just water for me,' said Giorgio.

'Half a glass won't hurt,' insisted Fabio, pouring the wine before dishing out two portions of lasagne.

'God I'm hot,' complained Giorgio. He had concurred with Fabio's advice to wear his skiing thermals underneath his uniform, but was wishing he hadn't changed until after dinner. After a couple of mouthfuls of lasagne, Giorgio noticed Fabio's notebook on the table. He picked it up to look more closely at some sketches on the top page.

'Looks like a nice place, a new commission?' he asked his architect partner.

Fabio, slim and well-groomed with a neatly trimmed

dark beard, hesitated. He sipped a little of his red wine, unsure how to respond.

'Not exactly.'

Giorgio would have let it go at that, but, deep down, Fabio wanted the matter discussed, wanted it to be out in the open.

'It's an old farmhouse I looked at a few days ago, about five or six kilometres south of Pescara. A bit of a wreck.' Fabio took another sip of wine. 'It's for sale,' he said quickly.

'But it's not one of your clients that's interested in it?'

'No.'

'So...'

'I know you like this apartment, it's very convenient...'

'But?'

'I've been thinking, maybe we could move somewhere bigger, with a bit of land. Somewhere we could do up together, where Mitzi can come and go as she likes. I just thought...'

Now that the suggestion was out in the open, Fabio dreaded what Giorgio's reaction would be. Giorgio put his fork down, stood up, and walked round behind Fabio. He put his arms around his partner's neck and gave him a hug.

'I think that's a wonderful idea,' he said. 'We'll go out at the weekend and I can see the place for myself.'

Giorgio returned to his seat and studied the sketches of Fabio's plans for the farmhouse with renewed interest.

'That's so exciting,' he said. 'I can't wait to see it. Mitzi'll be in seventh heaven.'

For the remainder of the meal, Operation Seahawk was temporarily forgotten, in favour of discussion about plans for the derelict farmhouse. Finally, with considerable reluctance, it was time for Giorgio to set off for his boat-watching vigil.

'Don't forget your phone,' said Fabio, noticing the device lying on the worktop.

'Can't take it,' responded Giorgio. 'Carabinieri radios only. Security issue.'

'You mean I won't be able to contact you?'

'Afraid not. Sorry Fab. Hopefully I'll be back before you leave for work in the morning. Don't forget to let Mitzi out for her night-time stroll.'

'I'll put a cat-flap in the door at our farmhouse, then she can have more independence. I hope you're going to be warm enough in the early hours of the morning, and please keep safe.'

'Don't fuss, I'll be fine. See you tomorrow.'

Lieutenant Alberico met up with his two-man back-up team in Ortona where he gave them a final briefing. They were to remain in their vehicle, which was to be parked on a road close to the castle. From that location, they could rapidly reach any section of the port or marina on receipt of a call from the lieutenant, if he spotted a suspect looking boat, with an indication of where the craft was likely to tie up. If Ortona happened to prove to be the destination for the people smugglers, Alberico would also call for assistance from one of the rapid response teams, as there were likely to be at least three smugglers and an unknown number of migrants, so the situation had the potential for considerable chaos.

'It'll probably turn out to be a very long and boring night,' he warned them, 'but we have to stay awake and ready, just in case. We'll be heroes if we manage to nab them.'

He made a final check that both his radio and flashlight were functioning correctly, before making his way to the vantage point at the far end of the long and slightly curved harbour wall, remembering how he had tried his hand at fishing from there with a schoolmate when he was younger. Lack of success at landing any fish, and a soaking one day from a sudden heavy rain storm, ended his time as a budding fisherman.

A group of professional fishermen were talking loudly on the quayside near one of several moored trawlers, while on the far side of the harbour there was still considerable activity. Alberico stopped to watch for a while as a container was hoisted from the deck of a large ocean-going ship on to the back of a low-loader truck that was waiting alongside. The scene was lit by harbour-side lights, as well as by bright searchlights from the bridge of the ship. Eventually the manoeuvre was completed and the lorry parked nearby, presumably, thought Alberico, ready for an early morning start to its final destination. The lights were extinguished, which seemed to be the cue for the fishermen to disperse, leaving Alberico in a lonely silence.

The hours from then on passed very slowly indeed for Giorgio Alberico on his night-time vigil. The stone steps seemed reasonably comfortable at first, but soon felt unbearably hard, and he began to feel cold despite the thermals. Notwithstanding the discomfort, he was aware of having momentarily dozed off a couple of times. He could see lights on a ship several kilometres out to sea, but otherwise, after midnight, the harbour was eerily devoid of activity.

At the apartment in Pescara, Fabio had been working late, putting some finishing touches to a proposal he was due to present the following day to some important clients. He looked at his watch. 'Mannaggia!' He hadn't realised how much time had passed. Having taken Mitzi down to the patch of open space behind the apartment building for her evening constitutional about an hour and a half earlier, she had wandered off, not returning when he called her, evidently intent on spending some time exploring the outdoors on her own. But now it was definitely time to return home for a small treat, before snuggling either into her own cosy bed, or otherwise on the bed with Fabio. He hoped it would be the latter, knowing how much he would miss having Giorgio next to him. Admittedly, Mitzi could be a bit of a pain, either with her exuberant purring, or her occasional preference for lying across his face, but it was a small price to pay for her affection. He grabbed the torch on his way out, wishing he had gone earlier to let Mitzi back in, and hurried round to the area of open land, surprised she wasn't already waiting for him outside the door. He was calling her name, willing her to appear, his voice rising in volume and anxiety each moment that she failed to come bounding towards him, anticipating being lifted so that she could rub her head against his face. Fabio broke into a trot, feeling his heart beginning to race and his mouth dry, but still incessantly calling Mitzi's name.

He negotiated a gap in the row of shrubs and trees that bordered the road, the light from his torch flashing this way and that as he ran along the side of the road, panic rising with every second that passed. Suddenly, laser-like, the beam picked out what Fabio was dreading he would see. She was partly concealed beneath a bush where Fabio rushed and fell to his knees in front of her, but he knew in an instant that she was dead. He gently picked her up, tears stinging his eyes. There was no obvious sign that she had been hit, but her eyes, so bright and playful in life, were closed. Her mouth was open, her little tongue lying to one side, where a small patch of blood had stained her ginger fur. Clutching her to his chest, Fabio carried the precious, lifeless body back up to the apartment, tears now running freely down his face and wetting his beard. He placed her carefully in her bed, curled as though asleep, her fluffy tail wrapped around her head.

'I'm so sorry, little one,' he said, gently stroking her fur. A feeling of guilt adding to the raw pain, Fabio stood and walked clumsily to lean on the kitchen worktop. He reached for the bottle of wine left over from the earlier meal and poured himself a large glassful. He then went to sit at the table, where he pushed aside his work on the architectural proposal, with no inclination for either sleep or work. How he wished that Giorgio was here to share the grief. He picked up his phone, tapped on Giorgio's contact symbol, then on the little phone icon, trying to think, while looking at a photo of those finely chiselled features in a little on-screen disc, how he was going to explain the tragedy to his partner. It was ringing, but something wasn't right. He was listening to the ring tone on Giorgio's iPhone. He turned and looked at the source of the sound, lying on the marble worktop. Angrily, he ended the call, and sat with his head buried in his hands.

Lieutenant Alberico's eyes opened with a start. He had dozed again, but for how long? Seconds, minutes? God, how he ached from sitting on the stone step. He stood up and stretched, rubbing his sore backside and thighs, looking out to sea where he saw a small, bright light. He checked further along the horizon, and there were the lights on the anchored ship he had seen earlier. Could this be another ship, perhaps? All feeling of tiredness vanished in an instant as he focused on the bobbing pinprick of light, the beam reflected every few seconds in the blackness of the water. As he watched, the light grew bigger and brighter. It was coming towards the shore. The light was low to the water, so a boat, not a ship, and travelling quite fast.

Alberico instinctively moved to the edge of the breakwater, as though a few metres would make a difference to his view, then suddenly the beam of light disappeared, seeming as if a cloak of invisibility had been thrown over the boat. He turned round to see a smaller light, nothing more than a powerful torch, emanating from beyond the bow of the moored container ship on the far side of the harbour.

'Being guided in,' Alberico said to himself. 'This is it, this is the one – it's happening on my watch.' He felt a rush of excitement as he fumbled to open the carrying case for his radio that was attached to his belt, already anticipating a commendation for the arrest of a gang of people smugglers. With fingers numb from the cold, he pulled the radio from its case, barely able to feel the equally cold plastic. The radio slipped, he made a grab for it, but only succeeded in batting the device further on its way out of his grasp. A corner of it hit the edge of the stone wall, sending it spinning outwards, to land with a gentle splash in the darkness of the sea. Alberico froze, unable to take in what had happened, until the muffled throb of a diesel inboard motor shook him back to reality. He couldn't use his flashlight to signal to the waiting back-up team, because it would be seen by the accomplice who was guiding the boat in to harbour. He was going to have to tackle them on his own. Moving as quickly as he could in the darkness, Alberico made his way back along the stone wall, past the stark outlines of the moored fishing boats, then along the inner harbour wall, partially lit by nearby street lamps. There were some low buildings at the town end of the wide dock area, next to a roadway, alongside which huge cranes stood like sentinels. In the harbour, beyond some smaller boats, Alberico could see the bigger shape of the container vessel. He waited in the shadow of one of the buildings, trying to formulate a plan in his mind, but eventually deciding that bluff was his best option. The run from his observation point had warmed him up, so it was with a more assured grip that he unclipped the holster and drew out his Beretta pistol, pushing off the safety catch. The feel of the gun in his hand boosted his confidence.

Alberico could tell by the chug of the engine echoing from the opposite wall that the boat was now within the confines of the harbour. The light from the shore-held torch was casting silvery shapes across small waves, when suddenly the beam picked out the boat's hull. The engine was slowed so that the boat came gently towards the quay, then a slight roar as it was thrust into reverse, sending clouds of white water bubbling around the stern, before a painter rope was hurled ashore and tied off to a bollard, first fore then aft.

Lieutenant Giorgio Alberico's moment had arrived. On another day, or even given a few more moments to reflect, he might have acted very differently, but he needed to perform his duty, and he was keen to prove himself. With flashlight in one hand and pistol in the other, he ran from the cover of the building to where the boat was newly moored.

'Carabinieri,' he shouted, 'everyone remain exactly where you are. Nobody is to come ashore until I give permission. You,' his shouting now directed at the man who had guided the boat in with his torch,' lie face down in front of me here, with your arms outstretched.'

The man obeyed his command, and Alberico took the opportunity to quickly turn and flash his powerful torch towards the hill below the massive black outline of the castle, praying that his back-up team would respond and come swiftly to his assistance. Not wanting to have his back towards the boat for more than a brief moment, he immediately turned to face it once again.

'Did you see that, Franco?'
'What?'
'A flashlight from down there, in the harbour area.'
'Didn't see it mate. Sorry.'
Franco was desperate for a cigarette, but knew he wasn't allowed to smoke during the Operation Seahawk

watch; something to do with the glow of burning cigarettes being visible at night. He was feeling tired and tetchy.

'Do you think it was the lieutenant?'

'Alberico? No, he'll call us if he needs us.'

'You think we should go and check?'

'We were told to "stay put" unless we get a call. Orders is orders mate.'

'I know, but – what if he couldn't radio for some reason?'

'What reason? He might be a stupid bloody officer, wet behind the ears, but he knows how to use a radio. Relax Renzo. If we see the torch again, we'll go take a look.'

Otto hadn't used violence before. He hadn't needed to. He was gripping with a tight hold the big spanner he had grabbed from the cab of the container lorry while the carabiniere was shouting his orders, but he was reluctant to use it. How much force would be needed to knock the guy out? If he didn't hit him hard enough, the carabinieri bloke would start firing that bloody gun of his. Otto had crept to within a few paces behind the officer. What if he looks around with his torch again? Perhaps it would have been best to just disappear, but Otto wanted the money. He was after more than just a quick screw with that red-head, Carla. OK, she was a prosy, but bloody hell she could turn him on. He wanted a whole night with her, and that wouldn't come cheap. Otto rushed the last few paces and swung the spanner with a heavy, clumsy blow to Alberico's head, just as the lieutenant was turning to the sound of footsteps. For a split second, he heard what seemed like a loud explosion as the heavy spanner made contact with the side of his head, then all senses were lost as he crumpled to the ground, blood already oozing from his wounded scalp.

The smugglers moved quickly. All twenty-five fee-paying migrants were herded from the boat into the truck's container, empty thanks to a business arrangement with the ship's captain. The container door was bolted shut, and Otto drove the lorry, without using his lights, along the dark strip of tarmac as far as the large lorry park alongside the coastal railway line, where he switched off the engine and lay flat in the tilted seat of his cab, waiting for first light when he could join other traffic leaving the port.

Just minutes after docking, the smugglers' boat was turning seaward in the middle of the harbour and was soon once again in open water, heading back across the Adriatic.

Lorenzo had been staring down into the darkness, watchful for any further flashes of light from the harbour.

'Franco, look, a light – there's a boat out there.'

'There's a boat. That's the sea. You have to expect boats on the sea. If you're still worried, try calling him. He'll have his radio on mute, so you won't be sending out a warning signal.'

Lorenzo didn't need any more persuasion, as he grabbed the radio and put in a call to Lieutenant Alberico.

'Dead. No ring tone. Nothing.'

Lorenzo and Franco looked at each other for a second before Lorenzo started the vehicle engine, slammed it into gear, and sped down the winding hill towards the harbour, while Franco lifted the Beretta M12S submachine gun onto his lap, his hand around the trigger guard.

Nineteen

'Take me through it again.'

Colonel Battista looked up with hard, unblinking eyes at the two carabinieri standing to attention in front of his desk. Franco and Lorenzo had expected to be going home after a sleepless night on duty, but instead they had been ordered to report directly to the colonel on the night-time events in Ortona.

'Like I said, Signore Colonel, we were in our vehicle at the prescribed location, waiting for a call from Lieutenant Alberico if he spotted a suspect boat. No call came, but at three zero seven hours, I saw a flash of light from within the harbour perimeter. This was not an agreed signal, so we continued to wait for a radio message. At three sixteen hours, in order to make sure the radio connection was functioning correctly, I put in a call to Lieutenant Alberico, but the lieutenant's radio did not respond. We decided to proceed immediately to the harbour where we found...'

'Where you found?'

'The lieutenant was lying in a prone position on the quayside. No other persons were present. A quick examination revealed what appeared to be a serious head wound. The officer had lost a considerable amount of blood. My colleague' – Franco glanced sideways at Lorenzo – 'immediately called for an ambulance, while I fetched the emergency first-aid kit from our vehicle and applied a bandage to Lieutenant Alberico's head wound.'

'I take it you had checked to make sure he was still breathing?'

'I did, Signore, yes, but noted that the lieutenant's breathing was shallow and slow.'

'And there was nobody else within sight?'

Lorenzo glanced at Franco.

'We believe we might have seen the light from a boat moving seaward from the area of the harbour, but no, Signore, there was no-one else at the scene.'

Colonel Battista stood up and walked to look out from his office window, onto a Pescara street just beginning its working day.

'So, we have an officer in a coma in hospital, not a single suspect apprehended, no sign of trafficked migrants or smugglers, no clues to work on, nothing. Big fat zero.'

There was silence in the room, as Franco nervously shifted his balance from one foot to the other.

'Alright, you may go,' said Battista at last, 'but make sure the desk sergeant has a written report before you go off duty.'

At that moment, Otto was parking his low-loader lorry with its empty container behind the rambling house situated between the railway line and the sea, a big wad of money in his back pocket. But all was not well with Otto. He was usually able to sleep in the cab of his truck, but last night he hadn't managed to get any sleep at all, and today he felt nervous and tired, and had developed a tick in his right eye. He kept seeing in his mind the carabinieri officer lying on the ground, blood gushing from the wound he had caused with the spanner, certain now that he had killed him. The carabinieri wouldn't let this rest, not with one of their own being killed. They wouldn't believe that he had only intended to knock the guy out, not kill him. Every sound made him jump, a car engine revving, or loud voices from the road outside. With a shaking hand, he lit another cigarette, wondering how long he could carry on like this, feeling like a hunted animal. The container would need to be delivered back to Ortona in a few days' time. At the far side of the house, four of the weary migrants were climbing into a car to begin the final leg of their journey, glad not to be in either a wallowing, sick-inducing boat, or a cramped steel container.

* * *

In another time zone, Sergeant Teresa Rossi was up, showered and dressed bright and early, not having adjusted to the UK being an hour behind Italian time. She decided that before breakfast, she would take a walk around the attractive-looking town of Alnwick, with its stone buildings and renowned castle. Having checked into the central White Swan hotel for the night, located in the intriguingly-named 'Bondgate Within,' she had already received one big surprise. The dining room featured décor from RMS Olympic, sister ship to the Titanic. Having watched the film, Teresa had visualised Jack and Rose dining in an identical setting to herself.

In her walk around the town, Teresa was surprised to see so few buildings of more recent architectural types. It had never really occurred to her that many of the towns in her native Abruzzo had been so badly damaged during the second world war that they had been virtually rebuilt, with concrete structures replacing the more traditional stone and brick.

She was about to cross the road in the town centre when she almost stepped into the path of an oncoming car. She held up her hand in apology to the driver, who had needed to brake sharply, then realised she had automatically looked to her left rather than right as she walked into the road, forgetting for a moment that the traffic here in England drove on the left.

Teresa's usual 'breakfast' was an espresso, possibly accompanied by a croissant. At the White Swan, breakfast was included in the price of her room, so when she returned to the hotel after her tour of Alnwick, she was determined to have what the menu called a "full English" breakfast, especially as it gave her a chance to pretend to be Rose on the Titanic once again.

She couldn't help giggling when the plate of food arrived at her table. She had never seen a meal like it, let alone attempt to eat it. Even the two slices of what looked like cooked prosciutto were enormous, and the thought of eating fungi and tomatoes and sausage at this time of the day seemed ludicrous, but Teresa Rossi was not one to shy from a challenge. When she hoped no-one was looking, she took a photo of the monstrous meal so that she could show it to people back home. Strangely enough, Teresa had to admit to herself that this strange assortment of food actually tasted good. She even followed it with a couple of pieces of toasted bread and some rather bitter orange jam. Thinking she wouldn't need to eat for the rest of the day, Teresa checked out of the hotel with still nearly two hours to go before she was due to call on Martin Renson, so she decided to familiarise herself with the route to his house.

She drove several kilometres down the road grandly called A1, then followed the satnav instructions to turn right onto a small minor road. She drove across some open moorland, then up a hill through a small village, until there was another instruction to turn right. She stopped the car opposite a small track. A sign at the side of the track read : Roseturn Farm. Private Road. Teresa got out of the car and looked along the track, but from where she stood, she couldn't even see the farmhouse that was Martin Renson's home.

* * *

Fabio had endured a miserable night. He had finished what was left of the red wine, and then drunk most of a bottle of sambuca, but it hadn't lessened the pain of having allowed the beloved Mitzi to be killed. How could he explain it to Giorgio? That thought was enough to shake him from a state of alcohol-induced torpor to realise it had been light for several hours, but Giorgio hadn't returned home from his night-time watch on Operation Seahawk. Why wasn't he here? Why hadn't he come home? He cursed again that he wasn't able to contact his partner, but Giorgio could have contacted him. Yet he hadn't. Fabio rose clumsily, putting his hand on the table for support, trying to think what he should do. He noticed the folder of drawings that he should be presenting to his clients, but quickly dismissed any notion of doing so. He wasn't sure whether to feel angry or worried that Giorgio wasn't home, wasn't here to share his grief, to say : "it's very sad, but it wasn't your fault. We'll get over it."

Without thinking very clearly, Fabio splashed some water on his face, grabbed his car keys, and went down to get his car from the apartment's garage. But instead of turning right to follow the familiar journey to his office, he turned left, the way Giorgio would go, towards the carabinieri headquarters in the centre of Pescara. The nearer Fabio drove into the city centre with its increasingly busy traffic, the harder he concentrated on his driving, especially after being the target of a long, angry blast from a horn after he had performed an uncharacteristically risky manoeuvre to join the correct lane leading to the river bridge.

He parked in a side street that Giorgio had shown him, then walked the short distance to carabinieri HQ. The lobby was already a maelstrom of activity, carabinieri officers and members of the public alike talking too loudly, arguing, waving arms, causing confusion. The reception office was empty. Whoever was supposed to be on duty had left their post, had gone out into the lobby, arguing with the rest of them.

'I wish to see Lieutenant Alberico,' declared Fabio, hoping one of the carabinieri would hear him and point out where he should go. No-one even turned to look at him.

'I WANT TO SEE LIEUTENANT ALBERICO,' he shouted above the hubbub. There was a sudden, momentary hush as people broke off their conversations to see where the shouting had come from. By chance, Lieutenant Olivia Macrini was just leaving the Immigration Checking office to pass through the lobby on her way to her desk on the second floor. She noticed that the sergeant on reception duty was about to march over towards Fabio, but she put a restraining hand on his arm.

'It's alright,' she said, 'I'll deal with it.'

Olivia was the only one of Giorgio Alberico's colleagues who knew Fabio, who knew of their relationship. She quickly threaded through the melee to reach Fabio, whose face showed the relief of seeing someone familiar.

'I'll just grab a pass badge for you, then come with me,' she said. She dangled a key in front of the duty sergeant to show she would be using an interview room, then led Fabio through a door at the back of the lobby, past a flight of stairs and some lifts, then along a drab corridor that was in need of re-painting, before unlocking the door of Interview Room No 2, where she ushered Fabio inside.

Fabio's relief at finding Olivia was wavering, with fear beginning to gnaw at him once again.

'Is he here? Is he coming down?'

They were sitting at a table on hard metal seats that were fixed to the floor. The buzz of the overhead strip light accentuated the pause before Olivia responded in the windowless room. Fabio started to feel claustrophobic, light-headed.

'Fabio, Giogio has been injured while on duty.'

'Injured? How badly? What happened?'

'We don't fully understand the circumstances, but he appears to have taken a blow to the side of the head. He's in hospital in Ortona.'

'Can I speak to him?'

'He hasn't regained consciousness just yet, but he's being well looked after.'

'He's unconscious? Oh my God! I have to go there, I have to see him.'

Olivia studied Fabio's unkempt appearance and the redness of his eyes.

'I'll take you,' she said. 'Wait here just for a couple of minutes while I clear it with my boss, then we'll go to the hospital.'

The drive to Ortona was quiet and tense. The usually garrulous Fabio sat slumped in the front passenger seat, looking with unseeing eyes at the passing landscape.

'Our cat, Mitzi, is dead.'

'Oh Fabio, I'm so sorry.' Olivia remembered how the ginger cat was so often the centre of attention, fussed over by both Fabio and Giorgio. There was another long silence while Fabio stared out of the window.

'It was my fault.'

Olivia shot a sideways glance at her morose passenger, desperately hoping that Giorgio would have regained consciousness by the time they arrived at the hospital, something to lift Fabio from his state of depression. She wasn't confident.

Ignoring the hospital car park, which by this time of the morning would already be full to overflowing, Olivia drove up to the security barrier and glared at the guard until he opened the barrier to allow the carabinieri patrol car to pass through. She parked within a few metres of the main hospital entrance, then, with Fabio trailing in her wake, marched to the glass-fronted information office.

'Please could you direct us to the ICU where there is a patient, Alberico, Giorgio, currently receiving attention.'

The information officer, normally reticent and abrupt with members of the public, if not downright rude, became suddenly helpful and welcoming when confronted with a carabinieri uniform. He directed Olivia and Fabio to the fourth floor, zone B, and even pointed out where the lifts were located.

Fabio was moving as though on autopilot, following Olivia into and out of the lift, letting her find zone B, and waiting in the corridor while she spoke to the doctor in charge of Intensive Care. As no infection was involved, he granted permission for Olivia and Fabio to enter the unit where Giorgio Alberico was on life support. The doctor was unable to give any clear indication when, or if, Giorgio would come out of the coma.

'It could be hours, maybe weeks, it could even take years,' he explained to Olivia, with Fabio out of earshot. 'The skull was fractured, but we don't yet know the extent of any cerebral injury. At the moment it's one of our GOK cases. God only knows,' he added, in response to her puzzled expression.

With her hand on Fabio's arm, Olivia guided him into the single-bed unit, but his sense of disorientation only increased once inside. Diminished by the high-sided cot in which he lay, almost hidden among a plethora of tubes and drips, sensors and monitors, was Giorgio's pale, mask-like face.

'Giorgio,' whispered Fabio, 'Giorgio, it's me,' he said,

with a little more volume. 'I want you back home very soon, we're – I'm missing you. Don't forget we're going to look at the farmhouse at the weekend. Please come back Giorgio. I love you.'

Olivia swallowed hard, as tears welled in Fabio's bloodshot eyes.

After another five minutes that felt like eternity, prompted by the arrival of a junior doctor who had come to check monitors and make notes, Olivia and Fabio silently left the room. Fabio turned for one last look at Giorgio before gliding, as though in a trance, back out into the corridor. Not a word was spoken between the two of them until they were back in the car and turning out of the hospital entrance onto the main road.

'He's not coming back,' said Fabio quietly. 'It's as though he's already gone.'

'Of course he's coming back,' said Olivia. 'Keep positive. The three of us'll have dinner together when he's up and about. It'll take more than a bang on the head to keep Giorgio down for long.'

Olivia's words of encouragement did nothing to lift Fabio's sullen mood during the journey back to Pescara.

Olivia insisted on taking Fabio's car key before delivering him to his apartment, explaining that she would come with another officer to bring his car back for him.

'I suggest you go to the pharmacy for something to help you relax,' she said, as she dropped him off at his home. 'I'm on duty this weekend, Fabio, so call me at any time. We can go and see Giorgio again.'

* * *

'A Captain Luciani at Pescara HQ wishes to speak to you, Major.'

'Thank you, Katia. Put him through.'

Katia transferred the call to Major D'Angelo's office.

'Pronto, Major D'Angelo speaking.'

'Good morning Antonio. Alberto Luciani here. You may remember we met in the New Year, at Major Micozzi's retirement.'

'Yes, indeed. I trust you are well, Alberto?'

'Very well, thank you. Colonel Battista asked me to contact you. The body of a young boy has been recovered from the sea here in Pescara, currently in the morgue at Chieti hospital. We understand you are leading the search for a missing boy, and wonder if you would come to look at the victim in case he's your MP.'

D'Angelo wished people would refer to Giovanni by name, rather than simply Missing Person, but he decided that his pique was more to do with the fear that Giovanni might be lying in a numbered compartment of a cold morgue, rather than any indifference on the part of Captain Luciani.

'I'll go and check, Alberto. Thank you for the information.'

'I'm going there myself, so shall we meet in reception in, say, forty-five minutes' time?'

D'Angelo looked at his watch. 'Yes, fine. I'll see you there.'

The proposed schedule meant that D'Angelo needed to leave almost straight away. He enjoyed a clear run to Chieti hospital, choosing to take the road past Buccianico which by-passed the town of Chieti, and he actually arrived a few minutes ahead of Captain Luciani. Both officers were familiar with the layout of the large teaching hospital, and despite D'Angelo's obvious tension over the forthcoming task, they chatted as they made their way to the morgue, where they found Dottore Sibona.

'I've been called in to perform the autopsy,' he explained.

'One of the consequences of fame,' re-joined Luciani, 'you don't get a moment's peace.' He winked conspiratorially at D'Angelo, trying to lighten the senior officer's sense of foreboding.

The three men watched as a morgue attendant pulled open the sliding drawer holding the boy who had been recovered from the sea the previous day. D'Angelo exhaled as he felt the tension ease from his taut limbs. One never quite got used to seeing death, especially when the victim was so young, but the instant D'Angelo could see that the boy in front of him wasn't Giovanni Mirelti, he couldn't help feeling a sense of relief.

The effect on Captain Luciani was quite the opposite. He stared wide-eyed and his body tensed.

'I saw him just two days ago,' he said in almost disbelief. D'Angelo and Sibona both turned to look at him.

'I swear,' he continued, as though to quell their perceived doubt, 'it's him, it's the boy I saw coming out of the hotel by the beach.'

Twenty

Leaving Dottore Sibona to carry out the post-mortem, D'Angelo and Luciani went to the in-house café where staff and visitors jostled for mid-morning refreshments.

'I thought when I saw him being escorted from the hotel that there was something wrong,' said Luciani, still trying to come to terms with seeing the boy dead, 'but this… Christ.'

It seemed strange to D'Angelo, listening to a sophisticated Roman accent in this setting. He wondered what his colleagues in Rome had made of his own rural Abruzzese accent all those years ago. No doubt he had been the butt of quite a few jokes.

'Let's see what comes from Sibona's autopsy. The boy was killed just hours after you saw him. Perhaps the man who was with him is your perpetrator.'

They had managed to commandeer a recently-vacated table in a corner near the cold drinks dispenser to sit down with their coffee.

'I'll get one of the IT gurus to help me try and put together an image of what he looked like. I need to go and interview the staff at that hotel as well. And…'

'What?'

'There was a government minister at the hotel. That's why I was there, to pick him up. He came out of the building just minutes after the boy and man.'

Luciani stared at his empty espresso cup, seemingly lost in thought.

'I'd better be getting back,' said D'Angelo, breaking the reverie. 'Are you waiting here for the autopsy report?'

'What? Oh, I almost forgot. Colonel Battista wants us to go and see him once we're done here. Sorry Antonio. His Master's Voice.'

* * *

Teresa Rossi had driven back for a wander around the Alnwick Gardens and a half-decent coffee, before returning to the entrance for Roseturn Farm shortly after eleven o'clock. The farm track, or 'Private Road' as it was called, was at least half a kilometre long, and ended in a circular driveway around a raised rose-bed in front of a large stone farmhouse with slate roof. Teresa parked her hired Fiesta alongside a silver Jaguar and a blue Range Rover. To the side of the farmhouse was a long, low outbuilding, where a man was tying a horse's leading rein to a metal ring embedded in the stone wall. He turned to look as Teresa approached him. He was tall, Teresa guessed around one metre eighty-five, well-built, with swept-back light brown hair and a strong, square-jawed face. The jodhpurs and riding boots he was wearing accentuated his muscular legs.

'Mister Renson? Mister Martin Renson?'

'That's me. How can I help you?'

'My name is Teresa Rossi. Actually I'm Sergeant Teresa Rossi, a member of the Abruzzo carabinieri. I understand you own a property near the village of Montenero?'

'That's correct.'

'And you were staying at that property last week?'

'You're well-informed, Teresa Rossi.'

'We're currently conducting some enquiries in the vicinity of Montenero, and looking for potential witnesses. Did you speak to any of your neighbours while you were there?'

Renson rubbed his chin with his hand, eyes narrowed in thought.

'Did I speak to any of my neighbours. I'll have to think about who I spoke to and who I didn't. Can you ride a horse, Teresa?'

'I had lessons when I was younger. I think I can remember how to ride, yes.'

'I see you're wearing trousers and trainers. I'm about to take my hunter here for a blow. My wife's mare needs some exercise, do you fancy joining me for a hack? I can probably find you a pair of boots and a hard hat.'

Teresa was taken aback by the suggestion, but she hoped she might get some answers, or at least some indication of whether Renson could be involved in a kidnapping, so, needs must…

'Alright. But don't bother with the hat.'

'Fine. I'll just find you those boots, and if you can wait here while I fetch Candy from the paddock, we'll saddle them both up and get going.'

It took most of the time that Renson was bringing Candy the mare back to the stable block for Teresa to squeeze into the boots, which were at least a whole size too small. She hoped Renson possessed a boot remover she could use when they returned from the ride.

'She's three-quarter bred and quite frisky,' said Renson, as he gave the girth straps a final tighten, 'but she's very willing.'

While Renson went to mount his big seventeen-hand hunter, Teresa swung up into Candy's saddle. The mare immediately took several steps backwards, nodding her head up and down, then jerked round sideways. Teresa could feel the power and energy of her mount, like driving a Ferrari when you're used to a Fiat.

'Like I said, she can be a bit frisky, but show her who's boss, eh?' called Renson, a little too gleefully for Teresa's liking. She squeezed the mare's flanks and pulled quite hard on the rein with her right hand to get Candy pointing back the right way.

'What command do you use to get them moving?'

'Walk on,' replied Renson, as he came alongside.

Teresa began to feel quite elated as she walked her horse along the farm track, through a gate to the right which Renson managed to open and then close behind them while still in the saddle, then followed at a canter along a path that cut across a large field, green with a promising crop of winter barley. They slowed to a trot through a copse of mixed woodland before emerging the other side to a hill of open moorland. With minimal encouragement from Renson, his horse, followed closely by Candy, broke into a headlong gallop up the slope of the hill, causing a flock of sheep, with their sturdy-looking lambs, to scatter to a safe distance.

Teresa felt a rush of adrenaline, that strange combination of excitement and fear, when you dared yourself to go faster, yet were aware of the danger. Renson glanced round a couple of times, presumably to see if Teresa was still in the saddle. She felt the wind blowing in her face, but all she could hear was the thunder of hooves. Beyond Candy's outstretched neck and pricked ears, Teresa's focus of vision was the summit of the hill, and the massive hindquarters of Renson's hunter. She saw Renson start to pull on his reins, as the powerful horse's head lifted and his pace slowed, so Teresa followed suit, finding it took considerable strength on her part to bring her mare to a halt at the top of the rise.

'Do 'em good, nice run like that,' shouted Renson. Teresa's heart rate was beginning to slow as she wiped some mud from her cheek. What would D'Angelo think of this? "All in a day's work, Rossi," he would say.

They rode at a gentle canter down the far side of the hill towards a large area of undulating woodland. Entering the woods, they walked between trees for a short distance until they came to a raised track about two metres wide, which stretched into the distance to both left and right.

'An old railway line,' explained Renson, as he encouraged his horse up onto the track. 'It was closed more than fifty years ago, but with all the line and sleepers gone, it makes a damn good bridle path. This way,' he said, setting off to the right at a trot.

After riding for about a kilometre, Renson once again pulled up his horse, and this time dismounted. Teresa did likewise.

'I want to show you something,' said Renson, leading his horse through the trees to the left of the track. They came out of the wood to the edge of a huge, disused quarry, the lower part of which formed a small lake.

'Half of Alnwick and several places further afield were built with sandstone from here. It used to belong to our family until three generations ago. It's how we originally made our money. Now, you wanted to ask me something.'

Teresa started to feel a prickling on the back of her neck. This could all go badly wrong. They were in a remote spot, and nobody knew they were here. The tone of Renson's voice had changed, just in those last few words, and his face had lost its appearance of benign affability to become menacing, almost threatening. She was determined to try and keep things as light as possible.

'Do you know any of your neighbours in Montenero?'

'You mean the ones in those farmhouses, close to my place?'

'Yes.'

'Not really, no. There's a guy called Pietro who I've spoken to a couple of times. Can I ask why you want to know?'

'Just the other side of Pietro's house lives a man called Bruno, Bruno Mirelti. His wife's name is Anna. They have daughters called Felicita and Laura, and a young son called Giovanni. Do you know that family at all?'

'Can't say I do. I'm only there for holidays, and what with the language barrier...'

'Giovanni is eleven years old, small, dark-haired. Do you think you might have seen him near your house?'

'Nope. What's the point of all this?'

Teresa unzipped the pocket of her fleece jacket and brought out her phone.

'There's something I'd like you to have a look at,' she said, scrolling through the last few photos. She noted that there was no mobile signal, international roaming having previously transferred her onto O2 from TIM, her Italian network provider.

'Does this mean anything to you?' she asked, handing the phone to Renson.

'If I'm not very much mistaken, it's a receipt for some food items. Compulsory with every purchase in Italy, as you well know.' He offered the phone back to Teresa.

'Could you go to the next image.'

Renson swiped the screen and looked at the hand-written message.

'So? Pagare la prossima settimana. That's "to pay next week," isn't it? What's Mirelti?'

'Mirelti is Giovanni's family name, and that message is written on the back of the receipt. It was found in your house, and I wondered if you might be able to explain it?'

'You've been in my house? How dare you. I don't know who you really are, Ms "Rossi", but I'm guessing you're some sort of private snooper. Who's paying you? My wife, is it?'

He thrust the phone back to Teresa.

'I'm carabinieri Sergeant Rossi, Mister Renson, and I'm investigating the disappearance…'

'Bullshit. You're no more carabinieri than I am. You're a dirty little bitch of an investigator snooping into my private affairs.'

Teresa shifted her stance slightly, and made a quick

assessment. Renson was powerful, weighing in the region of a hundred kilos, maybe a little more. She worked out a three-move – no, it would have to be four – a four-move sequence to incapacitate him, put him down. She relaxed, then tensed, ready for combat. Pre-emptive would be good, but unfortunately she would have to wait for him to make the first move. She was glad she was wearing the boots.

'If you were a bloke, I'd beat seven shades of shit out of you and leave you down there,' snarled Renson, flicking his head towards the quarry, 'but as it is, this is what's going to happen,…'

Teresa went off 'red alert'.

'…we're going to ride back to my house,' he continued, grabbing hold of her upper arm and squeezing it, 'you're going to get in your car and drive away, and never come near me again. Do I make myself clear?'

Teresa wondered if his hand round her arm, possibly causing slight bruising, constituted an assault, for which retaliation could be justified. Probably not. Pity. She was enjoying the mental image of Renson rolling on the ground with a dislocated knee and excruciating pain in his crotch.

'You have stated your wish clearly,' replied Teresa non-committedly.

'Good.'

'Before we go, I need to, er – relieve myself.'

'Yes, I dare say you do,' smirked Renson, pleased he had given her a fright. 'Go on then, hurry.'

Teresa ran through the trees, towards higher ground. After about twenty-five metres she stopped and checked the signal on her phone. Still nothing. She ran on, still going uphill, then checked again. One bar. Hoping that would be sufficient, she sent a text message to Inspector Armstrong.

> 'Urgent. Pl ask yr coll at Alnwick to send
> officer to Renson home. Teresa R.'

She pocketed the phone, and ran back down to mount Candy for the homeward ride, unsurprisingly without a word spoken between herself and Renson. She held the mare back as much as possible, slowing the journey home. Once back at the stable, she deliberately fumbled the unsaddling of her horse, then made a pretence of trying to yank a boot off.

'I need a boot puller. It's too tight.'

Renson blew out through his nose in irritation, then stalked off to fetch the wooden device from his tack room. Teresa kept glancing anxiously down the drive, willing a police car to come. When Renson dropped the boot puller on the ground in front of her, Teresa heaved and strained to remove one boot, then took a rest before attempting the second.

'Hurry up,' growled Renson.

This was it. End game. It seemed Teresa's mission would fail. She could think of no more excuses for delay, she would have to return home to Abruzzo without any answers, a question mark still hanging over the bizarre note found in Renson's Montenero house. After struggling with the second boot for as long as possible, she eventually had to admit defeat, as she put her other trainer back on. Renson was standing, hands on hips, watching her, as Teresa walked to her car and unlocked it. Another glance down the drive where she saw, in gaps between the trees and bushes, glimpses of a car, similar to her own, but coloured blue and white, coming towards the farm. She turned to look at Renson, unable to conceal a smile of triumph. He had now also spotted the approaching police car, watching it arrive with a look of puzzlement on his face.

The young constable parked, put his cap on, and walked to where Teresa had re-joined Renson near the stable block.

'Sorry to trouble you Mister Renson, sir,' said the constable awkwardly, 'I've been asked to attend a possible incident here.'

He looked from Renson to Teresa, expecting to hear a reason for his instruction to come.

'I wish to report verbal and physical threats against me by this man,' said Teresa, pointing to Renson.

'And you are, Ma'am?'

'I am Sergeant Teresa Rossi of the Italian carabinieri.'

Renson was staring at her, dumbfounded.

'You wish to lodge a formal complaint,' he mumbled, reluctantly fishing a small notepad put of his pocket.

'It depends,' she replied, looking at Renson. There was a short silence.

'I don't think that will be necessary, Dave,' said Renson. 'Let me speak to the lady in private for a few moments.'

Looking somewhat relieved, the police constable retreated towards his car.

'Do I press charges, or do I get some answers?'

'I have no idea what that note is about,' said Renson defensively, 'but I'll hazard a guess.'

He looked towards the policeman, judging him to be safely out of earshot.

'My wife is devoted to her law career, and spends an increasing amount of time in South Africa. She hardly ever comes out to our holiday home in Abruzzo any more. I've begun having a – relationship – with a young lady out there. It's most likely that she inadvertently left that receipt at my house.'

'What is the name of this lady?'

'Look, she's married, I'm married. Can't we just leave it at that?'

'I'm afraid not, Mister Renson. We're investigating what could be a serious crime, we have to make checks. Her name please?'

Renson looked at the ground, struggling with the consequences one way or the other. Teresa glanced meaningfully in the direction of the young policeman, hovering near his patrol car.

'Her name is Bianca. Bianca di Lello. She owns a business in Montenero, a butcher's shop. I presume either she owes Mirelti some money, or the other way round. That'll be all there is to it, I promise you.'

'Thank you, Mister Renson. If we're satisfied with the outcome of our enquiries, you won't be hearing from us again.'

'For what it's worth, I apologise for my behaviour. I thought you were… anyway, I've probably had punishment enough. I'm President of the rugby club, you see, and Dave Ormerod over there is our first fifteen full-back.'

Twenty-One

D'Angelo cursed himself for a fool as he ended the call and closed his phone. Teresa had rung him just as he was entering the basement-level car park beneath Pescara carabinieri headquarters, and what she had told him now seemed so obvious. Why hadn't he seen it for himself? The attractive woman with long chestnut hair at Renson's house had been Bianca di Lello. Renson's explanation about the written note also made sense : the butcher either owed money to Mirelti the rabbit-breeding farmer, or Mirelti the customer owed money to the butcher. Bianca would have to be spoken to, of course, just to be sure, but this episode now looked like only one more leaf blowing in the breeze. D'Angelo stopped on the small landing between the two flights of stairs and leaned back into the corner. He was still in that position when Captain Luciani caught up with him.

'Are you alright, Antonio?'

'Yes, fine. Thinking, that's all. Come on, onward and upward, as they say.'

Luciani grinned as the two of them continued on their way to Colonel Battista's office.

'Enter,' called Battista, after the customary pause. 'Ah, Antonio, pleasure to see you. You are well, I trust?'

'So far, so good, Edoardo, and yourself?'

'Fine, thank you.'

D'Angelo noticed a familiar-looking file, and his spirits sank. Battista was sitting behind his desk and indicated the two visitor chairs, but D'Angelo had walked straight round the desk, his arm outstretched, giving Battista no option but to stand and shake D'Angelo's hand. The close proximity of the two men emphasised D'Angelo's overwhelming physical presence.

'So,' said Battista, when they had settled in their respective seats, 'the boy in the hospital morgue, is he your missing person?'

'It's not Giovanni Mirelti, no, but…'

He put his hand towards Luciani, prompting the captain to impart his news.

'I saw that boy coming out of the hotel where I was collecting Signore Sartolini, the government minister, you may remember, Colonel.'

'You're quite sure it's the same boy?'

'Certain, Colonel.'

Battista drummed his fingers on the desk. Another murder to investigate, resources getting stretched.

'Dottore Sibona is doing a PM,' continued Luciani, 'he's going to contact me as soon as possible with preliminary results.'

'We'll decide how to follow up once you've heard from Sibona. In the meantime, Captain, you may return to your desk while we're waiting.'

D'Angelo and Luciani made brief eye contact as the captain stood and left the office.

'So, Antonio,' said Battista, shuffling a few papers

around on his desk, 'you haven't found the missing boy yet.'

'I'm afraid not.'

'How long has he been gone?'

'Four days.'

'Four. Mm. Little chance of finding him alive, then.'

'I like to think there's always hope, but…'

D'Angelo put his hand out, palm upwards, suggesting the colonel's prognosis may well be correct.

'I'll leave it to your judgement as to how long you keep looking.'

'Yes, Edoardo. Thank you.'

Battista slid the blue personnel file in front of him with an air of mystery, as though it was a playing card that could be the ace of diamonds, or could be the two of spades. He adjusted his wire-frame spectacles, then opened the file, making a pretence of reading details that he already knew.

'You've held the rank of major for a long time now,' he said, without looking up.

Understatement of the year, thought D'Angelo. He had once been one of the youngest majors on the force, now he's nearing fifty. Overlooked for promotion time after time. He didn't respond.

'You're a good officer, Antonio, but you're ten years my senior in age, and I'll be looking for my next move within three years.'

'You've done very well, Edoardo.'

'Dammit, Antonio, that's not what I'm getting at,' snapped Battista, now looking up from the file. 'Perhaps you've been held back by some, – some historical issues, but if you're going to move ahead, you should be here, where the action is. We've got some big cases live right now. You can't spend the rest of your career out among the olive pickers and fig eaters.'

D'Angelo kept his mouth clamped tightly shut. He knew that if he responded to that remark, it would end up as another adverse comment in the blue file.

'I'm not saying a missing contadino boy isn't important, of course it is, but here we're up against gangs.'

Battista stood and began walking around the room.

'Drugs, people traffickers. There are two nasty murders currently under investigation, and another from the end of last year that's still not closed. We need our best people working on the big cases.'

Battista returned to his seat at the desk and started turning pages in the file.

'As a young major, you were selected to spend some time on secondment to the New York Police Department, a prestigious posting.'

Here we go again, thought D'Angelo. Always, eventually, it comes back to this. It was a statement, not a question. He said nothing.

'Your assignment terminated prematurely. Tell me what happened.'

'I believe the facts are summarised in the file there.'

'Yes, the "facts" are written up here, but facts don't necessarily tell the whole story. You have a reputation for choosing not to wear a firearm. Would I be right in thinking that your reluctance to bear a weapon came from your experience in New York? I want to hear your side of it, Antonio. I need to understand.'

D'Angelo took his eyes off Battista and looked towards

the window. He rubbed his mouth with his finger, thinking, remembering. Should his lips remain sealed, condemning himself by silence, or does he try once again to convince a senior officer that his actions were justified.

'It was a long time ago,' said D'Angelo, his lame opening remark simply a ploy to buy some time. Battista sat watching him, silent and still, with his chin resting on steepled fingers, like a preying mantis sizing up a potential victim.

'I was there because they wanted to boost the numbers of Hispanics and Italian speakers in their police department.'

'And because of your experience in narcotics,' said Battista, tapping the file with his finger.

'It played a part,' agreed D'Angelo. 'There was a big problem with drugs in New York, but there were communities within the city that the police found difficulty in reaching. Back then, heroin was the biggest problem, a dirty drug at the best of times, but even worse when there were contaminated batches on the streets. These bad batches seemed to be particularly prevalent among the Latino population. Considerable numbers of kids were dying, and pushers were operating freely, in the streets, round the tenements. I was teamed up with a Puerto Rican detective, DS Valeria Martinez, with a brief to try and disrupt operations at the user end, while others concentrated on finding the bosses, some of them mafia. Some days I felt like we were actually making a difference, other times it felt about as useful as attacking a bear with a twig. We had been keeping an eye on a young gang member for several days. He was only seventeen, but he had been suspected of supplying drugs since he was about thirteen, and had risen to be quite a hot-shot, doing the rounds in his own exclusive patch in a brand new Mercedes. He also happened to be Puerto Rican. I knew we had to actually catch him in the act of doing a deal to hope for any chance of a prosecution, so we got in position ahead of him at one of his regular supply locations, myself close to where he would park his car, Valeria waiting twenty metres away to pick up the customer with their newly-bought fix. She knew what to look for. The heroin was hidden inside little rubber toy Disney characters. Can you imagine it – Mickey Mouse and Goofy models stuffed with heroin. On cue, our suspect turned up, and before long I saw him pass a small coloured object out of the car window to his customer, in exchange for a wad of dollar notes. I moved quickly. I pulled open the door and grabbed the key from the ignition, while at the same time telling the guy that I was a police officer and that I was arresting him on suspicion of supplying a class 'A' drug, and would he please step out of the car.'

'But he didn't.'

'No. Something about his demeanour immediately put me on my guard. He sat there, looking at me, then his eyes flicked down to the dashboard. His girlfriend was alongside him in the passenger seat, and I heard her say "no, Juan". I put my hand around the grip of my revolver and drew it a little way out of its holster. For a few seconds, nobody moved, then his hand flew to the glove compartment, he pulled open the flap, and grabbed the butt of a hand gun. I had fractions of a second to make a decision. I was a sitting duck. The thirty-eight calibre Ruger Service-Six revolver was a powerful weapon, and very unforgiving at close quarters. The explosions as I fired two rounds into his chest were deafening inside the car, then the girl was screaming, her hands over her ears.'

Battista turned over a few pages of the file in front of him.

'But that sequence of events was disputed, by both the girl and Detective Sergeant Martinez.'

D'Angelo remained stony-faced.

'I had to go and file a report straight away, then I was interviewed by three senior officers, but I regarded it all as routine, steps that must be taken if a member of the public is shot and killed by a police officer. I managed to get an hour or two of sleep, but when I returned the following morning, I was in for a big shock. I had seen the girl and Martinez being ushered into an interview room, which I had thought rather strange, but when I went back in front of the three-man panel, I was asked to hand over my badge and sidearm, and was told I was suspended from duty pending further enquiries. It was a complete hammer blow.'

'Detective Sergeant Martinez corroborated the girl's account of what happened.'

'Martinez had run to the car when I fired the two shots. The girl had got out of the car and was yelling at DS Martinez in Spanish. I was busy calling the station to report the incident and alerting them to the fact that there had been a fatality. I assumed Martinez was trying to calm the girl down until other officers and an ambulance arrived.'

'But perhaps that wasn't the case after all.'

'The girl had said that Juan was only trying to get his driver's licence out of the glove compartment when I shot him. The handgun he had been reaching for was on the floor well, under the steering column. The girl said I had pulled the gun out myself and dropped it on the floor.'

'And Martinez believed her?'

'I have always supposed that Valeria Martinez said what she believed to be the truth. She had nothing whatsoever to gain by doing otherwise, but she had been too far away to see what had actually happened. I think she convinced herself that she had witnessed what the girl told her.'

'And you were the one who was discredited.'

'Perhaps because I was the outsider, a hot-blooded Italian. Over the next few days, the boy, Juan, was described as being popular, God-fearing, who loved his Mom, although he might have been coerced by some bad men into selling a few drugs. I was painted as an out-of-control trigger-happy foreign cop.'

'But there was no trial.'

'No, they didn't want a trial. A quick dismissal and getting me out of the country was the preferred solution. They checked for my fingerprints on the boy's gun, but of course didn't find any. "Inconclusive", they called it.'

'But in Martinez's statement, they said you had…'

Battista scanned through the sheet of paper on the file

'… "boasted you would take this grubby little pusher off the streets," and I quote.'

'I never denied I wanted him locked up, taken out of circulation. In that moment when I was trying to arrest him, it was going to be him or me, and I made my decision. The irony is that he would probably have killed Valeria Martinez as well, then gone to ground, but…'

Battista slowly closed the file.

'I'm going to add some notes in here,' he said, tapping the file. 'Now while you're here, you can have your medical check and do a routine firearms proficiency test.'

Battista's internal phone bleeped.

'One minute, Antonio.' He picked up the phone. 'Battista.'

He listened for a few moments. 'Very well, Luciani, bring him to my office when he arrives.'

He replaced the handset.

'Dottore Sibona is coming here in person to give his report on the dead boy. You may be interested to hear what he has to say, so please join us when you're through with the MO and firearms examiner.'

Twenty-Two

'You don't smoke, then.'

'No.'

'Drink?'

'I take it you mean alcohol?'

The elderly, silver-haired man looked up with rheumy eyes, pale and placid behind bi-focal lenses.

'Beer when the weather's hot. Wine…'

'There's nothing wrong with a glass or two of wine a day.'

D'Angelo kept quiet. If the Medical Officer had asked him how much wine he drank, he would have been truthful and owned up to three or four glasses most evenings. Sometimes a whole litre. He wasn't going to dispute that one or two glasses would be fine, if only he could stick to that limit. Along with most of his colleagues, D'Angelo thought these medical checks were a waste of time, especially with this particular MO. He had retired as a civilian doctor, though no-one was sure if that was due to age or ineptitude, and then he had become Medical Officer in the carabinieri. Even the civilian family doctors played a very dubious role, being well paid for merely referring patients to an appropriate specialist department in a hospital, causing chaos in the hospitals. Everyone knew the system was faulty, especially the heads of A&E in the hospitals, but like so many faulty systems in Italy, nobody seemed to be able to find a solution. People just shrugged their shoulders and said "that's the way it is. It's Italy". D'Angelo accepted that routine medical checks were compulsory, so he remained acquiescent.

'Eyesight good, hearing fine. Any problem with bowel movements?' asked the MO in box-ticking mode.

'Most days I just sit in a small room and think about it, then let the matter drop.'

The MO's face screwed up in puzzlement at that remark, but ticked the box anyway.

'You're not in bad shape for your age, Major D'Angelo, but you're a bit overweight. How much exercise do you do?'

'Well, perhaps not quite as much as I…'

'Half an hour a day. That's what you need. Half an hour of exercise every day. Right, well I'm signing you fit for duty, please would you sign the forms here, here, here, here, and here.'

D'Angelo wondered if Italy used more paper than the rest of the world put together. He sometimes imagined great swathes of Nordic forest with signs saying : "Reserved for Italian Use."

D'Angelo stopped on his way to the underground small arms firing range and held his hand out in front of him. Good. Nice and steady. This shouldn't take too long. Part of the cost-cutting regime meant that fewer rounds were allowed to be used in practise these days. Most of the weapons training was carried out now using a simulator, but it was common knowledge that nothing could realistically replicate live firing. D'Angelo was already wondering why he had been summoned to hear the results of Sibona's post mortem as he rang the bell to alert WO Di Prinzio of his presence. The sound-proofed door was opened by the burly, bearded Warrant Officer, Marksman, First Class, ear defenders slung around his powerful bull neck.

'Good to see you again, Major,' came the deep, gruff voice. 'Entering the regional competition again this year?' said Di Prinzio, ushering D'Angelo inside and closing the door behind him.

'I'll give it some thought. Perhaps I should let someone else have a chance of winning.'

D'Angelo stepped forward to the firing point, where a Beretta pistol and pair of ear defenders were laid out on the table in front of him. He looked down the range to the big bank of sand at the far end before di Prinzio dimmed the lights, while leaving spotlights on the target area in front of the wall of sand.

'Three standard targets, three rounds in each target,' was the instruction as D'Angelo slid the safety catch off and donned his ear defenders. He balanced himself in his preferred position, known as the Fighting Stance, his right leg behind the left, knees slightly bent. He steadied his breathing and waited. With a click, the target bar swivelled to reveal three roundel targets, a black bull at the centre of each. It took just four seconds for D'Angelo to fire nine rounds. Di Prinzio pressed a button, and accompanied by a whirring sound, the three targets were carried on a wire to where he stood behind the firing point.

'Five bulls, three inners, one outer. Not bad in the time.'

D'Angelo smiled to himself. If anyone else had achieved that result, Di Prinzio would have acclaimed it as exceptional.

'The next test is slightly different. Fire rapidly if you assess the target to be appropriate.'

Six rounds left, thought D'Angelo. With two rounds per target, that means there will be three "appropriate" targets. His breathing wasn't quite so steady, and he felt the beginning of slight damp under his arms.

The wait for the first target seemed to take an eternity. D'Angelo felt the mounting pressure of nervous tension, as for the third or fourth time he moved his feet slightly to make sure he was properly balanced. Suddenly a life-sized photographic image appeared in front of him, a little to left of centre. A girl, attractive, blonde hair – looking at him down the sights of an AK47 rifle. D'Angelo rapidly fired two bullets into her forehead and she disappeared from view. Four rounds left, so two further genuine targets. He waited, wanting to cough to clear his throat, but didn't dare lose concentration. Another image flashed up, this time to the right. A man, angry-looking, snarling through a thick, dark beard, the ragged end of his turban hanging at the side of his face. He had one hand in front of him, finger pointing aggressively, the other arm by his side. D'Angelo lowered his Beretta. That could so easily have been a bad mistake. He felt the sweat under his arms and down his back. Next up was a woman, middle-aged, her hair tied back close to her head, mouth open as if yelling, her right arm poised to hurl something. The wooden shaft of a protest banner. Not appropriate.

D'Angelo quickly wiped the damp palm of his hand on his trouser leg, before taking a fresh grip on the butt of his pistol in time for the next image. A teenage boy, calm, clear-eyed, but with a machine pistol held with both hands in a firing position. A fraction of a second's pause, then two more rounds, one to the head, the second in the heart.

D'Angelo swallowed hard, and blinked some sweat from his eye. Don't mess up now, he told himself. Directly in front of him, a young black man, bandanna round his head, waving a red plastic pistol. Still one to go, thought D'Angelo. He waited. A smartly-dressed man, wearing jacket and tie, he could be a lawyer or bank manager. Not this one. But at stomach height he's holding – what – a heavy-calibre revolver. In quick succession, D'Angelo fired the first shot into the man's arm, try to stop his finger squeezing on the trigger, then the final bullet in his clip into the man's shoulder. Target disabled, not able to fire his weapon.

D'Angelo slid the safety catch back on and placed the empty pistol back on the table, along with his ear defenders. Di Prinzio put the lights back on full and finished scribbling some notes on his clipboard.

'Good work, Major. Your reactions aren't at all bad for...'

'Don't say it. For a man of my age. I hear that phrase too often these days.'

'Anything you want to say? About the test, I mean.'

'I take it I've passed?'

'Colonel Battista wants my immediate assessment, but between you and me, you don't need to worry. And incidentally, I was going to say your size. Usually the smaller, more compact shooters have fractionally quicker movements than the big'uns, but you seem to be an exception. All the best, Major. See you at the competition.'

D'Angelo knew what that had all been about, and he was thinking about the implications as he headed back up to Battista's office. The bastard wanted to know if he still had the bottle to shoot a boy, albeit a dangerous one brandishing a lethal weapon. Perhaps he should just jack it all in, retire from the force. He'd qualify for a pretty decent pension, and with his end of service pay-off, he could buy more land to add substantially to his Montepulciano grape production. What would Adriana think of that idea? Not a lot, but her level of disappointment couldn't go much higher than it is right now. 'First I'll find out what happened to Giovanni Mirelti,' thought D'Angelo to himself as he neared Battista's office, 'then hand in my resignation.'

Captain Luciani and Dottore Sibona were approaching from the other direction, so D'Angelo waited for them in the corridor in order that all three could enter the office together.

Battista had been studying some data on his computer screen, which he minimised as the three visitors settled in front of his desk.

'We're extremely honoured that you have come in person to present your findings, Dottore Sibona,' said Battista, with more than a hint of sarcasm. 'Please tell us what you have discovered.'

'The honour is all mine,' retorted Sibona. 'What I have for you at this stage comes with the usual caveats – it'll be two or three days before the labs come back with their analysis of the samples we've sent them, but I know how impatient you always are for something quickly to be working on.'

'I understand. Your speed is much appreciated.'

'I'll give you the facts along with what I offer as my interpretation of those facts. First, the easy bit. The boy was asphyxiated with the use of a length of cord, almost certainly the same cord that was tied to his ankle with a lump of stone attached to the other end.'

'So he was killed before he entered the water?'

'Precisely. There was minimal seawater in his lungs, so drowning didn't play a part in his death. Next fact, he had been circumcised, unusual among Italian boys unless they are Jewish or Muslim, so let's take a small leap of conjecture and say he probably belonged to one of those two faiths. Next, the skin between his first and second toes on both feet was hardened, consistent with wearing open sandals held in place by, say, leather or cord thongs between the toes on a year-round basis. In other words, not just wearing flip-flops for visits to the beach in summer, but living somewhere with a climate suitable for permanently using open sandals. Next, his diet. I've sent samples of stomach content for more detailed analysis, but I can tell you that his most recent meal appears to comprise food types mainly associated with the Middle East or North Africa – lentils, chick peas, falafel. In general, he wasn't particularly well-nourished, and also what little dentistry he had received wasn't of a high standard. All in all, gentlemen, my best guess, and it is only a guess, is that the boy was from one of the North African countries – Egypt, perhaps, or Algeria or Libya.'

'That's interesting, Sibona, very interesting. It does indeed give us a possible avenue to explore, bearing in mind the boy still hasn't been reported missing. What I suggest we do is...'

'I haven't quite finished, Colonel.'

'My apologies. Please, continue.'

'There are indications that he had recently been involved in sexual activity.'

'Sexual activity?'

'To put it somewhat indelicately, he had been buggered.'

'Good God. You said recently?'

'No chance of DNA evidence I'm afraid, the seawater has done a good job of washing away any possible traces of semen, but it would have happened some time in the forty-eight hours before his death.'

'It had already been determined that the boy died some time on Wednesday evening,' said Luciani, 'so he was possibly raped on Tuesday, but most likely on Wednesday.'

'If it was rape,' said Battista.

'He was under age. I think we can call it rape.'

'Your reasoning is sound, Captain,' said Sibona. 'You chaps are clearly more than guns, fast cars and pretty uniforms these days.'

D'Angelo couldn't help smiling, but Battista remained impassive.

'I won't go into details of the recovery of the anal passage after such an event,' continued Sibona, 'but Captain Luciani is quite correct in his assessment. I would say there's a seventy-five percent chance it happened on Wednesday, and twenty-five percent chance it was Tuesday.'

'So we have a possible motive for his murder. Thank you, Dottore, your visit has been very enlightening.'

'My pleasure, Colonel, and now, if you'll excuse me, I believe some students will be waiting for me down at the university.'

'Captain,' said Battista, when Sibona had left the room, 'liaise with the Communications Officer, and try to get as much coverage as possible in the local media – television and radio news networks, newspapers, the lot – you know what's wanted : we're looking for any information about a boy, aged about fourteen, possibly of North African origin, whose body was recovered from the sea on Thursday morning. Don't mention the strangulation at this stage. If anyone might be able to shed any light on who he might be, etcetera etcetera.'

'Yes, Colonel. There's another line of enquiry that I believe we should also look into.'

'What's that, Captain?'

'As I mentioned earlier, Colonel, deputy minister Sartolini came out of the hotel minutes after I saw the boy, so perhaps he saw him as well. I think we should ask him, it's worth checking.'

'Too speculative, Captain. No, we don't need to bother the deputy minister.'

'But Colonel, Signore, he may be a material witness, surely it wouldn't hurt to…'

'There are rumours, interrupted Battista, 'that Signore Sartolini may be seeking a move to the Ministry of the Interior. If those rumours are correct, and the move takes place, then Signore Sartolini will be our boss, yours and mine, Captain Luciani. No, we leave the deputy minister out of this business, and that's final.'

Luciani looked as though he had a lot more to say on the matter, and D'Angelo could see in the captain's face a sense of outrage that they would not be speaking to Sartolini. D'Angelo felt sure that Luciani wanted to speak to the deputy minister as more than a mere witness, and he wondered if Battista felt likewise. Could all three of them be complicit in obstructing the course of justice, he wondered.

'Yes, Colonel,' said Luciani, clearly accepting with difficulty his superior officer's command, and moving to stand up. 'I shall go and see the Communications Officer.'

'I would like you to stay a few minutes longer,' said Battista, putting his hand out to indicate that the captain should remain seated. 'Has any further progress been made in the investigation in the case of the drug gang murder?'

'Regretfully not, Colonel,' replied Luciani sheepishly. 'One of the officers assisting me on that case was assigned to Operation Seahawk, and people are reluctant to give any...'

'Yes, yes. I understand. No information coming from the streets. The warning to whoever thinks of defying the drug boss was very clear. Very clear indeed. Antonio, I presume you're familiar with the murder case we're talking about?'

'I've read the briefing notes, yes, Edoardo. It sounded – interesting. Some vicious retribution going on.'

'We're way beyond a few chancers and small-time crooks selling pills and dope to students. The drugs market is big business now, here in Pescara, in fact in the whole of Abruzzo. The stakes are high, and we've got a fight on our hands to try and contain it. You will have read in the notes that the boss is thought to be based outside Pescara itself?'

'This guy calling himself Rex? Yes, I noticed that.'

'Captain Luciani here has made a good start into the murder investigation, but I want to widen the scope of the enquiry, give it more prominence. You have experience in the drugs field, so I'm minded to appoint you as SIO for the case. I take it the MO gave you a clean bill of health?'

'He's not predicting my imminent demise.'

'And before you came in, I was looking at the results of your weapons test, kindly e-mailed to me by Warrant Officer Di Prinzio. Your score was very commendable.'

'Thank you, Edoardo.'

'Good. Luciani will be your 2IC, and we'll keep intact the team that's been working on it so far. You'll obviously have access to everything on file that was not included in the briefing notes. Do either of you have anything you wish to ask me or comment on?'

'No.'

'No, Colonel.'

'Right, let's get cracking. Good luck, gentlemen.'

Twenty-Three

D'Angelo woke on Saturday morning to a day that had changed its mood, much as he himself had done. The temperature had dropped, with fine, steady rain falling from a leaden sky. His sudden appointment as Senior Investigating Officer in what is currently Abruzzo's most high-profile murder enquiry was as puzzling as it was unexpected. Was Battista giving him a vote of confidence, a sign that the slate had been wiped clean of the NYPD blemish, and that his career could now be back on track, or was it a trap, an expectation of very visible failure, a guarantee of continued future rejection. He looked out at the front garden, where seats beneath a large sun-shading umbrella were now dripping with rainwater. Changing fortunes all round, he thought, as he poured himself a cup of the coffee he had made, while waiting for Adrianna and the girls to troop downstairs.

'I hope you don't mind, I want to take the Toyota today,' he said, when his wife appeared.

'Why, where are you going?'

'To the office. I've arranged… I've got a lot on, I'm going to be working right over the weekend.'

For a reason that D'Angelo couldn't properly quantify,

he didn't want to say that he had arranged to meet Teresa Rossi on her return from England.

'That means I'll be stuck at home if Marianna wants to take the Fiat.'

'No problem, Mamma,' said twenty year-old Marianna, without lifting her eyes from the screen of her iPhone. 'I'll get Patrizio to come and collect me if I want to go out anywhere.'

D'Angelo could see the annoyance expressed on his wife's face, but her eldest daughter's offer meant she had access to transport if she needed it, so there was little point in raising any further objection.

D'Angelo retrieved the carrier bag containing the dead buzzard from their chest freezer, and felt a guilty sense of release as he left the family home to drive through the rain on his familiar journey to work. He even sang along to a couple of former hits that were played on the car radio, until a break for the local news caused him to turn the volume up higher and to listen in grim silence as the announcer read the report about a mystery boy, about fourteen years old and of possible North African descent, found dead in the sea near Pescara. Does anyone out there know who he might be?

D'Angelo arrived at the carabinieri station ahead of Teresa Rossi, so he spent the time reading once again the file notes relating to 'Rex' and the Pescara drug gang murder, having already spent an hour the previous evening familiarising himself with the case, highlighting certain key facts. But when he heard Rossi arrive, he put the 'Rex' file to one side and concentrated his thoughts on Giovanni Mirelti and plans for the day ahead.

'Good morning Teresa, welcome back. Good journey?'

Emboldened by D'Angelo's use of her first name, and the 'off-duty' feel of working at a weekend, Rossi hoped she could get away with reciprocating the informal mode of greeting.

'Good morning Antonio,' she responded, with a big smile and all the confidence she could muster. 'I could certainly get used to this travel by private jet. I felt like a celebrity. Going back to Ryanair is going to be a massive downer, mixing with all the hoi polloi.'

'You got on alright with Giuseppe Damiano and his daughter?'

'They're really nice. No airs and graces for being wealthy business magnates, they treated me like an equal.'

D'Angelo smiled, knowing full well that Giuseppe and Patrizia Damiano would have warmed to Teresa Rossi's bright and effervescent personality. Teresa for her part decided it was diplomatic to avoid mentioning that she had been offered a job as Head of Security at the Damiano factory, an offer she had neither accepted nor declined.

'I'm sorry I sent you off on a wild goose chase, I suppose it was always something of a long shot. I should have thought of Bianca di Lello, though, as being Renson's chestnut lady friend and author of that note.'

'Renson got a bit nasty, he thought I was a private detective sent by his wife.'

'You did well, Teresa, I'm proud of you. Now, let's think about today's plan of action.'

'Is that the buzzard in the carrier bag? Can I have a look at it?'

Teresa was fascinated by the sharp-clawed, hook-billed

bird. She had seen them flying around, but never at close quarters before.

'You think now is the right time to bring in Pietro Fiorito?' she asked, dropping the still-frozen buzzard back in the carrier bag.

'There's a key to this puzzle somewhere out there, and I want to know if Fiorito and son hold that key. I would like to get them as much off-guard as possible, and they won't be expecting us to turn up at a weekend. Any small advantage is going to help. Now, you will need to be alone with Leonardo at some stage, and I think I know how we can fix that. Can you print off some documents that I can ask Pietro to sign.'

'What sort of documents?'

'Anything – insurance, health and safety, traffic regulations. About five pages, each requiring two signatures, should do the trick.'

'But why would he sign insurance documents?'

'Make sure they've been printed in a small font, and don't worry, I'll shred them all afterwards. You know what it's like, we're asked to sign documents all the time, but we never read what we're signing, even at the bank or the hospital. Everyone's so used to it that they just sign where they're told.'

'And what if he *does* see what he's signing?'

'I'll simply say we've made a mistake and given him the wrong forms. It should still give you enough time for a little tete-a-tete with young Leo.'

It didn't take long for Rossi to print off the forms D'Angelo wanted, so they were soon on their way to fetch Pietro and Leonardo Fiorito, with Rossi at the wheel of the 159.

'You said you wanted to speak to Bianca di Lello, and that we should call in to see Giovanni's family,' said Rossi, as they neared Montenero.

'Afterwards, when we bring the Fioritos back. Hopefully, we might be a bit further forward by then and have something to tell them.'

They found Pietro and Leo in a shed, cutting bamboo stakes for the tomato crop, and keeping out of the rain.

'What do you mean, you want us to come with you to be interviewed? Are you arresting us?'

'No, Pietro, we're asking you to voluntarily answer some questions.'

'And if I refuse?'

'Then we *will* arrest you. Easier all round if you come of your own free will.'

Pietro snorted and threw the bill-hook he was using to the ground in disgust.

'The boy stays with me at all times, alright? He gets easily confused, so I don't want you using your tricks to get him to say things he doesn't mean. Come on, Leo, we'll have to go and tell Mamma that we're going with these nice people for a while.'

* * *

There was a buzz of excitement at Pescara headquarters. A call had come from Ortona hospital with the news that Lieutenant Giorgio Alberico had regained consciousness, and furthermore that he had spoken a few words and seems to be coherent. Still weak, they stressed, but the doctor was very hopeful that Giorgio had not suffered any serious brain damage, despite the fractured skull. The feel-good effect of that news spread rapidly among the carabinieri on duty over the weekend, and especially for Olivia Macrini. A sergeant had been sent to the hospital to wait until Alberico was able to talk about events on Thursday night, hopefully to fill in the missing gaps – whether a boat-load of illegal immigrants had actually landed, and if so, what had become of them. There was also the question of why Alberico had failed to radio for help, and how he came to be lying badly injured at the dockside. For Olivia, it was just the feeling of elation knowing that her friend and colleague would recover, and that hopefully, in a few weeks' time, he would be back on duty.

Amidst all the excitement, she suddenly realised that Fabio wouldn't yet have heard the good news, so she rang his mobile number. Strangely, he didn't answer. Her call timed out and went to messaging service. That's very unlike Fabio, she thought, he usually can't bear to be out of reach of his beloved mobile.

For the next ten minutes, Olivia continued with her tedious job of the morning, which was to complete the reports still outstanding from the previous five days, then tried Fabio's number again. Still no response. She started feeling anxious. Unable to concentrate any longer on her clerical work, Olivia knew that no-one would begrudge her wanting to visit Giorgio Alberico in hospital, so she decided she would go to his apartment and collect Fabio, then the two of them could go to Ortona together, this time hopefully in a much better frame of mind.

She parked at the side of the road opposite the apartment block and went in the main communal entrance, then up the double flight of stairs to apartment number five. She rang the doorbell and waited, but Fabio didn't come to the door. She had heard the chimes coming from inside, so she knew the bell was working. She rang again. Still no response. Tentatively, Olivia tried the door handle and found, to her surprise that the door was not locked. She pushed it open a little way, calling Fabio's name. She walked inside the apartment a few paces and called again, then reeled slightly as she caught a familiar smell. Familiar, yet she had only smelt it once before. It was one of those smells that once experienced, never forgotten, a foul concoction of vomit, urine and alcohol that meant, to Olivia, only one thing. Her heart was pounding and her temples throbbing as she moved further into the apartment, on into the living room, where the stench was so bad that she clasped her hand over her face. *Ashes to ashes.* 'Oh God, Fabio,' she cried, the sight still a shock despite knowing what she would find. The once handsome, vibrant young man was slumped on the settee, vomit drying on his beard and down the front of his shirt, a damp stain on his trousers. *Dust to dust.* The skin on his face was like paper, and the once sparkling eyes were staring upwards, glazed and lifeless. On the floor in front of him a whisky bottle lay on its side, a little of the liquid forming a pool beneath the neck, and by his feet, to the left, the dead cat, Mitzi, was curled in her bed as if asleep. On the coffee table, Olivia could see two brown pharmaceutical bottles, both empty. Jumping into her mind, unbidden and unwelcome, was the stupid, puerile rhyme that the officer who had accompanied her the previous time recounted in a sing-song voice : *ashes to ashes, dust to dust, if the pills don't get you, the alcohol must.*

She jumped as a mobile phone ringtone broke the eerie silence. Following the direction of the sound, Olivia found Fabio's phone on the kitchen worktop, and she opened its leather-clad cover. Unrecognized caller. She left it to ring out and went back to the living room, where she opened a window to try and reduce the foul, clinging stench. She then took out her phone to call for an ambulance, as well as a Scene of Crime Unit just in case it wasn't suicide, even though she knew without any real doubt that it was. She jumped again when her own phone sprang into life with an incoming call. Another unrecognized caller.

'Hello,' she said, accepting the call.

'Hi Livvy, it's me.' Weak and muffled, but unmistakably the voice of Giorgio Alberico. 'The sergeant here has let me use his phone. I've been trying to call Fabs, but can't get hold of him for some reason. Can you see if you can contact him, and tell him he can come and visit? I'm in Ortona hospital, as you probably know.'

'Hi Giorgio. I need to sort a few things, then I'm coming straight in to see you. You get some rest now, OK?'

With a cold, sick feeling in the pit of her stomach, dreading the forthcoming encounter, Olivia made the other necessary calls.

* * *

Maria looked at the clock on the wall behind the counter and moved nearer to one of the speakers, the one in a corner near the electronic games and gadgets section of Party Pieces

For All, the shop where she had been sent to work. The final few outro chords were playing of the last number before a local news bulletin. She had already heard the news three times this morning on the in-store radio, but she needed to hear it again to be certain she heard it correctly. It had now dropped down to third item on the news, but as she listened intently, with a mixture of shock and disbelief, there was no doubting what the announcer had read. Young boy, North African descent, found dead in the sea, and they don't know who he is. The same icy shiver ran through her body, just like the first three times she had heard the broadcast. She was sure it was the same boy that she had seen being kept in the small bedroom at the house where she was herself boarded. Perhaps it had been an accident. Maybe he had gone for a swim and drowned, or fallen off the sea wall and banged his head. She had been through the possibilities over and over again in her mind, and still thought the idea of it having been an accident was highly unlikely, especially given how closely supervised they all were. Unless he had run away. Just as unlikely. The more she thought about it, the more convinced she became that the boy had been deliberately killed.

Maria couldn't turn a blind eye, pretend she knew nothing about him. She would have to ring that number, 112, the number she saw on a police car. It might get her into trouble, but it was a risk she had to take. Her grandma would say she was doing the right thing. They would take her back to the house at one o'clock when the shop closed for lunch, then she would use her secret mobile phone to call the police.

Twenty-Four

'I'm going to ask you again, Pietro, where were you and what were you doing on Monday evening?'

D'Angelo, with Teresa Rossi sitting next to him, glared across the table at Pietro Fiorito. Leo was sitting next to his father, mouth open.

'Wait a minute, I remember now. It was the night of the cup semi-final replay, right? Roma against Juventus. I went down to the bar to watch the match there.'

'Will anyone remember seeing you?'

'They certainly will,' chuckled Pietro. 'All the sad old bastards down there were supporting Roma. They should follow a decent club like Juve. I cheered and clapped when we scored, and I got a lot of glum looks and mumbled comments. Ha! We showed 'em.'

'From what I remember,' interjected Rossi, 'the goal was scored mid-way through the second half. Perhaps you weren't there during the first half.'

'Course I was there. Might have missed the first five or ten minutes, but I watched the game alright.'

'We'll have to check, of course,' said D'Angelo. 'Oh, Mannaggia! I forgot. I need to get you to sign the form saying you were here of your own free will, not under arrest and not under duress. Can you just pop out to reception with me for a moment and I'll find the form for you.'

'Leo,' said Pietro, getting to his feet.

'No, don't worry, Leo doesn't need to sign. You can sign on behalf of both of you,' said D'Angelo, ushering Pietro through the door.

'I think it might have stopped raining,' said Teresa to Leo, when the others had left the room.

He looked at her with a blank expression.

'Was it just you who saw the Mirelti boy on Monday evening, or did your papa see him as well?'

'Papa saw him too.'

'What did he say to him?'

There was a long pause. Come on, come on, thought Teresa, willing herself to stay relaxed.

'The Mirelti boy, he was cross. Shouted at me because I shot a bird.'

'Was this the bird you shot, Leo?' asked Teresa, lifting the bag containing the buzzard from beneath the table. Leo nodded, staring at the buzzard with wide eyes.

'Did he say horrid things to you?'

Leo nodded again. 'He attacked me.'

'Attacked you? What did you do?'

'That's when Papa came. He pushed the boy away.'

'Was the boy hurt?'

Leo shook his head. 'He ran away.'

'Back home?'

'No, the other way. Towards the road.'

Teresa could hear D'Angelo talking loudly in the corridor, giving due notice that he and Pietro were returning from the form-signing. D'Angelo opened the door to allow Pietro back inside.

'Teresa, can you just come and counter-sign the forms for me. We'll be back in a moment, Pietro.'

'What the hell is that?' said Pietro, pointing at the buzzard.

'Oh, that. It's the bird that Leo shot on Monday, isn't it Leo? We'll talk about it in a minute.'

'Yes, Giovanni was definitely at their place on Monday evening,' said Teresa excitedly as soon as she and D'Angelo were out in the reception area. 'Giovanni kicked off because he saw Leo shoot the buzzard. Pietro pushed him away, doubtless yelled at him to bugger off, then Giovanni ran towards the road.'

'Towards the road?' D'Angelo looked up at the ceiling, rubbing his chin. 'Why to the road, not home? Come on, let's have another go. Well done, by the way. Smart work, Teresa.'

D'Angelo and Rossi settled themselves back into the chairs opposite a sombre-looking Pietro and his puzzled son.

'So as I was saying, Leo shot that bird on Monday evening when he was supposedly chasing wild boar off your land. I know that, because I collected it from the butcher's on Tuesday. You see, Leo took it to Bianca di Lello, hoping it would earn him a few euros, sort of chicken in the sky, eh Leo? I've been holding back on you with another little snippet, Pietro. We have a witness statement that puts Giovanni Mirelti near your property at somewhere around seven thirty to seven forty-five on Monday evening. Do you have any comment you wish to make on that?'

Pietro exhaled loudly, and put his hands down flat on the table.

'OK, the boy was on my land.'

'On Monday evening?'

'Yes, on Monday evening.'

'Why didn't you tell us that before?'

'Because he had gone missing and you would have blamed me. I know how you stitch up people like us.'

'So tell us what happened.'

Pietro chewed his lip. 'The Mirelti boy saw Leo shoot that bird, and he went berserk. He was screaming and shouting, yelling that the buzzard was one of a pair about to nest, then he went for Leo with his fists and feet. Like a crazy thing, he was.'

'Did you intervene?'

'I told him to clear off.'

'Did you assault him?'

'No. I might have given him a little shove, that's all.'

'Was he hurt?'

'No way. He jumped up and ran off. And the blood on him was nothing to do with me.'

'Blood?'

'On his legs. He was scratched and his shorts were torn. He looked like he had been in a fight with a cat.'

'And he was still upset?'

'He was snivelling, yes.'

'Snivelling?'

'Well, crying.'

'So he was very distressed.'

'I suppose so. Because of that thing, I presume,' said Pietro, nodding towards the buzzard.

'And where did he run?'

'Out towards the road.'

'Not home?'

'Not home, no. Into the road.'

'Did you see him again after that?'

'No, that was the last I saw of him.'

'Think carefully, Pietro. You went out later to the bar to watch the football. Are you quite sure you didn't see Giovanni Mirelti after you saw him running from your property towards the road?'

'I swear it.'

'You lied before.'

'I'm not lying now. What I've just told you is the absolute truth.'

'Thank you for your co-operation, Signori,' said D'Angelo, as he dropped Pietro and Leonardo off back at their house. 'By the way, Leo, I should be able to let you have your shotgun back soon. But no out of season shooting, understood?'

Leo grunted a response, but Pietro stomped off in silence.

'Did you believe him?' asked Teresa, as D'Angelo drove the short distance to the Mirelti residence.

'Yes, strangely enough I did. What we need to figure out now is why Giovanni ran off, angry and upset, in the opposite direction to his home.'

The rain had stopped, but it had left a sparkle on the canopy of bright new leaves, and added vibrancy to the fresh growth of grass. The blooms on rose bushes planted at the ends of vine rows seemed to have been imbued with extra colour, as were the clumps of semi-wild irises, some of them white, some purple.

'I'll leave you at the Mirelti place while I go and see Bianca di Lello, assuming she works on a Saturday,' said D'Angelo.

'It's her own business, she'll be working alright. I'll see you later.'

Teresa had the familiar feeling of trepidation as she walked alone towards the house, but then noticed a man, quite youthful-looking, on the roof of one of the outbuildings. She decided to go and investigate, and on approaching the building she saw Bruno at the foot of a ladder.

'Good morning Bruno. Doing some repairs?'

'Rain's been getting in to the rabbit shed.'

'Is that your eldest son up there?'

'Francesco, yes. Come over from America for a few days. Adjusting some of the tiles to try and stop the rain. Any news on the youngest?'

'Well, there's been a bit of a development. I was hoping to talk to you all, keep you informed on what's happening.'

'You haven't found him then?'

'I'm afraid not. Not yet.'

'Go and tell that lot. They won't be bothered whether I'm there or not. It's like I don't exist any more.'

'I'm sure that's just the stress of the situation, Bruno. It's a difficult time for everyone.'

'It'll be a difficult time for me alright if I don't get this roof fixed, 'cos I'll be sleeping out here in the rabbit shed soon enough. Either that, or I'll be away back to my own village. Not wanted here now.'

Teresa couldn't think of anything she could say, so she gently touched his arm and walked away.

The front door of the house, usually open, was now closed, so Teresa had to knock and wait for Felicita to let her in.

'Hello, Felicita, not with Mario today?'

Felicita looked down at the floor, but said nothing. Teresa glanced quickly at Felicita's left hand, and noticed that the engagement ring was missing.

'Mamma, it's Teresa.'

'Who?'

'Teresa. From the carabinieri.'

'Oh.'

Teresa looked along to the far end of the room from where she had heard the voice, but could see no-one.

'Come,' said Felicita, leading the way.

Perched in one of the ancient easy chairs that were clustered in front of the television was Anna, or a version of Anna that seemed to have aged about ten years since Teresa last saw her. Her cheeks were hollow and lined, her red-dyed hair straggly, and her eyes dull.

'What is it?' she said brusquely.

'Hello Anna. I just wanted to let you know what's happening.'

'We can't even give him a decent funeral.'

'We're still looking, Anna. Is Laura at home today?'

'Down at the orto, picking broad beans.'

'Have you got a good crop?'

'Good enough.'

'I'd quite like Laura to hear the developments. Your orto is along the road, isn't it? I'll walk down there and meet her, then when we come back, we can all sit down and have a chat.'

'As you like.'

Teresa took a big breath of fresh air as she stepped back out of the gloomy house. God, she thought, the whole family are now victims.

D'Angelo did indeed find Bianca di Lello working in her butcher's shop. Teresa was right, people work hard if they're working for themselves. No wonder so many businesses are run solely by family members, thought D'Angelo. In fact Bianca wasn't alone behind the marble counter today, because she was being helped by a boy who looked no older than fifteen or sixteen. When she saw D'Angelo enter the premises, Bianca finished serving her customer and told the boy to continue serving on his own, then walked round to meet the carabinieri officer.

'Shall we talk outside?' he suggested.

They went out to stand by the wall at the edge of the apron area in front of the shop.

'My nephew,' said Bianca. 'He helps out when he's not at school. I think he wants to learn the business so that he might be able to take over from me one day.'

'How is he doing?'

'Not bad at all. I'll probably take him on full time when he finishes his education. So, Major D'Angelo, you've discovered my little secret.'

'He's told you then?'

'Yes, rang me yesterday. Sergeant Rossi is one of yours, I presume?'

'She's good. I'll be pushing her for promotion.'

'Major D'Angelo... I can't keep calling you Major D'Angelo. What's your first name?'

'Antonio.'

'I imagine your friends call you Tonio?'

'Some do, yes.'

'I shall call you Anton instead. That alright?'

'That's fine – Bianca.'

'I take it you want me to confirm what Martin told your Sergeant Rossi?'

D'Angelo took out his wallet and removed the receipt he had found at Martin Renson's house.

'I would like you to confirm that this is your writing.'

'Ah, the incriminating evidence. Yes, Anton, that's one of my little reminder notes to myself.'

'A reminder to what?'

'To pay for some rabbits Signore Mirelti had supplied. Always rabbits with Mirelti. No wild boar or buzzy birds.'

'Buzzards.'

'Buzzards. That's right.' Bianca laughed, and D'Angelo noticed how her face lit up.

'So you'll continue seeing Signore Renson?'

'I suppose so. I don't know.' Bianca leaned back against the wall, her face suddenly showing a serious expression. 'I married in haste, and too young. Nicolo, that's my husband, was working and earning money, so I thought that by marrying him I was gaining freedom and excitement, but I just swapped *my* Mamma and *her* rules for *his* Mamma and *her* rules. I found I was even less free than before.'

'Any children?'

'No – fortunately. I don't think Nicolo would have been very interested in children, and he's away for long periods with his trips to Germany, so all the responsibility would have fallen on my shoulders.'

'And his Mamma's.'

'And his Mamma's, true. The thing I had going with Martin Renson made me feel young and alive again, it boosted my confidence and gave me a sense of excitement – at least while it was secret. Maybe I'll feel differently now it's not a secret any more.'

'We're very discrete. We won't go shouting it abroad. But anyway, you've also got this – your business.'

Bianca turned and looked at her shop.

'Yes, I've got this. It gives me some independence. Nicolo has never shown any interest in it, thinks it's a waste of time.'

'You don't own it jointly, then?'

'No, I started it with a loan from my parents.'

'You seem to be doing alright.'

'I get by.' She smiled, showing a perfect row of bright white teeth, her eyes sparkling. A strand of her hair had fallen free and was waving in the gentle breeze, its chestnut colour illuminated by the sunlight. D'Angelo found himself wanting to tuck the stray strand back in place, then hold his hand against her face, keep it there. He felt a jolt like an electric charge in his crotch, and realised he was jealous of Martin Renson.

'You won't be pressing charges then, Anton?' she said, with her head to one side and a pert look on her face.

'Not just yet, Bianca,' smiled D'Angelo.

At that moment, Bianca's nephew came to the door of the shop.

'Zia Bianca, have we got any beef sirloin?'

'I'll be there in a minute, Luca.'

The boy disappeared back inside the shop.

'So we're parting as friends, Anton?'

'Of course.'

'Farewell then,' she said, leaning towards him. He accepted the invitation, and kissed her cheek. It felt soft and warm, and D'Angelo sensed again her delicate perfume, realising it reminded him of Renson's pillow. He put his hand on her waist as she turned, and he kissed her other cheek.

'I might have to call by some time to check that you're not selling any illegal meat.'

Bianca took a biro from the top pocket of her white coat and wrote a mobile number on the shop receipt that was still in her hand.

'Better come on a Wednesday. It's closed on Wednesdays, so there won't be any customers to contend with. Let me know in advance when you're coming,' she said, handing D'Angelo the receipt, 'so I can come and unlock the door and you can make your – little inspection.'

She smiled again, and walked to the door. Just before going inside, she turned and gave D'Angelo a wave, as if aware he was still watching her.

He wandered to his car in a haze of confusion, unsure if her last comment was a *double entendre*, or merely wishful thinking on his part.

Teresa, meanwhile, had managed to find Laura, who had almost filled two plastic carrier bags with broad bean pods.

'Let me take one of those,' offered Teresa as they started walking back towards the house. 'Lovely looking beans you've got here Laura.'

'Have some if you want.'

Teresa popped open a pod and put the first juicy bean into her mouth.

'Mm, delicious.'

'They always seem to taste sweeter somehow after the rain.'

The two of them walked in silence for a while, both eating a pod of beans.

'Felicita isn't with Mario today,' said Teresa, flinging the empty bean pod onto the verge.

'I think it might be off,' replied Laura, discarding her own empty pod. 'She hasn't really said anything, but I get the impression they've had a big argument, and she's not seeing him any more.'

They both decided to have a second pod of beans.

'I'm a bit worried about your Mamma,' said Teresa. 'She doesn't look well. Do you think she might need to see a doctor?'

Laura was staring down at the road in front of her as she walked.

'Don't know. She doesn't go to the doctor much.'

Teresa glanced sideways at her companion. So young, she thought, to be going through all this.

'It must be nice seeing Francesco again.'

'He won't be here long. His life's in America now.'

Once back at the house, they deposited the bags of broad beans near the sink in the small kitchen area, then Teresa suggested they all sit in the easy chairs close to Anna.

'Do you want me to fetch Nonna from her room?' asked Laura.

'No, I don't think we need trouble her. Perhaps you could pass on the information to her later. The first thing I want to tell you is that, for a while, we had our suspicions about the Englishman who has a holiday home here.'

'Signore Renson?'

'Renson, that's right. We thought it strange that he went back to England on Monday night, so soon after – you know. I went to England to speak to him, and now we're completely discounting him from our enquiries, so if you happen to hear any rumours about him, ignore them.'

'Mamma says it's them you should be talking to,' said Anna, pointing at the wall in the direction of the next-door neighbour Fiorito's house.

'Well, we've done just that, Anna. We took Pietro and Leonardo to the station this morning. What we found out was that Leo shot a bird, a buzzard, on Monday evening. Now, you told us that Giovanni went out to watch the buzzards, and we know how fond he is of all the wild animals and birds. It seems he saw Leo shoot one of them, which naturally made him very angry and upset. You mentioned, Laura, that Giovanni can be quite fiery if something bad happens, and Leo told us that Giovanni attacked him.'

'That's it then,' said Anna, 'that young ne'er-do-well turned his gun on our little Giovanni.'

'Apparently not, Anna. The father, Pietro, came out and pushed Giovanni away, then Giovanni ran out into the road, and that was the last they saw of him.'

'So they say.'

'We think they're telling the truth this time. Pietro also mentioned that Giovanni had scratched and bloody legs, and that his shorts were torn. Do you know if that happened before or after he left the house?'

Anna, Felicita and Laura looked at one another with quizzical expressions.

'None of us noticed,' said Anna, 'but it wasn't unusual for him to get scratched when he was out looking for things.'

Silence descended on the room.

'Perhaps when Giovanni ran out into the road, a car hit him,' suggested Laura, 'or one of those crazy delivery vans, then the driver panicked, hid him in the boot or back of the van, and dumped him in some remote spot.'

Anna gasped and put her hand over her mouth.

'That's feasible, of course,' agreed Teresa. 'It's a quiet road, and a driver doing such a thing would be very unlikely to be seen by anyone. We're keeping all possibilities open at the moment.'

All four of them turned their heads at the sound of a vehicle braking sharply and a car door being slammed shut. Padre Falcone was jogging as fast as he could manage towards their front door, a newspaper flapping in his hand. He banged on the door and opened it.

'Permesso,' he called, gasping for breath, 'can I come in?'

Anna, Felicita, Laura and Teresa all jumped up in astonishment.

'They've found him, they've found your Giovanni,' he shouted. He waddled to the pine table and spread his newspaper out. 'He's not alive, I'm sorry to tell you,' he blurted, hurriedly crossing himself twice, 'but now we can give him a Christian funeral, send his dear young soul to heaven, praise be to God.'

The four women crowded round him to look at his copy of the Abruzzo Times.

'They found him drowned in the sea at Pescara. They thought he might be from North Africa, and guessed his age at – let me see – about fourteen, but they're mistaken, it must be your Giovanni.'

'In the sea? At Pescara?' said Anna incredulously.

'I don't think we should jump too quickly to any conclusions,' said Teresa.

'But don't you see,' continued the priest, refusing to be distracted, and tapping the newspaper with a podgy finger, 'nobody knows who the little chap is. We'll have to go and tell them, and bring him home where he belongs. I'll do a lovely service for you Anna, really I will.'

'But why would he have been at Pescara? And in the sea?'

Speculation came to a halt as they heard another car arrive outside, and Laura went to open the front door.

'It's Major D'Angelo.'

'Let's see what he thinks about this.'

'Look, here,' said Padre Falcone, guiding D'Angelo over to the table. 'See, here in the newspaper, a boy found in Pescara, it must be Giovanni.'

D'Angelo glanced at the report and pulled his lips tightly together, making a sharp line of his mouth, as five pairs of eyes looked at him for a reaction.

'I don't know whether you will think it good news or not,' said D'Angelo quietly, 'but I saw this boy at the hospital morgue yesterday, and he definitely isn't Giovanni.'

Twenty-Five

Maria's hands were shaking as she scrabbled through the clothes in her small locker in the bedroom she shared with four other girls. Two of the girls were on kitchen duty, helping prepare lunch, while the other two were lying listlessly on their iron-framed beds. Maria doubted if the other girls would report her, but she didn't want to take any chances, so she glanced furtively behind her while her hand was closed around the small black mobile phone that had been hidden among her clean underwear. Satisfied that neither girl was paying her any attention, she slipped the phone into the pocket of her jeans, which thankfully were loose-fitting enough to conceal the hidden treasure. She crept onto her bed where she lay curled in a foetal position, waiting anxiously for the bell to announce lunch.

At last, the clanging bell announced that food was ready, which for Maria and the other Asian girls would comprise a version of South-East Asian cooking. It was a surprising, if not slightly bizarre, favour afforded to the girls, that they were given food more akin to that of their homeland rather than unfamiliar Italian fare. Perhaps the house manager thought they would be violently ill if they attempted to eat pasta or pizza, just as Italians wouldn't dream of eating non-Italian food.

Maria's room-mates rose from their beds and walked zombie-like towards the kitchen, with Maria following a few steps behind. Ironically, her stomach was so knotted with tension that she actually felt the pain that she was readying herself to sham.

As usual, the girls ate in silence, supervised by the house manager, but after just a few mouthfuls of her bowl of Bun cha, Maria clutched her stomach and groaned in agony.

'I must go to the bathroom, very urgent,' she wailed, walking doubled-up towards the door. Both the house manager and the cook dreaded any sickness among the girls. It would mean time lost from their work duties, and that would greatly displease Mister Lau.

'Go then,' said the house manager, 'but come back here as quickly as you can.'

As soon as she was away from the kitchen and out of sight, Maria dashed to the toilet and locked herself in, then turned the tap of the hand basin on full and opened the window, hoping any extra noise would disguise the sound of her voice, should anyone come snooping. Leaning out of the window to make her call, she dialled 112, and tried to calm her breathing so that she would be able to talk quietly but clearly. The call was answered almost immediately.

'Please give your name and the purpose of your call.'

'Maria,' she gasped, 'my name's Maria. I'm calling about the boy, the one in the news.'

'Do you mean the boy who was recovered from the sea?'

'Yes.'

'Do you think you know who he is?'

'Sort of. I think I know where he was staying before he was – I think he might have been killed.'

There was a pause.

'Please, I have to hurry, I can't talk for long.'

'Where are you calling from, Maria?'

She suddenly realised she didn't know the address of the house.

'I don't know – I can't tell you. I think I might have to go.'

'Please keep the call open, Maria. I'm going to transfer you to another officer.'

There was a click and another silence, as the carabinieri operator rang through to Operations.

'I've got someone on hold who might help ID the boy. Who's on operational duty today?'

'Captain Luciani, on 317.'

'Got that.' Luciani's phone buzzed.

'Luciani speaking.'

'Captain Luciani, I've got someone called Maria, sounds quite young, might be able to identify the dead boy.'

'Put her through.' Another click. 'Hello, this is Alberto Luciani here. Is that Maria?'

'Yes.' She started sobbing, overcome with the tension of the situation. Her thumb was poised above the 'end call' button of her phone.

'Did you see about the boy in the newspaper?'

'I heard on the news.'

'What can you tell me about him, Maria?'

'I saw him. He was at the house where I am. I saw him on – I think it was Thursday.'

'Where is your house, Maria?'

'I don't know.' Maria was crying again. 'I have to go now.'

'Wait just a moment, Maria. Do you go to school?'

'I work in a shop.'

'Which shop?'

'Party Pieces For All. Next to a bookshop.'

'Is the shop open this afternoon?'

'Yes.'

'Will you be working there this afternoon?'

'Yes.'

'Can you get away from the shop for a while, a drinks break or something?'

'No, can't leave shop. They're very strict.'

Luciani was puzzled. She sounded more like a slave than a shop assistant. Then it dawned on him. She *was* a slave.

'This is what I want you to do, Maria. What time does the shop open?'

'Half past two.'

'Alright, soon after it opens, I'll come in. I'll be in uniform. Drop something, anything, close to me, and apologise. Can you do that?'

'I think so, yes.'

'Well done Maria. I'll see you later.'

Maria stuffed the phone back in her pocket, washed her face and turned the tap off, then flushed the toilet. Tentatively, she unlocked and opened the door, relieved to find no-one outside, then crept back into the kitchen to finish her bowl of Bun cha in silence, wondering what the afternoon would bring.

At two forty, Luciani parked a few doors away from Party Pieces For All, and walked back to the shop. Once inside the brightly-lit emporium, he went to the till, where he was confronted by a fierce-looking Chinese lady.

'Sorry, Signora,' he said, 'routine check. You're one of the few shops open at this time, so...' He gave an apologetic shrug, his hands palm-upwards in the air. 'Just want to make sure you're giving a receipt with every purchase, in accordance with the law. As you know, under the Finance Act of...'

He stopped mid-sentence as Maria dropped a fluffy toy near his feet.

'Sorry, Signore,' she said, and started to walk away.

'You, Signorina, can you come back here a minute please?'

Maria stood meekly in front of him as Captain Luciani ostentatiously scrolled through some images on his phone until he found the one he wanted, then held it in front of him, looking from the screen to Maria.

'I have reason to believe you were involved in a theft from Comfy-Feet shoe shop on the fourteenth of April. I require you to come with me for possible identification by the shop owner. You are not required to say anything that may prejudice you at this stage.'

'No, officer,' said the Chinese lady behind the till, 'you must have made a mistake, she can't, she doesn't...'

'Very sorry, Signora, you just don't always know what these youngsters get up to when they leave work. Come along, Signorina, with me if you don't mind.'

'Well done, Maria, you're a clever girl,' said Luciani quietly as he escorted her to the patrol car. He opened the back door of the Alfa Romeo, and made a point of making sure she didn't bump her head as she climbed in. Luciani slid into the driver's seat and turned to speak to Maria.

'Am I right in thinking you're being held against your will?'

Maria appeared close to tears as she sat looking down at her finger nail, which she was clicking with her thumb nail, but saying nothing.

'Have you ever been to a gelateria?'

She shook her head.

'I know where you can get the best ice cream in Pescara, maybe the whole of Abruzzo. Let's go and have an ice cream, what do you think, Maria?'

She looked into Luciani's kind-looking face and nodded.

Luciani drove through a series of back streets until they ended up close to the lido.

'Here we are, Gelateria Ranieri.'

Luciani noticed how Maria looked around her as though seeking danger as they walked the few metres from the parked car to the ice cream parlour, then how she scanned the faces of the gelateria's other customers once they were inside.

'Do you want your ice cream in a cone or a tub?'

'Cone please.'

'You can choose any three of those flavours you like from the trays behind the glass panel. They're all of them good. In here, they still make all their own ice creams, not stuff delivered from a factory up north somewhere.'

Maria picked Pecan, Cream with Strawberry, and Banana as the combination of flavours to go in her cone, while Luciani chose double Coffee and Chocolate, then he paid at the till, and brought the receipt back to the lady who was serving. Maria watched with interest as her three ice creams were scooped from the trays and squashed into her cone, and after waiting for Luciani to be served, they found a table right at the back of the parlour, where nobody could sit behind them.

'Is it good?' smiled Luciani, after Maria had tasted all three of her flavours.

For the first time since he had set eyes on her in the shop, Luciani saw Maria smile.

'Don't let it melt and drip, so keep licking while we talk. I want to help you if I can. I'm not here to cause you any trouble, what I really want to know is whatever information you can give me about the boy. But let's start with you. How did you come to be here in Pescara?'

Maria realised that once this policeman learned the truth about her, she would most likely be sent back home. But that didn't really matter any more. Her life in Vietnam was better than her miserable existence here in Italy.

'I come from Ho Chi Minh city in Vietnam. My father used to have a tuk-tuk – you know, one of those motorbike taxis. We weren't rich, but we weren't poor. One day, he was taking my mother to the market, but there was a bad accident, they were hit by a truck and both of them were killed.'

'I'm so sorry Maria.'

'It was four years ago it happened. My brother and I went to live with our nonna, but she doesn't have much money, it was very difficult for her to look after us. Then we got some money from the truck company, as compensation for my parents being killed.'

'That must have helped your nonna?'

'A man came to see her, a Chinese man, and he told her that the best thing to do with the money was to send me to Europe where I could get a job, earn a good wage. He said that the compensation money would run out one day, but income from a good job is for life.'

'So your nonna paid the Chinese man to bring you to Italy?'

'Yes. He said that he knew people here who could give me a job, and I would get a – what is it – identity card, then I could go wherever I like, get a different job somewhere else if I like.'

'Are they the people you work for in that shop?'

'They don't give me any money, they say the money I earn pays for my accommodation and my food. I haven't been able to send any money to my nonna.'

'And this house where you're living, that's where you saw the boy?'

'Yes. I heard the house manager and the cook lady say that he is a Muslim boy, from North Africa.'

'When you were brought here, how did you arrive?'

'I came with others in a boat, then we were put in one of those big boxes they use to take goods on ships.'

'A container?'

'Container, yes.'

'Then did they bring you to the house here in Pescara?'

'Not straight away. First we went to another house, near where the boat brought us.'

'Do you know where that house is?'

'No, but it's near the sea. And on one side of the house there's a railway line. I could hear the trains going past.'

'So it's near where the boat landed, between the sea and a railway line?'

'Yes.'

Maria had finished her ice cream, having just put the last bit of cone in her mouth.

'Do you want anything else, Maria? A drink, perhaps?'

'No, nothing else thank you.'

'The boy you saw at your house, did you see him a lot of times?'

'No, only about twice. I thought it was very strange he was there.'

'Why is that, Maria?'

'He was very young, I don't know what work he could have done. And all the rest of us in the house are girls, like in the other house, the ones who work in the casino.'

'Casino?'

'Yes, Signore Lau's casino. He says the best girls can go and work there, lots of privileges.'

'Do you all work for Signore Lau?'

'I think maybe he owns the shops as well.'

'There are other shops?'

'There are two other shops we sometimes have to go and work in, yes.'

'What do you think happened to the boy, Maria?'

'I think maybe they killed him, but I don't know why.'

'What makes you say he may have been killed?'

Maria bit her lip.

'We're not allowed to go out on our own. When we're taken to the shop, we go in a car. I'm sure there would have been somebody with the boy as well, so I don't see how he could have fallen in the sea without someone seeing him.

That makes me think he was pushed in deliberately.'

'That's very interesting, Maria. You mentioned that you were taken to the shop in a car. Do you know what sort of car it is?'

'No. It used to be a big black car, but it's a different one now. Sort of silver, and not so big.'

Luciani pictured in his mind the large black Citroen he had seen when he saw the boy coming out of the hotel Sabbia D'Or.

'You've been very helpful, Maria. Now, you said you didn't know the address of your house, but do you think you might be able to direct me there in the car?'

'I think so, yes, but we would have to start from the shop.'

'Alright, I'll drive back to the shop and we'll see how we get on.'

Maria ducked down below the car window as they drove past Party Pieces For All, but then she was able to give Luciani directions to the house, with only one wrong turn which was quickly corrected. Luciani noted the address as he drove slowly past, then went part of the way back to the shop before pulling up in a parking space.

'Maria, I'm going to take you back to work and tell your boss that I made a mistake, and you're not wanted for shoplifting after all. You've been extremely brave, and I want you to continue being brave for a little longer. Very early tomorrow morning, some of my colleagues will come to your house and they will take everyone who's living there to another building so that we can search the premises.'

Luciani reached for his wallet and took out a card.

'This is my card,' he continued, giving it to Maria. 'When you are safe, and in a new building, show that card to someone in charge and ask them to ring me, then I will come and tell them how helpful you have been, and that we would now like to help you in return. Is that alright?'

Maria nodded, thinking she probably wouldn't be getting any sleep that night, she would instead be lying awake waiting for the early morning intrusion.

Twenty-Six

D'Angelo was once again alone in his office, staring at the picture of Rocky Marciano.

'Come on Rocco, give me some inspiration. Help me out here.'

Teresa Rossi had gone home in the 159 which, D'Angelo noted, she seemed to have commandeered for the time being. He hoped the Giulietta would soon be back from the repair workshop. He was trying to catch up with some of his work unconnected with either the Giovanni Mirelti case or the Pescara drug gang murder, but inevitably his thoughts kept wandering to one or other of those investigations. He knew that each day they remained unsolved, the greater the risk that they would end up as cold cases, gathering dust along with fading memories. He stood and walked over to the window to look out on the quiet weekend scene, when his phone rang with the 'home' ringtone. What now, he thought.

'Hello.'

'You're not driving are you?' asked his wife, Adriana.

'No,' said D'Angelo, thinking she was probably more concerned about possible damage to the car rather than any injury he might sustain if an accident should result in him talking on the phone while driving.

'Marianna and Patrizio have suggested we all go out for dinner this evening. They've booked a table for the five of us at that restaurant with the French-sounding name.'

'Le Clochard.'

'Yes, Le Clochard.'

'The tramp.'

'What?'

'That's what le clochard means in French. The tramp.'

'Oh. Anyway, I'm giving you plenty of notice so that you'll be home in good time. You won't be late, will you?'

'Presumably we won't be eating until eight-thirty or nine?'

'They've booked for eight o'clock, before it gets busy.'

'I'll be home in plenty of time, I promise.'

'Good. See you later then.'

'Bye.'

D'Angelo wondered if Patrizio wanted to celebrate his two hundredth patient or something. Nice enough chap, Patrizio, and dentists earn pretty decent money. Someone's got to fill or pull all those rotten teeth, but not something D'Angelo could imagine himself doing, however lucrative the reward. Still, probably better than being a chiropodist, he pondered to himself, dealing with smelly feet all day, or what about gynaecology? With that thought, D'Angelo re-awoke his computer screen and went back to the report he was trying to complete.

* * *

Colonel Battista was enduring a frustrating day. The morning rain had washed out his planned round with

Uberto, senior Notary at one of Abruzzo's oldest and most prestigious law firms, but Battista had stayed by himself at Miglianico golf club, having watched Uberto's maroon Maserati GranTurismo disappear towards the exit.

He had a coffee and read the newspaper, then decided, with the rain having eased to almost a drizzle, that he would have some practise shots on the driving range. He started with his trusty seven iron and, satisfied with how that was going, progressed up through the number four iron, number two wood, and finally his driver. That was working for him as well. Admittedly he sliced a couple, and hooked one badly enough for the ball to clear the safety fence and bounce off towards the car park. Good distance though. All in all, in this sort of form, he would have had a decent chance of beating Uberto today, and winning back his hundred euros. The rain finally stopped altogether, so Battista moved on to the practise green. It was his short game that so often let him down, so he took quite a few chip shots from various positions on the bank onto the green, then checked out his putting, trying to make allowance for how much slower the green was playing after that rain. He made up his mind that with or without a partner he would play at least nine holes, possibly the full eighteen, so he would have some lunch and then head out.

Ensconced at a table overlooking the portico, beyond which was the bright blue of the swimming pool, Battista ordered his favourite – ravioli filled with ricotta cheese and spinach with a butter and sage sauce.

'I'm sorry, Signore,' said the steward, 'that's not available today.'

With an exasperated sigh, Battista switched his order to tagliatelle with mushrooms and truffle.

'I'm very sorry, Signore, chef hasn't been able to get the truffle.'

'Mannaggia! What *is* available?'

'May I recommend the three-coloured fusilli with ricotta cheese, rocket and cherry tomatoes?'

'Go on then.'

'Any meat for secondo, Signore? We have some nice horse-meat today.'

'No secondo.'

'A quarter litre of wine?'

'Yes, but white, not red.'

Still miffed that he couldn't get his ravioli, but admitting grudgingly to himself that the fusilli pasta hadn't been at all bad, Battista changed into his golf shoes, but then found that his battery-powered trolley wasn't functioning. It was working fine when he brought it from his car to the clubhouse, but now it wouldn't budge. The ground was too wet for a buggy, so Battista grumpily dumped his golf bag into a club trolley and set off for the first tee. He should have known. Shots that worked well for him on the driving range didn't necessarily translate to the course, and his first tee shot flew straight into the stupid damn lake just a short distance in front of the tee, to the left of the fairway. The myriad croaking frogs seemed to be laughing at him, and a pair of moorhens scuttled into hiding in the thick bed of reeds, as though they were in mortal danger from his next shot. Even a passing crow cawed mockingly at the fun.

Fortunately, his two wood saw him safely onto the fairway, if a little too close for comfort on the right hand side, not far from the fence in front of some holiday villas, the roofs of which he had rattled a couple of times in the past. His follow-up shots weren't bad, but not good enough to prevent him going three over par. On the next two holes he managed a par and one over, then on the fourth his ball struck an olive tree and flew out of bounds, in fact it ended up in such thick undergrowth that it was another lost ball. Then his phone rang.

'Yes, Battista here.'

'Sorry to disturb you Colonel,' came Luciani's cultured Roman voice, 'but there's been a development in the people-smuggling case. I thought you might like to know.'

'I'm coming in. I'll be there in half an hour,' said Battista, already pushing his trolley back towards the clubhouse, not sorry for an excuse to abandon the course for the afternoon.

Luciani looked at his phone with a puzzled expression, not having expected that reaction from the colonel.

'Has this girl, what's her name? Maria – has she identified the victim?'

Colonel Battista's immediate immersion into work mode helped Luciani recover from the unusual sight of his boss in civvies, even though he still looked smart. Luciani wasn't sure about the yellow polo shirt, but each to their own. And then there was the lack of pique at coming straight in to HQ from the golf course.

'She's very young, I didn't want to put her through an ID of a cadaver, but I'm sure it's the same boy that she saw on Thursday.'

'So we have two important leads in our enquiry. Firstly, that the owner of the Blue Diamond club, Teng Lau, uses trafficked girls in his casino and shops, whether or not he's actually involved in the trafficking, and secondly, we have a rough idea where the migrants are held once they arrive.'

'Maria couldn't tell whether the truck had travelled north or south from where she had been landed, she felt disorientated in an enclosed container, but she did say it wasn't far.'

'We'll need a magistrate's warrant to search the casino, otherwise I imagine Lau will be smart enough to say we have no right to enter a legitimate business premises without legal authority, so get that organized. Have you thought about how we go about finding the half-way house?'

'I was hoping you might sanction the use of a helicopter, Colonel. We don't want to give warning to anyone who might still be at the house, but providing the pilot doesn't fly too low, he should have a good chance of spotting a likely premises.'

'What's he looking for?'

'We know the house is between the sea and the coastal railway line. I'm hoping the container lorry might still be parked outside. Unfortunately, the Port of Ortona vehicle movement records are very sloppy, so they haven't been a lot of help.'

'Has Lieutenant Alberico been able to give any assistance?'

'He seems to have had a relapse and is back under sedation, but while he was conscious, he told Sergeant Costa that he doesn't remember much about the incident, except that a boat with migrants on board definitely landed that night. It tied up in front of a container ship, and nearby there was a lorry with a container on its trailer.'

Battista stroked his chin in contemplation.

'I agree that it's worthwhile conducting a search, Captain. You have my authority to scramble a helicopter. Tell the pilot to try from ten kilometres south of Ortona to ten kilometres north.

'November Sierra Zero Four One to Control. Do you read me?'

'Control reading you loud and clear. Please state your current position, NS Four One.'

Battista and Luciani stopped pacing the floor of the communications room to look at the radio operator as she made contact with the helicopter pilot.

'Approaching ten KM south of Ortona, Control. Conditions excellent. Cloud cover has virtually disappeared, leaving clear visibility. There's a bit of high cloud, but I'm well below that. The sea's looking nice and blue and calm, by the way.'

'Any sign of potential target as yet?'

'Negative, Control. Too much distance at this point between railway line and sea. I'll keep you posted.'

Luciani looked round as a messenger came quietly into the room and handed Battista a folded piece of paper, before leaving just as unobtrusively. Battista unfolded the paper and read the message, then his mouth stretched in a mirthless smile.

'We can forget the casino visit.'

'Colonel?'

'The magistrate has refused a warrant, pending provision of proof beyond mere hearsay that a search of the premises is justified.'

'He what? We have a credible witness.'

'I strongly suspect, Captain, that the magistrate is a personal friend of Teng Lau's lawyer, who will by now have made a discrete phone call to his wealthy client, and all the young waitresses and escort girls will have been carefully spirited away.'

Luciani slammed his hand against the nearest wall, wondering how he was supposed to uphold the law in the face of so much corruption and collusion in high places. His thoughts were interrupted by the radio operator speaking again.

'Helicopter now one kilometre north of Ortona, ground target area looking more promising.'

'What assets have we got on the ground, Captain?' asked Battista.

'Two squad cars, one van. Five personnel in total, Colonel.'

'In Ortona?'

'Yes, Colonel.'

'Move them two kilometres north.'

Otto jumped in alarm when he heard the staccato hum of helicopter rotors, and hurried to the back door to peek outside. His breathing became steadier when he saw that it was flying quite high and following the shoreline, in which case it was more than likely taking tourists to view the trabbochi, massive fishing platforms unique to this stretch of Abruzzo's coast. He shut the door and fumbled for his cigarette packet to light up yet another cigarette, even though his mouth and throat were dry as sawdust, and his cough was getting worse.

Moments later, the comms room radio crackled once again into life, and the helicopter pilot's excited voice burst through to the operator's earphones.

'I have visual on your target, repeat I have your target. One hundred metres south of Tollo station, stand-alone three-storey house between railway line and beach, truck plus container parked at the rear of the property. You copy that?'

'Affirmative, NS Four One. Good work. Over.'

The radio operator called out the location details while Luciani was still talking to the convoy's lead driver, and before Otto had finished his cigarette, three carabinieri vehicles roared into position from the road, a Giulietta patrol car on each side of the house, a van sideways on at the front.

Battista and Luciani waited as patiently as possible for an on-site report, and before too long were rewarded with a call.

'We've detained a number of suspects, Colonel. We believe five are illegal immigrants and the sixth a trafficker. He appears to have a valid ID card in the name of Otto Brauscher.'

'Otto?'

'Yes, Colonel. He seems very edgy. Nervous as hell.'

'Let Border Security handle the illegals, but bring Otto here.'

'Understood, Colonel.'

'I'm going to interview Otto myself, and I want you in there with me, Luciani,' said Battista, with a look of cold determination on his face.

Luciani strode away from the communications room alongside the colonel, a spring in his step and glowing with pride.

Otto had been left sitting in the stark interview room for twenty minutes, his only company a silent and surly trooper standing in the 'at ease' position in front of the metal door. Everything Otto had been carrying in his pockets, including the wad of money and his cigarettes, and been taken from him and placed in a clear plastic bag. His belt and shoelaces had also been removed. When Battista and Luciani entered the room, the smell of sweat and fear was palpable as they sat at the table opposite Otto.

For fully ten seconds not a word was spoken while the two carabinieri officers stared at their prisoner. He looked a broken man. His thin brown hair was damp and matted, and beads of sweat glistened on his unshaven top lip. One of his eyes was twitching uncontrollably, and his clammy hands were in constant movement on the top of the table. His features were oddly distorted by the low-hanging light bulb in a white ceramic shade. Battista's eyes shifted to the identity card he was holding.

'Otto Giuseppe Brauscher.'

He looked up again to meet Otto's bloodshot eyes.

'Is that you?'

'Yes,' came the whispered reply.

'I beg your pardon?'

Otto cleared his throat. 'Yes,' he repeated, a little more audibly.

'How long have you been dealing drugs and smuggling illegal immigrants into the country, Otto?'

'No, not drugs. I've never done drugs.'

'You don't do drugs?'

'No, never.'

'You don't work for Rex then?' asked Luciani.

'Not Rex, no.'

There was another long silence while Luciani made a note in the file that was open in front of him.

'We'll keep to the people-smuggling then,' continued Battista. 'How many did you bring in this time?'

'Can I have a cigarette?'

'Not yet. We want some answers first.'

Battista slowly looked at Otto's identity card again.

'Brauscher. That doesn't sound like an Italian name.'

'My father was Austrian.'

'Would your father have been proud that his son was going to prison for people-trafficking?'

Otto suddenly looked as though he was close to tears.

'I just – I didn't think it was doing any harm.'

'But you knew you were committing an offence?'

'Someone I'd seen in the bar a few times said to me one day that I could earn extra money with my truck by taking a container a few kilometres from the port to Tollo station.'

'Easy work for good money, judging by the amount we found in your back pocket.'

'What we want to know,' interjected Luciani, 'is the name of your boss. Who pays you all that money for taking the immigrants to Tollo station?'

'I don't know any names.'

'You don't know who you're working for?'

'No.'

'Well who contacts you when you're needed to pick up a boat-load of illegal immigrants?' continued Battista.

'I get a text message.'

'What about the man in the bar. What's his name?'

'I didn't know his name. I haven't seen him for about four months.'

'What you're telling us is that you met some guy in a bar, you didn't know his name, but he persuaded you to commit a criminal act for which you would be handsomely paid. Is that about the gist of it?'

'It's not easy earning a living as a solo operator. His suggestion seemed too good an opportunity to miss. Can I have a cigarette now?'

'Not yet.'

Luciani picked up the thread again.

'You were asked before, how many people did you take to Tollo station on Thursday night?'

'About twenty-five.'

'Only five were found there. What happened to the other twenty?'

Otto shrugged. 'Taken away.'

'Did Teng Lau take them away?' snapped Battista quickly.

For a split second, Otto's eyes widened in surprise and his hands stopped working.

'Is Signore Lau your boss, Otto?'

'Who?'

'Lau. Is he the man you work for?'

'Never heard of him.'

'Quite a big shot. Owns the swanky casino on Viale Guglielmo Marconi.'

Otto shrugged again.

Battista looked at his watch. 'What would be your recommendation, Captain Luciani?'

Luciani leaned back in his chair and pulled his mouth down at the corners.

'Let him go.'

'Let him go?'

'We don't have enough to hold him, what else can we do?'

Otto's eyes were flashing from one officer to the other.

'Alright, here's what happens,' said Battista decisively. 'We issue a press release to say that Otto Brauscher was briefly detained and questioned in relation to a possible people-smuggling syndicate, he provided some assistance to the carabinieri, but was then released without any charge.'

'Then tomorrow, with your permission, Colonel,' continued Luciani, 'we will bring in Signore Lau for questioning regarding the employment of illegal immigrants at his businesses. With no connection between Otto and Lau, there shouldn't be any repercussions.'

Otto's eyes opened wide again, this time with genuine fear.

'No you can't, he's…'

'He's what? I thought you'd never heard of him.'

'Now you say the name again, I think I might have heard of him. It's rumoured he…'

'Go on.'

'He has a minder. They say he'll kill people if ordered by Lau.'

'Anyone you know of who's been killed?'

'It's only what I've heard. I don't know anything specific.'

'Let him go, Captain, and get that press release ready.'

'No, wait. There were whispers, nothing certain you understand, but a few days ago one of Lau's employees and a young Muslim boy...'

Luciani felt the blood drain from his face and his knee started twitching up and down. The realisation hit him like a thunderbolt. The boy and his guardian were compromised when he himself followed them from the hotel, and as a result they were subsequently murdered. He was partly responsible for the young boy's death. Luciani desperately wanted to go and get some water, but he couldn't leave now, Battista would roast him alive. He tried to concentrate on what seemed like distant voices as he listened to Battista continuing the interview.

'I can't see your life being worth very much when you leave here, Otto.'

'Please, I – I'll help if I can,' stammered Otto.

'Who is your contact? Who brings the people in? We have an officer who witnessed the boat landing.'

'But the officer is...'

'Is what Otto? Dead? Did you hit him too hard?'

'I didn't know, I didn't mean...'

Luciani snapped back into action. They've only caught one of the bastards, but it's the bastard who smashed Alberico's skull.

'What did you hit him with, Otto?'

'I just thought it would knock him out until we got clear,' sobbed Otto. 'I didn't realise...'

'Fortunately for you he was badly concussed but he's not dead. However, attempted murder of a carabinieri officer, you'll be looking at a long stretch, Otto. Have you ever been in prison?'

'No.' Otto's head was in his hands. 'I'm not like that.'

'What did you hit him with?'

'A spanner. From my truck.'

'Is the spanner still there in your truck, Otto?'

'Yes.'

Battista lifted his head a little, to make sure that the microphone in the light fitting picked up his voice clearly, for the benefit of both the recording and the officer monitoring the interview.

'To be clear, the spanner which you used to strike Lieutenant Alberico on Thursday night is in the cab of your lorry?'

'Yes.'

Battista sat back, satisfied that the Scene of Crime officers would be instructed to bag up the spanner as evidence.

'Can I have a cigarette now?'

'Sorry, Otto, didn't I tell you? This is a no-smoking building.'

Twenty-Seven

Even while he was getting ready for the evening family dinner at Le Clochard, D'Angelo was mulling over the call he had received earlier from Captain Luciani. They had made a breakthrough of sorts in the people-smuggling case, and had taken into custody the man who had attacked and injured the young carabinieri officer. That same man seemed to at least know of the existence of Rex, and Luciani would speak to the suspect again tomorrow to try and find out if he knows anything more about the drug gang boss. It was only a glimmer of a lead, but at least it was something, and D'Angelo was trying to decide whether to go to Pescara himself to interview the detainee, Otto, or leave it to Luciani.

'Does this necklace go with my dress?'

D'Angelo's cogitating was brought to an abrupt halt by Adriana's request for guidance. He dreaded these moments. Admittedly, giving advice on jewellery wasn't too fraught with danger, unlike the stress involved with giving an opinion on clothes. If he declared that a particular combination looked fine, he was accused of knowing perfectly well it looked awful, and he didn't care what his wife looked like in front of other people. If he said it didn't look quite right, he was just trying to pick fault with her for no reason and spoil her evening. It was a minefield. He chose option 'A'.

'It looks very nice. It matches the earrings, and picks out the blue of your dress.'

He didn't really know what he was talking about, but he had heard something like that being said, probably in a film, and thought it sounded plausible.

Adriana grunted and went back into the en-suite cloakroom, presumably satisfied with the appraisal. Happy that his decision-making was on point, D'Angelo made up his mind there and then that he would let Luciani get on with interviewing Otto, while he himself reviewed both the Giovanni Mirelti and drug murder cases alone, in the quiet of his office.

Patrizio had already collected Marianna and left for the restaurant by the time D'Angelo, Adriana, and younger daughter Gabriella set off, so the couple were already seated at a table in an alcove by the time a cheerful and enthusiastic waitress guided the rest of the family to their places.

'Encouraging to have some decent customer service,' declared Adriana, 'it's usually in pretty short supply around here.'

'I know what you mean,' agreed Marianna. 'Most of the shop keepers think they're doing you a big favour by allowing you into their premises, and as for you actually wanting to buy something, just too much trouble.'

'That's where the Americans have got it right,' said D'Angelo. 'You might find the "have a good day" syndrome a bit tacky, but at least you feel they value your custom.'

'If you think customer service is bad here, you should try Russia,' said Patrizio. 'I went there on holiday a couple of years ago, and customers there are treated with utter contempt. Russians have to be the rudest people in the world.'

Silence fell as Massimo, restaurant owner and chef, appeared round the corner of the alcove and placed on their table a tray holding a black bottle in an ice bucket and five glasses. Grinning widely, he started pouring the sparkling drink into the flutes.

'Prosecco, how lovely,' enthused Gabriella.

'Not Prosecco, Gabri,' said D'Angelo. 'Champagne, and a very good one.'

Glasses filled and placed in front of the diners, Massimo retreated back to the kitchen, still smiling.

D'Angelo and Adriana were looking somewhat puzzled, but Patrizio picked up his glass and held it aloft.

'With your permission, Antonio, I would very much like Marianna and I to become engaged to be married. Do I have your blessing?'

D'Angelo was trained to react quickly in unexpected situations, but on this occasion he stalled, and his wife beat him to it.

'How wonderful,' she said, lifting her glass, 'congratulations.'

'Of course you have my blessing,' said D'Angelo, trying to cover his delayed reaction, and preparing for the toast.

'To Patrizio and Marianna. Many congratulations, and a happy future life together.'

There was a buzz of excitement as Patrizio produced an engagement ring which Marianna slid onto her finger, amid gasps of appreciation from Adriana and Gabriella. D'Angelo had another sip of his champagne as he watched proceedings with a fixed smile on his face, but with mixed feelings in his head. Twenty years old, but to him she was still a child. His child. His mind flashed back to that helpless little creature in the maternity ward, then the months and years that followed, when she learned to crawl, and walk, and talk. She was always the quieter of the two daughters, and she seemed able to ease her way through life with very few traumas and without ruffling many feathers. He supposed that in married life, they would take over a floor of Patrizio's family home. Some girls would find that too suffocating, especially if the boy's mamma, Rottweiler-like, refused to let go. Quiet, gentle Marianna, however, would probably cope without any fuss. Perhaps she would go and work as the receptionist at Patrizio's dental practice, or even train as a nurse.

A flash distracted him. 'Turn your hand a little bit that way,' pleaded Gabriella. Another flash.

'I know we're not allowed to have phones at the table, Papa, but I've *got* to send some pics to Cocetta. Another flash as she snapped her glass of champagne.

The cheery waitress suddenly appeared, notebook poised, ready to take their orders.

'We're not quite ready, I'm afraid,' said D'Angelo.

'Don't worry, I'll come back in a few minutes. Shall I top up your glasses?'

She distributed the last of the champagne among the five glasses, and took away the empty bottle and the ice bucket.

'Come on then, let's choose what we're having,' said Adriana, taking on her motherly role.

After much pondering and discussion, and quite a few changes of mind, the family were finally able to place their orders when the young waitress next appeared.

'So that's mixed warm antipasti for three, and bruschetta for two,' said the waitress, checking what she had written on her notepad. 'Then for primi piatti we've got two potato gnocchi with tomato and pecorino cheese, risotto for two, and a chitarrina pasta ragu for one. Then for secondi you have two chicken all'erbette, two lamb Abruzzese, and one sliced chicken on a bed of crispy salad. As side dishes, three oven-roast potatoes and some vegetables of the day. Have I got that right?'

There were murmurs of assent from around the table.

'And to drink?'

'One sparkling water, one still water, a litre of cerusvuolo wine and a beer, please.'

'Patrizio has some other news,' announced Marianna, when the waitress had returned to the kitchen. Patrizio looked slightly abashed, yet at the same time quite pleased with himself.

'We're in the process of buying a second surgery, and I'll be in charge of it. We'll be equipping it with all the latest apparatus, really state of the art.'

D'Angelo found himself checking with his tongue for any cavities in his teeth, and he could have sworn that Adriana was doing likewise.

'Congratulations yet again. This is turning into quite a momentous day.'

The antipasti were served, and empty plates collected.

'Did I mention that I'll be needing the car tomorrow?' said Adriana, in a tone which suggested this was the first time it had been mentioned. Marianna turned suddenly from her private conversation with Patrizio.

'I'd like to take the Fiat,' said Marianna. 'I want to visit some of my friends, show them the engagement ring. Is that alright?'

'Of course,' said D'Angelo and Adriana together.

'Where are you off to?' asked D'Angelo, with forced casualness.

'I'm picking up Rosalinda and we're going to the Festa of the Madonna of the Woods, in Ripana. Do you want to come with us, Gabri?'

'Would that be the Madonna who appeared from the forest into the field where French soldiers were camped, and their horses, on seeing the spiritual apparition, knelt down on their front legs. The soldiers were so overwhelmed that at dawn the next day they broke camp and went away, leaving the good citizens of Ripana unmolested.'

'They built a church to the Madonna of the Woods in that very field.'

'Sounds as though an enterprising landowner who didn't know what else to do with the field got himself a good deal,' said D'Angelo.

'You're so cynical,' countered Adriana. 'These things mean a lot to people. Politicians and Governments come and go, with alarming rapidity in this country, but the church is always there for us. What else can you think of that was here way before we were born, and will be here long after we die?'

'Taxes.'

'Inflation.'

'What I'm trying to say,' continued Adriana, ignoring the barbs, 'is this : what other organisation do you know of that takes care of its own and relies on small contributions from all of us to keep it going?'

'The mafia?'

The sniggers forced Adriana to give up and resort to her wine.

'I will say this, though,' admitted D'Angelo, trying to atone for his wife's discomfort, 'the church here doesn't interfere in petty moral issues the way it used to, like calling for bikinis to be banned and so on. I was reading the other day about a country where an actress was put in prison because she wore a dress in public that was too revealing. The prosecutor said she was showing a lot of her legs.'

'How many legs has she got?' quipped Gabriella.

'She must have been Spiderwoman,' added Marianna.

D'Angelo smiled as the two girls giggled together, just as they did when they were, what, six and nine? Eight and eleven? Lord, how the years have flown.

'I bet you would go and watch a film starring a girl with eight legs, eh Papa?'

'Anyway,' said Adriana, cutting through the giggling and attempting to restore some sanity, 'what will you do tomorrow?' she asked her husband. 'Why can't you use a carabinieri vehicle?'

'Only the Forester is available,' he said, ignoring the fact that Teresa Rossi had taken temporary charge of the 159, 'and that is in the capable hands of Trooper Di Silverio who, you will be relieved to know, is on duty protecting you and everybody else at the festa tomorrow. In his mind, there will be a terrorist plot to launch an attack with grenades and automatic weapons, so he'll be ready to shoot at a moment's notice.'

'Di Silverio? Isn't he the one who calls you…'

'Yes, he's the one.'

'Calls you what, Papa?' asked Gabriella.

'Virgun, isn't it?' said Adriana, with a hint of a smirk.

'Virgun?'

'He thinks I'm afraid to use a gun because I never wear one,' explained D'Angelo.

'Yes, but vir-gun? Oh, I get it. Virgin gun.'

'Perhaps you could drop me off at work after you've picked up Rosalinda?' suggested D'Angelo, changing the subject.

'Fine.'

'Can I come with you Papa?' asked Gabriella. 'It's ages since I've been to the office with you.'

'Of course you can, Sweetheart.'

The primi and secondi courses had been served, and Marianna still had room for a semifreddo for dessert, while Patrizio enjoyed a tiramisu. They followed up with coffees, including liquors for D'Angelo, Adriana and Patrizio.

'Well, that's been an incredible evening,' said D'Angelo. 'Thank you, Patrizio, and congratulations to you both once again. If this were to be my last day alive on earth, I would die a happy man.'

'Why do you say that?' said Gabriella, her face clouding.

'Just an expression, Sweetheart. Don't worry, you're going to have to put up with me for quite a few years yet.'

Twenty-Eight

'Do you need to wear uniform on a Sunday?' asked Adriana.

'I'm working, so I wear uniform. You'll pick us up on your way back from the festa then?' said D'Angelo, climbing out of the car outside the carabinieri station.

'Yes, I'll text you when we're just about to leave Ripana.'

''Bye, Mamma, 'bye Rosalinda,' said Gabriella, also on her way out of the car. 'Oh,' she called, stopping Adriana from driving away, 'if you happen to see a stall with socks that have nice colourful hoops, can you get me a couple of pairs? Thanks Mamma, see you later.'

D'Angelo unlocked the door of the station and neutralized the alarm system, then he and Gabriella settled themselves in his office. D'Angelo had anticipated working alone on his problem cases, but he wasn't distracted by his younger daughter's presence.

He had extrapolated a list of significant points from the Rex and drug murder file, and this was the one he decided to review first, so he brought the list up on screen.

1. Victim's body tortured prior to death.
2. Small tattoo of hornet on victim's left wrist.

3. Possible links to South America. (Suppliers?)
4. Blue or green Renault van used to transport body.
5. Drug gang boss called Rex. (Assumed name?)
6. Rex operates the Pescara area, but is based outside the city.

'Where's the clue?' said D'Angelo out loud.

Gabriella looked up from her iPhone. 'I like clues,' she said. 'Come on, Papa, try me.'

D'Angelo pursed his lips.

'Alright, but whatever we say stays in this room, agreed?'

'Agreed.'

'A male murder victim was found dumped behind a small industrial unit near Pescara airport. There are six things we either know or can fairly safely assume. Number one, he had been tortured before being killed, finger and thumb cut off, cigarette burns and cuts to other parts of his body.'

'Yuk!'

'These are not nice people. In gang culture, mutilating the hands or fingers usually means the victim has been cheating, such as stealing more than his share, or setting up deals on his own. It acts as a warning to anyone else thinking of doing the same thing. Secondly, there was a small tattoo, a hornet, on his wrist. What would be your take on that, Gabs?'

'Probably just something he liked.'

'A hornet is a bit strange.'

'You mean it could signify his membership of the gang?'

'Or else a rival one. It's a possibility, don't you think?'

'What's next?'

'The examining pathologist believed the victim was originally from South America, something to do with his particular drug habit.'

'Like perhaps Colombia? That's a well-known source of cocaine.'

'Exactly. A lot of the supply lines start off there.'

'So the victim was somehow involved in the actual trafficking, not just distribution over here.'

'You're thinking like a true detective, Gabs. Maybe he was attempting a take-over from his Italian boss, so the boss put a stop to it, and sent a warning to his South American suppliers at the same time.'

'Sounds feasible.'

'Next, the body was taken to the industrial estate in a blue or green Renault van.'

'No registration number?'

'No.'

'Has anyone done a check on how many blue or green Renault vans are registered here in Abruzzo? There can't be a huge number.'

'That's a very good point, well done Gabri. I'll see to that tomorrow morning.'

'Next.'

'The drug boss is called Rex.'

'The king.'

'What?'

'Come on Papa, didn't you ever do Latin? Latin for king is rex.'

'I'm glad you've come in today. King. Makes sense, doesn't it, for the boss to give himself that title.'

'Anything else?'

'He seems to control most of the drug operations within Pescara, possibly the whole of Abruzzo, but he doesn't live in Pescara itself.'

'Hmm. I can't see that as being of much importance.'

'Well, that's our lot. Not much to go on, is it?'

* * *

In Ripana, Adriana had been forced to park half a kilometre from the town, with all the closer parking spaces already taken, then she and Rosalinda joined the throng milling in the streets. They hadn't progressed far when a yellow-vested marshal advanced down the middle of the road, moving everyone to the side, then music could be heard in the distance, as everyone waited for the band to come marching down the hill. Adriana and Rosalinda had missed the inaugural fireworks, as well as the more sombre procession which involved carrying an effigy of the Madonna of the Woods from her eponymous church to the town-centre piazza, but they clapped enthusiastically as the small mixed-age band went marching past.

The festa was an occasion to see and be seen, and to catch up with old friends you might not have met up with for a while. Adriana greeted Elena and Aldo, introducing them to Rosalinda.

'Such a nice family,' said Adriana when they had moved on, 'and their two boys have done so well for themselves.'

She then bumped into Carolina. 'She teaches history at the school in Lanciano,' explained Adriana.

People were browsing the numerous stalls, and discussing how much blossom had formed on the olive trees this year. There had been a couple of poor years for olives recently, either because the flowers hadn't formed in the spring, or olive fly larvae had spoiled the crop during the summer months. Everyone was hoping for a successful harvest come November.

Adriana and Rosalinda made their way slowly around Ripana in the midst of a busy, noisy crowd. At one time they passed Trooper Di Silverio and a colleague. Di Silverio acknowledged Adriana with a polite 'good morning, Signora.'

'Who was that?' asked Di Silverio's fellow carabiniere.

'The boss, Virgun's wife.'

'Wow. Glamorous, isn't she.'

Di Silverio looked round to see Adriana and Rosalinda disappear into the crowd.

'Trim figure. Too good for old Virgun, eh?'

* * *

In Montenero, Laura had received a phone call from a lady with whom she had a passing acquaintance.

'Is that Laura? Hello Laura, it's Lavinia Abbonizio here. I'm so sorry about your brother going missing like that, it must be dreadful for all of you. I've found out something this morning that might be helpful. I've just come back from visiting my aunt, I go and see her every Sunday you know. She's in her eighties now, but still quite spritely. Anyway, she saw one of your posters on the fish van when it called at her house, and she says she saw your Giovanni on Monday evening.'

'She saw him? Is she sure?'

'Oh yes, she's quite certain it was him. She said she thought he might have been in a fight or something, because he was crying, his legs were scratched and his shorts were torn.'

The blood was pounding in Laura's head. It *was* Giovanni that Signora Abbonizio's aunt had seen.

'Where was it she saw him? What time?' blurted Laura.

'It might be better if you go and talk to her yourself, dear.'

'Yes. Where does she live?'

'She's in the little end house of that row overlooking the road in Contrada Castagne. You know where I mean?'

'Yes, I think so. Thank you, Signora Abbonizio,' she said, ending the call. 'Mamma, I'm going out,' shouted Laura, 'can you tell Felicita that I've taken the Vespa.'

Moments later, Laura was zooming down the road on her scooter, heading for the hamlet of Contrada Castagne.

* * *

'And that poor young boy, Giovanni, was last seen running into the road from the neighbouring property?' said Gabriella, having asked her father if she could go over the Giovanni Mirelti case with him. 'Where does the road go?'

'To Montenero, but I think there are a few little side roads leading off it, probably to farms or isolated cottages. I'll tell you what, Gabri, you're better than me at working these computer apps, come and use Google Earth and we'll try and see what properties are off that road.'

'OK, here we go. There's a turning on the left side of the road almost straight away.'

'It's alright, I know that one, it goes to a holiday place. Keep going.'

'Another one here. I can't get down the track, but from the road it looks like an abandoned house.'

'The search team will have checked that one. Carry on.'

'Here's a slightly bigger side turning. There must be something along here because I can follow it with a camera view.'

'Follow it and see.'

'It's quite tricky. The road's fairly narrow with lots of bends. It was obviously filmed in the winter, which makes it a bit easier, without a canopy of leaves. Ah, look, a row of little cottages. It's obviously a small hamlet.'

'Come back a bit. There was a sign just back there.'

'OK, I've come back and turned round.'

'Slowly, slowly. There, look. What does it say?'

'Contrada Castagne.'

'Contrada Castagne. That rings a bell. Minimize that a sec while I check through my notes. Do you want a coffee, by the way?'

'No, we're too busy for coffee.'

D'Angelo scanned through his notes of meetings with various people in Montenero, then the word 'Castagne' jumped out at him. Filippo, the wood-worker, lives just past Contrada Castagne.

'Yesterday evening,' he said, 'you couldn't wait to contact your friend with news of Marianna's engagement.

Would you contact her just as quickly if the news was bad?'

'I guess so, yes.'

'So if, for example, I were to tell you that we wouldn't support you through university, you would tell her?'

'I would go round and see her. I know she would understand what it meant to me, and she'd be a shoulder to cry on, do her best to comfort me.'

'And an eleven year-old boy would probably do the same thing, right?'

'Eleven, before he gets all macho and independent, yes, he would.'

'Filippo.'

'Who?'

'Filippo, Giovanni's friend. Giovanni helped out in Filippo's workshop, and Filippo would teach him about birds and animals. On Monday evening, Giovanni was upset because he saw a buzzard being shot, so it's possible he would want to go and tell Filippo, a fellow nature-lover. Let's go over what we know about Filippo, and see if we can turn something up.'

* * *

Laura skidded to a halt outside the row of cottages and put her Vespa on its stand, then dashed up the short hill to the end cottage. The place seemed semi-derelict and hardly fit for human habitation. Scrawny chickens were scratching around in the dirt as Laura banged on the ancient and split wooden door. Nobody answered, and Laura wondered if the old dear was deaf. She decided to try her luck round the back of the cottage, where she found a stooped, grey-haired lady in well-worn black widow's clothes, busily plucking a chicken that was hanging by its feet from a post, fresh blood dripping down its neck and off its beak.

'Signora,' Laura called out, 'good day, Signora.'

The woman turned to face Laura.

'Signora, I'm sorry to disturb you, but I understand you saw my brother, Giovanni, on Monday evening?'

Laura pulled one of her posters from her pocket and unfolded it, showing the picture of Giovanni to the elderly but bright-eyed lady.

'Yes indeed,' she said, taking the poster from Laura and examining it carefully. 'Yes, that's the boy I saw. He was running down the road out there. Upset, he was, crying, and blood on his legs.'

'Do you know what time it was when you saw him?'

'Well now, it would have been somewhere around half past seven to a quarter to eight. You see, that's the time I call the chickens in for the night, stop the foxes getting them, you understand. I was rounding them up from my bit of land at the front there, overlooking the road, and that's when I saw the young boy.'

'Do you know where he might have been going?'

'Not much along there. There's Filippo Geniola's house, of course, but after that…'

She shrugged, and looked off into the distance.

'Filippo, the one who has a workshop in the village?'

'I believe he does, yes. He has friends on motorbikes who come and see him. He's a nice man, he came and rescued a baby owl that had got trapped in my chimney. A barn owl, he said it was called.'

'Thank you, Signora, thank you very much,' called Laura, as she turned and ran back down the earth path to her scooter. She decided to send a text message to the carabinieri man, Major D'Angelo, to let him know she was on her way to see Filippo. He had told her to let him know, any time, any day, if she discovered anything new. While she was tapping out the message, a Harley Davidson bike roared past her, up the hill away from the direction of Filippo's house. 'I hope that's not him leaving,' she thought to herself. She tried to send the message, but there was no signal. She was about to give up and put the phone back in her pocket, but then decided to try one more time, so she ran a little way back up the road, tried again, and this time was successful. She hopped on the Vespa and continued down the road towards Filippo's house.

* * *

'Let's find Filippo's house on Google Earth,' said D'Angelo. 'It must be just past that row of cottages.'

'Here we are,' announced Gabriella after a quick search, 'this must be it on the left. Looks like quite a big place, I would say it's a fairly typical three-storey concrete house, probably a fair bit of land with it.'

'I wonder...'

'What, Papa?'

'Marco took some aerial shots with his drone, I wonder if it came this far out. Let's have a look, shall we.'

D'Angelo loaded the file of aerial photographs, then clicked his way through them, halting at all the wide view shots.

'That could have been it,' said Gabriella, looking over her father's shoulder.

He went back to the previous long view.

'Yes, I see what you mean. There's the road, and that must be the end of the row of cottages. Not easy to tell, but you could be right. Wait a minute, what's that, behind the house, close to the trees. Can we zoom in on it?'

'I don't think you can zoom in, but, here, can I have a go, Papa. I think I can manipulate the picture so that we can make the area around that point into full screen size. It'll lose definition and be a bit fuzzy, I'm afraid, but – there. That's what you were looking at.'

'Hm. It is rather a blur isn't it. It's a building, though. Look at the shadow on the ground.'

'With a white roof.'

'Yes. Actually, it looks more like reflection.'

'It could be. Glass panels.'

'Solar panels. That's what they are. Solar panels on top of a small remote building.'

'Providing electricity? Or hot water?'

'Depends whether they're photovoltaic or standard solar panels.'

D'Angelo sat looking at the screen and thinking for a while.

'When I went to his workshop, I could smell marijuana.'
'So?'

'So perhaps Filippo has got himself a cannabis farm. Not just for his own use, but selling it as well.'

'By the way, Papa, shouldn't you check that text message that came through on your phone?'

'What? Oh, yes. It's from Laura, Giovanni's sister. She's

on her way to see our friend Filippo. Right now, I don't think that's a very good idea. I'll ring her and tell her to go back home. Mannaggia, no signal. I'll try again in a minute.'

'Do you know anything else about Filippo?'

'Not a lot. He does those wooden carvings.'

'Does he sell them?'

'I think so. I don't suppose he sells that many, though, not in a small place like Montenero.'

'What sort of carvings are they?'

'Animals and birds, mainly.'

'Are they any good?'

'Actually, yes, they are. Very good. There was one in particular, he said it wasn't for sale, but it was superb. A snake, sort of coiled and ready to strike. It even had red glass eyes. A snake.'

'You already said that.'

'Yes, sorry, I was thinking of something else. He checked the time, on a very expensive-looking watch, but I noticed he had a tattoo on his wrist.'

'Not a hornet by any chance?'

'Not a hornet, no. I wasn't sure at the time, but I think what I saw was the tail of a snake.'

'Like the one he had carved?'

'One of those big ones, I think they come from India, with a kind of hood behind its head.'

'I think they're called a Cobri, Cobra, something like that. Google it, then you'll get a picture.'

'I'll just try ringing Laura again first. No, still nothing. The coverage in some of those rural areas is hopeless.'

'I've found the snake for you,' said Gabriella. 'They live in Southern Africa, South Asia,…'

'That's like the one he had carved. Perhaps it's the same as his tattoo, not easy to tell, I only saw its tail.'

'King Cobra.'

'What?'

'King Cobra. That's what it's called.'

'King? Rex? Shit.'

'You don't think…'

'I don't know, but it's possible,' said D'Angelo, jumping up from his chair and rushing to open the small safe in the corner of his office.

'Listen, Sweetheart, stay here, keep trying to ring Laura. Get her number off my phone, I'll be taking mine with me.'

D'Angelo removed his Beretta pistol from the safe and pushed home a full clip of ammunition, then slid the gun into the holster on his belt.

'You got that number? I'll take my phone.'

'Papa, where are you going? You can't go on your own.'

'Got to, Sweetheart. Love you.'

D'Angelo ran out to the reception area, Gabriella following close behind.

'Hell, no bloody car.'

He looked at the board of keys, empty except for one.

'Bike. I'll have to take the bike.'

'I didn't know you could…'

'Gabri, keep trying that number,' yelled D'Angelo as he pressed the button to open the garage at the back of the station.

Gabriella was taking short, rapid breaths, trying to stop herself crying, as she ran back to her father's office.

D'Angelo fired up the Ducati Multistrada 1200 motorbike and, forgetting the torque of its powerful engine, flew straight across the road and bumped over the curb on the far side. He managed to get the machine under control, despite wobbling precariously, then opened up the throttle to roar up to the town centre junction. Seeing nothing coming from the left, he merely slowed down slightly before turning right and giving the bike full throttle on his way to Montenero.

Twenty-Nine

Gabriella had tried time after time to call Laura without success. She had finally given way to tears, the frustration of failed phone calls adding to fear for her father's safety. The only thing she could think to do was to ring her mother, but her mother's phone just rang and rang without being answered. She put her head in her arms and sobbed.

* * *

Laura rode into Filippo's drive, and left her Vespa on its stand to go and ring his doorbell, but there was no answer from the silent and seemingly empty house. That must have been him leaving on the Harley, she thought to herself, but it's worth checking round the back, just in case.

There was nobody around, so she was about to give up and leave when she heard a voice from beyond the copse of trees that shielded the back of the house. She walked through the copse and could see, just in front of the woods about seventy metres away, what looked like a stone turret, alongside which there stood a green van. Laura dodged behind a tree as a man appeared from around the back of the turret and leaned a spade against the side of the van.

Laura felt goose-bumps on her arms, some instinct or inner sense warning her of danger. Something was telling her that there was a connection between the spade and the van, because why else would he lean the spade there? Fear told her to stay away, yet she was determined to find some answers. The man disappeared through the door of the stone building, so Laura took her chance and ran the seventy metres to the green Renault van.

With a quick glance behind her, she opened one side of the van's back door, but what she saw inside the vehicle made her heart race, and a thumping inside her head made her feel dizzy and nauseous. Something was rolled up in a piece of green netting, the sort of netting that was used to collect olives during the harvest. She crawled inside the van on her knees, then started to unravel the green netting. Laura let out an involuntary shriek as she uncovered the top part of Giovanni's lifeless body, his face white in contrast to his matted black hair. Panting, her mouth dry, Laura shuffled backwards to escape the ghastly tomb, out of the back door of the van into a man's rough grip. With one arm held tightly around her neck to inhibit her scream, the other arm around her waist, he carried her in through the door of the turret-like building and flung her to the ground. A second man was standing inside the windowless, artificially-lit room.

'Christ, Laura, what the hell are *you* doing here?'

* * *

'I'm exhausted, I could do with a bit of a break,' said Rosalinda, having just bought a beautifully-decorated garlic holder from one of the craft stalls.

'Me too,' agreed Adriana. 'Come on, let's make our way down to the café, get away from the crowds for a while and have a nice cake with our coffee.'

They were both relieved to sit down in the quiet sanctuary of the café, away from the crush and noise, able to rest their aching feet.

'Is that your phone ringing?' said Rosalinda.

'Heavens, yes it is.' Adriana retrieved her phone from the inside pocket of her handbag. 'It's Gabriella. She probably wants to know if I've found her socks yet. Hi Gabri.'

'Mamma thank God Papa's gone on his own I don't know what to do he's in danger…'

'Wait Gabri, slow down, I can't understand what you're saying. Start again, love.'

'There's a man, in Montenero, he's murdered someone, and Papa's gone on his own to arrest him. I'm frightened, Mamma.'

'Who is the man?'

'His name is Filippo. Papa thinks he's a drug dealer.'

'Listen Gabri, there are some carabinieri here, I could get them to go to Montenero to help Papa. Where does this man Filippo live?'

'Near Contrada Castagne. I can get the co-ordinates from the computer and text them to you. Please ask them to hurry, Mamma.'

'Don't worry. 'Bye darling.'

Adriana snapped her phone shut and shoved it back in her handbag.

'Rosalinda, we have to go. We need to find those carabinieri we saw earlier. Antonio might be in trouble.'

Rosalinda jumped to her feet.

'Should we split up do you think? No, we'll never find each other again. We'll stick together for the search. Let's go.'

* * *

At first, D'Angelo had been slowing down for the bends in the road, but now he was hardly slowing at all, leaning in to each bend, trying to avoid the patches where the road surface was broken up, in some places temporarily repaired with loose gravel. He flashed between sunlight and shade like an actor in a flickering black-and-white movie. At times he had to take the centre of the road, in order to miss areas where bordering tree roots had pushed the tarmac into dangerous humps and troughs. Perhaps, he thought, Gabriella had managed to call Laura and warn her, or maybe he was wrong about Filippo, but he couldn't take the chance. He had to get to Montenero quickly.

* * *

The crowds at Ripana festa seemed even more pressing and claustrophobic for Adriana and Rosalinda in their desperate hurry to find the carabinieri. Trying to squeeze through the crush was a lot more difficult at faster pace, bumping into people and attempting to dodge around the slow ones. At last, Rosalinda, the taller of the two, caught a glimpse of distinctive blue and red uniform a few metres ahead.

'Quick, Adriana, we can catch them up.'

The final metres seemed to take the longest, but finally they reached Trooper Di Silverio, hands behind his back, threading his way slowly along the centre of the street.

'Excuse me, Di Silverio isn't it?'

'Yes, Signora,' he said, turning towards Adriana.

'We need to talk. Can we go over there, next to the stall, for a minute.'

In the comparative calm in the lee of the cheese stall, Adriana explained her husband's potentially dangerous situation.

'You must get there as soon as possible,' she explained.

'I must find my colleague first, he's…'

'There's no time. If we see him, we'll tell him where you've gone. My daughter has hopefully texted the GPS co-ordinates of the property – yes, here we are, can you make a note of them.'

Di Silverio tapped the numbers into his phone, looked around to check which direction he needed to be going to find his Subaru Forester patrol vehicle, then darted off on his mission to Montenero.

* * *

'You killed my brother. Why? I hate you,' screamed Laura, getting to her feet.

'I didn't want to, Laura, believe me.'

'You were his friend. Why did you kill him?'

'It hurt me to do it, but I had to,' said Filippo. 'I tried to think of a way to keep him alive. For two days he was living upstairs, up with my marijuana plants, even while the carabinieri were crawling everywhere, trying to find him. But he had seen too much, things he shouldn't have seen.'

'What are you talking about?'

'We had to punish someone, a guy called Hornet, who had got out of line. I had no choice. You can't let people who work for you start messing you around. Last Monday, Scorpion here and his buddy gave Hornet a going over. A bit messy, it was. Giovanni burst in looking for me and saw what had been done to Hornet, so I couldn't let Giovanni go after he had seen that. I'm sorry, Laura, truly I am. I liked the young guy.'

The small, round room was stark, like a prison cell, with its stone, windowless walls. A wooden ladder led up to the next floor via an open trapdoor, and, on a table which took up the centre space of the room, there sat an Uzi machine pistol.

'Now you've given me a real problem, Laura,' continued Filippo. 'I could have got away with Giovanni. The search would have been called off, the case would be left unsolved, while the kid was lying buried in the wood. But now there's you. You shouldn't have come here, Laura, you really shouldn't. Big, big problem.'

Laura was sobbing, making high-pitched whimpering sounds with each breath.

'I'm going for some ice,' said Filippo. He motioned discretely to the other man with a quick movement of a finger across his throat, then climbed the ladder to the trapdoor above.

* * *

D'Angelo turned off the road into Filippo's property and left his Ducati on its stand close to the Vespa, which he was sure was the same scooter he had seen at the Mirelti house. He cursed to himself as he drew his pistol from its holster and went to try the front door. It was locked, as was the garage alongside. Hoping to find a back door, or perhaps an open window, he moved quickly and quietly around the side of the building, finding two more doors that were also locked. He looked around for something heavy to smash a window, and noticed a low stone wall close to some trees. He went to collect one of the stones, then remembered the other building nearby, the one with solar panels on top, so he walked past the stone wall, through some trees, and looked across at the small tower with a green van parked alongside. He set off towards it with a loping run.

* * *

The long-haired, bearded man stood grinning at Laura for a little while.

'I'm known as Scorpion, see?' he said, pulling up his sleeve to show a scorpion tattoo on his wrist. 'The boss wants me to kill you, but not yet, eh? You and me can have a bit of fun.'

Laura shot a glance up at the trapdoor.

'Oh, don't worry darling. He'll be on the meth by now, in a little world of his own. He won't disturb us. Take your clothes off.'

With shaking hands and sobbing uncontrollably, Laura pulled her cotton top over her head and dropped it on the floor. 'Good girl, now the bra.'

Laura was shaking so much that she struggled to unfasten the bra, but finally succeeded, and slid it off her breasts.

'Mm, nice,' said Scorpion. 'I'm getting excited. Keep going.'

* * *

D'Angelo reached the van and noticed that its rear door wasn't properly shut. He opened both sides fully, and recoiled at the sight of Giovanni's partly uncovered body. He looked at the door leading into the turret, then crept around the outside, looking for another possible way in to the building.

* * *

'Come on, get those jeans off. That's it, now the pants. Lovely, lovely. I'm guessing you're a virgin, am I right, Laura? Now come and take my trousers off, unleash the beast. You'll see how big a scorpion can be. I'll tell you what, if I enjoy this, I'll hide you away somewhere safe, we can have fun together. Come on, Laura, you know you want to.'

* * *

Having discovered there were no other points of entry, not even a window, D'Angelo stood outside the door shielding his eyes. He reckoned that with no natural light inside, it might take a few seconds for his eyesight to adjust, and they may not be seconds he could afford to lose. The other big unknown was whether the door was open or bolted shut. He checked again that the safety catch of his Beretta was off, held his left hand for a moment above the door handle, then snapped it down, kicked the door open, and burst into the room, hugging the wall. Scorpion spun round, then reached for the Uzi machine pistol, managing to grab hold of it before D'Angelo fired two shots. Two small red holes appeared on Scorpion's forehead before he sagged to the ground, still clutching the Uzi in his lifeless hands, brain and blood spattering behind him.

Laura sank to the floor against the stone wall, clutching her knees together and crying pitifully, as D'Angelo dropped the gun into its holster, then took off his jacket and put it round her naked, quivering body. She was trying to speak, but no words came out. D'Angelo squatted on his haunches.

'It's alright, Laura, you're safe. Come on, let's get you out of here.'

Her eyes, wild with terror, were looking past D'Angelo to the wooden ladder.

'Have you just shot one of my best men?' said Filippo, also armed with an Uzi, which he was pointing at D'Angelo. 'My problems seem to be mounting,' he continued, descending the ladder. 'First her, now you. Take the gun out, with thumb and forefinger, and put it slowly on the table. That's good. Perhaps you've given me a chance after all. I'm going to have to arrange a tragic accident, a fire that kills both of you and the boy.'

D'Angelo noticed that Filippo's speech was slurred, and his pupils were dilated.

'Indulge me for a minute, Rex,' said D'Angelo.

'Clever man. I've forgotten your name.'

'D'Angelo.'

'D'Angelo, yes. You're smart, D'Angelo.'

'What happened to Hornet?'

'Got above himself, tried cutting me out of deals.'

'Too close to his South American buddies?'

'That's right. Birds of a feather, eh, D'Angelo?'

'Birds of a feather. It was birds of a feather that brought Giovanni here. Why did *he* have to die?'

'*She* knows.'

'He s-saw what they did to Hornet,' squeaked Laura.

'See? Now you've all got to go,' said Filippo.

* * *

Di Silverio didn't know whether to carry on or try to reverse the Subaru Forester out of the narrow and increasingly overgrown track through the dense woodland. 'Bloody useless satnav,' he yelled in frustration, 'nearly reached my destination? I'm totally bloody lost.' He pressed on for another ten metres before the track disappeared completely. He put the vehicle in reverse and turned in his seat to look behind the car in order to try and extricate himself, but suddenly noticed through the trees a strange building he remembered from a few days ago, when he was searching for the missing boy. It was like a small tower not far from a house, empty and locked up when he had checked it. Perhaps the nearby house was the one that his satnav was trying to lead him to. The GPS signal couldn't be that far out, so it was worth a try, he thought. He switched off the ignition and scrambled through thick, clinging undergrowth, stumbled over an ancient length of wire, and eventually managed to force his way out of the wood just a short distance from the stone tower.

Di Silverio remembered that the house was off up to the left, so he started to skirt the tower in the right direction. He hadn't gone far when his attention was caught by a vehicle, a van, parked on the other side of the tower. Noticing that both of the van's back doors were open, he approached to take a closer look, then stopped in his tracks when he realised that the object partly wrapped in green netting in the back of the van was the body of a small boy.

He tensed and drew his hand gun, turning and checking the area in a three hundred and sixty degree arc. He crept towards the tower and put his ear against the solid wooden door, sure he could hear voices from inside, muffled and indistinct though they were. The back of his neck was prickling, but there was no running away – he had to go in.

In a move similar to D'Angelo's, taught to him in firearms training, he flung the door open, saw a man with a machine pistol start to turn the weapon towards him, and dived back out to the side of the doorway, just in time to avoid a hail of automatic fire.

Filippo kept his finger on the trigger for a little too long. The extra second gave D'Angelo enough time to grab his pistol from the table and go into the well-drilled routine from his sessions on the firing range. "*Good grouping, Major D'Angelo. Three in the heart, two to the head. Well done, quick and accurate. Not at all bad. Good reactions for a man of your…*"

D'Angelo looked down dispassionately at Filippo's crumpled body. "*Is that why you don't carry a gun, Major D'Angelo? I think you quite enjoyed that.*"

D'Angelo holstered the pistol and stepped hurriedly outside to check on Di Silverio, who was on his hands and knees beside the door.

'Are you alright? Were you hit?'

Di Silverio shook his head and staggered to his feet, wiping his mouth with his sleeve, hoping D'Angelo hadn't noticed the traces of vomit.

'Well done,' said D'Angelo, putting his hand on the young trooper's shoulder, 'your timely intervention saved the day.'

D'Angelo removed the radio from its pouch on his belt and called Pescara HQ.

'Major D'Angelo here. I need some resources. Send a mortuary van, three deceased, two adult, one child, all male. And contact Social Services, see if you can get hold of a trauma counsellor, there's a teenage girl who's going to need some help. Where am I?' D'Angelo looked round at the van, where Giovanni's body was visible through the open doors.

'Paradise Lost...'

From the top of a nearby tree, a golden oriole started to sing its beautiful summer song – "you're a hero, you're a hero." D'Angelo turned back to see Laura step from the building, wrapped in his jacket. She stood still in the sunlight, looking up at the trees.

'... and Found,' murmured D'Angelo.

Postscript

Thank you for reading *Sweet Song, Bitter Loss*. If you enjoyed it, please take a few minutes to post a review – it would mean so much.

Best wishes,
Paul Hencher.